The Greek Escape

Karen Swan is a *Sunday Times* Top Five bestselling writer. She is the author of twelve other novels. She previously worked as an editor in the fashion industry but soon realized she was better suited as a novelist with a serious shopping habit. She is married with three children and lives in East Sussex.

Come to find her at www.karenswan.com, or Instagram @swannywrites, Twitter @KarenSwan1 and Facebook @KarenSwanAuthor.

Also by Karen Swan

The Greek Escape

KAREN SWAN

PAN BOOKS

First published 2018 by Macmillan
an imprint of Pan Macmillan
20 New Wharf Road, London N1 9RR
Associated companies throughout the world
www.panmacmillan.com

ISBN 978-1-5098-4062-5

1 3 5 7 9 8 6 4 2

A CIP catalogue record for this book is available from the British Library.

Typeset by Palimpsest Book Production Limited, Falkirk, Stirlingshire
Printed and bound by CPI Group (UK) Ltd, Croydon, CR0 4YY

Visit www.panmacmillan.com to read more about all our books
and to buy them. You will also find features, author interviews and
news of any author events, and you can sign up for e-newsletters
so that you're always first to hear about our new releases.

For Ells

Just keep swimming.
(With occasional yoga. And pauses for wine.)

Prologue

She fell backwards through the air, picking up speed quickly, her green silk dress flapping loudly against her skin like a startled bird's wings. Her hair streamed upwards, framing her last view like willow fronds as she plummeted silently through the night. It had all happened too quickly for her to feel any fear and there was a strange calmness to knowing that it would all be over any moment now. These past few months had broken her and so, perhaps, this was not the calamity it seemed as her eyes watered and her body braced. Perhaps it was merciful. Kind, even. This was not living. It was no life.

She would be gone, yes.

But she would also be free.

1

Chapter One

New York, early July 2018, six weeks earlier

'Right, nobody panic,' Xan said, standing up from his chair on the other side of the desk and waving his arms at them in a panicky manner. 'But I need thirty penguins for a black-tie party in East Hampton. Now.' He pushed his hands towards them both in a point. 'Go!'

'I *love* penguins!' Poppy gasped, swinging from side to side on her spinning chair, all gangly limbs, and sipping on a green juice.

Chloe sank her chin into her hand. 'Why do you need penguins at a black-tie party? Or is that just a ridiculous question?'

'Seriously?' Poppy deadpanned. 'I can't believe you even need to ask.'

Xan walked around the bank of desks and came and sat on the pile of paperwork between theirs. 'The client wants them to mingle.'

'Mingle. Huh,' Poppy nodded, as though their sociability was the pertinent point. She finished typing an email and gave a loud exhale. 'Well, just so long as they don't want them serving the drinks. That really would be unreason-able.'

Chloe chuckled. God, she loved her job and the fact that this counted as just another day at the office. 'What time's the party starting?'

Xan pouted. 'Two hours.'

'Right,' Chloe said slowly; the Hamptons were a three-hour road-trip from here as it was, and that was before you counted in that it was late Friday afternoon and most of Manhattan was trying to get out there too. 'So then you're looking at a helicopter.'

Xan shrugged. 'I'll get a Tornado if I have to – have you ever *spoken* to that woman?' Chloe shook her head. 'She makes Melania look low-maintenance.'

Poppy guffawed. She had the type of Julia Roberts mouth that reached beyond the outer edges of her eyes when she smiled – which was a lot. She was a curious contradiction of extremes – rail-thin body and super-tall, but with oversized eyes and fluffy baby-blonde hair. She was one of the most senior members of the team and yet she wore her authority lightly – anyone walking in off the street might mistake her for an intern.

'I've just put a hold option on the Augusta Grand at the TSS heliport. I think it'll be big enough to take thirty penguins, don't you?' Xan mused.

Poppy's eyes danced again. 'Oh, intriguing maths question! How many penguins does it take to fill an Augusta Grand? What *is* the cubic volume of an average penguin these days?' she asked, looking at Chloe with an earnest expression.

Chloe sat back and swung in her chair too. They spent much of their days like this. 'Depends, Pops. Are we talking Emperor, or your common-or-garden Antarctic variety? Otherwise, it's like comparing apples and pears.'

4

'Apples and pears? Stairs?' Her voice was plummy and far too enunciated to pull off mockney convincingly, just as its lanky owner wasn't fooling anyone with her carpenter dungarees; Poppy Langham was a viscount's daughter with half the sheep in Shropshire grazing on her family's land.

'I have no idea what you're talking about,' Xan sighed with a tut as they collapsed with laughter beside him; sometimes, being the only English people on the team was as foreign as coming from Mars – and just as fun.

'It's the cockney rhyming slang we told you about, remember?' Chloe said, patting his knee. An avid Anglophile, Xan was often in thrall to their niche colloquialisms, although he rarely managed to deploy them correctly himself and once told their boss, Jack, on the way out to lunch, that his new car was the bee's legs.

But even he had no time for a lesson in the finer points of English slang today. 'And that helps me with my penguins how?'

Poppy put her feet up on the desk – red and white chequerboard Vans today – a clear sign she was ready to work. 'Right, well assuming a chopper transit time of thirty minutes, that means we've got ninety minutes to track down a colony.'

'Ninety?' Chloe queried. 'I'd go with seventy. It's rush hour, the traffic to the heliport?' She gave a shrug.

'You're so right,' Poppy nodded. 'Seventy minutes. That's what you've got to work with to hunt them down.'

'Well, all this maths advice is great,' Xan said sarcastically, picking up her juice and finishing it off, the sucking of the straw making a wonderful feature of his cheekbones. 'But besides the cubic volume of a penguin and allowances made for rush hour, can you tell me *where* to find the damned birds?'

There was a brief hiatus in discussions.

'Hmm.' Poppy gave a mournful sigh, tapping a finger against her generous lips. 'I definitely know where you *can't* get them.'

'The zoo?' Chloe posited.

'Exactly so,' Poppy marvelled, pointing at Chloe as though she were a gameshow contestant on a lucky streak. She looked back at Xan with a stern expression. 'The paperwork's a bitch. You're looking at a week, basic.'

'Okay, so not the zoo. How about the—'

'Aquarium?' Chloe suggested.

He nodded. 'Yeah, exactly. The aquarium.'

Poppy pulled a pitying expression. 'Same problem.' She waggled her very-chewed Bic at him. 'What *you* need is a private collector.'

'Or an eccentric billionaire?' Chloe cut in. 'There's bound to be one who keeps them as giant chess pieces or something.'

'Very true,' Poppy said, nodding in agreement.

'Yes, but *who* has a private collection of penguins on the eastern seaboard?' Xan asked, looking panicked. 'I mean, I know several ornithologists – Bob Truman has . . . owls and falcons? Some eagles too, I think.'

'Trump probably has a flock of flamingos at Mar-a-Lago you could borrow,' Chloe offered.

Xan repressed a shudder. 'That really would mess with the dress code. It's supposed to be a black and white party.'

'Oh. Bummer.' She leaned back in her chair, swinging side to side in half-circles, her eyes pinned thoughtfully on a commuter ferry sailing down the East River. The sun was skimming through the tower blocks at a sharp angle as it slid down the walls of the sky, lending the water's usual green tint a coppery patina. She reached for her new Dior cat-eye shades – she always left a pair dangling over the corner of her screen for just such emergencies – arching her eyebrows questioningly at Poppy.

'Mmm. Very nice,' Poppy said approvingly. 'Are those the ones Charlize Theron had?'

'Yeah, I saw them in Barneys. You like?'

'I *love*. Can I try them on?'

'*Hello?* My penguins?' Xan interjected as they began playing dress-up. 'I'm running out of time here. How far north do you think we can go in a chopper to get back to the Hamptons in time for the party? We could be nudging into Maine, maybe even Quebec?'

'Yeah, maybe,' Poppy agreed, admiring her reflection in the tiny mirror Blu-tacked to the corner of her screen.

'I mean, Canada's cold,' he continued as she pulled a pout. 'It's freezing. They've got to have penguins.'

Poppy gave him a sad shake of the head. 'Penguins are indigenous to the Antarctic Circle, babe. Canada has *bears*.'

Chloe gave a mournful sigh. 'If only she'd asked for bears!'

'Now that certainly would be a party no one would forget . . . It'd be a black and white and red dress code pretty damn quick,' Poppy giggled, amusing herself.

An idea came to Xan, his face brightening. 'Wait – never work with kids or animals, right? But *some* people do. That's their specialism. So that's what I need – the name of an animal trainer. Someone in film.'

'Sounds good,' Poppy nodded, handing Chloe back her glasses.

Xan gasped again, becoming animated now. 'Oh! There was that Jim Carrey film a few years ago, wasn't there? That had penguins. Oh, oh! What was it called?' he asked, snapping his fingers excitedly as he tried to recall the name. '. . . *Mr. Popper's Penguins*!'

Poppy did a full revolution in her chair, her ridiculously long legs zigzagging to keep her feet off the ground. 'I *loved* that film! We bunked off a geography field trip to go and see it when I was in the Upper Fifths.'

'I think I must have missed it,' Chloe wrinkled her nose and did a spin of her own.

'Oh babe, you've gotta see it.'

'Right – so we just need to find out who supplied the birds for that,' Xan mumbled, giving up on their help and rushing back to his side of the desk. 'They might have a contact on this coast . . .' His voice trailed off. '. . . What's this?' He read something on the screen before looking up at Poppy. 'You've already sent me a number?'

'Oh. Yeah,' Poppy shrugged. 'The guy owns a wildlife reserve in Vermont; he hires out some of the animals to certain events to fund his conservation activities.'

'But . . . but why didn't you just tell me that in the first place?' he almost shrieked. 'I've just wasted ten minutes standing talking to you.'

'Not wasted, Xan. The journey is the destination, remember,' Poppy grinned, shrieking as an açai berry was flicked her way.

Chloe laughed, returning to her own work. As the Corporate Partnerships Director she didn't have to get her hands dirty dealing with the weird, wacky, bizarre and often outright strange requests of their members. Rather, it was her remit to find inroads with companies with overlapping synergies and customer demographics to theirs, securing deep discounts and ready access for their members. Invicta was already the premier luxury concierge club across Europe and although America was a relatively new frontier for the company, operations here were growing faster than anywhere else globally; she had only been based in the New York office for five months but, as in London, much of her time was spent networking, breakfasting, lunching and generally schmoozing for the greater good, with the result that she already knew the city more intimately than most of its born-and-bred inhabitants. They say it takes three winters before someone can call themselves a New Yorker but she already had her ear to the ground of this city, she had taken its pulse and she knew exactly what would make its heart beat faster – be it a new Soho House outpost, the opening of Ian Schrager's latest hotel or Scandinavia's Noma doing a $2,000 per person, one-off pop-up dinner at members-only club Spring Place. Since arriving in February, she had thrown herself into her work with the zeal of ten men and there was not a five-star hotel bar she hadn't drunk in, a Michelin-starred restaurant she hadn't dined in. Poppy was as much her dance-floor partner as she was her desk-mate and Chloe had started to become accustomed to seeing photographs of the two of them in the social pages several mornings a week. But if it sounded great – it was great – her definition of luxury had changed, and as she began to feel her new roots graft to the bedrock of this city, nothing was more enticing than the prospect of a quiet night in; there was only so much top-end living a quiet former Brownie from Northumberland could take.

'Yessss,' Poppy said, putting the phone down and giving a little fist pump.

'What?'

'That was the confirmation I've been waiting for, to say that Alexander can have a week's exclusive use at the new Soneva resort in the Maldives. It doesn't open for another month, but you know how he gets about his privacy.'

Chloe did indeed know. Poppy was a lifestyle manager for the top-tier clients; she only ever handled five at a time – a membership fee of $200,000 a year bought her almost-exclusive attention – and Alexander Subocheva was the top banana. An old-school oligarch, with a mining, hotel and electronics empire with outposts around the world, he lived one of the most extraordinary lives on the planet. Absolutely nothing was off limits to him. When he had wanted to ride motorbikes down Big Sur with Tom Cruise, Poppy had arranged it. When the world's only remaining privately owned Leonardo da Vinci had come up for auction, he had sent her along to get it for him so that it could be hung above the bed in his private jet. This holiday sounded entirely reasonable under the circumstances; he might as easily have asked to vacation on the moon as there.

'Nice.'

Beside her, Poppy's fingers tapped on the keyboard as she fired off a happy email to his executive assistant.

'How's Pelham, by the way? Did they get out okay?'

Poppy groaned. 'Only just – not that *he* knows that.' She had spent most of yesterday trying to charter a fully skippered yacht to sail her favourite – rather beleaguered – client Pelham, Lord Hungerford, from Belize to Tulum after their driver, heading for the jungle, had called to say they'd been targeted by Guatemalan bandits and were being followed. Poppy, who remembered the 'flexibility' of official authorities there from her gap year, had calmly told him to head for the coast and she'd deal with the rest; Chloe had over-heard her – it had been like she'd been giving directions to the pub. 'As far as he's concerned, we changed itinerary because of the weather forecast.' She grinned. 'Poor Pelham.'

Chloe couldn't help but laugh. It was a refrain she heard a lot: 'Poor Pelham'; after thirty years' philandering, gambling and squandering of the family fortune, he'd had an epiphany when his fourth wife ran off with his stepson from his second marriage, and had spent the best part of the last year trying to win back his first wife, Clarissa – 'the love of my life and the best thing that ever happened to me, but I was too bloody blind to see it,' he'd moaned down the phone to Poppy. He and 'Rissa' had settled into a comfortable friendship over the years – she had chosen to forgive his betrayal 'for the children's sake' – but although she was happy as his 'companion' in their newly warmed-up relationship, she refused to countenance moving to anything more formal again, despite Pelham's ever more extravagant declarations of love. He had been trying to propose for several months but kept being thwarted in his attempts, not just by Rissa's stubbornness but by various acts of God too, and now . . . lawless South American bandits.

'So anyway, Elle and I are hitting Montauk this weekend if you fancy it?' Chloe said, flicking through a ritzy brochure outlining a projected luxury property development in the Swiss Alps; she was negotiating a deal for their members to get first dibs and buy off-plan, and she had a meeting pencilled in for the following week to tie down terms. 'We're getting the 7.09 p.m. Jitney.'

'Ugh, I'd love to but I really can't.' Poppy flopped again, throwing her long limbs out like a starfish, head tipped back so that her hair dangled down almost to the base of her chair. 'I've got to stay here, just in case. Alexander's got his big dinner tonight and I cannot afford for a single thing to go wrong. He's got it all so top-secret.'

'Why the big fuss?' Chloe could only imagine the combined net worth around that particular dinner table – equivalent to the GDP of a lesser European power, perhaps?

'He's rooting out some potential investors for the hotel chain; he's pretty keyed up about it so I need everything to go off perfectly.'

'Which it will.' She knew better than anyone the effort Poppy had gone to. As her neighbour, she had overheard everything from the genesis of the idea to its execution. Alexander's brief had been: 'Something spectacular, unforgettable. A statement of my unique vision and pioneering luxury.' And so Poppy had come up with a silver-service dinner on an iceberg.

The logistics had been formidable – high winds, and the inherent fragility of the iceberg that had been identified as best suitable for the job meant arriving by helicopter wasn't an option, and Poppy had not only sorted out the catering and travel logistics to get the select few guests to Greenland, but had also arranged for each of them to be measured – wherever they had happened to be in the world at that point – for bespoke reindeer-hide suits that would be ready and waiting for them to change into on the jet. Once they landed, dog-pulled sledges and drivers were waiting on the ground to transport them to the safest disembarking point off the mainland (which was changing daily due to the ice melt) from where a Rib of ex-Navy Seals would take them to the iceberg. An ice sculptor had spent the past three days carving a turned staircase for them to walk up and a fleet of butlers were going to be waiting at the top with trays of perfectly chilled vodka. It was incredible, ridiculous. Exactly what passed as normal for a man like Alexander Subocheva.

'Well, it's a shame you can't come tonight – we're hitting that new steak place in Amagansett – but the spare bed's still free if you want to swing by,' Chloe said. Elle had rented a tiny cottage in Montauk for the summer season but Chloe was so often spending the weekends in it too, that she was chipping in with the rent. Strictly speaking it was a two-bedder, but Poppy wasn't too grand to sleep on the small two-seater sofa-bed in the living room, her bare feet dangling over the end of the mattress.

She put down the ski resort brochure and reached for her bag. Friday six o'clock meant it was officially the weekend. She was outta here.

'Hmm, Sunday day could be good. What time will you be leaving to come back?'

'Not till late. If you got the first bus down—'

Poppy gave a lopsided grin. 'Alternatively, Alexander will be back by then. If he's choppering in to his compound, I might try to cadge a lift with him.' Her phone rang again. 'I'll text you, let you know.' She picked it up and shot Chloe a wink as she drained the remains of her water bottle. 'Hey, Mike, how are you? Still in LA I see . . .'

Michael Greenleve, music producer, cockney as a pearly king but now a high-roller in LA. Chloe felt she almost knew Poppy's clients by heart too. Sitting in such close proximity meant conversations were rarely private and, as such, Chloe knew he liked rock but not reggae, took his steak rare, smoked only Partagás Serie D cigars, was on his third wife, had just ordered the new invitation-only LaFerrari Spider, had mistresses in both the Hills and Jamaica, where he did a lot of his recording (both mistresses knew about the wife but not each other), and was currently committed to a high-intensity interval-training exercise programme that had seen him rushed to emergency care twice – without a single conversation explicitly about him ever passing between them.

'Down to San Francisco . . . ?' she heard Poppy's voice receding behind her. 'In a sub . . . ? Ohmigod, Mike, that sounds amazing! . . . Yes of course I can. When were you thinking . . . ?'

Montauk, Long Island, the next day

Embers from the beach fire twisted in the air before them, performing gymnastic leaps and arcs against the blushing dusk, the cool beads of condensation sliding down the beer bottles in their hands. Chloe was sitting in a low-slung Adirondack chair, her bum almost grazing the deck, her long bare legs extended up onto the low balustrading of the stoop with a view of the surf crashing beyond, the soundtrack from inside the bar just a mellow backbeat out here. She was examining her toes and wondering whether the baby-blue polish had a touch of the hypothermic about it as Elle, sitting beside her, caught up on her Instagram feed.

They had enjoyed another of their signature lazy days on the beach, although the definition of lazy here was quite different to her understanding of the word when she had lived back in Chiswick: instead of a lie-in, hangover, greasy spoon brunch and an afternoon on the sofa or, if the weather was nice, lying on a blanket in Dukes Meadows, her Saturdays here consisted of a five-mile hike around the Point, a

Pilates class and a game of beach volleyball, before she could justify a prolonged flop on the sand all afternoon.

Chloe pressed her fingers to the skin by her eyes; it felt salted and tight now, in spite of her crazed SPF30 habit that saw her reapply layers every ninety minutes without fail. But then, she had Celtic blood, it was obvious just from looking at her; her father had always described her pale skin and freckles as being like nutmeg sprinkled on milk. She'd inherited his hazel-green eyes and her mother's luxuriantly thick auburn hair – she wasn't made for five hours on white sand; she was built for northern winters and cable-knit sweaters, gathering logs and drinking cocoa.

Elle, on the other hand, was born to days like these – almost six feet tall and of Ghanaian descent, her blue-black skin gleamed defiantly right back at the sun, her limbs so long and lean it was like lying next to Naomi Campbell, skin as taut as a trampoline. The only thing to bother her in this landscape was getting sand in her hair – a magnificent Afro that easily added another five inches to her height. Beside her, Chloe couldn't have looked more like a former hockey-playing English schoolgirl if she'd tried. A soul singer with a voice like warm honey and ginger, Elle was born to the stage – her voice demanded it, her physique commanded it and subsequently, she held something of a niche cult status in the cabaret bars and party scene of downtown Manhattan. No party could swing without her. She was always the most vibrant and fabulous person in a room – helped by a penchant for colourful vintage clothing – and Chloe was still occasionally taken aback to think that this bird of paradise had so completely taken her under her wing. The first time they'd met had been at the Strand bookshop on 12th and Broadway; they'd both reached for the same title when there was only one copy left. Elle, who had got her hands on it first, had suggested sharing it and meeting up for coffee to discuss it afterwards. The coffee, ten days later – they had both raced through the story – had segued into dinner and then dancing in a club in SoHo, and just like that, a friendship had been born. They'd barely left each other's sides since and with Poppy frequently joining them too, Chloe had felt the first buds of her new life here begin to flower.

'So where d'you wanna eat?' Elle asked, dropping her head back on the chair and looking at her with a desperate expression. She did this a lot, her hunger coming on in sudden, violent bursts; when she needed to eat, the word 'now' was always silently attached to it.

Chloe's eyes narrowed in consideration. She was always hungry, not just sporadically. 'Are you feeling burgers? Or pizza?'

'Right now, I'm vibing both.'

'Well let's go to Navy Beach, then. It's closest and we should be able to get a table quickly.'

'Sounds like a plan,' Elle said, tucking her long legs in and standing up. It was like watching a baby giraffe waking up. 'I'll get the tab. My turn.'

She disappeared inside, the top of her hair brushing the doorway. Chloe stared out to sea and watched the last of the boats coming back in from a day on the water, the lights of the marina further along the headland already flashing beacons. She tracked the lights with her eyes, barely bothered to move her head. She didn't want to move; she felt limpid and relaxed, the beer adding a gentle buzz to the warm night. She would sleep well tonight, she already knew, and she hoped Elle didn't want to go clubbing later, that they could let their evening drift to a drowsy close. Clubbing meant more drinks and small talk with nameless men, eye contact and suggestive dancing. And whilst that worked for Elle, these easy hook-ups, they were a complication she didn't need; not yet. She kept trying to get herself there but she wasn't in that place yet. It was too soon.

Her own phone rang on the deck beside her chair and, for a moment, she was tempted to leave it. Especially when she saw it was from work. She picked it up *because* it was from work.

'Hello?' she asked quizzically. No one from the office ever called her at the weekend.

'Chloe? It's Jack.'

'. . . Hi, Jack!' She couldn't hide the astonishment in her voice. Jack Mortimer was one of the company's founding partners, a good-looking, tall, former public school boy with a flop in his hair that would make Hugh Grant sigh with envy. He had rowed for Cambridge and was what her mother – who had a gift for summing people up with neat accuracy – would have called 'an old-school playboy' with a renowned love of the cards, horses and women. He was famously horizontal most of the time, but caught at the wrong moment, on the wrong day, he could be offhand, mercurial and quick-tempered – a cat with claws. 'What's up? Is everything okay?'

'Not really, no.' He sounded distracted. 'Look, where are you?'

'In Montauk.' Her eyes fell to the inky horizon again.

'Oh great,' he muttered under his breath. 'Practically half-way to London then.'

What? That wasn't remotely true, although clearly it was undesirable to him that she wasn't still on East 10th. Something was wrong. She rose to standing, going to lean on the balustrade. The last wink of day was barely a slit on the horizon, night's dark chariots pulling down jet curtains, the sea breeze beginning to pick up. 'Jack, what is it? What's wrong?'

'Look, Chloe, I need you to get back to Manhattan.'

'Okay,' she said slowly, wondering what was going on. 'I can leave first thing, but—'

'No. I need you to get back here, like, now.'

'*Now?*' she spluttered, looking at the beer bottle in her hand; it was her third. A gentle numbing fuzz was beginning to settle over her. 'But why? What's happened?'

There was a pause and she could almost hear his struggle in the vacuum.

'Jack?' Her hand gripped the phone more tightly, her eyes pinned to the boat on the horizon now, as though she needed something to hold on to. She felt the anticipation build in her with every breath, fear beginning to creep like a mist.

'There's . . . there's no easy way to say this, Chloe . . . there's been an accident.'

'. . . Are you okay?'

'Not me.' She heard him take a deep breath. 'It's Poppy.'

'*What?*' Chloe gasped, feeling the blood pool to her feet as she forgot to breathe.

'She was hit by a car as she left the office tonight. Some fucking idiot careered onto the kerb –' He swallowed. '. . . The driver fled the scene. The police are looking for him now but by all accounts it happened so quickly, it was over and he was gone before people even knew what was happening.'

A car driving onto the kerb? No. This couldn't be happening. 'Do they think it was a terrorist act?' Chloe whispered, scarcely able to believe she was asking the question. Two minutes ago, it had just been another regular Saturday night . . .

'No. At this point, everything suggests a drunk driver. Hit and run.'

She scrunched her face up at his answer; was it preferable? Where was the comfort in it being an accident, knowing that it was simply random, just plain bad luck, the ultimate case of wrong place, wrong time?

'But is she okay? I mean, she's okay, right?' She saw Elle, who had come back now and was standing by their chairs, questions on her face as she took in Chloe's urgent tone.

There was a pause. 'We don't know anything yet, the doctors will only liaise with next of kin. But from what I understand, she's still unconscious.'

'Still? What do you mean, "still"?' Her voice was shrill, tight as a wire.

'According to eyewitnesses at the scene, she hit her head on impact.'

Chloe gasped again. 'No!'

'But . . . but on the plus side, the paramedics were there within minutes. She's going to be fine, Chloe,' he said with determination, as though that alone would decide it. 'She'll pull through this. Poppy's strong.'

Chloe didn't answer – exactly how strong did you have to be to take on a car and win?

She couldn't process this. She couldn't think straight. It was as though the world had tilted ninety degrees on its axis and her feet were sliding . . . 'Have her parents been informed?'

'Yes. We've booked them on the next flight out. They'll be here by morning.'

'I'll collect them from the airport then,' Chloe murmured, gathering herself, trying to rally.

'No need. I've already told them I'll do it.'

'But there must be something *I* can do.'

'There is, it's why I'm calling. I need you to get back to Manhattan and pick up Poppy's client load.'

Chloe's jaw dropped. *'Me?'*

'I know it's a lot to ask. This is all a lot to take in. Trust me, I *know.*'

'But, Jack,' she stammered, trying to keep up, to make her brain function. Why was he even thinking about work at a time like this? 'I don't do front-of-house, for one thing. I'm nowhere near experienced enough. I don't have the contacts or the . . . the nous to handle her clients.'

'Give yourself more credit, Chloe, you're easily up to this. Tom told me how you stepped in when they had vacancies in London.'

'But that . . . that was a different level. General membership – tickets to a Bieber concert, dinner reservations at the Firehouse. I'd be no good with the big boys.'

There was a pause. 'Chloe, please. There's no one else I can ask.'

'What about Serena?'

But it felt like treachery even suggesting it. Poppy didn't have the darkness in her to hate anyone but if she had, she would have hated Serena Witney. Serena was the only other VIP lifestyle manager in the New York office, but the two women couldn't have been more different, and it was no accident of design that their desks were at opposite ends of the office. Whilst Poppy's clients adored the warmth, bohemianism and witty irreverence that belied her formidable professional capabilities, Serena's admired her for a service

20

that was cool and clinical. She was never late or unprepared, tired or anything less than immaculate, and she looked upon her own clients' successes as a proud mother would, basking in the reflected glory. Poppy had no objection to that, as she'd muttered to Chloe many times over lunch, stabbing her kale with her fork, but she did object that Serena was neither a team player nor an adequate manager to the more junior associates on her desk and only ever seemed interested in engaging in a battle of egos with *her*. Poppy handled Serena's brittle nature the best way she knew how – by taking the mickey – and when she'd joked that Serena had only ever taken the job to land herself a rich husband, Poppy had seen the glimmer of fear in her eyes and subsequently repeated it at every possible opportunity.

'Serena handles Lorenzo Gelardi,' Jack said with barely repressed weariness.

'Oh. God, yes.' How could she have forgotten? Lorenzo Gelardi was Serena's own pet mogul, heir to a shipping fortune which he had taken and built up into a world-leading logistics empire. The fact that he and Subocheva despised each other – Alexander's model wife had once been engaged to Lorenzo – only served to further polarize Serena and Poppy's positions and embed their own rivalry. If the men were to find out they were both clients of the same concierge company things would become difficult enough; there was simply no question of both of them being handled by the same lifestyle manager too.

'So you can see why I need you back here and holding the fort – pick up Poppy's client list and keep them happy, that's all I'm asking. Just until she recovers. Which she will.'

'Of course.' Chloe nodded, hearing his optimism, wanting to feel it. She watched a wave barrel towards the shore, rearing up as though holding its breath, before smashing down into oblivion. She watched the foam bubble and hiss before it sank into the sand. She couldn't believe this was happening. Poppy – mown down. By a drunk. Just a regular Saturday night out . . .

He heard her silence and registered it as disapproval. 'Look. I know I must sound like a heartless git talking about clients at a time like this, when all any of us cares about is Poppy pulling through. Believe me, I feel demented about it, I want to kill the bastard who's done this to her. But there's nothing I *can* do, and sitting around, out of our minds and letting everything go to pot, isn't going to help her – and it could actively hurt us; she wouldn't want that. She would know we can't leave her clients dangling whilst they're waiting for her to get better. They all adore her, of course they do, but let's not fool ourselves – if we don't keep their juggernauts rolling in the interim, someone else will. Their sympathy will run short if they can't continue their own lives as normal.'

'Jack,' she sighed. 'I hear what you're saying, but there must be others better placed to fill in for her than me. Xan, for example. I'm the newest member of the team here.'

'Yes, but you've also worked for the company overall for longer than any of them. Not to mention you fit the profile – Poppy's clients like an unflappable English voice at the end of the line.'

'Yes! Because her father's a peer of the realm. They like the nobility by association. I don't have that. My father was a maths teacher.'

'Listen, you sit next to Poppy, you overhear her conversations, the tone she uses with her clients, what they like. You know them, even if you don't know that you do. Trust me, there's no one better qualified for this than you.' He took a breath. 'Plus, Poppy would choose you to cover for her, you know she would.'

Chloe closed her eyes, knowing he was right. She tried to think, to pull herself together. 'Did the iceberg dinner go to plan, do you know?'

'I haven't heard otherwise so I assume so. Subocheva's never slow to make his displeasure known, let's face it.'

'Well I guess that's something. She had been planning it for weeks. Did you know she even had special reind—'

'On to the next, Chloe,' he said briskly. 'That's old news. Subocheva will already be on to the next thing so you must be too. It's why I need you back here. You need to get up to speed with where he's at and find out exactly what he needs next.'

'But what if I *can't* do it, Jack?' she winced, winding her fingers in her hair. 'I don't have Poppy's contacts, her imagination.'

'Fake it till you make it. Just keep smiling and saying yes. Nothing's impossible, only time-consuming. Come to me or Tom if you hit a wall.'

As if. 'I guess,' she agreed, biting her lip nervously.

'Look, you're not alone in this, Chloe. We'll support you in every way we can but you need to remember *you're* doing this to support Poppy. It's the best way you can help her right now. We're all left hanging, not knowing how she is or what's going on. The only thing we can do is keep the balls in the air for her till she gets back and starts trying to convince everyone she's really a cabbie's daughter from Peckham.'

Chloe tried to chuckle, smile even, but the horror of her loud, lanky friend stretched out on a hospital bed with

God-only-knows-what injuries meant her body wouldn't obey. 'You're right. It's for Poppy. She'd hate for her clients to be let down. I think . . .' She frowned as something came to her. 'I think it's Pelham's daughter's birthday next week. I'll need to check the file.'

'Do that.'

'And . . .' She thought back, recalling Poppy's phone conversation as she'd left the office yesterday. 'I think she was setting up something on a sub for Mike Greenleve.'

'Sub? As in sub*marine*?'

'Yes.'

She heard him sigh again. '. . . Okay. Then check on that, see where she got to with it. But this is good. This is what I meant, Chloe – you're the only one for the job. You know more than you think you do. All those little snippets and passing details. You just need to think back to things you heard and tap in. It's all in there. Just come back here and start getting up to speed with what she was working on; I'm in Palm Beach at the moment – flying back in an hour – but we'll touch base again tomorrow. Hopefully by then there'll be some update from the hospital too.'

'God, I hope so,' Chloe said with urgency. 'Please God let her be all right.'

'We've just got to keep calm and carry on,' he said, before ringing off. Chloe stared at the phone, marvelling that he'd actually, in all seriousness, used the tea-towel cliché.

But he was right. What other choice did they have?

Chapter Two

Hotel Crillon, Paris, July 2018

Elodie swung a crossed leg as the house model struck a pose, the girl's eyes fixed on a painting behind her head. She recognized the look in those eyes all too well, the particular blankness that comes from a severely restricted diet and nights spent drinking tequila, the detachment that is inevitable when you are just a frame, a glorious accidental conflation of long bones and tight skin, startlingly visible and yet invisible at the same time.

She brought her attention back to the dégradé tweed cloth of the girl's jacket instead, the jewelled buttons, the rich ivory-coloured tulle that was so flattering in European light during the winter.

'Now, that could work for the Amfar Benefit in New York at the beginning of October,' murmured Raquel, her stylist, who was sitting beside her and clutching a printout of her formidable social engagements for the next four months. 'The cut would be divine on you.'

'I have a jacket just like it.'

'Yes, but that's in LA and, to be honest, I was never sure about the neck on it. Besides, if we got them to cut this one in the berry colourway, I think it would look so much more vibrant against the dress, don't you think? It's a bit too wed-dingy all in the cream like that.'

Elodie didn't reply; already she could feel herself being worn down by her stylist's relentless, voracious acquisitive-ness.

'And that shade of red is so your colour,' Raquel added.

It was decided then.

The atelier mistress standing off to the side, a vision of effi-ciency and discretion in a white work coat, nodded her head and the model kicked her foot forward, spinning round on the spot and sashaying from the room, just as another entered in a midnight and white feathered gala gown.

'Now this, this,' Raquel said, with a buzz of excitement in her voice, 'should be just perfect for the Breast Cancer bene-fit next month. If they can get it done in time.' She raised her head and addressed the atelier mistress directly. 'Is that possible, Madame Dubeau?'

'Of course. It would be prioritized, naturally.'

'No – it's sleeveless,' Elodie said, raising an objection. On this, she wouldn't be pushed.

Raquel's threaded eyebrows arched to a perfect point as they always did on this subject. 'But your arms are exquisite, Elodie, so slim.'

Elodie gave a tiny dismissive shake of her head and held her tongue, knowing her silence was more powerful in put-ting across her displeasure.

Raquel looked back at Madame Dubeau with a sigh. 'Could sleeves be put on this style or do you think they would detract?'

'*Peut-être*, a narrow bracelet sleeve in the silk chiffon? Or a balloon style in the silk mousseline? We could get the atel-ier to make up a toile showing the different looks?'

The house model – staring at the same painting behind Elodie's head – shifted her weight onto the other hip. There, but not.

Raquel looked back at her. 'What do you think?' Her tone was confiding, intimate. 'I think it's a toss-up between this and the Valentino.'

'Valentino?' Elodie queried. There had been so many. How could she be expected to remember?

'Yes, red satin – you know the one, tiny little bow at the neck, trapeze line, very skinny arms?'

'Ah,' Elodie nodded, not quite sure if she genuinely did remember it or if Raquel's earnest tone had simply convinced her she did. 'Well, if the Valentino's already got the sleeves . . .'

'You're right of course. I doubt Karl would thank us for tinkering with the fine-tuning of his creation.' Raquel looked over at Madame Dubeau. 'We'll pass on this.'

Madame Dubeau nodded again and the model kicked her foot forward in the identical fashion of the previous girl, leaving the room just as the elevator 'dinged'. Everyone looked up and Elodie felt that frisson that she always felt when her husband walked into a room. It was as though the molecular set-up actually changed – compressed somehow, sucking out the air, making the colours shimmer.

She watched as he strode down the outer hall, walking through the open arch to the drawing room of their suite, his eyes pinned upon her. He had been away for seventeen days now – Berlin, London, New York, Chicago and elsewhere besides; he didn't usually leave her for so long.

Her eyes followed his every move, her heart beating harder as it always did in his presence, but she didn't stir from her seated position on the little gilt chair and she watched as he took in the scene – little girls playing dress-up.

'You ladies look like you're enjoying yourselves.' Amusement curled in the words like a sleeping cat. His dark-suited silhouette, strong-shouldered and compact, looked hard-edged and blocky in the elegant, ethereal room where extravagant domed displays of white peonies – as big as snowmen's heads – sat on spindle-legged tables, and the pale-celery silk-lined walls were hand-drawn with wispy chinoiserie.

'Darling, you remember Madame Dubeau from the Chanel Atelier,' Elodie said in a quiet voice. 'And Raquel, of course.'

'Of course,' he murmured, inclining his head fractionally in agreement even though Elodie knew he had absolutely no idea who the sleek-bobbed brunette to her right was. He had met Raquel a dozen times before but he always greeted her as a perfect stranger. '*Enchanté*, ladies.'

Another model stepped through from the spare bedroom that was being used as the dressing area, a startled look crossing her face and causing her to falter momentarily in her long-legged stride as she saw the client's husband's sudden, unexpected bulk behind the silk sofa, an almost violent intrusion of masculine energy in what had been a cocoon of feminine activity. But then again, power and the illusion of it often had strong effects on people. It stunned, sometimes frightened, other times excited.

The poor girl resumed her walk – suddenly, the task looked difficult, the jet-beaded evening dress ridiculously *de trop* in the mid-morning light.

'Raquel and I are refreshing our memories of the collection. We have a busy autumn schedule coming up,' Elodie said, watching him watch the model who had struck her pose and was now frozen on the spot, trembling like a deer, eyes unblinking on that damned painting behind her.

'But is this necessary?' her husband asked with a hint of a wry smile climbing into his eyes. 'All this . . . drama?' A fractional tip of his head indicated the immaculate, serenely quiet room. 'If you need a new wardrobe, my love, just buy the lot.'

Beside her, Raquel startled as though prodded by a red-hot poker. 'Sorry?'

But Elodie fell ever more still. She knew what her husband wanted, what he was really saying.

'Darling, you're too good to me,' she said quietly, holding his gaze for a moment before turning back to the other women in the room. 'And you're busy, Madame Dubeau, I should have realized there are so many others who need your attentions; I'm being selfish detaining you here.' She smiled, allowing a beam of radiance to escape from her as she rose from her seat and formally ended the proceedings. 'Could you please arrange for one of everything in my size, excluding the previous dress? But we'll take the jacket from Look Twelve in the berry red. And my usual requirements apply.' Nothing above the knee. No bare arms. No extreme cleavage or cut-outs.

'*Bien sûr*,' the atelier mistress nodded, too elegant to allow her jubilation to show on her face as the house model clipped past at a pace. 'And would you like it to be delivered here, or to one of the other addresses?' They had five on file for her.

'Here's fine.' Her hands were clasped in front of her but impatience was folded in the gesture and Madame Dubeau, understanding, discreetly took her leave. They had her measurements. The finer details could be arranged another time.

Raquel, on the other hand, was oblivious to Elodie's subtlety, her almost-black eyes bright with the excitement that came from coolly dropping half a million on a single designer's collection for a season's worth of parties.

Elodie headed her off at the pass, leaning forward to air-kiss her cheeks. 'It was so good of you to arrange this, Raquel, thank you. I'll let you get back to your day. You must be so busy at this time in the couture schedule.'

'Oh – well, yes,' Raquel stammered as Elodie took her hand in her own and shook it lightly. The butler was standing waiting by the arch to lead her out. 'But we'll need to talk about the Valentino. I still think—'

'Absolutely. I'll call you.'

'And I've got Dior booked for Thursday.'

'Wonderful.'

Elodie's stillness had been cultivated over many years; her stunning looks had exposed her to a lifetime of hungry stares and jealous scrutinies which she had always struggled to endure. She had never enjoyed being in the limelight, never liked having her photograph taken, and her wedding day, in which she was subjected to all those things, had been an agony. It had been many years before she had come to notice how her guarded demeanour actively unnerved people, that the more quietly she spoke and the more still she became, the more agitated and restless they became in turn, as though they had to fill and occupy the vacuum she created. Usually they could endure a few minutes at most before they were compelled to move off, leaving her to the peace she craved.

She was working it right now, seeing how they scattered.

She smiled but said nothing, her dark eyes blank and unreadable, and Raquel scrabbled for her bag, shoving in the notebook with her elaborate – but quite unnecessary – sketches of each outfit she had earmarked for her client. 'Such a fabulous decision; the entire collection's to die for; you'll be a vision,' she said, blowing extravagant kisses as she dodged sofas and side tables and followed the butler through to the ante-hall.

Elodie waited for the click of the suite door closing before she slid her eyes over to her husband's. He was waiting, one hand reached out to her, the palm up and open.

'Shall we, darling?'

Chapter Three

New York

The office had been designed with the wow factor in mind. Visitors, upon stepping out of the lifts, were faced with a double-height space – the advantages of taking the top two floors of an old factory – and a run of wall-to-wall khaki steel windows that looked straight onto the river. But if the carcass of the building was industrial, the fittings were super-luxe, with matt-black walls and banks of ivory leather desks grouped in rectangular clusters through the open-plan space. What enclosed spaces there were, were smoked-glass cubes of various sizes – the smallest for receiving guests and confidential tête-à-têtes, others for bigger department meetings, and the biggest of all for Jack's office. The idea behind it was inclusivity – no hidden agendas, no political power plays behind locked doors and shuttered windows – but it had led to something of an office ritual to lay bets on the colour and design of Jack's dandy socks each day as he came in and invariably pushed his shoes off, whilst sitting at his desk. (If she remembered correctly, Friday's had been Dennis the Menace motifs on black.)

The Poggenpohl kitchen, at the opposite end, just down from the lifts, boasted four Gaggia Naviglio coffee machines and a vast Meneghini La Cambusa fridge, which was freshly stocked with sushi every morning for employees to nibble on at will; the kitchen abutted a vast soft-seating area put together from vintage orange-velvet Bellini chairs, with board games and noise-cancelling headphones left out for anyone who needed them. The pièce de résistance, however, had to be the giant graphic world map that ran one full room height along the nearside wall. White on a black background, tiny lights flickered on it intermittently like peeping stars on a cloudy night, indicating requests coming in from members across the globe and providing an at-a-glance guide to which regions were awake and active at any given time.

Chloe wasn't sure she would ever forget Jack's partner Tom Elliott's face when he had received the architects' final invoice, but Jack had been adamant – how could they promote a luxury lifestyle to their customers if they didn't deliver it to their staff? It was about 'integrity', Jack had insisted; that was his favourite word whenever he was trying to get his way on something. But perhaps he'd had a point – *Architectural Digest* had run a feature on Invicta's new American headquarters when the space had been unveiled and plenty of other features had run on it since, buying them invaluable publicity and inculcating them on the radar of Manhattan's most asset-rich, time-poor denizens.

But there was no wow factor for Chloe as she walked in now, at almost midnight on a Saturday night. On her way in, she had seen the whirl of blue lights, police tape flickering around a protected area further down the street, and the sight of it had almost made her throw up. Poppy. She knew that was where it had happened, she just *knew* it. Her friend's favourite juice bar was half a block along. Had she been going to get herself one, a treat after yet another Saturday in the office?

She stood for a moment, staring at Poppy's desk. Nothing tangible had changed. It remained exactly as Chloe had left it the evening before, except that the drained cup of green juice was now in the bin; but her chair was left on a half-spin, facing away, as though she'd jumped out of it – which was quite likely, knowing Poppy.

At the very end of the space, the lights from the out-of-hours desk pooled onto the corridor floor, the team's voices just a low murmur behind the door as they dealt with the bread-and-butter requests of securing restaurant reservations, getting members onto club VIP lists and booking last-minute hotel suites.

Chloe sank down, weak-kneed, into her friend's chair and looked around her with teary eyes, the evening's earlier beers beginning to make her head throb. Tentatively, as though trying on the space for size, she ran her hands over the smooth surface of the desk, her eyes hopping like a robin over the eclectic gathering of miscellanea – a fig-scented candle almost burnt to the base; a black and white photo of Poppy with her four siblings, all of them dangling from the giant sweeping branches of an ancient yew tree; the pink starfish she had bought in Little Exuma in March and used as a completely useless paperweight; the patchouli and rose otto meditation mist she would spray, 'Omming' loudly, whenever Serena click-clacked past looking officious; the severely chewed lids of her favourite red Bic biros; a half-empty pack of spearmint gum. And Chloe knew without opening it that there was a small pot of Marmite in the top right drawer, 'for emergencies'.

34

Poppy's desk was barely five feet from her own, and yet everything looked different from this vantage. She had an unobstructed view to the kitchen and lifts, which from Chloe's desk were partially hidden by an exposed brick pillar, and the small mirror affixed to the top of her monitor, which Chloe had assumed was for applying make-up during one of her famous quick-change transformations – Poppy had a model's chameleon-like ability to transform herself with a quick twist of her hair and a hint of dress – actually reflected not just the main glass-walled meeting room but also the happenings on Serena's desk and in Jack's office behind her.

To her right, the white world map winked, so unbalanced with demands as to seem that it might tip over. The West Coast was speckled with pinpricks still but the body of the country behind it lay in darkness; Europe was only just stir-ring and wouldn't hit peak activity for another few hours yet, but it was lunchtime in China and the Asian continent was ablaze with flashing lights. It had always struck Chloe as peculiarly meditative to see the way the lights steadily swept across the wall throughout a day.

She checked the time in Greenland – almost 4 a.m. there. Was Subocheva still there? Chloe didn't know anything of his itinerary once the iceberg dinner was completed, although the fact that Poppy had been in here today suggested she had been following up on his plans. Pulling open one of the side drawers where she knew Poppy kept her client folders, she found the five names she was looking for: Subocheva, Mike Greenleve, Pelham, the film director Christopher Proudlock and Rosaria Bertolotti, the opera singer. It was their lives – global, connected, demanding – that had domin-ated Poppy's every waking hour and now, until she came back, they would dominate Chloe's.

With a weary sigh, she sat back in the chair, her double espresso still steaming through the sip-slit in the lid, and began to read. It was time to get up to speed.

Monday came round with two sweeps of the map, the bright lights swinging east to west like a prison-ground's search-light, the out-of-hours teams switching shifts as night turned to day and back to night again. She had spent the entire weekend camped out here and she had the stiff, aching body to prove it, only returning to her apartment to catch a few hours' sleep before coming back to read and revise Poppy's files like a cramming student. She had learnt about her newly adopted clients' careers and family lives, the exact locations of their international homes and the favourite suites and hotels they preferred to stay in when travelling, their dietary requirements, allergies and cosmetic surgery histories, musical and cultural tastes, preferred designers, names of their pets, the cars they drove, the schools their children went to, the dates of their birthdays, their families and loved ones. She had trawled their social media accounts, making notes of anything extra she thought to be pertinent in shot, and even though she had yet to meet any of them face to face, she felt confident she now knew them better than their mothers, spouses, kids, best friends or bosses. She had the three-sixty view on them, the profile that only built up when their multiple different public faces were super-imposed onto one body in a way that could never happen in life. The business associate would never know her client as a friend; the mistress would never know her client as a spouse; and the friend would never know her client as a business rival. But she did, and their every peccadillo – be it a specific Mont Blanc fountain pen for signing a contract, or forty-eight white long-stemmed roses for a new lover – was on her list and in her head. She had done all she could and now it was Monday and the phone would ring. It would begin.

She had arrived early, partly because Jack and Tom had scheduled a conference call with her at eight and partly because her nerves were making it almost impossible for her to sleep anyway. She had been awake since five and, after abandoning a meditation session halfway through, had jogged the eighteen blocks from her apartment to here, showered and had her feet under the desk by seven.

'—Oh, Chloe. *You're* here.'

Chloe looked up at the voice. Jack had written to the team over the weekend, informing them of Poppy's accident. It wasn't just another Monday, this wasn't business as usual, and as everyone started arriving, the mood in the office was distinctly muted. Poppy's vivacious irreverence had made her the beating heart of the team – she was already missed, Chloe was already not enough.

She pushed back in her chair, fingers interlaced. 'Hi, Serena.' Chloe saw the question on her colleague's face as she took in the sight of Chloe in Poppy's chair, her Vans-stickered headphones over Chloe's ears. 'Yes. Jack's asked me to cover for Poppy till she's back.'

'Really?' she drawled, as though the word was elasticated.

Chloe found the surprise in her voice offensive, the intimation being that she was back office only, not good enough to interact with the prize clients; it was Chloe's exact fear, and within a few words Serena had hit upon it. 'Yes. I did some client-facing work back in London.'

'I never knew that.' Serena nodded as though deciding to

let it pass. 'God, it's so terrible though. I couldn't believe it when I heard. It's so unbelievably distressing.' She didn't look that distressed; in fact, she looked immaculate in a black shirtwaister dress, strappy pointed flats and Michael Kors shades on her head pinning back her long dark hair. It seemed she too had been at the beach this weekend – how long ago Saturday seemed already – for her cheeks and forehead were more tanned than Chloe recalled. She could imagine her, poolside in East Hampton, a chilled drink beside her. Not so very different to how she herself had found out of course, but she could bet their reactions would have been very different. 'How's she doing now? Has there been any further news?'

Chloe looked away, disgusted. As if she cared! This was just gossip to Serena; the woman clearly either didn't know or didn't care that Poppy's life hung in the balance. 'Not that I've heard,' she said in a tight voice, picking up one of Poppy's battered biros and beginning to tap it frantically against the desk.

Serena hesitated, watching her, seeing how Chloe wouldn't return her gaze: she was as closed as a clam. Her eyes skimmed Poppy's desk as though it might be contaminated but she stepped closer and leant against the edge of it, lowering her voice. 'Listen, Chloe, I'm not going to pretend Poppy and I were close. Clearly we weren't what you'd call friends, but what happened to her – it's the most terrible thing. I wouldn't wish that on anyone. I hope more than anything that she'll be okay.'

Chloe looked back at her, seeing the concern writ large over Serena's face. Of course she did. Who wouldn't? There was no room for petty office politics at a time like this. 'I know,' she relented, feeling bad for her intial harsh thoughts.

A sigh escaped her. 'I just wish the hospital would tell us more.'

'Jack's email said she was in a coma?'

The very word made Chloe shudder. 'Induced, yes,' she clarified, as though that somehow made it better, implying that the medics really did have control of this situation. 'She sustained a severe head injury, apparently.'

'My God,' Serena whispered, looking horrified. 'I *still* can't believe it. It all feels like such a horrible dream.'

The word you're looking for is *nightmare*, Chloe thought to herself, wanting to scream. 'I know. It's just terrible.'

Xan came in, his skateboard tucked under one arm and trilby on. His desk was on the other side of the bank to Poppy and Chloe's, Serena's narrow back turned to him, and he arched an unimpressed eyebrow at the sight of her there, cosying up to Chloe.

Chloe didn't respond, Serena was watching her.

'Still, trying to look on the bright side, this is a great opportunity for you. You must be so excited.'

Chloe frowned. 'I'm sorry?'

'To be taking on Poppy's clients. That's no mean feat, she's got some big names on her list – impress them and you could springboard into any job you wanted.'

Chloe blinked. Did Serena really think that she was concerned with her own career trajectory under these circumstances? 'As I said,' she replied in a strangled voice, scarcely able to believe she had just fallen for Serena's duplicity, and aware of Xan's flabbergasted expression behind Serena's back, 'I'm only sitting in for Poppy till she's well enough to come back. I'm very happy in my own area. *This* is not something that I want.'

'Oh, of course. *I* know that.' There was a pause and

Chloe saw Serena was making no move to head off. 'But if I can offer you a friendly word of advice,' she said, leaning in slightly. 'They're tricky characters, Poppy's clients, and they don't suffer fools. Not to mention, Poppy has a way of inveigling herself into people's lives – I'm not sure even *they* realize how much they depend upon her. I know from experience that it's a very intimate relationship, one that takes months – if not years – to nurture; there's a chance they'll resent you for not being her, you should be aware of that. It won't necessarily be an easy ride, these next few weeks.' She reached out and patted Chloe's arm, before straightening up. 'So if you need a friendly steer at any time, you know where to find me, okay? I'd be only too happy to help.'

'Is that bitch for real?' Xan hissed, throwing down his hat furiously.

'I know . . .' Chloe murmured, watching her go. The phone on the desk rang and distractedly Chloe reached out to answer it. 'Invicta, Chloe Marston speaking,' she said on autopilot, spinning back in her chair and watching in the small mirror as Serena reached her own desk and fluffed her sleek hair with a toss of satisfaction. '. . . Hello?'

There was a pause. 'Oh. I wanted Poppy Langham. I thought this was Poppy's direct line.' It was a woman's voice, an accent and annoyance in the words.

Chloe winced, bringing her full attention back to the caller; Poppy's number wasn't listed, only clients had the direct line which meant . . . Rosaria. It had to be Rosaria Bertolotti, her only female client. Serena's words were still ringing in her ears . . . *they'll resent you for not being her*. 'Yes, yes it is. I'm afraid Poppy is unavailable at the moment.'

'*Unavailable?*'

Apparently the word made no sense. 'Yes. I'm going to be covering for her for the next couple of weeks.'

There was a stunned pause. 'But why? Where is Poppy? What is going on?'

Chloe hesitated; she had been rehearsing what she would say since she'd heard the news on Saturday night, but saying the words out loud and actually stepping into these people's lives . . . it was becoming real now. 'I'm afraid it's bad news. There's been an accident and Poppy's in hospital. She was involved in a road traffic accident at the weekend.'

Chloe heard the woman's intake of breath. 'My God.' Her tone had changed completely.

'I'm really sorry.' She wasn't quite sure what she was apologizing for.

'. . . Will she be okay?'

'We think so. We hope so. The doctors aren't releasing much information yet, it's still very early days.'

There was another long pause.

'I'm so sorry to have to be the one to break the news to you,' Chloe continued, hoping she wasn't talking too fast, that the words weren't coming out as a nervous gabble. 'But I want to reassure you that you will continue to receive the same support and expertise in her absence. As I said before, my name is Chloe and I work very closely with Poppy and—'

There was a quiet click.

'Hello? . . . Hello? Are you still there?'

The connection was good and Tom Elliott's open, country-clean face beamed into the room as clearly as if he actually was sitting across the table; she could almost smell his usual double-shot coffee and Armani aftershave drifting through the air.

'. . . hoping to operate later, *if* the swelling's gone down enough,' Jack was saying on her right-hand side and looking haggard. He appeared to be growing a beard, although not by design, and it looked to Chloe as if he had spent as much time at the hospital as she had at the office.

'Jesus, it still doesn't seem . . . it doesn't seem real,' Tom muttered, rubbing his face and looking agitated, no doubt frustrated to be so far away. He was what her mother called a 'doer', preferring always to be in the thick of things, helping, sorting out problems, dismantling crises. It made him both a great manager and a pain in the backside. 'But, I'm sorry to say that word is getting out already,' he sighed. 'Liv's just told me everyone's already beginning to talk about the accident—' Liv was his PA and one of London's best-connected girls about town.

Jack interrupted, a frown crumpling his laughter-lined brow. 'When you say everyone, you mean . . . ?'

'The Soho House crowd; the Condé Nast girls; plus Mills overheard some people talking about it at the polo in Windsor yesterday,' Tom said, counting off his fingers. 'Apparently #prayforpoppy is getting a thread on Insta.'

'Great, so then it's only a matter of time before the paps come sniffing,' Jack groaned. 'They love nothing more than a toff in crisis. I can see it now: *Aristo totty left for dead in hit and run drama.*'

'Jack, don't,' Chloe winced, looking down at her hands.

'Sorry. Sorry,' Jack replied quickly, looking pained at her expression. 'That was a stupid thing to say.'

Tom looked over at Chloe with concern. 'How are *you*

doing, Chloe?' Chloe stared back at him accusingly; like he cared. 'You and she were good friends, I gather.'

'We still are,' she said more sharply than she had intended, but his use of the past tense, as though Poppy was already dead . . . gone.

'Yes, right, that's what I meant.' Tom shot a look at Jack – neither of them was doing a good job of navigating the emotional minefield.

She inhaled deeply, pulling herself back in. 'I'm fine.' She brought her gaze back to his though her expression was more guarded now. She couldn't allow this to get personal.

'And are you up to speed on her clients?'

'Yes. I spent the weekend mugging up on the files,' she said briskly. 'I feel I'm good to go.'

'Have you spoken to any of them yet?'

'No, I wanted to check everything was clear with both of you before I made contact,' she said, before remembering. 'Although, actually, that's not quite true – someone did ring in half an hour ago asking for Poppy and I had to tell them.'

'Really? Who?'

'Well, she hung up before I could get her name—'

'Her? Rosaria Bertolotti then?' Jack said, interrupting her. Chloe shrugged.

'Why did she hang up?' Tom enquired.

'Shock? Upset?'

'Well that's not good! If she needed Poppy and Poppy wasn't there . . .' He looked stressed. 'See? This is exactly what I mean, Jack. We need to contain this. Manage it properly. We can't have her clients finding out after the rest of the bloody world.'

Jack forced a wry smile; he looked too exhausted to do

any more than that. 'Tom, relax. It was one call. Chloe will deal with it, won't you, Chlo?'

'Of course. I'll ring her back after this to introduce myself properly and make sure she – and everyone else – is up to speed on events.'

'Good,' Jack smiled, but Tom still looked concerned, his gaze lingering on her with worried eyes. Chloe tried not to take it personally, his evident fear that she was going to somehow sabotage or jeopardize the company's relationship with five of its most lucrative clients.

'Well just try to anticipate their needs, okay?' he said, shifting in his seat and putting on that earnest but chummy expression he always pulled at their team-bonding gigs. 'Be . . . be proactive, not reactive.'

'Right,' she agreed, like she didn't know that already. 'And so with that in mind, I'm going to propose meeting each of them for drinks, breakfast, lunch, dinner, whatever they can accommodate as soon as possible – and assuming they're in the country. I may know them inside out but it would allow them to get to know me too. Some proper face time would be good, help to really break the ice.'

'Great idea,' Jack agreed. 'As soon as they meet you, they'll be crazy about you. What's not to love, right, Tom?'

Tom met her gaze and blinked back at her through the screen. 'Yes, right.'

Chapter Four

'Okay, now we're getting somewhere,' Chloe sighed, clapping her hands once and pressing the palms together with a pleased expression as she sat back in the chair.

'Success?' Xan asked from his side of the desk. If she and Serena had come back from the weekend with tans, he had had go-faster stripes buzzed into his hair.

'Finally! I've spent the past hour chasing Poppy's clients. It's only five people. Five phone calls. How hard can it be, right? Let me tell you – it's like hunting bloody spies!' She began counting off her fingers. 'Pelham's incommunicado in the Gulf of Mexico, fishing for marlins.' One finger. 'I've left a message for Alexander's assistant in Moscow – according to *her* assistant, he's in Geneva today – but she hasn't come back to me yet.' Two fingers.

'Ah yes, the warm and cuddly Anjelica.' Xan smiled. Subocheva's executive assistant was renowned for her frosty demeanour. 'Well, you won't hear back from her till she's run background checks on you.'

'How reassuring,' Chloe said wryly, hand still in the air.

'Hey, who can blame them?' Xan grinned. 'A strange woman calling on Poppy's line? Just because you're paranoid, it doesn't mean they're not out to get you, am I right?'

'Well I doubt they'll find anything on me apart from an

unpaid parking ticket in Ladbroke Grove and some late library books,' she groaned, forgetting about her countdown and lacing her hands behind her head as she let herself slip back into the memories of her old life for a moment: oozing poached eggs on rye for breakfast at the Daylesford Deli, delicate pink tulips from Wild at Heart, the way the sunlight pooled at the bottom of the bed warming her feet, those crushed vintage linen sheets she'd found at Portobello Market, the drawer – his drawer – which was full to bursting with his spare shirts, pants, toothbrush, socks, condoms . . . No! She snapped back into focus, sitting upright again with a jerk that made Xan frown. 'Uh, anyway, LA's still asleep so I won't try Proudlock or Greenleve till after lunch. But I did just nobble Rosaria Bertolotti's assistant; that was her I was speaking to just now. I'm going over to her hotel for coffee.'

'Nobble?'

'Snaffle. Catch. Get hold of.'

He nodded and she could see he was making a mental note of the new word. 'Well are you going now? Cos I'm doing a one-time-only, never-to-be-repeated doughnut run in a minute. I figure we could all do with a sugar boost.'

He was right. Chloe glanced around the room. The usual buzz that made their office sound more like a coffee shop than a workplace was distinctly absent today, small groups sitting clustered on the sofas, shaking their heads sadly. As though there was no hope.

'The meeting's not for another hour; apparently I was *lucky* to catch the great soprano, as she's flying out to Brazil at lunchtime,' she said, shutting down her computer briskly and grabbing her bag. Their hopelessness wasn't something she would share, or tolerate. She needed to get out, to breathe and get some headspace; she had been cooped up in here for too long now. 'But sadly, no doughnut for me. I'm quickly going to show my face at the Berluti brunch first. I said I'd swing by and clearly they won't be up to speed with the . . . changes here yet.' She had spent much of last week setting up this exclusive private viewing for their members at the Madison store.

'Where's our soprano staying?'

'The Hallmark on Fifth.'

'Corinthian suite?' Xan enquired.

'Yes. Know it?' Chloe asked, checking her hair and make-up in the little screen-mounted mirror. She applied a dab of lip gloss and smoothed down her men's-cut olive trousers, opening up the neck of her crisp, pale-pink shirt.

He nodded. 'Marble bath. Good views of MoMA from that side too.'

'Okay, good to know.'

'If you see Gordon, the concierge, remember me to him. We go way back.'

Chloe smiled – Xan was all of twenty-four; how far back could they possibly go? 'Okay, I will, thanks. Wish me luck.'

'Why? What did luck ever do for you that we can't?' Xan called after her as she walked over to the lifts. She chuckled as the lift doors opened. He had a point.

'Oh, excuse me,' she said, as a man stepped out and almost walked straight into her.

'My mistake,' he said distractedly, seemingly not seeing her – which was a shame; he was *gorgeous* – as he was overwhelmed, like everyone else, by the magnificent space that greeted him. She stepped into the lift and pressed the button to go down, watching him scan the enormous open-plan office. Everyone reacted this way.

He turned back. 'Excuse me, this is Invicta, right?' the man asked after her.

'That's right. Who are you here to see?'

'Poppy Langham.'

'Oh—' The doors began to close. 'Oh!' Frantically, she pressed the 'doors open' button and after a few seconds, the man, who had been rudely sliced out of sight, reappeared again and she jumped out of the lift like a gazelle clearing the grass. She gave an embarrassed smile. A cartoon entrance wasn't the sleek first impression she'd have hoped to give.

'Uh . . . I'm afraid Poppy's not in today but my name's Chloe Marston, I'm covering for her.' Chloe took him in more critically as she put out her hand – early thirties, muscular build, five eleven, longish mid-brown hair that curled over at the front, dark-brown eyes and a week-old beard. He was wearing jeans, Adidas trainers and a navy polo shirt, and she got the impression clothes didn't interest him much.

'Joe Lincoln,' he said, shaking her hand with a grip that made no allowances for their discrepancy in build or height. 'Is Poppy on holiday?'

'Uh, no. She's been . . . unavoidably detained,' Chloe smiled, trying to guess the nature of his appointment with Poppy; there had been nothing in her diary for this morning.

'Really? Because when we met up last week, she gave no indication she would be away. We arranged to meet up here.' His voice was brisk, his gaze disconcertingly direct.

'Oh, right,' Chloe said, even more baffled. Poppy never missed an opportunity to eat or drink out if she could possibly help it and as such, almost never arranged meetings at the office. 'And what was the purpose of your meeting?'

'To discuss membership.' His tone suggested 'what else?'

'Oh, I see,' she said, understanding now. Poppy had given

him a card at some party, drumming up business as she did everywhere she went – people always wanted her in their lives once they had met her – and now he had come knocking, liking the idea of red-carpet tickets and being on all the right guest lists. 'Well it's not actually Poppy you need to see; she's one of our VIP managers and she—'

'Yes, exactly.'

'I'm sorry?'

'We had discussed her becoming my lifestyle manager when we met up last week. I'm only in town for a couple more hours so I said I'd drop in when I was passing.' He shifted his weight onto the other foot, looking restless now. In spite of his low-key attire, he had the brisk, direct manner of a man whose time was important. And valuable.

'Oh.' Chloe didn't know what to say. The VIP managers only ever looked after five members at a time – it was all that was reasonably possible given the number of hours they had to devote to each one at this level – and Poppy had a full book. Why had she told this man he could join her client list? 'Um, please, I'm forgetting my manners,' she said, smiling and ushering him away from the lifts. 'Won't you come this way and we can talk more privately in one of the meeting rooms?'

'Fine.'

She led him over to the meeting room that was opposite Jack's office, behind her own desk, desperately trying to get his attention as they passed. But Jack was on the phone, sitting on the edge of his desk and looking out of the opposite window, his back to them. She could tell by the high set of his shoulders that it wasn't a pleasant conversation. Was he on the phone to Poppy's parents? The hospital?

She closed the door, instantly silencing the low hum of

amiable telephone chatter behind them. The idea behind the transparent walls had been inclusivity, but sitting here now felt more akin to being on a stage, there to be watched, judged for stepping into Poppy's shoes without, seemingly, a second thought – for it hadn't only been Serena who had been startled to see she had been the one chosen to pick up the slack.

Over Joe's shoulder, she could see Xan's surprised look at her volte-face back into the office. She shrugged her eyebrows at him, trying not to smile as he pulled an outrageous expression, clearly approving of the very attractive man before her; he bit down on his crooked index finger excitedly.

'Please take a seat. Can I get you anything to drink – tea, coffee, matcha, a juice?'

'No. Thanks,' he added as an afterthought, spreading his arms over the top of the low white leather tub chairs. He took in his surroundings at a leisurely pace.

'So, I'll start by apologizing, Mr Lincoln.'

He looked straight at her and it was like being hit with a dart. 'Joe, please.'

'Joe,' she nodded. 'I'm afraid you've caught me on the hop. Today has been . . . unusual for lots of reasons.'

'I'm getting that. When's Poppy back?'

'Well that's the thing, we don't know.'

He frowned.

'I'm afraid, the truth is, Poppy was badly injured in a car accident at the weekend. She's in hospital.'

'Jesus.' Joe frowned, looking sterner than ever. 'Is she going to be okay?'

'We don't know that either. She's currently in a coma.'

'Christ, that's terrible.' Joe sat further back in the chair, staring unseeing out of the window for a long moment. 'God, I'm sorry to hear that. She's really great. I like her a lot.'

'Yes. Everyone loves Poppy.'

He looked at her again. 'And so *you're* filling in?'

As though she was something he'd found under his shoe. So much for first impressions. 'Yes. It's been a shock for all of us, the entire team, and we're all just trying to . . . keep things going as best we can until we know more.'

He shook his head, still distracted by the news. 'You make it sound bad – her chances, I mean.'

Chloe hesitated. Did she? She felt gripped by panic that the worst might happen and yet refused to succumb to that morbid lethargy of her colleagues; she felt impelled to keep moving, keep doing stuff. She had thought that felt like the right thing to do. 'I'm sorry, I don't mean to sound gloomy. We should know more tomorrow. They're hoping they'll be able to operate then.'

'Christ,' he tutted, looking out of the window, his gaze far-reaching on the river. 'I was speaking to her only last week. Thursday I think it was.'

'I'm sorry. I know this must be a shock.' She wondered why she was trying to make him feel better when Poppy was *her* colleague, *her* friend.

He looked across at her, his expression neutral, and she knew this empathy wouldn't occur to him. Poppy's accident was a tragedy, yes, but also an inconvenience.

'So . . . if I can just clarify a few things with you. Poppy said she could take you on as a client?'

His eyes narrowed. 'Yes, why? Is there a problem with that?'

'Well, not a problem exactly but you see, our VIP managers

only ever take on five clients at a time and Poppy already has five, so –' She spread her hands out apologetically. '– I'm not quite sure why she said she could take you on.'

Joe frowned again – it was a particularly forbidding look and she felt her stomach clench anxiously. 'Well nor am I. What was she doing, wasting my time, if she knew she couldn't look after me?'

'I'm sure she wasn't trying to waste your time,' Chloe said hurriedly. 'She must have had a very good reason for telling you such a thing; Poppy is the best of the best . . . But perhaps she meant for you to be handled by one of our other VIP managers?'

'I don't want anyone else. I want her and I was very clear on that when we met last week. My rapport was with her.'

'Of course, yes, I understand.'

'Otherwise I'd have called back the other concierge ser-vices that have been on my tail for months. All my associates use Quintessentially.'

'Yes, they're very good,' she agreed, knowing the com-ment was intended as a threat. Quintessentially had been first in, the ones to formally create this business and they were Invicta's biggest rivals. Tom had even been at school with some of the founders; they moved in the same social circles.

'I'd never even heard of Invicta until I met Poppy and I'd certainly never considered using such a service until her. But there's something about her. I liked her.'

Everyone did. 'Yes,' Chloe smiled. 'I quite understand.'

He stared at her, as though noticing her properly now. 'How long have you been working here?'

'Me? Well, actually I'm new to New York. I've only been in this office a few months so I'm still finding my feet with some of the finer details, but for the company itself, I've worked for them almost since the beginning, so five years now. I was the first person they hired in the London office.'

'London, right. That accent.'

'Yes. Worked my way up from tea girl, after uni.'

'So then why aren't you a VIP manager if you've worked here for so long? You obviously didn't come over to New York to be a VIP manager. You said you're only covering for Poppy.'

'That's right. Just until she's well enough to come back and pick up the reins again. I usually head up our Corporate Partnerships. It's my job to synergize our client database with brands that will appeal to them, be they lifestyle companies, travel deals, latest technologies, or social happenings.'

'Synergize,' he murmured, a faintly mocking note sounding in the word. His eyes narrowed as he openly scrutinized her, making no apology for the fact. Finally he nodded. 'Fine. I can see you're decent, hard-working and eager to please.'

Chloe blinked at him, certain he'd just described her childhood Labrador, Inca. Could he have been more patronizing? 'Well, thank you,' she said in a bristly tone, trying to hide that she'd taken offence.

'Yes. I think we can work together.' He nodded again, like he'd just made a momentous decision. 'I'll sign.'

Her mouth dropped open. 'But . . .' Had he already forgotten what she'd just told him a few minutes ago about Poppy's books being full? Or did he simply ignore what he didn't want to hear? 'The problem is, Joe, I don't think I can sign you. As I mentioned before, Poppy's book is full.'

'But *you'd* be looking after me.'

'Yes, along with Poppy's other clients. That would be six in total. Too many.'

'I hardly think I would tip the scales, my requirements are fairly precise. I'm not interested in any of that "chef's table" bullshit.'

She suppressed a sigh. It was a shame that face – and body – belonged to such an obnoxious man. 'Oh. So what are you looking for?'

'A house. In Greece.'

'You want me to find you a house in Greece?' she repeated.

'That's what I said.'

'Then you need a realtor.'

'No. I tried them. I'm looking for something . . . extra special. I don't want what everyone else can get. Ideally I want you to find me something that isn't even on the market.' He held up a hand and began counting off his fingers. 'It's got to be private, in at least thirty acres of its own land; have converted outbuildings, all services, needs to be immediately habitable—'

'Uh, where in Greece exactly?' she interrupted.

'One of the islands. I don't mind. Show me a shortlist,' he shrugged.

Chloe stared at him. So much for not being demanding!

They stared at each other for a moment and she could feel his will muscling in on her, bullying her. 'I'm correct in thinking that your sign-on fee is $200,000, right?'

'Yes.'

'That's a pretty princely sum for you to find me the house of my dreams.'

Arrogant too, then. But he was right – two hundred thousand, ready money, surely couldn't just be turned away, could it? And although she didn't know what Poppy's motives had been for bringing him in, they surely had to be

54

sound; Chloe hadn't been exaggerating when she'd told him Poppy was the best of the best.

Chloe bit her lip, her eyes sliding over his shoulder to the sight of Jack, still on the phone. 'If you could just give me a minute? I need to have a quick word with my boss.'

'Sure.'

She got up, making for the door, aware of his eyes following her like she was a curiosity. 'And you're quite sure I can't get you anyth—'

'No.'

Trying not to break into a run but moving as fast as she could, Chloe darted across the corridor, knocking on Jack's door but letting herself in anyway, before he could even reply.

'I'm on the phone,' he said, visibly irritated, as he pressed a palm over the mouthpiece.

'I'm sorry, but this is really important.'

Jack sighed. 'Tom, I'll have to call you back,' he said, before hanging up. 'What is it?'

'That guy sitting in the office behind me,' she said, not daring to jerk her head in Joe's direction in case he was watching.

Jack peered round her quizzically. 'What about him?'

'He'd arranged to see Poppy this morning – as a potential new client.'

'Well, direct him over to the general membership team, then.'

'No. As a VIP client.'

'*What?*'

'Exactly.'

'But Poppy's already got her quota.'

55

'That's my point. Did she mention it to you? Did you know she wanted to take on someone else?'

'No, she never . . .' He frowned. 'Well actually, she texted on Saturday saying she wanted an early meeting with me this morning. Could be that maybe?'

Chloe shrugged. 'Maybe, I don't know, but he's being really insistent. What do you want me to do? I've tried telling him Poppy can't take on any more clients but now he's saying he'll go along with me until Poppy comes back. He wants us to find him a holiday home in Greece.'

'Why doesn't he get a realtor then?'

'Because *anyone* can get one of those, Jack. He wants something that isn't even up for sale.' She crossed her arms. 'He's not taking no for an answer but I don't think I can do this. He's difficult, and cocky and arrogant. A complete ego-maniac. I've got enough to deal with as it is without adding *another* client to the list.'

Jack sank down into his chair and stared up at the ceiling. Grey-blue moons cradled beneath his eyes. It was several moments before he sat upright and looked back at her. 'Unless he isn't going to be superfluous.'

'What do you mean?'

He chewed his bottom lip thoughtfully. 'Poppy mentioned she thinks Pelham Hungerford could be a flight risk. He only signed up in the first place when his latest wife left him – and because he's a friend of her father; but apparently he's about to propose again or something?'

Chloe rolled her eyes. 'Well supposedly, but he's not doing a very good job of it.'

'Perhaps not, but if the lucky lady does say yes, and he's got someone to look after him again . . .'

Bugger. Chloe sagged. 'So then maybe that was why Poppy was teeing up this guy?' she murmured.

'Possibly. What's his name anyway?'

'Joe Lincoln.'

'And what does he do?' Jack asked, crossing his arms and ankles. 'What do we know about him?'

'Nothing yet, I haven't got that far. So far he's mainly been interviewing *me*.'

He was quiet for another minute. 'Okay, look, we have no way of knowing what Poppy was thinking bringing him in but we'll have to assume she had a good reason for it; she clearly knows something we don't and until she can tell us what's going on herself, I think it's best if we just go with it. We don't want to let her down, do we?'

'No,' she mumbled.

'Go sign up your Mr Lincoln and find him that house of his. Greece, was it? I've got a couple of contacts in Athens I'll put you on to.' Jack's gaze drifted over to the conference room opposite and Joe Lincoln's profile. He had got up from the chair and was standing by the window, on the phone, one arm raised above his head as he looked down upon the city like a phoenix in the sky. He was standing slightly in profile and, even from here, Chloe could see the sinews in his neck plucked out like violin strings as he issued commands of some sort down the line. 'He looks a real pussycat,' Jack said wryly, shooting her a sideways look.

'Just what I was thinking,' Chloe murmured, opening the door and wondering exactly what she had let herself in for.

Chapter Five

Chloe felt sure her smile was slipping, even though the cramp in her cheek muscles told her otherwise. She waited patiently while Rosaria tapped out her words on the tablet and waited for them to be held up.

No lilies, it read.

'Okay,' Chloe said, feigning interest as she made a note of it in her book.

'Signora Bertolotti is highly allergic to lilies, they must never be in her presence,' added Maria, the assistant, as her mistress began writing on the screen again. 'And if roses must be given, they should be long-stemmed and the thorns removed.'

'Got it.'

'Also, they must be pale pink or yellow or white but never red. Signora Bertolotti does not deal in clichés.'

'Uh-huh.'

They waited again, the soprano's fingers tip-tapping on the tablet the only sound in the room.

Chloe's eyes skimmed the suite impatiently. It was old school with French-polished brown furniture and swagged silks at the window; white tulips peeped from crystal globe vases and the cream carpet was lightly etched with a pale-grey lattice design. There was no sign of the marble bath from where she was sitting. Her tummy rumbled – she had missed the Berluti brunch on account of having to sign up Joe Lincoln and take payment for his membership. His bank was a small Swiss one she had only encountered a few times in her career, very discreet, very private. They had set up a further meeting for later this afternoon so that she could begin to build a profile for his portfolio before he flew out again; he hadn't been happy that they couldn't do the pre-liminaries there and then, but she had explained in her best patient voice that her appointment here had already been arranged and that she was, in fact, on the verge of being late for it.

She had rushed away as quickly as she could but still arrived here several minutes late, much to Rosaria's evident displeasure, and Chloe had felt on the back foot with her ever since.

Waiting, still waiting for the next commandment, her eyes fell to several voluminous dress bags hanging from a port-able clothes rail set near the door, a six-strong set of Louis Vuitton cases stacked in a tower ready to be brought down to her car. The two shih-tzus, Dolly and Princess, who had greeted her with ferocious yaps, were now blessedly dozing on one of the armchairs opposite, their paws twitching as they scurried in their dreams.

Rosaria herself was striking, albeit tiny at five foot one, her pale oval face only just beginning to soften at the jawline, her eyebrows like sliver moons framing sharply almond-shaped eyes. Disappointingly, her long hair, which was famously dyed a blue-black to look jet dark under the opera house lights, was twisted up and hidden beneath an orange silk turban, and her heavy curves that translated so well for classical tragedy were obscured this morning by a Japanese kimono. She wore a light muffler at her throat so that, besides her face, all that could really be seen of her were her small, ringed hands and pedicured feet. She was like a softly padded silken bundle, silent and still; such was the life of a resting soprano. She never used her voice between perform-ances – according to Maria, who had greeted her at the door, Rosaria wasn't scheduled to speak before six o'clock, Rio time – which meant this 'get to know you' meeting wasn't going according to Chloe's plan; she'd had more personal interactions with her postman.

Rosaria lifted the tablet again.

Arrange dinner with the President.

Oh dear God. Chloe felt her stomach drop. 'Of America?'

'Brazil. There is a state dinner after the performance tonight,' Maria clarified. 'Clearly it is an oversight that the invitation has not come through. The president and Signora Bertolotti are close friends. He would never have invited her to perform and not dine. It is an administrative error.'

'Uh-huh,' Chloe nodded, not believing a word of it. 'And have you contacted his office?' As Rosaria's executive assist-ant this fell within her jurisdiction, surely?

'Of course not. It would embarrass the president if we were to point out the error ourselves. We must employ a more diplomatic channel.'

'Meaning me?'

'Exactly.'

Chloe nodded, wondering how exactly she was supposed to garner a seat at a state dinner with the president of Brazil, *tonight.* Friday's mingling penguins seemed small fry. 'Okay, well sure, I'll definitely do what I can.'

Rosaria's eyebrow arched to a point.

'Which means I-I'll sort it,' she said hastily. 'Don't worry.

It'll be arranged by the time you touch down.' Chloe swallowed, her stomach plunging like she was in freefall. This was madness. On the side table, her phone buzzed and she saw Joe's name come up. He was texting her the address of where they should meet before he flew out of the country.

She suppressed a sigh, looking back at Rosaria with her stitched-on smile. She figured she should quit whilst she was ahead. Her client's requests needn't necessarily stop at dinner with a president. 'Okay, well, this has been great; I had better stop taking up your time; you should rest before your journey later. I'll get that dinner sorted out for you.' She cleared her throat, not at all sure how she was going to pull it off. 'But in the meantime, I'm so glad we had the opportunity to do this and talk face to face. It's wonderful to meet you in person at last; I've always been a terrific fan of yours—'

Rosaria nodded, clearly used to this bit.

'—And I hope you too feel this has been helpful?' Rosaria gave a sort of nod. 'I just wanted you to be able to put a face to the voice, so to speak. Anything you need, I'm only a phone call away. Please don't feel that anything changes for you just because Poppy's . . . away.' To her surprise – and dismay – they hadn't asked after Poppy once, and Chloe had found herself explaining Poppy's absence like a child explaining to her teacher that the dog ate her homework. 'Your needs are my priority and I'm really excited and honoured to be working with you.'

The eyebrow twitched again.

'*For* you.'

Her phone buzzed again as she stood, picking it up, but it slipped from her hand, falling onto the water glass beside it and tipping it over. It was only water, yet the way both women flinched, it may as well have been claret pouring onto the carpet.

'Oh, goodness,' Chloe mumbled, looking for something with which to mop it up; but the clatter had woken the dogs who now began barking again, one of them jumping from the chair and beginning to spring at her feet – and perilously bare ankles. 'I'll . . . I'll get a towel from the bathroom, shall I?' she asked, just as the dog positioned itself directly in her path.

The yelp, heart-stopping though it was, was nothing to the cry that followed it, as Rosaria leapt from her semi-recumbent position with surprising agility. 'Princess! My baby!'

Maria gasped in shock at the unscheduled sound of her mistress's voice, and Chloe looked between the two women with even more horror, as the injured dog was scooped up in one moment and Rosaria belatedly clutched her throat in the next, sacrificing herself for love.

'Ohmigod, I'm so sorry, I didn't see her there, I didn't know she . . .' Chloe whispered, barely able to use her own voice now either. 'Is she okay?'

Chloe herself wasn't sure which 'she' she was talking about – dog or owner? – but her enquiry was met with stony stares as the dog continued to yowl and whimper, and Rosaria's hand stayed at her throat. Beside Chloe, the water glass had finished emptying its contents onto the floor, a large puddle spreading through the fibres, but Chloe had a feeling no one cared about the damned carpet any more.

'I'll let myself out and leave you to get . . . settled,' she said quietly, nodding, trying to smile as she picked her way across the room and dodging the other dog, which was now also running in agitated circles between the coffee table legs and her own. 'Have a . . . have a safe flight.'

Never had she been so happy to close a door behind her. She slumped against the corridor wall with her eyes closed, wondering if she'd just managed to lose her first client.

Her phone buzzed again and she groaned. If that was Joe, chivvying her . . . How the hell did Poppy do this, day in, day out?

All good so far?

It was Jack.

'Just peachy,' she muttered bitterly to herself, striding down the corridor and on to the next appointment.

If it hadn't been for the fact that he had already paid the sign-up fee upfront, Chloe would have thought this was a prank. The meeting place with Joe was a stark contrast to the lavish opulence of Rosaria's hotel: a rickety trestle table, just one of many, set amidst a street food market in Greenwich Village. Pigeons were hopping on the ground hopefully, a group of courier cyclists walking around awkwardly in their cleat shoes, bikes left in a tangle nearby. There were vast queues at the various food carts, their wares written on blackboards, a vivid buzz of lively conversation that drowned out the sound of the traffic just a few metres away.

It was as far from anything she might have suggested as it was possible to get – there was no roof, much less a Michelin star! – and part of her wondered whether that was the point; she had the distinct impression he didn't like playing according to the rules and that what impressed others left him cold. Reverse snobbery?

'Hello again.' He looked up from his phone. It was a

bright, sunny day and her own image was reflected back to her in his shades. 'Sorry I'm a bit late. The meeting overran with my other client.' It was the story of her life today.

He didn't reply but looked mildly irritated. Clearly none of the VIPs liked to believe anyone else's time was more valuable than their own.

'This place is great,' she said brightly, looking around at the cluster of food carts set up in a large, open square around them and selling everything from specialist breads and cheeses to Korean kimchi, Vietnamese pho and Keralan curry. There was even an English fish-and-chip van, only they were selling truffle fries and vodka-battered scampi.

'Yeah, well, it's not the kind of place that needs concierge membership to get into.'

She looked at him, somewhat taken aback. It seemed a very odd thing for a man who had just dropped $200,000 on that very thing to say. He pushed a coffee towards her. 'For you.'

'Thank you.'

'It's Sumatran. Made with Mandheling beans,' he said, as though that would mean something to her.

A foodie, she noted mentally, smiling as she sipped it – before her eyes widened in surprise. 'My God, that's so good!' she exclaimed, pushing her fingers to her lips as though pressing the point.

Even with his sunglasses on, she could tell he was pleased. 'Exactly. Have you eaten?'

'Uh, no . . .' She looked around at the assembled choices. None of them really allowed for ladylike eating. They were all of the napkin-at-your-neck, dribbles-on-the-chin variety.

'Like Mexican?' he asked.

'I'm always partial to a taco,' she smiled, suppressing her horror at the thought of tackling one in front of him.

He frowned. 'They don't do tacos like you'd know them. It's Mexican food at its finest. Their chilaquiles and aguachiles are excellent.'

Chila-whats? She looked over to see a black truck with Chimichanga written on the side in clean white font. 'Let's do it.' She shrugged, taking the path of least resistance. She went to pull her legs out from under the trestle so that they could stand in line to order, but to her surprise, Joe merely turned towards the truck, raised an arm and signalled 'two' with his fingers. She saw the woman inside nod and signal back.

'They'll bring them over,' he said, turning back to her.

'Oh. Great.' She slid her legs back under, wondering what he had just ordered for them both. 'I didn't know they do a waiter service here.'

'They don't.' He offered no further explanation, the intimation being that clearly he was a good customer, or they knew he was a powerful one at least.

A tiny pause bloomed; she felt unaccountably stilted in his company. He wasn't much older than her and yet he behaved as though he was, forcing a breach between them. 'So tell me about yourself, Joe. What is it you do?' she asked, figuring they may as well get down to business seeing as he wasn't big on small talk.

He threw her a level look. 'I have an engineering company.'

'You're an engineer? Gosh, now I wouldn't have guessed that.'

'No? What would you have said?'

Her eyes skipped over him appraisingly, taking in the

sculpted physique evident even beneath his innocuous clothes. If it wasn't for the shaggy hair, she'd have said he looked like a commando and he wasn't a sharp enough dresser for architecture or anything design-led. But precious few jobs enabled someone to earn at the heights required to drop two hundred grand on a concierge membership – or join a Swiss bank, for that matter. 'Something scientific perhaps – bio-tech? Or IT maybe? You look like you could've designed an app.'

'On account of the beard?' Bemusement softened his gaze a little.

She smiled. Busted. 'Maybe. Engineering's not an area I know much about, I'm afraid. Do you enjoy it?'

'There are challenges I enjoy, and I like the logic running through it. I guess you might say I've always liked making broken things work.'

She smiled, trying to imagine him as a little boy with his Lego. She was an aunt now, to her big sister Kate's son Orlando, so she was becoming well acquainted with the finer points of toddler construction.

'Do you have to travel much for it?'

'More than some, less than others.'

'Which is your preferred airline?'

'It depends where I am. American for domestic, BA or Swiss for Europe, Emirates for long haul.'

'Do you have a PA?'

He looked at her with something akin to suspicion. 'Why?'

'It'd be good if I had a chat with them at some point so that I can help them help you with your travelling logistics. Seventy-five per cent of the requests we receive are travel-related – you know, people flying in to a new city and wanting to know the best place to eat, shows to see, that kind of thing. I could collaborate with them on that, make sure you're getting the best possible experience wherever you are.'

'I like to keep my business and personal lives separate and this is strictly a private venture. Besides, I have zero interest in following the crowd. I like to explore places myself and trust my own instincts.'

He gave a small shrug to their surroundings, indicating this place was a case in point. It wouldn't feature on any magazine 'hot spots'; you didn't need to be on a list to get in. She looked at him, trying to work him out. Did he want their services or not? There was something prickly, almost reluctant about him, as though he disapproved of her and what she represented, which was ridiculous because *he* had been the one insisting that she took him on this morning.

He didn't seem like most of Poppy's other clients – at least, not what she assumed them to be like (although Rosaria had hardly welcomed her with open arms just now either; perhaps Serena hadn't been so off-base with her warning after all?). But sitting beside her, she had always overheard Poppy chatting to her clients with a chummy playfulness; everything was upbeat and exciting, her clients viewing her services as the cherry on the top of their ice-cream sundae lives. But Joe had a flat, almost unenthusiastic directness that she would have expected if she'd been sell-ing him a phone or a car. Then again, he'd thought he was getting vivacious, well-connected, smart-as-a-whip and thin-as-a-snake Poppy and ended up with good, ole faithful Labrador her; she supposed it would take a while for him to adapt.

'That's fine,' she smiled. 'No problem. So then let me get

some basic details from you – age, background, education, marital status, that kind of thing,' she said, pulling her note-pad from her bag.

'Is that strictly necessary? I'm really not interested in all the fluffing bullshit. I don't need you to pander to my ego and send me fruit baskets on my birthday. I've already told you what I've signed up for.'

She took a breath. This bit wasn't supposed to be the hard work. 'Joe, I assure you this is standard procedure for VIP members. Regardless of what you may start out wanting from us, that is bound to evolve and I need to build up a profile of who you are and what you like so that I can better anticipate what you'll need from me. We'll be working together closely. I need to get to know you.'

He inhaled deeply, the gesture seemingly bored and defensive at once. 'It's not like there's much to tell – I'm thirty-four, born in Vermont. My parents are retired. I have a younger brother. I'm not married. No kids – that I know of,' he added, seemingly in all seriousness. 'I went to MIT.' He shrugged, as though that was all there was to tell. An entire life condensed into one breath.

'Well,' Chloe smiled after a pause, knowing she could have pretty much got that information off Facebook. 'That's a great start.' She pressed her hands together, wondering how to get him to soften. What had Poppy done to get him on board?

A couple of women walked up, carrying takeaway boxes of pad thai. 'Can we sit here?' one of them asked, indicating the other end of the table. All the other tables were taken.

Chloe looked at Joe to check he was happy with that; this was his patch after all. He might not like having strangers sitting so close, especially when they were having what he was clearly finding to be an intrusive conversation. But he gave a relaxed shrug.

'Sure.'

She eyed the food hungrily. It really did look – and smell – incredibly good.

'So, um, what else?' she mused, trying to bring her concentration back to work and off her stomach. 'So I'll need your address – or addresses, if there's more than one. Also, details of your doctors, surgeons, dentists, next of kin, tailor, barber, things like that. I've emailed a form over to you so if you could get it back to me as soon as possible, then I can add it to your profile.' He looked back at her in silence, seeming incredibly bored, and she guessed he usually had people to do this for him; but if he insisted on keeping this strictly in the private realm ... 'Obviously, the sooner I know all I can about you, the sooner I can start helping you and anticipate your needs.'

The look he gave her suggested she would never be able to anticipate his needs but they were interrupted by the woman coming over from the truck with two steaming plates of chilaquiles. Chloe's mouth started watering instantly as she saw that they were quartered corn tortillas, topped with tomato salsa and grilled red snapper. All was forgiven. The smell was divine.

'There you go, Joel.' Her black hair was wildly curly, held back by a red cloth hairband, stacks of rubber bracelets up her tanned arms. And her accent was thick, dancing almost. She was South American-looking.

'Thanks, Ariane.'

Chloe smiled her thanks in silence. 'Primarily then, the most helpful thing you could tell me is what it is that you want from me? Apart from the holiday house, I mean.

You're saying you don't personally care about where's hot or not, but if you need to be somewhere or have to impress a client, we can help. Our reach is global.' She watched him begin to eat with typically male concentration, as though this was the first food to pass his lips in a week. 'Equally, if you need anything logistical to be arranged that might be out of the remit of your PA, I can sort that for you – jet charter, a helicopter, a bulletproof car? You name it; I can order you a rickshaw in Bangkok with three minutes' notice if that's what you'd like. Whatever you need.'

He stopped eating and looked up at her from under his thick brows. 'Right now, I just want a holiday house in Greece. Can we talk about that?'

She felt a rush of intense dislike at his curtness – did he need to be so rude? But she forced a smile anyway. She was doing this for Poppy. For some reason Poppy had felt she needed him, so Chloe would do this for her; she would do *anything* for her, if she would just promise to be okay. 'The house. Okay,' she sighed. 'You said somewhere private, thirty acres—'

'Four bedrooms in the main house, minimum. Plus I'll need outbuildings on the land, although it's not crucial that that's in place yet.'

'Okay,' she said, eating as daintily as she could, trying not to splash salsa on her shirt and having to suppress her moans of satisfaction; this food was incredible. *Could* she get some sort of deal set up here for the members? she wondered. Or would these indie types run a mile from the idea of becoming 'corporatized', bought somehow? 'Do you want landscaped gardens? Olive groves?'

'Don't care at this point. That can be decided later.'

'And are you after any particular style of building? Manor house? Contemporary build? Farmhouse?'

'So long as it's secure and private, I don't care. I'll judge when I see it. It's about the location and privacy, first and foremost.'

'And what's your budget?'

'There isn't one.'

Her hands stalled mid-air. 'No upper limit *at all*?'

He shook his head but didn't look back at her. 'Nope.'

She allowed herself another bite of her lunch. '. . . And you said *anywhere* in Greece?'

'One of the islands.'

'You don't want to narrow it down a bit more than that?' She couldn't quite keep the sarcasm from her voice. 'One particular sea perhaps – Aegean? Ionian?'

He didn't rush to answer, seemingly savouring this last bite of lunch. But having finished eating, he pushed the plate away, pressing the napkin to his mouth momentarily. He looked back at her with a smile. 'Tell you what, Chloe – why don't you surprise me?'

Chapter Six

'. . . honestly, Chlo, I could have died, *everyone* was staring!' Kate's big green eyes widened even further, the red wine glass in her hand sloshing around alarmingly as she shifted position. In the background, her husband Marcus was on his hands and knees constructing an intricately designed wooden train track on the floor, even though it was almost midnight over there, with tunnels, suspension bridges, junction boxes and multiplex engine sheds adding to the mathematical complexity of getting all the negative and positive ends to match up. Kate must have had to pick her way over it like a cartoon burglar just to get to the sofa.

'Well, that'll teach you for trying to show off. Just because you did Grade Five tap, it doesn't mean you know your Savasana from your Malasana.'

'My what?' Kate spluttered.

'Precisely. Arse from elbow is my point. You're in the wrong class, Sis. You're going to end up getting injured. I don't get what the big deal is. Just move down to the Beginner class.'

Kate's eyes widened. 'But you see – there it is: *move down.* Implied failure. Before I've even begun!'

Chloe tutted. Only Kate could turn a resolve to shift the baby weight into a crusade to be the best in the class, and now it wouldn't be enough to get into these poses, she'd have to do them deeper, hold them longer than anyone else. 'Must you turn everything into a competition?' Chloe chuckled, herself sitting cross-legged on her bed, cheeks still flushed from her boxing class as she ate her well-deserved burger.

It was still light although the steamy heat of the day had gone and the traffic was thinning outside on Perry Street. A couple of pigeons were roosting, cooing loudly, on the black fire escape that criss-crossed the building, passing directly outside her vast, arched bedroom window. The window had been the reason she had rented the apartment; though the entire flat was barely bigger than her sitting room in London, that architectural feature and the wonderfully distressed brickwork had captivated her immediately. No matter that there was no view, that being only on the fourth floor meant she looked onto walls; she had a window and a fire escape and if it was good enough for Holly Golightly, it was certainly good enough for her.

The plantation ceiling fan whirred in the middle of the room, flickering the flame of her favourite scented candle on the wooden mantelpiece. On the opposite wall, only seven feet away, almost so close she could turn it off with her foot, the TV was on, on mute.

'Thanks for the support,' Kate groaned. 'You don't understand what it's like having a tummy like Jabba the Hutt. Just wait till you have a baby, then we'll see who's competitive at yoga.'

'Okay. Sure.' Chloe licked some ketchup that was dribbling down her finger. She heard Kate sigh loudly at her refusal to enage.

'What have you just been up to anyway? You're looking very sporty.' Kate took another sip of her wine, sleepiness beginning to impinge upon her features. Orlando still awoke early and she was already going to have less than six hours' sleep tonight, but these catch-up sessions were important to them both and Chloe's job – with the amount of after-hours socializing it entailed – meant that grabbing a mutually convenient time, what with the five-hour time-lag to factor in too, was no mean feat.

'My boxing class.'

'You're still doing that? I thought you'd moved on to barrecore.'

'No. Too much plinky-plonky piano music for my taste. Not to mention I've got the flexibility of a brick. Boxing seems to suit me.'

Kate arched an eyebrow. 'Because you still need to hit the bejesus out of something? I thought you said you were getting past the anger now.'

'I am. I have. I just still like punching stuff.' She gave a careless shrug but didn't meet Kate's eyes. 'Go figure.'

'Hmm,' Kate said suspiciously, looking for signs of the cracks that had propelled her across the ocean that now separated them. A small silence bloomed but Chloe refused to be drawn. Plenty of people liked boxing. It was a brilliant stress reliever and gave great definition in the arms. It didn't have to signify anything more than that. Kate, reading the cues, changed the subject. '. . . So, has there been any more news on Poppy?'

Chloe flinched at the question. She flinched every time she thought about it. 'The operation was a success – they think – but they're still keeping her in the induced coma for another few days to allow the swelling to go down. Until she wakes up, we won't know if it worked or not.' She remembered how Jack's mouth had barely moved as he'd relayed the update to the team that afternoon – the no-news coming off as bad news. Everyone felt uptight and upset, the continuing uncertainty of the situation keeping them off-balance; Xan had looked like he was going to cry, the girls on the membership desk had collapsed into another morbid huddle on the sofas.

But Kate wasn't one to flinch or look away. She liked facts. Certainties. 'What are the possible outcomes?'

Chloe held up a weak hand and began counting off her fingers. 'Full recovery. Speech problems. Motor problems. Or . . . or she doesn't wake up. That's pretty much the range.'

Perhaps it was the bald way in which she had expressed it, but Kate looked visibly startled by her words. 'Oh, Chlo,' she whispered, sympathy shining from her eyes.

It was almost more than Chloe could bear. She always knew the world was okay if her big sister said it was. So to see sadness, loss of hope, despair . . . 'Oh, she'll go for the first one, don't you worry,' Chloe said defiantly. 'There's no way Poppy will miss the company's summer party next month. She's been looking forward to it all year.'

'Yes, of course she will.' Kate squinted, seeing the tension in Chloe's face. 'Have you been able to see her yet?'

Chloe shook her head. 'No. It's still family only. Even Jack can't get in. I've sent flowers, of course, but I think they'll be dead before she sees them.' She bit her lip hard as she stared at a sliver of onion, pale and translucent, on her plate. 'Not that that matters a damn.'

'No, of course not,' Kate agreed, matching her stoic tone, as though sensing that Chloe needed that strength from her. 'Well at least you're doing all you can on a practical level. That's all you can do right now. How's it been with her clients?'

'Hmm, yes, about that.' Chloe groaned and settled the ketchup-smeared plate on her thighs, her shoulders slumping wearily. 'Mixed bag. I had a nightmare with one of them on Monday.'

'Why, what happened?'

'I almost killed the woman's dog and in so doing, made her scream when she's not even allowed to whisper – she's a famous opera singer, Rosaria Bertolotti?' Chloe added, seeing Kate's confused expression. 'She never, ever speaks before noon.'

'Oh, right.' Kate pulled a 'get her' face. As a former counsellor for trauma victims, she didn't have much sympathy with such things as strained vocal cords. 'First world problems' was her favourite phrase, uttered at least twice an hour.

'And this was after she casually insisted I get her seated at a state dinner with the president of Brazil that night.'

'Holy shit! And did you?'

'Of course.'

'But how?'

'Tickets for a meet and greet with Selena Gomez at her concert in Rio next month for the daughter of the Communications and Engagement Manager.'

'But that's blackmail,' Kate gasped, looking delighted.

'No, it's inducement. You can be sure the president would have thanked me for my efforts anyway; I didn't know it at the time, but according to Xan, the president and Rosaria had been having a raging clandestine affair for years until she broke it off when she fell for some conductor. But he died of a heart attack a few months back and so now it's . . . game on, again.'

'Right,' Kate breathed, looking both rapt and appalled at

once. 'Any other "inducement programmes" you've got going on?'

'No. The rest have been well behaved so far; in fact, it's been fairly quiet these past few days. Most of them aren't in New York at the moment and I think they're still getting used to the idea of me. It's such a shock to them all. They rely on Poppy so much, not just practically but emotionally too; I don't think they realized just how much until they heard what had happened. One of them actually started crying when I told him about the accident.'

'Ah bless.'

'Yes.' Pelham had taken the news particularly badly, but then he had a stronger emotional link to Poppy, having known her since she was a child; he had rung off quickly, his voice suddenly hoarse, promising to call back with a date for tea at his townhouse in Greenwich when he was next in town. Proudlock, the film director, had been momentarily stunned but soon recovered himself and in the next breath had asked for both a suite at Hotel du Cap and a boat with a helipad to be moored at Cannes for two days during the film festival – oh, and for his dry-cleaning to be picked up. Greenleve hadn't yet returned her call; he was holed up in a recording studio in Hawaii where he'd had all wifi and mobile connections cut with 'the outside world' – a deliberate ploy intended to concentrate the energies of his current hapless artist, who was in the throes of a very public and well-documented heroin addiction; according to his assistant, he wasn't expected to surface for another four days or so. She was meeting Alexander Subocheva for the first time for drinks tomorrow – she had only got as far as speaking to his executive assistant up till now, having passed sufficient background tests to get past *her* assistant. As for Joe Lincoln, who was of course fully up to speed on the situation, he had zipped off to France for some meetings and she hadn't heard from him since their lunch on Monday.

In fact, after her initial baptism of fire on Monday morning, the week had settled into its usual, familiar routine and she had been able to keep up to speed with most of her ongoing projects in her old sphere. So far, she was keeping all the balls up in the air and Jack – who had finally shaved, at least – was looking less stressed.

Chloe pulled her hair up into a ponytail, keeping her arms up there, elbows pointing out as she sank back into the pillow. 'Have you spoken to Mum? How is she?'

'Good. Busy with her herbaceous borders, of course. Everything's going *wild*, she says.'

'She says that every year.'

'Exactly. And she's worried about you, naturally. Thinks you're too far away.'

'New York is not far away. I may as well be in Cornwall as here; they're both a day's travelling from Alnwick anyway.'

'Well, she frets about you working too hard, being lonely, lost in the city, pining for—'

'So all the usual stuff then?' Chloe said crisply.

'Precisely. She's coming down next week. We've got tickets for the Summer Exhibition at the Royal Academy.'

'You should have asked me!' Chloe pouted. 'I could have got you in on the opening night.'

'Me and Mum mingling with Tracey Emin? Can you really see it?' Kate giggled, peering over the top of her now almost-empty wine glass.

'No,' Chloe chuckled. 'Perhaps not.'

A vehement curse from the back of the room made Kate

turn around. Marcus was up on his knees, with his hands on his hips and a face like thunder. 'This bloody thing. We're short one tight turn again; more bloody long turns than you could shake a stick at, but no more tight turns. Honestly, it's the same every sodding time! I'm fed up with it, Kate. What am I supposed to do? The damn thing won't fit without it; do I redesign the entire bloody thing from scratch? I'm getting the early train tomorrow but I promised Orlando I'd get this done for when he came down in the morning. I mean really—'

Kate gave a weary sigh and turned back to the screen with a knowing look. 'Someone's about to blow a gasket. I have to go.'

'Of course. Duty calls. Speak soon.'

'Love you, babe.' Kate blew a kiss at her.

'Love you too.'

Chloe pressed disconnect and sank back against her pillow, her plate still balanced on her lap, the sudden quiet blooming like a bloodstain as Kate's crazy, chaotic world was severed from her own and she was alone again. She imagined her mother back home in Northumberland, kneeling on her daisy-printed foam pad and furiously weeding the begonias, Radio 4 playing beside her, bedsheets flapping on the washing line, the Cheviot hills distant sentries on the horizon.

It felt a world away from here – even the wind there was different: cool and fresh and tinted with the scent of clover and moss, cows grazing in the neighbouring field, their slow footsteps heavy on the dewy grass; whilst here, Chloe awoke to horns and shouts and the rattle of shop shutters being pushed back each morning. It wasn't worse, per se, just different – because she did love it here. The pulse of the city energized her; it had synched with her own, dragging her up to the light again precisely when she'd needed it most. She had just never imagined that her life would ever lie in *this* heaving mass of light and noise. She had always known she wouldn't stay in Alnwick, of course – her ambition needed more, her curiosity demanded it – but six months ago, her future had still looked very different from this reality: different backdrop, different accents, different ending.

She reached for the remote, flicking the channels and trying to find something that wasn't an advert, when the FaceTime tone rang again.

'Kate?' she asked, looking distractedly for the mute button.

'Not quite,' said a male voice.

She looked at the screen in surprise. *Him.* He was sitting in his study at home, a small narrow room with a vintage film poster of *The Leopard* on the wall behind him and a red Anglepoise lamp on the desk. The light cast an unflattering brightness on his face, highlighting the bags under his eyes and ageing him fifteen years.

'Please!' he said, seeing how she went to press disconnect, the set of her mouth betraying her determination not to even set eyes upon him. She didn't want him to see anything about her; it was unavoidable at times, of course, but she wouldn't give him the satisfaction of catching her in her t-shirt, eating on the bed. Alone. 'Please don't hang up! I have to tell you something!'

She paused and she could see him immediately scanning the space behind her, taking in the pom-pom lights she had draped over the mirror, the exposed brickwork, the dusty-pink velvet scatter cushions that sufficed for a headboard.

His eyes came back to her and he had the grace at least to look abashed for snooping. 'Any word on Poppy?'

'How would I know? Jack's more likely to confide in you than me,' she said in a brisk tone.

There was a small silence. 'Your hair looks great short, by the way. When did you cut it?'

She didn't reply. Did he really need to ask? Cutting her flame-coloured mane – the thing he had loved most about her – into a sharp-pointed crop had been the first thing she'd done on arriving here.

'I keep meaning to say how good it looks but it's never . . . never quite the right time.'

She glowered at him. Funny, that.

His eyes skittered over her, drinking her in in a way that wasn't possible anywhere else. 'I guess I never imagined you . . . I always thought of you as long-haired—'

'Yes, well, I fancied a change.' Sarcasm hung from the words; they both knew it was the understatement of the year. Change of hair? Change of life, more like.

He nodded. 'You look incredible.'

'You said you had something to say? I doubt it was to pass comment on my hair.'

He looked abashed, his boyish features flinching at the harshness of her words. 'Yes, right. I guess I wanted you to know first – I'm going to come over. Early next week, most likely.'

She felt her blood run cold. '*Why?*' The question was sharp, a demand for explanation, as a deep frown creased her brow. She didn't want him out here. He had to stay over there, far away, with an ocean between them. It was the deal she had single-handedly drawn up and signed for them both. Him there, her here. It was the only way she could do this, move forward.

'Morale? To be helpful? We all need to pull together at a time like this. I can't bear being back here knowing that you . . . that you're all going through this alone.'

'We're not alone.'

'You know what I mean, though.'

She didn't reply and the silence around them grew loud. Yes, she knew exactly what he meant and she felt a rush of fury burst through her. He didn't mean 'them all'. He meant her. *She* was the one all alone and he knew it. This was just a ruse, a way for him to get his foot in the door, to get face to face with her when she'd switched continents to deny him exactly that chance. How *dare* he come over here! She reached forwards again and she saw the panic gather in his true-blue eyes again.

'Chlo—'

For a split second, their eyes met and she felt the golden thread that bound them to one another snap tight again. She had hoped it had been cut but now she saw it had been merely hanging slack all this time, and he was simply going to come over here and wind her back in, like a spool of thread he could turn at will, anytime he liked . . . No. She wouldn't allow it. Their relationship may have been conducted on his terms, but their separation would be on hers. That much she could control at least. 'Do not come here. I mean it. Goodbye, Tom.'

Paris

The light from the low candles bathed the tables in a honeyed glow, making the crystal glasses glitter and the bejewelled guests preen. Above their heads, upturned banks of lilac, sugar-pink and white orchids dangled down from the ceiling in thick cascades like a meadow in reverse, the room's supporting pillars so thickly wadded with tens of thousands of cream roses that the entire space was wholly transformed into a sylvan garden bower. In the middle of the room sat the happy couple, the bride in Dior couture and not even pretending to eat her lobster, the groom listening to one of his team, who was bending down to talk in his ear.

Elodie sipped her Cristal slowly – she never drank much these days anyway, she had learnt the hard way what happened to beautiful girls who drank too fast – pretending to listen intently to the man on her right. Fifty-seven, Albanian and with the jowls of a mountain dog, he was nonetheless one of her more interesting dinner companions, recounting the time his diamond mine in Angola was stormed by militia whilst he toured with the Russian trade minister.

'That is a particularly special stone you have there yourself,' he said, taking her right hand in his and inspecting her engagement ring, a seven-carat emerald-cut yellow diamond.

'Thank you. My husband has a fine eye.'

'It is a necessary skill when one has a fine wife.'

'You flatter me,' she demurred, pushing down the first prickle of nausea. 'What did you present to your wife on your engagement?'

'Which one?' He laughed.

Elodie kept her smile in place and waited, deploying her stillness to effect again.

'It was a ruby and diamonds setting, I believe.' He pulled a confiding expression. 'Although, do not test me on that, it can be hard to keep up.'

Elodie looked down the table at his current wife, the fourth incumbent, and could see that, as types, she and this other woman weren't so very different: both reed slim, with long dark hair and brown eyes that seemed overly large in their faces. She knew that to a man like him, they were inter-changeable. Disposable.

She looked across the table at her own husband, amongst his own kind in this crowd of power players, except for the fact that he didn't play by their rules. For him, marriage was for life. He would be hers and she his, for always.

He was listening to something the woman to his left was saying, his gaze impassive on the spot in front of his plate as she spoke but, even from across the table, Elodie could tell he was disagreeing with every word that left her lips. There was just something in the set of his mouth, the tilt of his head, invisible to all but her. She knew him so well, his body language a book she could read, like a dog able to decipher her master's non-verbal cues.

He glanced up as though feeling the weight of her stare, their eyes locking into a hold and she felt that sudden lurch in her stomach that was so familiar to her now and yet still managed to shock every time. His lips curved into a smile and she knew what it meant, the promises it held. He had flown in for the wedding especially – the bride was one of her closest friends after all – but he would be gone again by the time she woke tomorrow, their time together as fleeting as rainbows.

Beside her, the Albanian touched her hand as he refilled her glass and she froze into statue-like stillness, for there was intimacy in the gesture, an unwanted familiarity she had been at pains to avoid. Only her eyes moved, back to her husband's gaze, and she saw the tiny twitch of his finger on the tablecloth.

She knew what that meant too.

Chapter Seven

New York

'How are you, Steven? It's good to see you again,' Chloe smiled, shaking the club manager's hand as she approached the bar. She might be a newbie to the city but she was already one of their best customers.

'It is a pleasure to have you back, Miss Marston,' he replied.

'I hope I've arrived before my guest?' she asked, looking around the opulent space. Coming to the Rarities bar was like stepping back in time – it was decorated in rich plum and damson tones with mahogany fittings and plush carpets, marble busts at the windows and life-size portraits on the walls. Chloe had chosen it specially – a members-only bar with an annual fee of $10,000. She had made exhaustive enquiries to check whether Alexander had ever visited; to her satisfaction, it appeared he hadn't, which made it an ideal location for their first meeting. It was never easy finding novelty for the super-rich, they had usually been everywhere and done everything, and although ten thousand was but pocket change to a man like him, she was pleased to have this small advantage at least. It showed him that in spite of his reach, she had knowledge and contacts where he didn't and that Invicta's services were still pocket change for a man of his wealth.

The club was also guaranteed to be quiet – they made a point of never reserving more than two-thirds of the capacity so that members could always be sure of getting a seat – as well as discreet; celebrities often came here for a drink, away from fawning members of the public wanting selfies and autographs, and some of the biggest deals in the financial world were brokered between its walls.

'Where would you care to sit? There are two seats by the window.'

Chloe shook her head. She knew from Poppy's notes that Alexander travelled everywhere with a security detail that wouldn't like him sitting in plain sight. 'Somewhere quieter – a corner ideally.'

'Absolutely, follow me.'

He led her across the room, through a narrow corridor and into an adjoining drawing room. 'Will this do?' he asked, motioning to two enormous wing chairs in the furthest corner. It was dark, dimly lit there. A trio of men in suits were seated at the sofas in front of the fireplace nearby – close but not too much so – and she saw an off-duty NFL star on the other side of the room in deep discussion with a woman who was clearly not his TV anchor wife.

'Perfect.'

'I will bring over the menus, and your guest when he arrives.'

Chloe walked over to the corner, deliberating which chair to choose – would he prefer the one that faced into the room, giving him a clear view of their neighbours and anyone who came in? Or the one with its back to the room, protecting his privacy and hiding his identity from whoever else came in?

She decided he would prefer the latter – although she could always move if she was wrong – and settled herself into her seat facing the room.

Discreetly, pretending to check her phone, she watched the NFL player, who was now touching the knee of the woman who was not his wife; she tried not to listen in on the conversation of the businessmen on the sofas, who appeared to work in Commodities and were planning a trip to a private club later. Their conversations passed in a low, agreeable murmur as ten minutes went by. Fifteen. She rang in to the office to check she hadn't missed any messages and Xan was regaling her with his latest 'nightmare' request when she heard fresh voices and looked up.

'He's here,' she whispered, cutting over him as he was in full flow about just how hard it was to get the Port Authority to agree to 'Marry me Lisa' being beamed onto the Statue of Liberty. 'Sorry, Xan, gotta go.'

Two men were standing in the corridor – she could see them reflected in a mirror from where she was sitting – and at first she thought they were both the bodyguards, such was their stature. But then her gaze locked with the slightly smaller man – if anyone six foot tall could be described as 'small' in any way – and the room, the city, seemed to fall away.

He had deep-set grey-green eyes that seemed as if they ought to belong on a wild animal – a snow leopard perhaps, or a lynx – and short, thick, light-brown hair. He was muscular, with a rugby player's physique, but somehow he seemed to take up even more cubic space than his size suggested, as though he had an aura that added to his bulk. She had seen photographs of him, of course, but they had failed to capture his energy; on paper he looked dull-edged, slow and wary, regarding the camera with overt suspicion, but in the flesh, there was a bladed sharpness to his movements, an intensity of focus that drew every eye his way.

He walked over, stopping in front of her. It was like having a Lamborghini bear down upon her at 200 mph, only to stop bumper-to-knee and she was surprised to realize she was now standing too. 'Miss Marston.'

Even if she hadn't been, she would have said 'Yes.' This was what power did – it had a tangible presence, transfixing people, changing them. 'Mr Subocheva, what a pleasure,' she said, hoping he couldn't see her nervousness. He shook her hand, never dropping his eyes from hers and she felt like she was being X-rayed, seen from the inside out. 'But please, you must call me Chloe.'

'And I, Alexander.' His accent was thick, tumbling the words into a delicious richness. He held her hand for a moment longer than she anticipated, still assessing her, the fractional overstep just enough to force her back a pace mentally, and set her off-balance. It was an assertion of power.

'I hope this suits you, meeting here?' she asked, indicating towards the cosy corner she had bagged. 'I find it's nicely private, whilst still having some atmosphere.'

'I like it very much.' He waited for her to take her seat again before he took his own, his bodyguard walking over to the nearest empty chair just off to the side of them and pretending to read a cigar magazine. 'I had thought there were few secrets left to me in this city but I see I was wrong.'

Behind him, she could see the businessmen looking over, undisguised curiosity on their faces. An apex predator was in the room and everyone there knew it.

Steven came over with the menus and Chloe pretended to study hers as he explained to Alexander the rarity of the drinks served here, hence the club's name. In many instances, he was saying, they were serving the last remaining batches in the world of those elite malts and distillations.

'I'll go with Chloe's choice,' Alexander said, handing back his menu without looking at it. 'It will be a good test of whether she is a woman whose judgement is to be trusted.'

Chloe's lips parted in a surprised smile; she saw the anxious smile on Steven's face. 'Well, then, in which case we'd love the Black Tot,' she said confidently. 'Do you like rum?'

'I am Russian. I like every spirit.'

'Well this is a very special one,' she smiled. 'Historically, it was believed that sharing a tot of rum helped breed kinship among sailors in the British Navy. It was a practice observed for over three hundred years, and when it was discontinued in 1970, the last remaining stocks were stored in government warehouses and now only come out for special occasions – such as Prince William's wedding.'

His eyes never left her face once. 'Then I look forward to trying it,' he said, elbows splayed, his fingers pressed together in a steeple. 'But before we go any further, tell me, how is Poppy?'

The smile widened on Chloe's lips. He was the only one of her clients – apart from Pelham – who had cared still to ask. Greenleve seemed to have forgotten, having suddenly resumed contactability this morning and called her three times already today with various nefarious requests but not asked after Poppy once; Proudlock had been much the same, tutting at all the right points for all of two minutes in their initial conversation, but then he hadn't mentioned her since that day either – not a single enquiry as to how the surgery had gone or whether she had yet woken up; and of course Rosaria, silently tapping out her demands on a tablet, had been far more concerned by Chloe stepping on her dog's paw than the prospect of Poppy undergoing neurosurgery. 'Well, we're beginning to think we may have reason to be hopeful. Every day she gets through is another day she gets stronger. They operated to remove a blood clot from her brain on Monday.'

He looked genuinely concerned. She had been hit on Saturday night and today was now Thursday. 'But she hasn't woken up yet?'

'No, they're keeping her in an induced coma until the weekend at least; they're monitoring the swelling.'

'But her family is with her?'

'Yes, they flew over on Saturday night; they've been by her side ever since.'

He watched her intently, his quick eyes noticing all her little fidgety quirks such as how she raked her hair back when she was nervous, or the way she rubbed her index finger and thumb in circles when she was anxious. In fact, within two minutes of being in his company she felt more 'seen' than at any other point since moving here. 'Is she getting the best care? Who are her doctors – have they been checked out? My motto in all things is trust – then verify.'

'I understand from Jack – my boss – that she's receiving excellent care; they have a very strong trauma team by all accounts.'

'I hope it goes without saying that if anything is required . . . anything at all . . .'

'That's incredibly generous. Thank you. I'll make sure that is passed on to her family,' she said.

Alexander sighed, sitting back slightly. 'I did not believe it when Anjelica told me; I was convinced it must be some sort of joke.' He glanced up at her from slightly lowered lids.

'But I am sure you already know that Anjelica is not one to make jokes.' He delivered the line with a flat tone but she sensed amusement in it.

'No, quite.' Her own telephone conversation with the woman – when she had finally rung back to arrange this meeting – had been so brisk, Chloe had half thought she was communicating in Morse code.

He frowned, his mouth set in an exasperated line. 'I hate . . . I hate not being able to *do* anything about it. Helplessness is not a feeling that sits well with me.'

'I know, that's the worst part of all of this. Just the waiting; waiting and seeing. But there is literally nothing more to be done. The doctors say their job is finished, it's now just a matter of time.'

There was a long pause as he looked at her again, watching, assessing, judging. 'And so you are here, taking the reins.'

She took a deep breath, feeling like she was pitching for the deal of her career. 'Yes, and I hope that's not too disruptive for you. These are exceptional circumstances, clearly, but I appreciate that your relationship with Poppy is a close one and that it must be unsettling to suddenly have someone new looking after you.' She had spent the week trotting out these words in various fashions but still she couldn't shake the tinge of bitterness she felt at having to say them, as though the inconvenience to these people was in any way on a par with the disaster that had befallen Poppy.

'I had reservations, yes. There are not many people I trust and I like to look in the eye of anyone I work with.' He nodded, his gaze like a grip, holding her up, pinning her in place. 'I expect you have already read up on me, so tell me about you. Who *is* Chloe Marston, my new lifestyle manager? And don't leave anything out. I am sure you know perfectly well my researchers will dig it up one way or another.'

There was that look again – amusement hiding in the shadows of still eyes. Or was it not a joke? It was impossible to tell with him.

'Well, I'm twenty-six, from a place called Alnwick in Northumberland in the north-east of England. I'm the younger of two girls; my sister Kate is four years older than me and living in London. She got married a few years ago and has a little boy, Orlando, so I'm an aunt now and fast becoming an expert in tank engines.' It was a light-hearted quip but perhaps he didn't get it, for his expression didn't change. 'I played hockey for my county, I'm mad about most sports – skiing, water-skiing and tennis particularly. I studied Spanish and French at Warwick University. What else? . . . Um, I spent a couple of years working for a ski-hosting company in Verbier before I got the job at Invicta – in fact, that was how I met Tom and Jack, the founders. They stayed in the chalet where I was working and we hit it off; they had been doing everything themselves from their flat in Fulham for a couple of years and I was their first hire when they got their initial round of funding and started to grow the business . . .'

'And look at it now. Thirty-two offices worldwide, 584 staff, turnover of twelve million pounds annually.' The figures tripped off his tongue like the alphabet and she snatched a glimpse of the business brain that had brought him such success. But the Invicta figures, impressive though they were for a young company, were absolutely nothing to the size of his empire which spanned everything from mining interests in east Africa, to luxury hotel groups in Europe and Asia and cabling technology in mainland America.

'I know, it's incredible what they've built up; so quickly too.'

'Do you enjoy your job?' he asked.

'I love it there, I love everything about the job – the variety, the daily challenges, no two days are ever the same. Ordinarily, I'm the Corporate Partnerships lead here; I only relocated from London five months ago.'

'And why did you move?'

There was a question. She gave a sort of chuckle, wondering what she could say. 'Well, Jack needed help developing that side of the business here for one thing. It wasn't practical to keep managing all our link-ups from London alone. There's big business here that we weren't tapping into, and our membership here belongs to a different culture; it's a different clientele. We need to make sure we're offering a personalized fit, whilst still maintaining a global reach. So that's my remit.'

His eyes narrowed, as though alighting upon something. 'What was the other thing?'

She had the feeling he hadn't heard a word she'd just said. 'Sorry?'

'You said they needed help developing that side of the business here for one thing. What was the other?'

Her mouth opened but it was a moment before any sound would come out. 'Well, I had always wanted to live in the Big Apple of course,' she said, her finger and thumb rubbing together. 'It was the ultimate dream come true for a country girl like me.'

'. . . I see.' His expression changed, and it was as though an arctic wind had blown through the door. She felt suddenly cold, chilled. He went to stand. 'Well, it was nice to meet you, Miss Marston.'

'W-wait!' she said, jumping to her feet and staring at him in alarm. What had she done wrong? 'Where are you going?'

'I believe I was very clear that I cannot work with people I don't trust. And it seems I cannot trust you.'

What? 'But you can,' she protested desperately, not caring that the men on the sofa had stalled their conversation to openly listen to theirs. The bodyguard was on his feet too. 'Please—'

'No, you are lying to me. And if you would choose to deceive me over something as trivial as this, how could I ever trust you on the important things?' He glowered at her, those eyes which had been so warm and approachable just moments before, now fathomless and blank.

The bodyguard was standing by his shoulder now, looking down on her as though *she* was a potential risk to her client. She stared at Alexander, panic coursing through her like a pinball, that he was leaving, that she had blown it again. First Rosaria, now him.

He turned to leave.

'I . . . I had my heart broken. The man I loved got engaged to someone else,' she blurted out, her own eyes suddenly hot and wet. She felt humiliation that she had to say it out loud, to have her weakness and shame paraded in front of him. Him, of all people! 'That was why I came here. I couldn't stay in London after that.'

Alexander paused, his chin tilted up interestedly.

'I'm s-sorry,' she stammered. 'I should have just come straight out with it, but I didn't think it—' She swallowed. 'I didn't think it would be interesting, or . . . or appropriate, even, to confide something personal like that to you. It's not supposed to be about me.'

He took a step closer to her. 'Of course it is,' he said strongly. 'Don't you see? This relationship *is* personal. If we go ahead, you will know more about me than my own wife. My mother. Do you think that can work if you are a stranger to me? Do you think it is not relevant that you have uprooted your life because of this man, that you have had to start all over again?'

She swallowed, shaking her head anxiously as his eyes held her up again as surely as hands under her arms. 'I'm sorry.'

'I have to know you will be honest with me. I require – no, I insist – upon full disclosure every time, no matter if you think it is unimportant or trivial. *I* will decide what matters.'

'Absolutely. Of course.'

'I am a man with many enemies, Miss Marston – it is impossible to reach my station without them. It is part of the process and I accept that. But it means my friends become even more important. Trust is everything.'

She nodded, blinking rapidly to push back the wetness in her eyes.

He stared at her for a long moment and it was like watching the winter snows melt on a meadow – beauty, colour and softness emerging from the frozen blanket. 'So, you came all the way to New York to escape the man who broke your heart, huh?' He nodded. 'That tells me you are impulsive, strong, independent . . .'

He was leading her back in to a second chance, an opportunity to redeem herself, to save this situation. 'Yes. It was a sort of "now or never" moment,' she said quickly. 'I found out on the Thursday. I was here by the Monday.'

'A woman with the courage of her convictions, I like that.' He looked impressed, his sternness all but gone now. 'But tell me this – is New York far enough away from him, this man?'

'Oh yes, plenty far,' she said quickly. 'It's over. Done.'

Steven came back with their drinks, hesitating as he saw their toe-to-toe stand-off, the bodyguard hovering. Alexander gave an almost imperceptible nod and the bodyguard stepped away, Alexander stretching one arm out to receive his drink.

'Then that deserves a toast,' he said as she received her drink too. 'You know, we have a saying in Russia: you do not miss the cow until the barn is empty.'

Chloe fixed her smile in place. Huh? Joe Lincoln had pretty much likened her to her Labrador and now Alexander Subocheva was likening her to a cow?

'Whatever your Englishman did, he must know by now he has lost something very precious.'

Was he right? She thought back to her conversation last night with Tom, him wanting to come over here, chasing her down.

'I, on the other hand, make a point of appreciating the cow. I have built my career by seeing opportunity where others see only difficulty; I do not let my cows leave the barn.' He smiled. 'I mean to say, Miss Marston, that his loss is now my gain. So I propose a toast to absent friends—'

'Absent friends,' Chloe said with hearty agreement.

'But also to us – I believe this is the start of a beautiful working relationship.'

She let him clink her glass, the sound sonorous and sweet as she allowed herself to relax once more, victory snatched from the jaws of defeat. 'To us.'

Chapter Eight

'Listen, the dude is paranoid as,' Xan said, standing on his beloved skateboard and jigging side to side on it beside her desk. 'I heard the Kremlin, the FBI *and* Lorenzo Gelardi have got tails on him.'

'Oh, *you* heard this?' Chloe grinned, sitting back in her – Poppy's – chair and sipping her coffee. 'Well I didn't know you had eyes in the FBI,' she teased. 'Why didn't you say? That shit can be useful.'

Xan pouted. 'You did well to wind his neck back in, is what I'm saying.'

Chloe spluttered at his surprisingly correct deployment of a British colloquial phrase. 'Oh, Xan!' she said, crossing her hands above her heart like a proud mother. 'My work here is done.'

His eyes brightened. 'Yeah? Did I get it right?'

'You can move to England and live like a native,' she laughed, just as her phone rang again. 'Hello, Chloe Marston speaking,' she said, watching as Xan air-punched his way off, in search of more gossip and hopefully a bag of peanut M&Ms. 'Oh hey, Mike, how are you? How's the album coming along today?' It turned out that when Mike was 'back in contact', he really was back in contact. He called at least every couple of hours and Chloe felt she had a better grasp on his week than her own.

'Fucking slowly, since you ask,' he rasped. 'Turns out our lovely lead singer, thanks to his four-day bender last week, has come down with what looks like a nasty case of the clap – balls the size of coconuts and pus oozing from . . . well, I don't like to be indelicate but let's just say it was from a place where pus shouldn't ooze.'

'Yikes, I'm sorry to hear that,' Chloe replied, covering her eyes with her hands and trying not to gag.

'Yeah, 'e's in a right state; rolling around, groaning – although that's probably the comedown as much as anything.'

'Comedown?'

'From the smack. We're gonna need a medic out here quick, someone we can trust to keep quiet. I can't get anyone local, it'd be all over the island quicker than a dog with two dicks.'

Chloe pulled another face. 'No, quite.'

'Sort it for me, will ya? We only got the studio booked another two weeks and at this rate, we ain't even got a B-side. I need him doing that thing he do by tomorrow.'

'Absolutely. I'm on it. I'll text you an ETA when I get it.'

'Thanks, babe.' And he was gone.

Chloe shuddered; even just the conversation made her feel grubby. 'Right, I need a doctor in Hawaii,' she murmured to herself, clicking open the West Coast file. 'Doctor in Hawaii . . .'

Behind her, an uptick in the buzz of conversation registered vaguely as she scrolled to see who headed the team in the LA office, her ears picking up on the sound of chairs being scraped back, greetings hailed. She punched the number in the phone and pressed it to her ear, listening to the ringing tone as her eyes slid to the small mirror on the corner of her screen. Jack was coming out of his office. Lifting her head, she saw why.

'Well, well, well, the prodigal son returns!' Jack said wryly, leaning against the doorframe and watching as Tom moved slowly through the room like an A-lister on the red carpet.

Her jaw dropped open at the sight of him. This couldn't be happening. Not only had he defied her express wishes that he not come here, he must have pretty much caught the next plane after she'd hung up on him; she clearly remembered he'd said he was coming out next week! Had he known she'd try to dodge him again – take some annual leave or hide out in the Hamptons for a bit once she heard he was coming over anyway? Ducking her head down low below the line of the screens, she watched the action, her heart pounding at triple time that he'd caught her on the hop, unaware and unarmed. She glanced in the small mirror again to find her cheeks were flushed and she cursed herself for reacting to him.

She watched as Tom got to his old friend, stopping several metres short and throwing his arms out. There was a pause before Jack walked into them, the two men back-slapping one another like brothers, genuine affection flowing between them. They had been friends since prep school, sharing almost a lifetime of memories together.

'How are you holding up, mate?' Tom asked.

'All right. You know how it is.'

'Yeah, I do. You look like shit.'

Jack cracked a smile, running a hand through his floppy hair. 'What are you doing here? Did I miss a memo?'

Tom gripped Jack by the shoulder and squeezed. 'I just wanted to show my face and give my support. It's been a crap week, right? I thought you could do with a helping hand. I bet you've barely slept.' Jack shrugged but the dark circles under his eyes told the truth. 'How's she doing, our Pops? Any change?'

'Same. Holding on.'

'Shit, mate, I'm sorry, I know what she means to you. All of you,' he said, suddenly inclusive, sweeping his arm round and collectively, psychically, gathering the team in his embrace as his gaze swept the room.

In the mirror, she saw his eyes find her – or rather the back of her – the phone still in her hand even though the ring tone in her ear was now a disconnected alarm. They stayed on her for a moment, the confidence in his expression flickering momentarily, like lamplights during an electrical surge.

'The papers have gone nuts back home,' he said, pulling his gaze back to Jack.

'I've seen. I've been fielding calls from reporters all week.'

'Just hang in there. They'll lose interest soon.'

There was a pause. '. . . Mmm.'

Tom frowned but Jack simply nodded his head in the direction of his office and walked into it. Tom glanced back at the office, taking in their group quizzical look. 'Everyone, drinks at the Howard at 6 p.m. tonight, on me. I hope to see as many of you as possible; it'll be good to catch up. We could all do with a little light relief after the week we've had.'

His eyes slid over to her back again – still inert, still all he could see of her – before he followed Jack into the glass office and closed the door.

The rest of the team dispersed, that familiar buzz of chatter filling the room again as their two leaders stood with crossed arms and deepening frowns. What were they discussing? Chloe wondered, spying from her make-up mirror. She watched Tom as he began to pace, looking good – so good – in his skinny brick chinos and pale-blue shirt. His swept-across hair was longer and he'd lost a little weight from when she'd seen him last; both changes suited him, goddammit, making a play of his already sharp cheekbones and emphasizing his blue, lively eyes.

'Well *that* sounds fun,' Xan said, across the way, eyes dancing with mischief.

She lifted her head up to see him properly. 'Huh?'

'Drinks tonight with our handsome co-founder. It's not often he blesses us with his presence. You gonna come?'

'Oh –' She pulled a sad face. 'Can't. I've already got plans.'

'Yeah?' He looked crestfallen. Without Poppy, their little gang felt fundamentally diminished. 'Not even a quickie?'

'Sorry, I'm going for dinner with Elle.' She felt bad about lying, but then again lies were simply part of the landscape with Tom. Always had been. They tainted everyone he touched.

Xan smiled affectionately at the mention of the name. 'And how is that girl?'

'She's great. She's got a new gig now at that cabaret place in Midtown. Oh, what's it called?'

'Not Feinstein's/54 Below?'

'Yeah, that's the one.'

Xan gave a low whistle. 'Then she's going places. She'll get a recording deal no problem if she's playing there.'

'Hopefully,' Chloe sighed. 'She's so good, she deserves to find an audience.'

'With that glorious hair and bod of hers, I can already see the album cover,' Xan said with a sigh. 'Glitter eyes, liquid satin . . .'

'We'll make sure you get the styling credits.' She chewed on her pen lid, watching him. 'So you're actually planning on going to the drinks tonight then?'

'Of course. We *love* it when Tom comes over.' Xan winked at her.

'I take it that's the royal we?'

He shrugged happily.

'You're not his type,' she grinned.

'How would you know?'

'Because I know his fiancée.'

'Spoilsport.' Xan wrinkled his nose and disappeared below the parapet again.

Chloe stared at her screen for a moment, not seeing it or her reflection in it, but Tom's fiancée Lucy, with her symmetrical smile and perfect teeth, sleek blonde hair that never had roots or frizzed in the rain, her neat figure and predilection for ballet pumps that seemingly encouraged her to hop and skitter lightly, like a fawn. Tom had told her he was going to break it off with her, promised her; he'd said that it was only the fact she was so fragile that had stopped him before . . .

She blinked, breaking the reverie, shaking off the spell. What did it matter what he'd said? It was bad enough that she'd believed him for so long. But he had made his choice, finally, and she'd made hers. Her life was here now and she had a client with a client with the clap. She was needed!

Picking up the phone again, she dialled LA and got down to business.

It was a hot night, one of those times when the very walls of the city seemed to sweat, disgorging its citizens onto the streets, people swarming everywhere – sitting on the steps of the brownstones, leaning against the walls of bars, bare feet kicked over the balconies of terraces and tiny verandas. She walked home at a shuffle, still eating the popcorn she hadn't finished on her own in the cinema; it was cold now and not how she liked it, but holding the box against her chest, one hand dipping in every so often, it was something to do. She felt restless and agitated, like a night moth that couldn't settle, throwing itself at the lights, wings beating frantically.

When she rounded the corner onto Perry Street and saw him sitting on the steps of her building, it wasn't surprise that she felt. Deep down, she had known he would come looking for her, just as he had probably known that she wouldn't go to the drinks. They knew each other too well. The only time he had ever surprised her had been on that Thursday lunchtime, when she'd seen him – *them* – coming out of Asprey on Bond Street with bright eyes and loving kisses, the cab whisking her past in silent dismay, her face pale behind the glass as if she was watching through a TV screen, a voyeur of her own tragedy.

By the time he'd realized she knew, she was already in New York, taking up the new post she'd created for herself. Jack had been taken aback by the sudden speed of it, naturally, but Tom – unable to tell the truth – had been forced to corroborate her story, and the transfer had gone unquestioned; Jack had been trying to get her over here for years anyway.

And her escape had largely worked. Apart from accidentally picking up his FaceTime earlier in the week, she'd done well at avoiding him, making sure they were never alone on conference calls, blocking his emails on her personal account, his texts. What was there to say anyway? Asking another woman to marry him was hardly accidental. And if she was being honest, it had been on the cards all along, Chloe had just refused to face up to it. She had wanted to believe the promises he whispered in her ear – that Lucy was more of a friend than anything else, that accepting her father's seed money in the business made it difficult to extricate himself from the family, especially when a return on his investment was all but impossible during their rapid global expansion roll-out. Chloe had told herself over and again, as she spent Christmas and birthdays without him, that he was simply trying to do the honourable thing, the right thing, by a woman and her family who had bound him as tightly to them as any wedding band. He was in a fix, already beholden to a woman he didn't truly love by the time she came along, and many times over the years Chloe had ended it with him, refusing to be the 'other woman' as first one deadline, and then another, slipped past and still he was with Lucy. But he always won her back; it was simply impossible to avoid him when she had to see him every day in the office, and it was just too hard to resist his anguished looks of longing across the room as she resolved, this time, to be strong.

But things were different now, for he hadn't simply let things continue to drift with Lucy, he had actively made a life decision whilst Chloe slept on the other side of the bed. So what did he possibly think he could say to explain this time? Did he really believe he could make things better between them, that they could be friends at least? No, she had broken the loop at last and freed herself from him. She had had to leave the country to do it, but she had done it.

She stepped back behind a tree, watching him as he sat on the steps in the lamplight, his elbows on his knees, his phone in his hands. Every time a car passed, or a couple approached, he looked up, that familiar bright-eyed expression on his face. There was no way past him without going past him. He was making himself unavoidable and she realized she had been wrong when she'd told Alexander New York was plenty far away from him. It wasn't.

In her bag, her phone rang and she pulled it out, keeping her eyes on Tom all the while. She didn't trust him not to steal a march on her, behind this tree.

'Yes?' she asked distractedly, her voice a half-whisper as she watched him sigh heavily, weary now. He had had a long day – a transatlantic flight, full day at the office with Jack, drinks after work . . . He must be tired, wondering why she was not home at just gone midnight, who she was with . . .

'Chloe?'

'Yes.'

'It's Pelham.'

She sank against the tree and closed her eyes. 'Hey, how are you?'

'On a bit of a sticky wicket, since you ask. I'm in a suite at the Carlyle – or rather I was—'

He was in New York? The man was like a grasshopper. In his sixties and on a plane more often than most men changed their socks.

'—Only, I had thought perhaps I ought to stop beating about the bush and take a more . . . direct approach.'

Chloe frowned, not quite sure what he was trying to tell her.

'Nothing else has worked, you see? And I thought maybe she wanted me to be more . . . forthright, more manly.'

Uh-oh. Chloe winced, bracing herself for what was coming.

'So I took the liberty of letting myself into her room after we had parted ways for the evening.'

'. . . And she didn't appreciate that?'

'I'll say. She took exception to my "presumption", as she put it, and threw me out. So now I'm in the corridor. In my birthday suit. Without a key.' He sounded like he was about to burst into tears. 'I didn't quite think it through properly, you see.'

Chloe watched Tom as he undid and retied the lace on his shoe. He was a brogues kind of guy.

'Pelham, don't worry, I can sort this. I'm just getting in a cab now,' she said, raising her arm as she saw a taxi with its light on coming down the street. 'I'll be with you in five. Just stay where you are. Don't move.' She couldn't have a peer of the realm caught in such a compromising position – the press would be as bad for them as for him. She rang off just as the cab pulled alongside her. 'East 76th,' she said, jumping in and slamming the door shut.

The windows were open and she suddenly heard her name.

'Chloe!' Tom called, getting to his feet and running after her. 'Chloe, wait!'

She saw the driver's eyes slide over to the rear-view mirror, taking in the sight of the floppy-haired Englishman chasing them down the street. 'Drive on,' she said to the driver, not looking back. 'The Carlyle, please.'

Chapter Nine

Provence

Elodie walked quickly through the market, the extra-wide brim of her straw hat obscuring almost all of her face as she kept her gaze firmly on the cobbles. Sandalled feet passed by her small field of vision, the chequered cloths of the stalls fluttering lightly in the breeze, the scent of lavender and roses threading through the air as she moved with purpose, with intent, off the main avenue and into the smaller back-streets. The shadows on the ground were sharply defined and she walked in and out of them with blinkered haste, never stopping to browse the window displays or pop into one of the many boutiques, oblivious to the gazes that snagged on her and followed her narrow retreating back as though somehow knowing she was set apart from them.

The building was nondescript, tall and narrow with smoky lemon walls and peeling powder-blue shutters, blending perfectly with its neighbours on the strip, the brass plaque beside the door rubbed almost smooth with age.

She walked on tiptoes up the stone steps and turned into the reception area on the right. The receptionist – new; he deliberately kept them on a short rotation – looked up as she walked over the terracotta tiles towards her, past the yucca plant whose leaves were thick with dust. Standing by the desk, she saw three pairs of feet, already parked – one in Havaianas, one in brown suede lace-ups, the other in faded red leather Avarcas sandals.

'*Le médecin*, ten-thirty,' she said in her quiet voice.

The receptionist checked on her screen. 'Thank you, madame. If you would like to take a seat?'

Elodie sat in the chair she always chose – the hard-backed ladder chair in the corner, furthest from the door and windows, her head down so that the hat brim flopped, revealing only her jaw and mouth. Ignoring the magazines on the coffee table, the small TV mounted on the wall, the messages on her phone, she crossed her legs and waited, only the fast swing of the action betraying her restlessness.

It was another eight minutes before the door opened and she looked up – showing a partial view of her face for the first time – as the nurse came out.

'The doctor will see you now,' the nurse said after a pause, looking straight at Elodie.

Elodie rose, the motion fluid and self-contained, and she walked in silence across the reception area to the consulting room. She closed the door behind her and the doctor looked up from his desk, pen still in his hand as he finished writing his notes. His dark curls had grown longer since their last meeting, and were verging on the unruly, his skin more tanned as summer hotted up.

'Elodie.'

Slowly, she reached up and removed the hat, her dark hair falling forwards to frame her face as though protectively. Too late.

The pen fell from his fingers, his mouth going slack at the sight of her. 'My God, what has he done?'

Chapter Ten

New York

Chloe traced the hopscotch lines on the ground with her foot while Elle grappled behind the curtain. 'Are you in yet?'

'. . . Almost!' Elle panted, an elbow suddenly punching the fabric out, followed by the sound of a zip being pulled and a deep groan. 'Yes!' The curtain flew back and Elle struck a model pose with an exaggerated hip pop and a pout on her lips. 'Whaddya think?'

'Wow!' Chloe said, startled by the newly dramatic zigzag silhouette of a woman whose Amazonian height already turned every head.

'I know, right?' Elle agreed, stalking out, one hand on her hip and turning to look back at herself in the mirror. Chloe looked at their reflections, thinking how incongruous they looked together – Elle towering over her, ebony skin gleaming in the midday sun, hair pulled back into an Afro-bun today, her curves shoehorned into a tiny strapless red polka-dotted ruched dress that had probably last been worn to someone's prom in 1984; and then her, pale-faced and looking drawn with remnants of yesterday's mascara still smudging the skin around her eyes, and practically invisible in a black vest, slides and cutoffs. Chloe licked her

109

index finger and tried rubbing away the remains of mascara again.

'Can you sit in it?' she asked.

'Don't need to sit,' Elle said dismissively. 'I can walk in it and I can . . .' She took a shallow laboured breath. 'I can breathe. Just.'

'You should totally get it,' Chloe said, sipping on her juice, head tipped to the side as Elle struck pose after pose. 'You look incredible. I couldn't get those angles with a protractor and ruler.'

'But where will I wear it?' Elle pouted, even though they both knew without a shadow of a doubt that Elle would be getting it regardless.

Chloe considered for a moment. 'Come to the private view of the Basquiat exhibition on Monday. I'll get you in.'

'Yeah?' Elle's eyes lit up. 'This'll be perfect.' She struck another pose before looking at Chloe. 'What will you be wearing?'

'Nothing as fabulous as that. It's work for me, remember.'

'It doesn't mean you have to dress like a nun,' Elle said, jogging her with her elbow as she sashayed back into the precarious cubicle and started getting changed again. 'And it's time to stop living like one too, by the way. Did you ring that guy whose number I gave you?'

Chloe winced. She'd been hoping Elle would have forgotten about that. 'No.'

'*No?*'

'Not yet I mean.'

The curtain whisked back, Elle looking indignant and not at all concerned to be flashing her underwear to the rest of the flea-market shoppers. 'Chlo! Why not?'

'Because it's not the right time.'

'Bullshit. When is it ever not the right time to hook up with a hot guy?'

'There's too much else going on. Work's mental – I've just had the week from hell trying to pick up Poppy's clients, get to know them, keep them happy.'

Elle, who had been about to disappear behind the curtain, stalled, regarding her with suspicious eyes. 'And? There's something else.'

'No there isn't.'

'Yes there is. There was an "and" hanging in the air there, I heard it.'

Chloe bit her lip. Elle was like a bloodhound, always able to pick up a scent. 'And Tom's come over.'

'Shut the front door!'

'I wish I could. But he was sitting on my steps last night so I couldn't even get *to* my door.'

'The freaking nerve of the guy! What did you do?'

Chloe shrugged. 'Ended up staying at the Carlyle. One of my clients was there so I had to pop over anyway; I know the concierge there really well so I lied and said I'd lost my house keys and they just gave me a room.'

Elle arched an eyebrow, looking indignant and impressed all at once. She clicked her fingers. 'Just like that?'

Chloe shrugged. 'Our client bases completely overlap. They scratch my back, I scratch theirs.'

'Jeez, I am so in the wrong industry,' Elle tutted, pulling the curtain back.

Chloe turned away, walking along the hopscotch lines again, her gaze lifting up and out to all the other stalls set up in the school playground; overhead the High Line meandered in gentle curves, voices drifting like smoke in the air above them.

Browsing here on a Saturday morning had become one of her favourite things to do since moving to the city; she liked the bustle, the slow shuffle, the thrill of hunting for unspecified treasures. Unfortunately the minuscule size of her apartment meant she couldn't indulge as much as she'd like. The weekly market was known for its vintage furniture stocks but one Moroccan pouffe would pretty much cover the only spare floor space available; jewellery and old books were admissible however and she loved rifling through the antique French linens that were neatly folded and piled in stacked towers on the trestles. There was something so appealing to her about the old smells, timeworn textures and faded colours to be found there. It was so different to what she encountered during the week, where everything was shiny and new, perfect and box-fresh: supercars and 800 thread counts, four-figure flower arrangements and diamond chandeliers, where consumption was king and what you had defined what you were. But this market, appearing as if by magic in this Chelsea elementary school playground every Saturday morning, brought her back to herself, cherishing the individual, the lost, the unique. It was her New York Portobello.

'So what are you gonna do?' Elle called.

Chloe turned back, retracing her steps, one hand resting on an old analogue black-and-white TV set which was sitting on an Ercol table, beside a rack of vintage fur coats. 'Same as I have been doing – blank him.'

'But he's here now. He's come all the way *here*. You can't avoid him now, you're in the same city, same country again. And even you can't stay at the Carlyle every night.'

'Nah, I won't need to, this isn't about me. He's only come over because of what's happened with Poppy.'

'Oh, come on, you don't believe that!' Elle scoffed.

'Actually I do. I've been giving it some thought and if this was really about me, he'd have come over before now. I've been here *five months*, Elle. This is a team morale-boosting session, he told me. And I believe him.'

'Yeah, so that's why he was sitting on your steps last night.'

'Two birds, one stone. Trust me, he's always been one for efficiency. But he's a fast learner too and I've made it perfectly clear I have absolutely no intention of speaking to him.' She studied her nails, wondering if she should go for a manicure after this. 'He won't bother me again,' she mumbled.

Elle sighed, stepping out of the cubicle, the dress draped over one arm as she came over and squeezed Chloe with the other. 'Neither one of us believes that. I don't care what you say, you'll have to talk about it with him at some point, you know you will. You can't go out with someone for four and a half years and break up without either one of you ever saying a single word about it. I mean, that is fucked up, sister.'

'Well, he managed to get engaged to someone else without ever saying a word about that, so . . .' Chloe said tartly.

Elle's dark eyes were large and round and shining with concern. 'He's come here to win you back, and we both know it.'

'No.' Chloe's brisk tone shut the topic down immediately. Or rather, it was intended to—

'He's had time to think, that's what it is. He's realized what he's lost now, that's the thing,' Elle said with a wise expression.

'Oh my God, not you too! I am not a cow that's left the barn.'

'A cow?' Elle asked, looking lost.

'Oh—' Chloe checked herself. 'Nothing. It was just something Alexander said the other day.'

'Alexander?' Elle arched an eyebrow, instantly forgetting Tom. 'And who, pray tell, is he?'

'Cool it. Alexander Subocheva. He's one of my clients now.'

Elle's pink-glossed mouth dropped open. '*You're* looking after Alexander freaking Subocheva?' she gasped.

'Sssshh!' Chloe said, pressing a finger to her lips and checking no one had overheard. 'It's not public knowledge.'

'Shit, you have hit the big time, baby! It's all glamour, glamour, glamour from here. He's like . . . a billionaire!'

'Yes. He's also still a flesh and blood person, not so very different from you and me.'

'Except when you cut him, he bleeds gold.'

Chloe chuckled, shaking her head as Elle reached in her purse for a twenty-dollar bill and handed it to the stall owner, who – barely looking up from her phone, a cigarette stuck to her lower lip – stuffed the dress in a brown paper bag and almost shoved it back at her. Elle's mouth pursed into a perfect, unimpressed pout, looking back first at the woman, then at Chloe. 'See what I'm sayin'? Alexander Subocheva doesn't have to put up with this shit.'

They wandered in easy silence for a while, peering at old coral necklaces and onyx ashtrays, wool naval overcoats and 1920s feathered headbands.

'What do you think?' Chloe smiled, flipping open a black marabou fan and fluttering it in front of her face, eyes lowered coquettishly.

'Oh la la, Lady Marmalade,' Elle smiled, picking up a smaller white one beside it and copying her, beginning to sing with a low smoky purr. Chloe laughed, performing a sort of dance alongside her, their wrists twirling, feathers shimmying as they tried to open and close the fans in a single snapping movement. 'Huh, harder than it looks,' Elle said, wrestling with hers.

Chloe, her nose tickled by the feathers, sneezed four times in quick succession. 'Hmm, maybe not,' she said, replacing the fan on the counter and giving the stall owner an apologetic smile.

A girl walked past them, eating a falafel wrap.

'Ohmigod, that smells so good,' Elle groaned, her nose in the air and almost trailing after her.

'Shall we get something to eat?' Chloe asked, knowing Elle was just about to realize she was absolutely starving.

'Hell, yeah. Where are you thinking?'

'Actually, I've got an idea,' Chloe smiled. She led the way out of the flea market and back onto the street. In the couple of hours it had taken them to slope around the market, Chelsea had hit peak weekend mode – the pavements were crowded with couples ambling hand in hand, young families pushing babies in strollers, runners pounding the streets with tied-back hair, earbud wires dangling and iPhones strapped to their arms.

'I know a place you're going to love,' she said, leading the way through the crowds. 'I came here with a client earlier in the week. I'd never have known about it otherwise.'

Elle pulled a face. 'It doesn't have a fancy dress code, does it? I know what kind of place you go to with your clients and, trust me – I'm not dressed for it.'

'And I am?' Chloe grinned, indicating her bare legs and tatty shorts to Elle as they walked briskly, shopping bags swinging as they dodged and wove round the crowds. The street food market was only six blocks away and when they arrived, the crowds were already thick.

'Oh my God,' Elle drawled, taking in the buzzy scene. 'You took a client to *this*?'

'Well, rather, he took me.' She grabbed Elle by the arm. 'Come over here, you've got to try the chilaquiles at this Mexican place.'

'Chila-what?' Elle blustered. 'Is that some fancy name for a taco?'

Chloe laughed; hadn't her reaction been exactly the same? 'Trust me, they do those too but the food here is unlike any Mexican food you've had before. It's gonna blow your mind. They even add pomegranate seeds to the guacamole. It's so pretty you don't know whether to eat it or wear it.'

They walked past trucks selling sweet sourdough dough-nuts, olive breads, lobster rolls, pastrami cuts; Chloe stopped at the end of the line for Chimichanga Taqueria. The aroma drifting from the cart was delicious and Elle both closed her eyes and clutched her stomach in a display of appreciation and anguish; waiting for food wasn't her strong point.

The line shuffled forwards and soon they were tantaliz-ingly close to the front.

'What'll it be, ladies?' asked the curly black-haired woman who had served her and Joe the other day. Ariane, was it? She didn't appear to recognize Chloe at any rate.

'Apparently I've got to have the chila-thingies,' Elle called up to her.

'Make that two,' Chloe added.

'Two chilaquiles,' the woman called to a line of people work-ing behind her, their backs to the market as they chopped chillies and peppers at lightning speed and ground avocadoes with pestles and mortars. 'Any drinks with that?'

'A couple of beers,' Elle said.

'That'll be sixteen bucks,' the woman said, holding out her hand.

'I'll get this,' Chloe said, holding out the notes before Elle could reach for her purse. 'It's my turn.'

'Okay, thanks.' Elle squeezed her arm gratefully – she was perpetually broke, spending what little money she had on her beloved vintage finds. The two of them scanned the rest of the food market as they waited with watering mouths. Almost all the trestles were taken.

'Do you want to wait for this and I'll go get us some seats?' Chloe asked.

Elle shot her a bemused look. 'You? The English girl? We'd be here all day with you *queuing* and saying "sorry" every time someone stole your seat.' She patted Chloe on the arm with a laugh. 'No, sweetie, you wait for the food and I'll go find us somewhere to sit. Leave this with me.'

Chloe grinned, watching her bold friend sashay into the fray, paper shopping bags swinging from her hand. Sure enough, within a minute of standing ominously above a couple who'd finished their meals and were selfishly lingering, she'd bagged them some places.

Chloe looked around the market with interest as she waited; there hadn't been time to take in the detail with Joe the other day and when she'd mentioned it to Xan on her return to the office afterwards, he'd told her about the one on Union Street too. She kept wondering about some kind of tie-up for their members . . . but how? The very appeal of a place like this lay in its accessibility. She didn't think the stallholders would be particularly amenable to the idea of hooking up special deals for an already over-privileged elite – but that only served to make it *more* desirable in her eyes.

To paraphrase the late, great Groucho Marx, her members wanted to belong to any club that wouldn't have them.

'There you go.'

She turned back to take the food, already almost able to taste it—

'*Joe?*'

He looked down at her in surprise, frozen, the bowls outstretched in his hands in front of him. 'Chloe.' He looked every bit as stunned as she was.

'What . . . what are you doing here?' she laughed, unable to hold it in. Of all the unlikely scenarios! His face was a picture; he didn't look quite so superior or arrogant now. In fact, he looked lost for words.

'I got back from France yesterday.'

As if that had been her point! 'No, I mean – what are you doing *here*?' She motioned to the street food market.

'Oh! Yeah, I'm helping out.'

No shit, Sherlock! she thought to herself, but she couldn't wipe the surprised expression from her face. This was literally The Last Thing she could have expected to see. What next – Alexander Subocheva manning stalls at a jumble sale? Was it a pro-bono thing?

'It's run by some friends of mine and they get real busy so, occasionally, if I'm tooling around, I pitch in for an hour or so. Just to get them through the lunchtime rush.' He shrugged, taking in her still astonished expression. 'What? It's fun. It gives me a complete break from my routine. Plus it's helping with the jet lag today. There's no chance of sleeping here.'

'Oh yes, absolutely. Absolutely,' she agreed, trying not to stare at the sight of him in a long black apron. Bizarrely, he somehow made it look sort of . . . manly.

A little silence pulsed.

'Actually, I was going to call you on Monday anyway – find out how the property search is going?'

She cracked open another smile; it was somewhat ironic to be discussing a money-no-object holiday home with the man serving her a posh taco. 'It's going well!' she laughed, shaking her head. This was crazy. '. . . Uh, so I've made lots of calls and spoken to some contacts in the region; they've helped me identify some islands I think best fit your brief, so now I'm researching those more closely and I'm getting a shortlist together. I'm hoping I should be able to show something to you soon.'

'Good, I can't wait to see—'

'Joe! Two panuchos?' the woman taking the orders called over, shooting him an impatient look.

He looked back at her, pulling a face. 'I'd better get back—'

'Of course, yes. You're needed,' she said, beginning to laugh all over again. Did Ariane know she was bossing about a major captain of industry?

'It's not that funny!'

'Oh, it really is!' she guffawed. She had a proper case of the giggles now as she took the plates off the counter, her face red with suppressed bluster. 'You must go . . . but it was good to see you.'

He looked down at her, seemingly bemused by her hysterics and, to her surprise, as their eyes met she felt a tiny spark inside her stomach, like a pilot light trying to ignite. His entire demeanour was different from their first meeting – weekend feels? 'Call me.'

The laughter died in her throat and she swallowed hard. 'Yes. I will.' It was a professional order, of course, nothing more, but in that flash of a moment, in another light or another life . . . She walked over to Elle, feeling high, and somewhat bewildered.

'Well?' Elle breathed dramatically. 'Don't keep me hanging. Who the hell is he and did you get his number?' Her words came out in an unbroken rush.

'His name's Joe and I've already got it. He's a client.' She rolled her eyes.

'He's hot!'

'He's a client,' Chloe sighed, handing over Elle's plate, but Elle was still too busy eyeing him up to notice.

'Wait a minute, what's he doing making chickadoo-things or whatever you call them, if he's a client of yours? I don't want to think how many he'd have to make to afford your fees.'

'It's his friend's truck, he's just helping out. He owns an engineering company.'

'You know that for a fact, do you?' Elle asked, her eyes still pinned upon him. 'I ain't never seen an engineering boss look like *him* before. Don't they need to be bald and short-sighted?'

'I have performed due diligence,' Chloe smiled, glad her back was to him as she began to tuck in. She had confirmed his details at Companies House and was satisfied that everything checked out, but the company website was one of those artsy ones that was big on ambient lifestyle shots and images of their projects, but precious little on the personalities running the show. Google hadn't produced much more – he didn't have any social media accounts that she could see, and there weren't any paparazzi images of him at industry events or charity circuit parties, which chimed with his lack of interest in using Invicta to get on the city's hottest

VIP lists; he was as elusive and discreet as his Swiss banking card.

Chloe took a bite of the chilaquile and slumped with happiness. 'Ohmigod that's so good,' she moaned, running the words into one another. Coming to eat here after their Saturday morning market mooch might have to become a habit, she thought to herself.

'So he's hot *and* rich *and* generous – tell me more.'

'Can't, client confidentiality.' Chloe dabbed the corner of her mouth with her finger, sure she was dribbling, it tasted so good.

'Oh, don't give me that,' Elle admonished, her eyes still on him. 'You can at least give me his number.'

'I definitely can't do that!' she guffawed.

'Why? Do you want to date him?'

'Elle, he's my client,' she repeated with a groan.

'So then you can give me first dibs. Can't you *engineer* a meeting?' She laughed wildly at her little joke.

'I'm there to fulfil his requirements, not dictate them.'

'Hmm, and wouldn't I just love to fulfil his requirements,' Elle said with a wicked grin. 'Hey, you could always invite him to that Basquiat retrospective you were telling me about.'

Chloe smiled; her friend was incorrigible. A veritable man-eater. Turning round slightly, her eyes slid over to him again – he was chatting and handing over plates to another set of eager customers. But what was she going to do? Even if she was looking – which she wasn't – he was a client and that made him the last person she could ever go on a date with. No. Whatever . . . whatever that *moment* had been back there, she just had to suck it up.

'Come on, help a girl out,' Elle pouted. 'I got me a dress and a party and no date.'

Chloe collapsed into a grin. 'Well, I could send him an email flagging it up,' she said slowly, licking sauce off her fingers. 'I guess there's no harm in that.'

Chapter Eleven

Even with heels, the dress was a little long. Elle could have worn it with flip-flops and it would have hung perfectly, but on her, the cornflower-blue silk puddled on the floor.

'Dammit, silver heels . . . silver heels,' she muttered to herself – they were the only ones with the requisite height to keep her from tripping on the hem – squatting as best she could in the dress to get a better look at the shoe boxes piled under her bed. She still couldn't get used to having *quite* so little space. Her shoes had to be kept under the bed, her coats hanging from a drying rail above the bath and the shelf that ran high up on every wall in every room of the apartment, which she had thought such a quirk when she'd rented it, was positively groaning from the weight of lidded boxes storing everything from underwear to hairbands to wooden spoons.

She found the heels wrongly packed in a box with her tax returns and went back to the mirror again. Behind her, in the reflection, was proof of the carnage that had been involved in getting her to this serene point – dresses strewn all over the bed, various bras for different necklines dangling like caught fish on the bedstead, shoes toppled like bowling pins, powder, blusher and eyeshadows sprinkled on the dressing table . . . Yes. She twisted one way, then the other, trying to get an all-round look. The dress didn't quite achieve the same feats of engineering as Elle's Cyndi Lauper redux dress, but nonetheless the wide twisted chiffon straps and the wrap-over bodice did wonders for emphasizing her hip-to-waist ratio. Chloe couldn't stop looking at her own reflection. Put on a tiara and she'd be a veritable princess! She never got dressed up like this – her job meant enabling it for others, not for herself.

She caught herself, suddenly chastened. *Her* job? Hers? It was Poppy's. It was Poppy who ought to be standing here, dressed up to the nines and ready to sparkle. Instead she was . . . she was . . .

The buzzer rang, making her jump. His driver, no doubt. She skittered over to the intercom and spoke into it. 'I'll be right down!' she called brightly, trying to sound calm, in control and professional.

It was six exactly and frankly she needed another quarter of an hour before she'd be properly ready. She still had to backcomb her hair at the roots, that wing eyeliner to correct and she hadn't settled on a pair of earrings yet . . . Still, he wasn't a man to be kept waiting. She sat on the bed, buckling the sandals as best she could, but the bodice of the dress was so tight, it was a miracle she could breathe, much less bend.

The buzzer went again. 'Yes, I'm coming. I heard you the first time,' she muttered out loud and to no one in particular, hobbling over to the door again.

'Hi. I'll be just a minute,' she said cheerily into the intercom. Didn't this driver know it was rude to turn up somewhere on time, that women cannot be rushed when getting ready for an evening out? 'We're like paintings,' she mused to herself, putting in her stud earrings that she'd left on her bedside table and appraising her reflection; the silver shoes were – blessedly, as hoped – just high enough to bring the hem off the floor. 'Ready when we're ready.'

She pouted, struck a pose, then another. She considered Instagramming it; Jack was big on his staff showing their followers snippets of the glamorous lifestyle they offered access to, but – as the buzzer went again – there was no time now. Perhaps when they were there.

Without bothering to reply this time, she pulled the door closed on her apartment and went down the stairs as quickly as she dared in the dress, throwing open the building door with a flourish and a smile a few moments later, only just stopping short of a 'tada!'

And it was as well she did, because to her surprise, two men were standing together rather awkwardly on the top step, clearly both vying for the intercom.

'Tom!'

'Chloe—' He jumped to attention like a soldier on parade, a flamboyant bouquet of yellow freesias – her favourites – filling his arms.

The man to her right, in a driver's uniform, nodded his head with a taciturn expression. 'Miss Marston?'

'Yes.'

'If you're ready?' he said, motioning towards the sleek black limo idling on the street. The windows were blacked out completely.

'Absolutely,' she said, picking up her skirt daintily to see her feet as she walked down the steps, moving after him as though there was no one else there.

'Chloe, wait,' Tom said, an incredulous note in his voice as he reached for her, awkwardly, the flowers threatening to spill from his hold.

'No,' she snapped under her breath, pulling herself out of reach. 'I'm busy.'

'Doing what?' His eyes raked over her, desperation in them, and she knew she looked good. If Elle had been here, she would have made her pop a hip. 'Where are you going?' He seemed to have forgotten he was holding the bouquet, cradling it in his arms like a sleeping baby.

'That's none of your business,' she replied coolly.

'Who is that? Who's in the car?' he asked, peering at the blacked-out windows of the limo, but to no avail. Chloe could have told him those windows were bulletproof; if they wouldn't let a sniper's rifle do its worst, his jealousy had no chance.

'As I said – none of your business.' Let him stew, she thought, pleased by the anguish in his boyish features.

'Chloe, wait—' He let the flowers drop as he caught her by the elbow this time and his touch singed her skin, making her blanch. 'Give me a time then, a place. Tomorrow – we can have Sunday brunch. Please, we have to talk.'

'No, we really don't.'

'This is crazy. You can't keep avoiding me.'

She pulled her arm away from him but there was no hurry in the movement; it was like peeling back a plaster, inch by inch. 'Can't I, Tom? Like this, you mean?' She moved down the steps with glacial dignity. 'Can't I?'

'It is good of you to step in at such short notice,' Alexander said as the car pulled away, the tail-lights of the taxi in front casting them in a red glow, her heart still at a canter.

Had he witnessed the scene just now as Tom doorstepped her? How could he not have done? He was just too much of a gentleman to comment on it. Did she look as flustered as she felt? She glanced back to find Tom picking up the flowers off the step, their heads down in his limp arm as he watched them glide into the night.

'Are you kidding? A night at the Met? Who doesn't love that?' she lied through a bright smile, trying to slow her breathing down. Adrenaline was racing through her, the lies coming one on top of the other, first to Tom, now him. She wondered what Alexander would say if she told him the man responsible for her continent swap was standing right there, back on those steps.

'You look beautiful – if I am allowed to say such a thing?'

'Thank you, you're very kind.' She had borrowed the dress off her contact at Barneys and the tags were still in for return on Monday, sticking against her skin; she wouldn't be at all surprised if she was imprinted with a reverse Elie Saab logo when she got in later.

'Would you like a glass of champagne?' he asked, indicating the bottle of Krug that sat nestled in a bed of ice between them.

'How lovely,' she accepted. A drink was exactly what she needed right now. She imagined she could still feel Tom's hand on her skin; it had been their first touch since what had been unwittingly their last night together, back in February.

She watched as he peeled back the gold foil and popped the cork effortlessly. His might was implied in every movement, though he didn't move much. Perhaps that was why.

'So have you seen *La Trav* before?' she asked, plumbing into the small talk that came so easily to her these days, chattering about nothing of consequence and keeping the big conversations on mute. It was the definition of her New York nights.

'Many times, but not this version. You?' The city flickered

darkly behind him, smoke-tinted behind the extra-thick windows. He handed her the glass before returning the bottle to the ice. Chloe faltered – was he not going to have one too?

'Uh, it's one of my favourites – I think because the soprano is so prevalent, it's easier for me to sing along. I can never get anywhere near the low notes of *The Barber of Seville*, for example, even in the shower.'

He nodded, seeming amused by the idea.

'How long are you in the city for this time?' she asked, sipping the champagne slowly and wishing she hadn't accepted it now. Did it appear unprofessional? Was he inwardly disapproving? Had she failed a test?

'Just a few more days here then back to Europe, for most of the summer I hope. My wife does not like me to travel so much.'

'It must be hard for her when your businesses demand so much attention. Does she ever travel with you?'

'No, she has no interest in sitting in hotel rooms whilst I attend meetings and dinners; frankly I would not want her to be exposed to half the characters I have to do business with. And of course, she has a very busy life of her own; she is very involved in several charitable projects.'

So far, so predictable, Chloe thought behind her polite smile. Charity work and shopping would define her days.

'Anjelica is very good at making sure our schedules co-align as often as possible; we try never to go more than a week apart, but recently my business concerns have been . . .' He sighed wearily. 'Complicated.'

'Yes, I saw, I'm sorry,' she said, marvelling at his understatement. Even if she hadn't spent most of last weekend reading a thick file on his business interests as part of the in-depth profile Invicta kept on him, his companies had been dominating the headlines of the financial papers for all the wrong reasons recently – allegations of sexual harassment at his hotel group had been leaked and resulted in a series of resignations by several senior female personnel; on top of that, the proposed $12.2 billion merger of his One Stop highways travel plaza business (a US-based subsidiary of his Black Pearl hotel group) with the budget motel chain Traveller's Rest, had been referred to the Federal Trade Commission.

He looked at her. 'You read the business news?'

'Of course. I like to get a broad picture of the climate and trends; many of our clients are in that world so it pays to keep abreast of the current events.'

He looked displeased as he looked straight ahead; in spite of his light, quick eyes, he had what Kate would call a 'strong' profile: heavy brow, fleshy nose, prominent jaw. 'So then you know that the sale of one of my companies to a partner brand is being shot down by the anti-trust agencies?'

She had read that the Department of Justice was filing to prevent the deal on the grounds that the new company would control a 62 per cent stake of the travel accommodation market in up to nine states. 'I do. I'm sorry, that must be a blow. I can only imagine the amount of work that went into putting the deal together in the first place.'

'Yes. Fifteen months of talks and negotiations. It has been an *interesting* week,' he said mildly. 'My lawyers had covered every angle before we went public. It is very strange to them – and me – that this has happened. Assurances had been made in the relevant quarters that our dominance in the handful of states in question would not be a problem.

What is nine states out of fifty-two, after all? Certainly not a monopoly. The technical requirement for that classification is controlling 25 per cent of the given market.'

Chloe quickly did the maths. Nine states out of fifty-two was a fifth of the market, or 20 per cent. So why *was* the deal being held up? Was he implying it was being deliberately ambushed? And if so, by whom? 'Is there nothing that can be done to rescue it?'

'Only structural remedies.' And when he saw the blankness in her expression he added, 'Divestiture of some of our other businesses. I have been "advised" that selling off my main hotel group would benefit the deal greatly.'

'So will you do that?'

'No. Never. I have made it very clear to them that I would never even consider it.' The words rounded out under pressure, his accent a thick and rich gravy upon them. She was surprised when he gave a low laugh, shaking his head at the very idea; it was both mocking and incredulous.

'Can I ask why not?' Her mind was working fast, trying to understand his position. She knew he had got his hands dirty making his seed capital in mining in Russia and was a multi-millionaire by his early twenties; that he had made his second fortune in home electronics, before finally sealing his billionaire status with the acquisition ten years ago of the Black Pearl group. According to Poppy's notes – made in her trusty red biro – the luxury hotel chain was the crown jewel in his empire, encompassing a major five-star hotel in every European capital, and it had given him the cachet of international class, of discernment by association – or rather, outright ownership. 'It sounds like that company is particularly special to you.'

'Yes,' he said, beginning slowly. 'If I lost everything and had to start again from nothing, I would throw everything I had into getting back that one company. It is the only one that matters.'

'Because it is profitable?'

'It is my *least* profitable business,' he chuckled. 'That is why the Department of Justice thinks I am crazy for rejecting their so-called offer. One Stop, on the other hand, can't stop making money. Even my advisers are telling me I am crazy to try to do this deal and sell it off.'

'Then why do it?'

'Because the monies from that sale would give me the capital injection I need to expand Black Pearl without having to take in external investment.'

She thought back. 'But wasn't the point of your iceberg dinner to attract interest from investors?'

His eyes narrowed. 'I see you and Poppy have been talking.'

'No, no,' she said quickly. 'Not talking. But I sat next to her. I inevitably overheard some things from time to time.' She gave an easy shrug.

'It was a back-up option. As soon as I began to suspect my rivals were interfering with the merger, I set up this other plan but it is not what I would choose. I work better alone. I am not what you would call a team player. Boards don't like me and I don't like them.' He gave a wolfish smile.

'I see,' she said slowly, trying to keep up. 'I still don't understand, though, why you want to sell one of your most successful companies to grow the most unsuccessful one?'

He gave an amused smile. 'It is illogical, I agree, and it is the very first time in my life when I have allowed myself to pursue a project that is not geared to maximum profit. But I feel I have perhaps earned that right. If not now, when?' He gestured around him, the move taking in the plush quilted leather of the limo, the uniformed chauffeur, the city itself: he was master of it all. 'But you see, those hotels – each one of them – represent everything my early life was not – comfortable, warm, well stocked, safe. When I was a boy in Novokuznetsk, my mother would stand in the queues for five hours for bread, soap, sausages . . . And when she was not queuing, she worked three jobs as a cleaner. Yet it was still not enough. Some days I was so hungry, so riddled with stomach cramps, I could not stand straight.'

'My God.' She frowned, appalled. 'What about your father? Where was he?'

'He worked in the steel factory but he left us when I was six, when my youngest brother was born. He had cerebral palsy; there was very much stigma attached to disability in those days, it made our lives much harder, but to have handed him over to the state, to a so-called *home*, would have been tantamount to abandonment. He would have been left to wither. My mother knew this, my father too – but still he wanted my mother to choose between them. So she chose my brother.'

'She sounds like an incredible woman,' Chloe said softly; she could see the anger still simmered in his blood, a quiet hurt that had not yet been extinguished.

'She was.' His eyes narrowed. 'And I vowed to avenge her when my father left, abandoning *us*.'

'And did you?'

'Yes. The factory my father worked in was the first company I bought. I fired him myself.'

Chloe felt a chill. This was a man who had been chiselled from rock – he was as hard on the inside as the outside, shaped by forces beyond his control. 'That must have been . . . satisfying.'

'Yes it was, but I did it for my mother, for her pride. I wanted to make her life better.' He looked ahead for a second, a small knot of muscle spasming in his jaw. 'One time, when she was an hour from the front of a line, she collapsed and had to be moved out of the way; she had arthritis in her knees and the pain was so bad. She lost her place and had to start again.'

Chloe gasped. 'But surely someone could have helped – got the bread for her? Or helped her get to the front?'

He gave a dark smile. 'You think like a westerner – you do not understand what it was like then; this was communist Russia, everything was rationed. People were just trying to survive. Kindness was weakness; if you got, then they might not. Who could take the chance?'

'It must have been terrible growing up like that.' She could scarcely imagine it. Her own childhood, though plain by Tom and Poppy's standards – whilst they had skied every winter, she had stayed at her grandparents' croft in Scotland; they had had ponies, she had cats; they had had land, she had a garden – was still blissful in its normality. She had been warm, she had been loved, she had never gone without.

He gave a shrug. 'I know what it is to suffer, to go to bed at night wracked with pain because my body was so starved of food, but I cannot regret it; the hunger in my stomach became a different sort of hunger and made me what I am today. It has driven me on to all this.' He indicated again the gleaming car, his evening suit, the glittering lights of Manhattan itself. They drove past the grand crusted façade of the Waldorf Astoria – not one of his hotels; or at least, *not yet*.

'So when they say I must divest of the very thing that represents my life journey, it will not happen, even though the hotel game is just a vanity show. There is almost no money in it.'

'There really isn't?' She was fascinated. No one had ever given her such honest insight before.

He shook his head. 'If I buy an established hotel in a prime city, I pay a high premium for that; with new management we can usually increase the yield by five per cent, if we really dig, perhaps seven per cent.' He shrugged. 'It is nothing really, no margin. But I still won't sell.'

'I can see why it matters so much to you.'

'Black Pearl is my legacy. It is the empire I will pass on to my future sons – God willing. The merger may have been black-flagged, but there is always another way.' He looked straight at her. 'I like to say Adversity is simply Opportunity turned inside out.'

'I like that,' she smiled. 'I'll try to apply it the next time I feel the universe has got it in for me.'

He nodded back but she saw genuine warmth in his eyes now. It had been a frank and enlightening conversation and she felt they both understood each other better; certainly she felt he was beginning to trust her. In the course of this one short car journey, she had made meaningful contact at last with her most important client and one of the most powerful men on the planet. She had been right in what she'd said to Elle about him the other day – cut him and he wouldn't bleed gold; he was flesh and blood and sweat and tears, a man grown from the bones of a starving young boy.

Their car was pulling up outside the Lincoln Center plaza and the security guards jumped out to open the doors. She smiled as she imagined Elle's face at seeing her now – gliding out of the limo in an exquisite gala gown, a billionaire by her side. They walked up the steps together and into the magnificent, teeming lobby, its split staircase and cascade of galleries awe-inspiring at any time of day but particularly tonight. The safes of Manhattan's grandest dames had been opened and the guests were out-glittering the chandeliers: sapphire cuffs, ruby tiered necklaces, bauble rings, even tiaras . . . Chloe felt bare by comparison; it wasn't the dresses that did the talking here but the jewels. She was wearing her usual diamond stud earrings but they were so small even her newly short hair covered them and automatically, her hand rose to her chest, picking out the exposed sweep of her neck, back and shoulders.

As if reading her mind, Alexander scanned the room and looked back at her. 'Always so *de trop*. When will these people realize even diamonds cannot compete with the beauty of young skin.' Chloe was taken aback by the compliment but it made her hand drop down and she stood a little taller. 'My wife has more jewels than she could possibly wear, but to me, she never looks more beautiful than when her skin is bare.'

Chloe smiled at him. It was a romantic thing to say and she liked that he clearly idolized his wife, that in spite of all his wealth, she still held the power.

Heads had turned at their entrance, but it was a moment before Chloe realized there was no immediate clamour to greet them; none at all, in fact. Although Alexander outgunned almost everyone here financially, that wasn't the same thing as being liked and she guessed that many of those 'enemies' he had referenced in the Rarities bar the other night were here in this building – businessmen and bankers he had edged in deals, grudges worn on the lapels of those expensive dinner suits.

They stood there for a moment, an island in a sea of glittering guests – alone, isolated, publicly ostracized. Chloe felt her cheeks begin to burn. Everyone was looking . . .

She saw Alexander's bodyguards – one watching him, the other the crowds – begin to lead the way up the stairs, parting the crowds like the wake on a speedboat. Alexander held out an arm, a surprisingly chivalrous gesture, and she slipped hers through it. 'Let us go to my box, there is always too much talk at these things. People wanting to score points and compare. But we are here for the children, are we not?'

There was scorn in his voice but not just because of the social snub. His philanthropy was well documented and through the charitable foundation that bore his name, he had established various schools and hospitals back in Russia. The aim of tonight's show was part of the effort to raise ten million dollars for a children's welfare project in Syria. But, she wondered, as they climbed the steps conspicuously, people moving aside, whispering at their backs, how many other people here even knew – much less cared – which charity tonight's performance was supporting? Most of them were more preoccupied with being seen by the right power brokers and society hostesses.

Their path to the box was unimpeded, thanks to the heavies in front, and they took their seats above the masses. The auditorium was filling rapidly, ripples of laughter and delighted greetings rising like balloons through the air. Everything was red and gold, lavish and opulent. Below the stage, the orchestra was already warming up, strings being tightened and waxed, pipes cleared and polished, chairs scraping back, stands being adjusted up and down a couple of inches.

Chloe saw a few people she recognized – Invicta gold clients – and she waved friendly greetings, before seeing the small jolts of recognition and then disapproval on their faces as they clocked her date for the night. She felt another kick of injustice on his behalf. He was a ruthless businessman, of that she had no doubt. But wouldn't anyone be, after a child-hood like his? How many people here would have survived his upbringing? Who else here had lived through the very same poverty and hardship that they were raising funds to overcome tonight?

None of them, and she wondered how he bore it all, the constant scrutiny and judgement that accompanied him wherever he went. He didn't seem to court attention and yet it clung to him. She had seen it herself the first time she had set eyes on him at the bar last week. Beside her, Alexander was still and quiet and yet he was the undisputed nerve centre of the room, the source of all energy. The more he looked away, the more they stared. He was all the more imposing for his refusal to engage with their games, customs and social mores and although she could feel their collective disdain, she sensed their envy too; they still wanted what he had. The still wanted to be him.

The house lights dimmed and a hush fell upon the crowd, everyone settling in for the next hour. The orchestra took up their instruments but the conductor made no move to begin. Instead, the spotlight found a diminutive woman in black lace walking across the stage.

'Ladies and gentlemen, before the performance begins, I want to make a short announcement,' she said. 'As you are well aware, this gala performance is being held in aid of the

Rebuild charity, which is committed to developing schools and playgrounds for children in war-torn areas around the world. Tonight, we are looking to raise ten million dollars for a primary school in Raqqa and your generosity in coming here tonight means we have already made a strong start in reaching that number.'

She looked around the auditorium, her hands clasped together in front of her chest. 'So it gives me *immense* pleasure to be able to share with you all now, that the remaining sum has been donated in full by a benefactor who is a true friend both of Rebuild and the Met—'

A gasp zipped along the rows, an instant hum of whispers rising like cicadas at dusk.

'—And whilst the donor has requested anonymity, it is only right that we should take a moment to give thanks for such an outstanding show of generosity and benevolence to which we are all hugely indebted. If you could all join me in a round of applause—'

She didn't need to ask; the claps quickly became a thunder, people rising to their feet and cheering. A ten-million drop was not insignificant, even in a city with Manhattan's wealth.

Alexander stood too, clapped too. Chloe looked across at him and he gave a small shrug and nod, as though impressed, as though surprised.

But she knew. Cut him and he would bleed. Because somewhere beneath that flint rock exterior was a very large, hard-beating heart.

Chapter Twelve

Squeaks and beeps. That was the soundtrack to the hospital. And blue was the colour palette – blue scrubs, blue chairs. The scent was antiseptic and fear.

Chloe sat where she was, watching the multitudes come in and leave in a never-ending carousel through the revolving doors, tears, panic and pain the universal tickets that gained entry no matter the race, religion, gender or age. She had been sitting here for almost two hours now and seen a little girl wheeled in, a paramedic kneeling on her chest; she had seen a man dragged between two friends, a bullet hole leaving a snail trail of blood behind him; she had seen a screaming little boy with clingfilm wrapped over his reddened torso. She had seen more than she had ever wanted, but she still hadn't seen her friend.

She had another attempt at the crossword. Five down was driving her nuts.

Understand wise words and oscillate.

She chewed on the pen, trying to keep her mind mobile and elastic, trying not to think about how bad it must have looked when Poppy had been wheeled in here eight days earlier. Who was living with the image of having seen her, bloodied and broken, that night?

The lift doors pinged open again and she looked up

reflexively, even as she expected the disappointment of another stranger's face. Only, this time, she recognized the bone structure of the woman walking towards her: a high forehead and broad cheeks, fine-boned hands and elegant ankles. She was a striking woman, the sort who looked as grand in wellies or an apron as in a ballgown. Her hair was cut in a short bob and she looked put-together in pearl earrings, even though her trousers were creased and there was a small tea stain on her shirt – trembling hands, no doubt. Her complexion was pale beneath her make-up and her smile took effort, as though being winched up on strings.

Chloe rose to standing, her breath held.

'You must be Chloe. I'm Rosalind, Poppy's mother.' Her voice was clear, albeit quiet, as though the fact of her words couldn't be relied upon any more.

Chloe wanted to say it was a pleasure to meet her at last, but the words got stuck in her throat. Where was the pleasure in this?

'Poppy has told us so much about you.'

'She's awake?' Chloe's body stiffened with sudden hope.

Rosalind hesitated. 'Not yet.' The words seemed like steel rods being pulled from her bones. 'But the doctors have begun to withdraw the medication that's been keeping her under. She should wake up any time in the next few hours.'

'Oh God.' Chloe felt a rush of panic. She had pulled Poppy's mother away from her bedside, just as the prospect of her daughter regaining consciousness was suddenly a reality. 'And you're down here with me? I mustn't keep you.'

'I should have clarified – she'll wake any time in the next few hours, *to days*,' Rosalind continued kindly. 'It's fine for a few minutes.'

Chloe stared at the flowers she'd brought, not sure what to say suddenly, and she felt a crisis of spirit that Rosalind was the one to have to find conversation, to comfort her.

'I'm sorry you can't see her yet. They're being terribly strict about who can and can't visit,' Rosalind apologized, as though she was personally responsible for hospital policy. 'But hopefully over the next week, if all goes to plan . . .'

'Absolutely. We've all been desperate with worry, at work I mean. Everyone loves Poppy. She brings the entire team together. Every day we keep asking Jack if there's any news.'

'Yes, he's been a great support to us, sorting out our hotel arrangements, transport and the like. He's even been sending over hot meals for us.'

Chloe winced. Hot meals. Why hadn't she thought of it?

Rosalind was watching her, seeing the recrimination, guilt and shame crossing over her face. She gestured to the seats behind them and they both sat. 'It's a great comfort to us to know that Poppy is surrounded by so many people who care about her. It can be hard knowing if that's the case when your child lives so far away.' She smiled. 'Well, I imagine your parents must feel the same, don't they?'

Chloe nodded. 'I've only been here five months. My mum still calls me weekly to check I'm eating enough fruit.'

'You all grow up too quickly, that's the problem,' Rosalind said sadly. 'One moment Pops was eleven and doing dance routines in the drawing room and bounding round the garden with Rollo – our Lab; the next, she was living out here and flying in private jets . . .' She shook her head in bafflement. 'It was all so fast. We were worried it would turn her head, this lifestyle. She was always such a down-to-earth girl and money always corrupts in the end, doesn't it? We've seen it happen to friends of ours. It's hard not to think that if she'd only been doing a normal job, this would never have happened.'

Chloe knew that Poppy's family, though rich in assets and heritage, were cash-strapped compared to the rich elite that now hobnobbed at their table. 'Oh, you can't think like that,' Chloe said, reaching over to touch her arm, seeing the despair wash over her face like a storm surge, 'what ifs' and 'if onlys' taking root. 'It was just a horrible case of being in the wrong place at the wrong time.'

'Except it wasn't though, was it?' Rosalind's blue eyes shone bluer through budding tears.

'. . . What?' Chloe's voice became hollow, tympanic; and she felt an arrow of fear at the way Rosalind was looking at her.

'Didn't Jack tell you? The CCTV shows the driver deliberately swerving.' Rosalind shook her head, as though baffled, mystified, the words not making sense. 'How could anybody *do* that?' she whispered. 'To my little girl?' Her voice split, cleaved in two like a seasoned log, and she dropped her head into her hands, weeping silently as Chloe, mechanically, automatically wrapped her arms around her, Rosalind's words knocking against her ribcage and skull like hammerblows; they didn't make sense. This had been *deliberate*?

'Do they know who? Why?' Chloe asked, when Rosalind began to regain herself. 'Do they have any leads?'

'No, nothing,' she shrugged. 'The registration plates were stolen; and they lost track of the car over Brooklyn bridge. A couple of cameras not working, apparently.'

There was a long pause as Chloe tried to digest what she was being told, a cold clammy chill rippling over her skin. 'But is she safe now? What if . . . what if . . . ?' She couldn't finish the sentence: what if they came back?

'There's a police officer outside the room,' Rosalind said, dabbing her eyes with crooked fingers, and steadily regaining her composure. 'Hence why security is so tight.'

Chloe blinked at her, feeling her own breathing speed up, the panic begin to rush. She had never imagined, not once in this crazy week when she'd thought she'd been so helpful standing in Poppy's shoes, going shopping and to the opera and sparing the blushes of randy, elderly men in hotel corridors, not once had she considered that this was anything other than a tragic accident, a matter of passing the time until her friend came back. 'So they don't have any leads at all?'

'None. No names, no motives,' Rosalind said, her eyes glazed with fear. 'All we know is that someone out there tried to murder my daughter.'

'Open up!' Her fist hurt but she kept on banging. She didn't care whether security was called, or the police. She wouldn't stop until—

The door opened and Jack, dressed in sweat shorts and pulling a t-shirt over his head, looked back at her in bewilderment. 'Jeez, what the hell, Chlo?' he said, looking to see whether there was anyone else with her in the corridor.

'Don't give me that,' she said, angrily pushing past him into his hallway. Her entire apartment would fit into his hall. 'When were you going to tell me what's really going on?'

He blinked, looking confused. 'With what?'

'With what?' she echoed in disbelief. 'With Poppy! I've just come from the hospital.'

'Fuck, is she awake?' He was rigid with attention now. Almost everyone reacted the same way.

'No, Jack!' she almost yelled. 'She's not! I'm talking about the fact that it wasn't a hit and run at all – like you said. That the police are investigating it as attempted murder!'

'Shit.' He sighed, visibly slumping. 'You'd better come in.'

She threw her arms up in the air as if proving that she already had.

'I mean wine. We need wine,' he muttered, ushering her through.

She followed him into an open-plan space, floor-to-ceiling windows on two sides giving a view of the treetops on the west side of Central Park. Overscaled cubed sofas were arranged in a U-shape with faded, shaved-back rugs on the floors and a matt-black concrete-topped kitchen at the far end. His interior designer had clearly decided to let the view do most of the decorating.

He pulled a bottle of rosé from the fridge whilst she, like everyone else, walked over to the windows and looked down – as a relative newcomer to the city, she still hadn't got used to the dramatic drops which were just part of life for real Manhattanites; Jack's apartment wasn't even considered to be that high on the fifty-third floor.

'Here.' He handed her a glass and jerked his head towards the sofas. 'Come. Let's sit soft and talk.'

Reluctantly, still mad with him, she did as she was told, glaring at him from over the top of her wine glass as she sipped and he fidgeted.

'Look, I get why you're cross with me but I swear, I was doing what I thought was best – for everyone. For the team, the company, our clients. If it gets out that this is a police investigation—'

'It's going to, Jack! There's no way something like that can be kept secret.'

'I know. And I wasn't trying to keep it secret as such, I just wanted . . .' He exhaled, looking beaten. 'I just wanted to buy us some time. It's been such a headfuck this week; everyone's really low about the accident. Can you imagine what would happen to morale if they found out it wasn't an accident at all but that someone had targeted her?'

Chloe winced, unable even to hear the words. The very idea of it was disgusting, diabolical. 'They must have some leads.'

'I know, I think they do too but they're not sharing at the moment.' He shrugged. 'They interviewed me last Sunday, routine stuff – wanting to know if I knew of any problems in her personal life, whether she'd made any enemies at work—'

'Enemies at work?' she laughed drily. 'Do they *know* what we do? We make people's lives better, nicer, prettier, funner.' She tutted. 'And yes, I know that's not a real word,' she said before he could. 'But how could she have any enemies from that?'

'That's precisely what I told them,' he sighed, drinking deeply and almost clearing the glass in a single gulp. He looked across at her. 'I don't suppose she ever mentioned anything to you? An irate ex? A client who wanted more? You sat together.'

She frowned, scanning her mind, wishing it could work like a computer program looking for bugs. But it didn't. She was flawed, forgetful and stressed, most of the time more preoccupied with her own problems, Jack like a screensaver in her mind. 'No . . . nothing like that.'

'You're sure?'

'As I can be. I'm certain I'd remember something like that.'

He sighed. 'Yeah. That's what I thought.'

She looked at him, staring at his profile as he looked out over the famous city skyline. 'Jack—'

He glanced back at her; her voice had dropped and softened, all the rage from five minutes earlier now spent. 'Yes?'

'If we don't know *why* this happened to her, how can we be sure that . . . that the person who did this isn't going to go back and try again? They're still out there; they could just be waiting – waiting to see whether she wakes up or not. And if she does . . . ?'

'You mustn't think like that,' he said sharply. 'She's safer now than she's ever been; there's an armed guard outside her door.'

'I know, but—' Her voice was tremulous and her eyes glistened. 'The only consolation in this week has been telling myself that the worst has already happened; that every day that's passed has meant Poppy was getting stronger, better, safer. But what if that's a lie? What if this is only the beginning? No one seems to have any idea why this happened to her or what this person wants from her—' She could hear her voice growing shrill.

'Chloe, do you see now why I didn't tell you? Why I'm keeping it from everyone for as long as I can? All it does is sow panic and fear and confusion.'

She nodded, looking away, trying to keep the tears back. It didn't help to fall apart on him. It didn't help Poppy.

'Right now, we all need to be clear-headed and . . . calm,' he said with a heavy sigh, sounding exhausted himself. 'We have to stay calm.'

She wiped the tears away with the heel of her hand, not caring that she was probably smudging the vestiges of last night's mascara. She stared at her hands. 'Is this why Tom's come over? Does he know too?'

'Yes. Well, no—'

She frowned, confused.

'I mean, yes he knows about the police investigation, but no, I don't think it's the only reason he's come over here.'

She took another gulp of wine, trying to hide her expression behind the glass. 'What then?'

'Personal reasons.'

Her heart went into a gallop.

'P-personal? But what's happened?'

Tom sighed heavily again. 'It's him and Lucy,' he said darkly, rolling his eyes. 'I think it's all off.'

'Off?' she mumbled, repeating him idiotically, but her brain wouldn't work properly. She felt assaulted from every angle. She stared into her glass but she felt him watching her, a silence blooming. 'But didn't they just get engaged?'

'Yeah. But listen, don't repeat any of this, the last thing he needs is his personal life becoming office gossip fodder. I'm only telling you because I know you and him go way back; the two of you ran that office from the start.' There was a pause as he watched her. 'I'm surprised he hasn't told you, actually.'

'Well we . . . we haven't really had a chance to catch up yet,' she mumbled. 'It's all been so crazy.'

'I guess.'

She ran a finger around the rim of her glass. It was no small amount of wonderment to her that Jack had never seemed to guess the relationship between her and his business partner; for the first month here, she'd been waiting for him to instigate 'the chat', where he would confide his suspicions or just come straight out with it. But he never had. Obviously, with Jack being based over here and her and Tom back in London, it had been easier for the two of them to be together without being rumbled; and they had always taken extraordinary precautions to make sure they were never seen together by the team – that they didn't arrive at or leave the office at the same time, that they didn't use nicknames or pet names, that she never sat in his office and no incriminating emails were sent. 'Do you know why?'

'No idea, he's being tight-lipped on the matter. But everyone's pretty stunned – as you know they've been together since uni days; Lucy's practically part of the furniture. It's been "Tom and Lucy" as far back as anyone can remember.'

'Right.' It was certainly all she could remember. Lucy had got to him first – that was what it came down to. It simply didn't matter that he loved Chloe more, that they both knew they were meant to be together, that their love was like a heat that kept her warm even when he wasn't around. Lucy was fragile, a beautiful but frail creature who had never believed she was quite good enough for her highly social, rarely-there parents. She had low self-esteem, made manifest by an eating disorder in her teens and a heavy reliance on smokes and chianti now in her twenties. Tom hovered over her more like an anxious parent than a boyfriend, never quite sure if she was 'okay' to be left for long periods.

Jack shrugged. 'Lucy's in a right state by all accounts.'

'That's awful,' she mumbled.

Jack shrugged. 'Yeah, although . . . I dunno. I sometimes think these long-term relationships can . . . sort of peak, you know? You're together for so long, you can't imagine not being together. But that doesn't necessarily mean you're the best match going forward. Life moves on. People change.'

Chloe shot him a look, checking whether there was a question behind the statement. Besides, what would he know about going the distance? He considered anything that went past the weekend a long-term relationship. 'I guess.'

He regarded her interestedly. 'What about you? Are you with anybody?'

'Me? God, no,' she said briskly, shaking her head just the once and hiding her face behind her glass again. 'What?' she asked, as he continued to stare.

'Nothing.' He shrugged. 'You're just such a dark horse, that's all. You never talk about yourself.'

'Because it's genuinely not interesting.'

'Oh I doubt that,' Jack demurred gallantly. 'I think you underestimate yourself, Chloe Marston.' He glanced out at the illuminated skyline. '. . . I only ask because Tom said he thought you'd been seeing someone in London.'

'Did he?' She tried not to look overly engaged in the conversation, even though it had made her heart skip two beats. 'I wonder why he thought that.'

'So, there wasn't some big break-up then? That wasn't the reason for finally relenting and coming over here with so little notice?'

Exactly so. 'Nothing so dramatic, I'm afraid.'

'Huh,' he nodded, when she made no move to elaborate further. A silence stretched, cat-like, between them. 'Well, anyway, Tom's in bits, it's all a right mess,' he said finally as they both looked out onto the skyline. 'I reckon he's come here to clear his head; put some space between them and get some perspective on the Lucy thing, you know?'

'Yes.' But she wondered where the truth really lay: did he want more space from Lucy? Or less from *her*? 'So how long's he going to be out here for?'

'A week, maybe two? A lot will depend on what happens with Poppy, of course.'

'Where's he staying?' She asked the question as lightly as she could.

Jack's eyes darted back to her. 'The Howard, I think.' A quizzical frown puckered his brow. 'Why?'

'Just wondering. I was at the WestHouse the other day and made a new contact with the concierge there; I like what they've done with the refit and they're keen to get on our lists, so they've offered me a good rate. I just thought if he wanted to test-drive somewhere new for us . . .' She gave a lackadaisical shrug for good measure.

'That's worth knowing. I'll let him know; see if he can swing by sometime next week.'

They lapsed into a small silence, their eyes on the city still at full tilt outside the windows; the first lights were already being switched on, punctuating the tower blocks like a Tetris screen.

'Well, listen, I should get on and leave you to your Sunday – or what's left of it,' she said, leaning forward and replacing her empty glass on the coffee table. 'And . . . I'm sorry about earlier – I shouldn't have just turned up here unannounced and almost knocked your door down. I just—'

'It's okay, Chloe, I totally get it. It was a big shock to me too.'

She stood, her gaze unseeing upon the city spread out below them. It was almost more than she could imagine, bear – to think that that driver was out there, somewhere in those streets, getting away with it . . .

'But listen, Chlo, I think it would still be good to keep news of the investigation quiet until there's a compelling reason *not* to. We don't want rumours starting or the clients getting spooked. The fewer people who know at the moment, the better.'

'And who is that then?'

'You, me and Tom.'

She nodded, wondering whether she could keep it from Xan; he had an innate ability to tell when she was being evasive about something. 'Okay, sure.'

She walked slowly towards the door.

'Things will get better from now on, you'll see. It's been a week since the accident and Poppy's survived both that and the surgery. Every day that passes she's getting stronger. We'll be back to normal in no time.'

She nodded but it didn't ring true. They were in the business of providing the spectacular, the extraordinary, the rare; they moved through a world of bespoke experiences in which there were no limits. Frankly, she wasn't sure any one of them would know what 'normal' was if it came up and punched them in the face.

Chapter Thirteen

'Don't do it, Chlo,' Kate said in her most warning tone. 'I mean it. You've only just started getting your life back together again. Do not let him in.'

'I'm not, but—'

'No buts!' Kate said, jabbing a finger at the screen, eyes wide and serious.

The two sisters stared at one another from different sides of the ocean.

'But what if what Jack said is true about him and Lucy—?' The words raced together defiantly, too fast to be stopped, the question needing an answer; *she* needed an answer.

'Then why's it taken him five months to dump her, huh? Why didn't he do it the moment he lost you?'

Chloe's mouth opened but no words came out; they never did. She had never won an argument against her sister. She wanted to say something about missing the cow but she couldn't organize the words into a coherent order. Espresso martinis would do that to a girl.

'Because he's a bloody idiot, that's why.' The finger jabbed again. 'And besides, you don't know he's the one who dumped her, do you? For all we know, she dumped him! And now he's turned his attention back to you, thinking you're an easy target, a sure thing.'

Chloe's face crumpled at the brutality of her sister's honesty.

'Oh!' Kate's face came right up close to the screen. 'Oh, babe, I'm sorry, I didn't mean it like that, please don't cry.'

'No, no you're right, I know you are,' she sniffed, pressing the heels of her hands to her eyes, not wanting to smudge her mascara. She was still drunk, still wearing the fancy Zimmermann dress she'd put on after leaving Jack's apartment to go to the bar with Elle. She had wanted to escape, to pretend everything was fine and dandy, even if only for a few hours – her conversations with him and Poppy's mother that afternoon had left her reeling and in need of a vent. Not to mention she hadn't dared stay at the apartment in case Tom came over again. She didn't trust herself, especially not now she knew things had changed. Her head was all over the place; the world felt like it had been set on its side and she couldn't think straight any more. She was trying to do the right thing, she wanted to do it . . . but then the crashing disappointment she'd felt at coming home to find him *not* on her doorstep only compounded her miserable confusion.

She knew she ought to sleep; it was two in the morning, she couldn't start her new week on four hours' sleep; she had to be on top form in case Pelham or Rosaria or Alexander or any of the others rang in. And yet still she'd spent the several hours since getting in, wandering around the flat with a vodka in hand like some sort of tragic *Blue Jasmine* figure. It always went like this – her trying to resist, Tom wearing her down even in his absence.

Kate, on the other hand, was not drunk and emotional from a night on the tiles. She was in her dressing gown, puffy-eyed from another night of subsistence-level sleep and already with a Stickle Brick caught in her hair. It was seven in the morning there, but she'd already been up for an hour and a half with Orlando and she'd known even just by the ring tone that her little sister was in crisis.

'You're right. I have to forget him. Move on,' Chloe said in a wobbly, slurred voice. 'Whatever's going on with him and Lucy, it's none of my business.'

'Exactly. You're too good for him, babe. Don't waste your time on some idiot who doesn't know how lucky he was to have you. You deserve more.'

'I do. I'm a strong, independent woman,' she repeated like a mantra, but without any accompanying conviction. 'I've built a new life for myself—'

'Well, *sort* of.' Kate wrinkled her nose.

'Huh? I moved to a new country,' she said indignantly. 'How is that not a new life?'

'You're still working at his company.'

Chloe glowered at her. 'Th-that is not a helpful osverbation.'

'I'm just saying it makes it hard to keep the guy out of your life, that's all. If you want to move on, you also need to move job.'

'I *like* my job,' she cried. 'Why should *I* be the one to go? He's the liar! He's the cheat! Isn't it enough that I left my homeland, the country of my birth? My *family*?' she said dramatically. 'He can go! It's the very least he can do!'

'Uh – it's his company? Look, I totally agree in principle but this is a hard one to fight against,' Kate pointed out. 'Just go to one of your competitors instead; do the same job somewhere else and you'll get to piss him off too,' she said gleefully. 'You won't be free of him till you do, you know that.'

Chloe did know that – and it was precisely why she hadn't done it, somehow unable to make the final cut that would set them both adrift from the other. It was one thing to leave the country, to swap a continent to escape him, it was quite another to lose touch completely. She couldn't imagine a life where he wasn't in it, even if it was just in the background or through a screen, a name at the end of a memo. Her anger and humiliation had sustained her for these past few months, driving her to rebuild with a sunny smile and complete immersion in other people's lives; sorting out their problems had been the salvation she'd needed, as it meant she didn't have to wallow in her own. But now he was here, and Lucy was off the scene and it was getting harder to keep the anger going *all* the time.

'I can deal with him at work,' she mumbled.

'Hmm, I hope so.' Kate made her point with a hitched eyebrow and dubious stare. 'Just don't forget how he made you feel, okay? Because, trust me, I remember exactly how you sounded when you rang from the back of that cab. You were in *pieces*. You can't go back to that, Sis. Don't let him do that to you again.'

She nodded. Firmly. Decisively. 'I won't.'

In the background, Orlando wandered through with his nappy in his hand, prompting a small shriek from her sister and they said their goodbyes quickly as they always did, blowing kisses across the ocean. Chloe sat back, slumped on her bed, clutching Marmalade – her tatty childhood bear who had followed her from home to university to London, and now here – and staring at the single forlorn long-stemmed freesia Tom had managed to push through the letterbox after she'd left for the opera last night. It was a little bit mangled, some might say crushed, from where someone had trodden on it. But if she closed her eyes, she could still feel her arm glow from his touch. And that was precisely the problem – because no matter what her big sister said, she still remembered exactly how he made her feel.

'Oh my God, did the cat die?' Xan asked, a look of horror on his features as she crossed the floor to the desk.

'What cat?'

'Your grandma then?'

'Oh haha.' Chloe stuck her tongue out at him and let her bag drop to the floor with a thunk. She had thought the cream vintage Valentino skirt-suit – a bargain at the Saturday flea market – had done a pretty good job of detracting from her exhausted pallor. 'You are glowing with radiance too, darling.' She sipped harder from her coffee and sank down into the spinny chair. Automatically she began swaying herself from side to side, soothed by the comforting motion and wishing she could close her eyes and go back to sleep.

'What did you *do* that's left you so broken?' Xan persevered, his chin cupped in his hands, watching her. He gave a stage-worthy gasp. 'Did you hook up with someone? Tell me *everything*.'

She opened her mouth, ready to slap him down – since when did she ever hook up? – when she saw a familiar gait in her peripheral vision. Tom was several metres away, walking from his temporary office in the meeting room, behind her desk, towards the kitchen. She knew he was getting a tea – strong, no sugar, *dash* of milk – he always had a cup of tea at ten, but his mere presence was like a scent, something tangible she could grab.

A small smile curved her mouth upwards. She may not

have slept a wink, but that didn't mean she couldn't pretend it was down to more interesting reasons than pacing all 335 square feet of her apartment most of the night.

'No,' she said in a provocative voice.

'You did hook up!' Xan gasped. 'I can tell.'

'I don't know what you're talking about,' she said primly, refusing to make eye contact and instead sitting far too upright, Miss Moneypenny-style and booting up the computer. Predictably, Xan went into a spin.

'Was he hot?'

'No comment.'

She registered that Tom had stopped walking and was loitering by the desks nearby, picking up a magazine and pretending to flick through it.

'Then give me a name at least. Something to work with. Come *on*. This is news.'

Instead, she raised her eyes to Xan's and pressed a silencing finger to her lips, a discreet tip of her head towards Tom making him glance towards their boss. 'Not now,' she mouthed.

Xan sat back, scandalized and delighted, quietened for the moment at least.

'Well *I* went to Cape Cod,' he said, instead picking up the conversational slack and speaking in an entirely unconvincing way. 'Caleb's been on for weeks about going so we finally went over, but you know, it *so* wasn't all that.' He rolled his eyes but Chloe wasn't paying attention. Tom, hearing the conversation had switched topic from her social life to Xan's, had tossed down the magazine and resumed his stroll to the kitchen. Chloe couldn't help but notice several of the younger girls followed in his wake a few moments later, a small group congregating around the kettle like horses around water; there was certainly as much head tossing and hair flipping going on. Did they know his engagement was broken? He was an attractive man and highly eligible; she knew he wouldn't be single for long, not once word got round.

He only caught her staring the once, his eyes easily catching hers across the room as he stood almost a head taller than his acolytes. Neither one of them smiled, wretchedness in both their gazes, and she made a point of being on the phone when he passed back several minutes later.

She wanted to cry.

She heard the door to his glass office close and saw Xan watching him take his seat again.

'Right, the coast is clear,' he said, getting up and walking over to her side of the desk and plonking himself down in what had once been her chair beside Poppy's. 'I want to know everything. And don't leave out the juicy bits.'

It had been precisely the morning she didn't need – thanks to the Carlyle debacle last week, Pelham Hungerford's engagement hopes were now hanging by a thread and he felt it required a grand statement of love to keep things together. They were now in Vienna, so after twenty minutes of intense wall-staring, Chloe had suggested a private cruise on the Danube that evening, with petals being scattered from the bridges as they passed beneath. Pelham had loved it and she had just sourced the boat and was finalizing hiring a private chef to put together a menu for them, when Rosaria Bertolloti had called in. She was in Argentina but the hotel had run out of San Pellegrino water; they had offered Perrier but her dogs only drank San Pellegrino – what was more it had to be poured from the glass bottles, thank you very much, not plastic ones. 'They can tell,' she'd said, before hanging up and leaving Chloe to the task of sourcing glass-bottled San Pellegrino stockists in a two-mile radius of the hotel. Then Proudlock had remembered his winter tyres hadn't been changed off his Maserati and he was going to be back in the country next week – could she see to it? So she had.

And now she was here, in a conference room seventy-two floors up and waiting to see the CEO of the property development company that had won the contract for a development of fifteen super-luxury chalets, a five-star hotel and two twelve-apartment buildings in Andermatt, Switzerland. A rare decision by the Swiss Federal Council had meant the properties could be purchased by non-Swiss nationals and she was keen to get them under the noses of Invicta's clients.

Being here was also a valuable chance to get out of the office – all morning, as she had hit the phones, working her contacts and tapping her resources, she had caught Tom's eyes on her in the reflection of the small monitor mirror. He couldn't see her watching him watching her, but that almost made it worse; she wasn't sure how much more she could take. It felt like the oxygen was being slowly sucked from the room, leaving her light-headed and breathless.

The door opened and a red-haired woman in a navy pant suit came in, a slim MacBook Air under one arm. 'Chloe, thanks for coming.'

'The pleasure's all mine, Helen,' Chloe said, rising to shake hands with her. 'I've been dying to see what you've got for us. It sounds incredibly exciting.'

'I'll be honest, *we're* incredibly excited about it,' Helen beamed, sitting down opposite her in one of the turquoise-velvet chairs. 'The location is just spectacular and of course, it's so rare to get an opportunity to make something like this available to the international market. Switzerland is prime but such a closed shop.'

'Exactly why I thought our clients would want to know about it.'

'You did well to get in first. We're anticipating strong demand,' Helen said. 'I've had Quintessentially on the phone twice daily for the past fortnight. They're not happy we won't take a meeting till we've seen you.'

'Well, I guess you snooze, you lose,' Chloe smiled; she had known this was a good fit for their clients and she'd been first off the blocks to negotiate the exclusive on it. It was her job to make sure that Invicta's members would be the first to get eyes on the development, first refusal would be theirs; she was damned good at her job and she still bristled at Kate's suggestion that she should have to give it up to escape her ex. 'Let's see what you've got.'

Helen opened up the MacBook and picked up a small remote on the table. 'Tell me, how are things at the office?' she asked, as a screen slid down from the ceiling and an overhead projector whirred into life. 'I heard about your colleague's accident. I'm sorry.'

Chloe nodded, hating being reminded of it, having to talk about it in polite muted terms when she wanted to scream and tell everyone that it was no accident. 'Thank you. It's been a tough time but she's hanging in there. All indications are good.'

'I'm so glad to hear that.'

An image of a pristine alpine landscape – jagged mountains tearing into the sky – came up on the screen, just as there was a knock at the door. They both looked up.

'A Mr Elliott from Invicta to see you?' an assistant said, peering in. 'He apologizes for being late.'

Helen frowned. '. . . Okay. I thought it was just going to be the two of us.' She glanced across at Chloe who could only shrug in reply – now she really couldn't hide her shock. 'But that's fine. Show him in, please.' The assistant disappeared and Helen looked at Chloe again.

'I'm sorry, I didn't realize Tom was coming,' Chloe said, embarrassed. Tom's games were going to make them look incompetent and unprofessional. It was one thing doorstepping her outside her apartment but did he really think he could stalk her meetings too? 'He's our co-founder, over from London for a while and wanting to sit in on some of our projects here.'

'Hey, that's great from our point of view,' Helen said. 'Backing from the top can only be a good thing.'

The door opened again and Tom came through, looking lean and polished in a navy suit and pale-pink shirt with no tie. He always looked as though he'd just come from a run and shower, his skin bright, foppish hair gleaming. Chloe looked down, hating the way her heart accelerated at the sight of him – instinct, habit – as his eyes instantly sought hers.

'Forgive the intrusion, I hope I'm not too late?' he asked, shaking Helen by the hand.

'Not at all. We're delighted you can join us.'

'Well I was keen to make it; I know for a fact we've got names on the London books that are going to be hugely interested in this project of yours,' he grinned, rubbing his hands together. 'Hey, Chlo.'

'Hi, Tom.' She gave her best benign smile.

'Please, take a seat,' Helen said. 'You haven't missed anything. We were just about to get started. Can I get you anything – tea, coffee, water?'

'Not at all,' he said, taking the chair beside Chloe and sitting down in it with a contented sigh. 'Everything I need is right here.'

'. . . We'll be in touch,' Tom said, shaking Helen's hand vigorously as the lift doors slid open and he followed Chloe in.

Chloe watched as they closed again, silence filling the small space. There were two other people in there: a white-haired man in a pinstripe and a ponytailed young woman in a Banana Republic dress – Chloe knew that because her label was poking up at the neck and it was taking all of her self-control not to tuck it in for her.

No one spoke, their eyes on the blue LED numbers that counted down at alarming speed. Seventy-one, seventy, sixty-nine . . .

'Well that was certainly very interesting,' Tom murmured. 'They've done a great job with the spa. And I loved the colour palette. What did you think?'

'I agree,' she said back, equally quietly.

'It's an interesting fusion of styles. Sort of Asian luxe, but with a rustic vibe.'

'Yeah.'

The man in the pinstripe coughed a little, shifting his weight.

'And the nightclub looks good. Not seedy. It looks like they've really thought about the lighting.'

'Crucial.'

She felt his stare get heavier. 'I suppose if I was looking for niggles, I'd say it's a shame the height in the garages isn't a little better – a Range Rover might be pushing it; we should get measurements to be sure. And the nearest helipad's half an hour away, which is tedious. It might be worth seeing if that point is moot,' he mused.

'Sure.'

'There's still time at this stage.'

'Absolutely.'

The doors opened again and the man walked out. Level fifty-six.

Fifty-five, fifty-four, fifty-three . . .

'I liked the bar area though, didn't you?'

'Mm hmm.'

The girl in front shuffled and turned slightly, clearly trying to glimpse the two people involved in this one-sided conversation. Tom smiled at her, that easy, happy-go-lucky grin that made everyone like him and want to be his friend. The girl smiled back – no doubt loving him even more on account of his accent – before tightening her ponytail as she reluctantly faced the doors again. Chloe stared at the Banana Republic label again.

'And the lobby for the hotel was spectacular. My God, that chandelier, did you clock it?'

'Hard not to.'

'That's really got the wow factor. Yes.' He inhaled heavily. 'There's no doubt our clients will love it. *Love* it. I can already think of a few people who'd want a first gander.'

'Great.'

Her eyes stayed on the display. Twelve, eleven, ten . . . Come on, she willed it. Don't let this elevator stop and that girl get out before they got to the ground floor. She couldn't be alone in here with him. She just couldn't.

Five, four, three . . . Yes, yes.

To her dismay, the doors opened and the girl – casting another rueful smile at Tom – walked out. Chloe felt her jaw tighten, her limbs loosen as she stared out into the corridor, debating whether to get out here too. The doors started to close and she could feel – actually feel – Tom's anticipation that he'd got her where he wanted at last: trapped, cornered, forced to look, to listen. He had moved position already, turning to face her—

A man leapt in, appearing suddenly in the diminishing rectangle of light between the sliding doors, one moment not there, the next, absolutely filling it. 'Thank God,' he panted, throwing them a wry look before straightening his jacket and pressing the button for the lobby.

Thank God indeed.

Giving a stiff nod, no trace of his smile now, Tom stepped back again and Chloe closed her eyes, never more grateful for the company of a stranger.

They reached the ground level just seconds later and Chloe walked out first, taking long-legged strides, her eyes dead-ahead on the rushing, swarming street as she crossed the marble lobby. Tom was a half-stride behind, staring at her in what she knew would be disbelief that she could keep this up, be so very stubborn.

'Chlo – I thought it was the right thing to do.'

The sentence had no context, it should have made no sense, but she knew from his tone of voice what he was telling her. It was the only conversation between them, the wall they had to scale.

She didn't stop walking.

'It was Burns Night and all the old crowd was there . . .'

Her heart rate sped up at his justifications, excuses. She didn't want to think about it, knowing the details wouldn't make it better. If she could just get to a cab . . .

'They're all marrying off, having kids. People were beginning to ask questions, wonder why me and Lucy weren't following suit—'

She pushed the glass door with a violent, angry shove, not bothering to hold it open for him but he was right with her, the toes of his shoes flashing in her peripheral vision with long-legged strides as she kept her head down.

'You know what it's been like with her; you know I've tried telling her. But one minute she's fine, the next she's crying and telling me no one's ever loved her, that she feels so afraid and anxious—'

Chloe closed her eyes, trying to push him from her thoughts. Blah, blah, blah, the same old story. He'd been giving her this patter for the last four years and she knew only too well about Lucy's problems – her own life had been put on hold and given over to that poor woman's concerns as she tried somehow to do the right thing by her, to make sure she was okay before Chloe could truly be with the man she loved. She had put her own needs second for all that time, racked as she was by the guilt that Lucy had the first claim on him and that had to count for something. But no more. At some point, she needed to come into play too and although his engagement precluded her from his and Lucy's equation once and for all, that was still the resolution she had finally made for herself when she'd decided to move here and start again.

Her arms swung harder, her chin defiantly up in the air.

'You know what she's like—'

This wasn't helping; did he actually think it was?

'—I just couldn't think, Chlo, I couldn't think of what to do to make things right – I wanted you but I couldn't bear to hurt her either.'

'Well, clearly proposing was the perfect solution to your

dilemma,' she said sarcastically, still not slowing down. 'Excellent. Great plan. Well done, Tom.'

'Chloe, wait.'

It was the sudden quietness of his voice that stopped her. There was no great exclamation of anguish, no high passion or abundant flowers this time, just a man with his mistake. He had stopped walking and was looking after her with a look of such brokenness, such longing, she felt her spirit almost leap out of her body and into his arms.

'I got it all wrong, I know that. But you have to believe me when I say that in the moment of asking her, I honestly thought it was the right thing to do. The weight of everything in my life was coming down on that side, we'd been together so long, everyone expected it: our families, our friends – I thought that had to be the path for me, even if I didn't feel it.' He shrugged. 'I swear I was going to tell you myself; I tried, several times, but somehow every time I went to do it, the words were so diabolical . . .' He frowned. 'To tell *you* I was marrying someone else? It made no sense to me. I felt desperate, I couldn't see any way out – protect her but keep you. And then, the whole thing became like a runaway train. I'd no sooner asked the question than it all took on a life of its own, like it was nothing to do with me any more and I was just a bit part in the whole charade.'

'No, *I* was the bit part, Tom!' she cried in disbelief, hardly able to believe what she was hearing – he thought he was the victim in all of this? 'Me! I'm a fucking footnote, nothing more. You kept telling me to keep the faith, that we would be together. For four years I waited for you to do the right thing – by all of us! But you didn't, you were too much of a coward. And you know what? I don't think you ever had any intention of leaving her for me. You were just using me.'

'No, not using you! Never that!' he said, desperation in his eyes. 'Christ, I wish things had been different. I wish to God I had met you first, or at the very least, broken up with her back then, right when I first met you. But you walked into the office a fortnight after her father signed the cheque and I was already trapped. He wasn't investing in Invicta because he believed in *me*, he was investing in the business that he believed was going to bankroll his daughter's future life. He signed up knowing I was going to be his son-in-law. That was the unspoken deal. He knew it, I knew it – and you did too. I was straight with you!'

'Yeah, you were – up until the part where you went to Asprey and bought her a ring.'

'I was a fucking mess, Chlo!' He gripped his hands in his hair, seemingly pained by the memory. 'Every time I tried to break it off, she'd start crying, putting all this emotional pressure on me and, you're right, I was a coward – I'd bottle it. We'd been together so long by then and she made me feel like I was *abandoning* her.' He shook his head, wild-eyed. 'She wouldn't let go even though things were different between us and the relationship was clearly failing. I had completely retreated from her, emotionally, physically . . . I didn't want to be with her, I was becoming . . . cruel. I hated what I saw as her weakness.' He looked baffled and ashamed. 'I thought at the very least she would tire of my indifference and dump me. I kept hoping and praying for it anyway, but she never did.' His mouth stretched with bitterness. 'She wanted that fucking wedding and she wasn't going to throw in the towel on the small account of me not loving her.'

Chloe blinked, feeling herself tremble at his words, her arms wrapped tightly around her body as though shielding herself from a polar wind.

'I couldn't see a way out.' He took two steps towards her. 'It was only when she was choosing the ring that I realized just how completely she knew this was going to go down – which ring, which shoes, which flowers, the names of our future kids . . . Our lives were totally mapped out. That was the moment when I finally realized I couldn't let it go on any longer, even if it did destroy her.' He ran his hands through his hair, his face crumpled with disbelief. 'I didn't care any more. I was going to finish it, I *swear* I was. I went round to your flat that weekend to come clean and tell you what had happened. I just wanted a fresh start and I knew I had to be honest with you about what I'd done and how close I'd come to fucking it all up. But when you didn't answer and then I heard from Jack that you were *here* . . . ?' He raked his hands through his hair, holding it tight as he relived the moment. 'I swear to God it almost killed me on the spot. I was frantic. Desperate. I had no idea how to reach you or contact you. You were blocking my calls, my texts. I couldn't bear that you'd found out and I couldn't even try to explain.'

She swallowed, remembering how efficiently she had cut the ties of communication between them, ghosting him.

'And . . . as the weeks went on and it was clear you didn't want to know, I tried telling myself perhaps you'd done the right thing; that it would be easier for us both to move on if you were here and so I tried going with that. Bloody hell I tried! I was determined to forget you, Chlo. And I thought I was doing okay. I had got to a point where I could hear your name and not have to cut the meeting short. You were gradually becoming just . . . a mirage, an idea of someone.' He shook his head, his shoulder slumping an inch. 'Or at least I thought you were, until I saw you in that meeting again the day after Poppy's accident. You had your new haircut, you looked so . . . strong, so beautiful – and that was when I knew that I'd never get over you, that I had already fucked everything up and my life would never be right again without you in it.'

He took another step closer again, within touching distance now.

'I didn't sleep for the two nights after that; then on the third day, I finally did it – I told Lucy that I couldn't marry her, that I loved someone else and I got the first flight I could to here – where I've spent almost every waking moment just trying to get in the same sodding airspace as you.' He gave a small groan.

She cracked a half-smile, worried that the movement might make her crumble completely. She had no defences left. He had hurt her, yes; devastated her, in fact. But he had suffered too. Perhaps more so, in many ways.

Kate wouldn't get it, nor would Elle. Nor would his friends, or family. Jack. It was going to be complicated, she already knew that.

He closed the gap between them, both oblivious to the seething traffic, honking horns and jumping lights, the short-tempered pedestrians muttering under their breath to swerve them as they raced to meetings and appointments in the blistering July heat. 'Tell me there's still some hope.'

She blinked, barely able to hear the words over the rushing of blood in her ears. But then, she'd always liked watching that mouth. Kissing it . . .

'Maybe a little,' she murmured, refusing to make it too easy for him.

'Yeah?' His face brightened, his muscles visibly softening. 'Even though . . .' His voice trailed off.

'Even though . . . ?' she prompted.

'Well, I overheard about your date at the weekend,' he said quietly, holding her hands in his and looking down at her, his blue eyes more puppydog than she'd ever seen before. 'I mean, I wasn't eavesdropping or anything like that but I wondered if . . . if it was that same guy picking you up in the limo . . . I mean, I realize I don't have any right to even ask—'

She felt a wave of relief wash over her at the sight of his evident anguish, glad her role-play with Xan had been such effective torture. She smiled. 'I may have come all the way to New York to escape you, Tom Elliott, but you cast a long shadow.'

'Thank God for that,' he muttered, pulling her in towards him suddenly and kissing her as though they were standing on a sandbar in the Indian Ocean and not on the corner of East 40th and Park.

'Never leave me again, Chloe,' he whispered.

'I won't.'

'Do you promise?'

'I promise.'

Chapter Fourteen

Provence

The water splashed noisily into the bath, amplified by the rose-quartz walls; the scent of lotus oil pungent even with the tall open windows. She looked down upon the gardens manicured to perfection, narrow cypresses planted at exact five-metre intervals all the way around the estate, lavender beds snaking in geometric shapes, orange and lemon trees dotted with colourful fruits. It took a team of eight full-time groundsmen to keep it looking that way; they were always there whenever she went to the windows, walking back and forth, pushing their wheelbarrows or carrying their spades or forks over their shoulders like civilian soldiers; sometimes, when it was bad, she felt like they were there to keep her in. Spying on her; reporting back.

It was a ridiculous notion of course. They were just gardeners. But did they ever wonder about her, always standing at the windows, staring out at them, hiding away? She rarely received visitors any more. Did they comment among themselves about the gravel drive that scarcely ever required raking, so few cars travelled across it? Or had that gone unnoticed too? She was hidden in her palace, forgotten.

The water sounded high in the bath and she turned back to close the taps, catching sight of her reflection in the mirror. The sunny garden backlit her and she saw her slim silhouette outlined through her cotton nightgown, her long dark hair swept across one shoulder. For a moment, she was startled by her own loveliness. It wasn't a vain thing to admit to; purely objectively, she could see for herself the pleasing symmetricality of her features, the lissom length of her limbs, the Bambi-like appeal of her large brown eyes in her face. But she took no joy in it; it was the reason she was here, like this.

Letting the gown slip off her shoulders and twisting her hair into a knot, she climbed into the bath, closing her eyes as the warm oily water closed around her. She sank down to her earlobes, feeling how the muscles relaxed; they were always as hard as stones these days, as though braced . . . Her masseuse – on the days she was allowed to come – couldn't understand it.

She took a deep breath, knowing it couldn't be put off any longer. With superhuman effort, she turned her head to the side and forced herself to look at the tiny stick she had left on the side of the bath. In the two minutes that had elapsed, two dark lines had come to show in the window.

She looked away again, feeling the cold swirl in her bowel that she always felt when she was afraid. Feeling dizzy, she bent one leg for balance, planting the foot on the bath floor, her knee poking through the water. Her fingers traced the bloody frill on her thigh, the bruise fading fast now; once it got to the yellowing stage, it was usually pretty quick. In fact, she could barely make out that it had been a footprint a week ago.

She looked at the stick again – the two lines still there.

That wasn't something that would disappear so easily. It wasn't something she would be able to hide.

Much less protect.

New York

Xan looked up in surprise as she reached for her bag. 'Out again?'

'Is that a problem?' she asked archly, checking her reflection in the small mirror and glancing at Tom too whilst she was at it. He was on the phone but there was a looseness in his bones that hadn't been there this morning and she wondered whether there was in hers too, whether anyone else could see it? She felt physically different in her body since their kiss earlier. Awake. Alive again.

She reached for the tinted lip gloss in the drawer. It was Poppy's but the two of them had always shared it.

'You only got back an hour ago and we've got that first aid refresher course at five. I was assuming we would be partners. You're the only one I'd let give me mouth-to-mouth.' His eyes slid over to Tom's office. 'Well, one of two.'

Chloe giggled, combing her fingers through her hair lightly, lifting it at the roots. 'I wish I could stay; clearly nothing would be lovelier than an hour of CPR with you, but needs must, I'm afraid. I'm meeting Helen Fletcher to sign the paperwork on the Andermatt deal. She's been getting the legals to give a final sign-off; Quintessentially have been hot and heavy on their case so I want this thing put to bed.'

'Can't I come with you?' he sighed, sinking his head into a hand, his elbows spread on the desk. 'I've spent most of my afternoon bowing and scraping trying to get access to the Royal Collection at Buck House.'

'The palace?' she frowned. 'But why?'

'Got a client heading over to London next week and he's made it his life ambition to see each and every one of Vermeer's remaining thirty-six paintings.'

'Niche.'

'Yeah – and two of them belong to your beloved monarch.'

'Ah.' She was struggling to open the tin lid on the lipgloss pot.

He looked at her hopefully. 'I don't suppose you've got any ins with the royal household?'

She thought for a moment, dabbing two fingertips of gloss onto her lips. 'Actually, I do know the President of the Royal Academy; he'll have connections with the Royal Collection. Leave it with me, I'll put a call in,' she said. She checked her hair and smoothed her brows with a wetted finger. She considered the pull-bow on her blouse. Did it look a bit uptight? She gave it a tug and the black chiffon ends flopped prettily against her cream jacket. Much better. She didn't look quite so much like she was going into a planning meeting now. Her gaze flicked back towards Tom again, in the mirror. His eyes were on her and she felt herself swell with happiness. She straightened up. 'Well, enjoy the course.'

'Where are you going for this meeting anyway?' Xan asked suspiciously, taking in her 'undone' look and flushed cheeks, spinning on his chair as she began to walk round the desks.

'The Howard.'

His eyes widened. 'Oh! So when you say "sign the paperwork", what you actually mean is "drink cocktails in the Blond bar".'

'Do I?' she giggled.

'Yeah. That would explain this new . . . *vibe* you're working.'

'Vibe? Me?' she mocked, barely able to meet his gaze.

'Hmm.' He looked across to Tom's office again and Chloe wondered whether Xan had caught him staring. But she could hardly turn around to check. 'Isn't the Howard where Tom's staying?' he asked in a sly voice. He had a super-sleuth's nose for conspiracy and deception.

'Is it?' she asked innocently, taking the opportunity to turn and look over for him. 'Well, he's not there now,' she shrugged, indicating that he was on the phone in his office. 'Toodlepip, chum.'

'Toodle*what who*?' he cried in sudden excitement, forgetting all about Tom and running after her as she sashayed over to the lifts. 'Is that your cockney slang thing again?'

There were distinct disadvantages to trying to conduct a secret liaison when you were on 'how's your wife?' terms with the concierges of every luxury hotel in the city, Chloe mused, sitting in the Blond bar at the 11 Howard and pretending to Instagram. She had been here for an hour already, her meeting with Helen having been wound up in twenty minutes, the time it took them to sign, sip a watermelon mojito and shoot the breeze on the Basquiat retrospective happening that night – for which Chloe had been only too happy to put her name on the door.

Part of her wished she could have gone home to get changed into something more alluring than this cream suit, but then again, a tryst with her ex hadn't exactly been on the cards when she'd been getting dressed that morning and there wasn't time to pop back to the apartment now; Tom had a dinner booked in with Jack and one of their investors at nine, not to mention she needed to show her face at the Basquiat, so their time together was already bookended as it was.

She sat back against the velvet sofa, the second watermelon mojito chilling her palm as she finally had the time to wallow in the afternoon's events; it had been like a dream, all those things he'd said . . . She had made them up for him a million times during the last five months but she'd never thought she'd ever hear him say them, that they could actually be true.

She checked the time on her phone again – six twenty-five – and sighed. Time was taunting her in its lead boots; he'd said he'd be back here by seven, that would give them two hours if he agreed to be fashionably late for his dinner date. She thought he could probably be persuaded . . .

She finished her drink and stared at the glass, debating a third. Butterflies had taken wing in her stomach and her skin felt tingly, her eyes alight. She was restless, getting ahead of herself. Another drink might take the edge off, slow her down a bit . . . ?

She walked up to the bar. 'Another mojito, please,' she said, setting down the empty glass.

'Sure,' the bartender said, immediately setting to the task.

She leant against the counter and glanced around the space; it was already buzzing, filling up quickly, although not yet peak time, groups of friends were huddling on the teal banquettes, hesitant dates making conversation in the armchairs. The walls were golden-ridged like tide-rippled sand; an uplit wheat-coloured curtain hung from ceiling to floor; heavily foxed mirrors, not so much reflecting the light as absorbing it, creating a moody, mercurial vibe. Everything felt urban, sophisticated, seductive . . . Like her.

'One watermelon mojito,' the bartender said a few minutes later, setting it on a mat. She turned, making to head back to her original spot but it had been taken by another group. Oh.

Her hand reached instead for the bar stool beside her. She could always sit here and wait.

But then an idea came to her.

'Hey, I'll take this up to my room, that's okay, isn't it?' she asked the bartender.

'Sure. Which room are you in? I'll have it added to your account.'

'One forty-six. Elliott.'

'Done,' he nodded.

She took the drink with a smile, a swing in her hip and a glint in her eye as she walked through the bar. She could have taken the lifts but she was, to all intents and purposes, still a Londoner – she'd walk everywhere – and she climbed the industrial spiral staircase, plotting all the while.

This was good, better than waiting for him to collect her. He liked surprises. She recalled he had particularly liked coming over to her flat one evening to find her cooking his favourite dinner, naked but for an apron. 'In case of hot splashes,' she'd laughed as he'd spun her round to whisk it straight off.

She stepped onto the carpeted corridor, her eyes scanning the signs for which direction to take, her free hand already in her bag and rummaging for the key card he had given her earlier. He had anticipated the same problem with knowing the concierges as she had.

She sipped the drink as she went, feeling sexy and dangerous. Her! Chloe Marston, a badass for once.

Somewhere in the background she heard a door open, a woman's voice drift down the corridor like a sea mist. It was soft. '. . . have to do it again sometime.' Another tryst. This hotel was made for lovers.

Where was the key? She knew she had put it in the side zip pocket of her bag. With a sigh, she stopped walking and checked the bag properly: mints, a Sudoku puzzle book, her phone, lip gloss, two hundred receipts (or so it seemed), a pen . . . Goddammit. There was nowhere to put her glass, so she crouched to set it down on the carpet, grateful that she was wearing heels for once; it meant she could balance more easily.

'Absolutely. I'll make it worth your while—'

Chloe's head whipped up at the man's voice, just in time to see a sleek brunette step back from the doorway. No. No. *Her?* Why was she here? . . . Without hesitation, without time even to stand, Chloe rolled into the deep doorway immediately to her left, grabbing her bag and pulling it in after her. Her legs were an ungainly tangle, knees up to her chin, her blouse twisted, her mouth hanging open in shock, eyes as wide as if she'd been throttled and she knew that someone, somewhere, would be watching this on a security camera, witnessing her drama unfold.

'—Call me. Day, night – there's never a wrong time—'

The man's voice again. It rattled her bones, made her world quake – because an English accent in New York City was as conspicuous as a red rose in the snow and she knew exactly to whom it belonged.

'Thanks, I'll bear that in mind,' the woman purred, her voice coming closer to Chloe now. She was on the move.

Too late Chloe caught sight of her drink still sitting, conspicuously, in the middle of the corridor: a single watermelon mojito left on the carpet, ready to be inadvertently kicked by some passer-by. Serena would see it, though, she noticed these things; she would see it and come over here and how would Chloe explain why she was huddled in a ball at the foot of a stranger's door, just down the corridor from Tom's room?

She scrunched her eyes shut, wanting to press rewind and go back to just a few minutes earlier, when she'd been feeling sexy and uninhibited and free and happy. This couldn't be happening. Not again. She was back in that cab on Bond Street again, watching her life pause then buckle, crushed by external forces bigger than her. She wanted to scream. She wanted to cry. She wanted to punch him, to kick her. Instead she lay huddled like a street rat, listening to Serena's velvet padded footsteps on the carpet draw closer and waiting to be stripped of her pride too. She could already anticipate Serena's superior look of glee as she came upon her, balled up, trying to hide . . .

Only – the footsteps stopped and the 'ding' of an elevator halfway up the corridor was followed a moment later by the slide of doors. Chloe frowned, her breath held as she heard her colleague's stilettos tap on the aluminium plate floor as she walked in. A few seconds passed – possibly a lifetime – and then the doors closed again, taking Serena away and with her, Chloe's hope, her trust, her future.

For a moment, she was grateful for this one small mercy that she hadn't been seen; her pride had been preserved if nothing else. Rolling onto her knees, she waited as a hushed silence prevailed again, nothing moving in the hotel corridor, and, on the surface, everything went back to how it had seemed just a few moments earlier: her wish had been granted and Tom was in that room down there, waiting for her.

Only it hadn't been *her* he'd been waiting for; he'd told *her* he wouldn't be back here till seven. She was simply second in line – again – and everything he had said on the street had been lies. There wasn't a word of truth in it. How could there be?

She didn't know how long she sat there, on her knees, her heart beating in her chest like a boxer's glove against a punchbag, but eventually it occurred to her to move. Slowly, holding the walls, she pushed herself back to standing and stood there, trembling, in the middle of the doorway as the questions continued to rush at her like stinging bees – how long had it been going on with Serena? Were there others?

Part of her wanted to storm his room and beat the hell out of him, to hurt him with her fists the way he'd hurt her with his kisses. But the tears streamed silently down her cheeks because she knew the answers didn't matter. Nothing he could say now would undo what she had just seen. It was actions, not words, that she trusted and she had been an idiot to expect her fate would be any different to the woman's who had gone before her; he had cheated on Lucy with her (or was it the other way round?) so of course he would cheat on her with someone else. That was what he did. It was who he was. What was the famous quote? When you marry the mistress, you create a job vacancy? And it had been uttered by a man who could well have been one of their clients, no less. A billionaire, one for whom the normal rules didn't apply. Hadn't Rosalind said to her at the hospital that money corrupts? Well, Tom had bought his own hype. He had spent so much time catering to the whims of the rich, the vain, the shallow, the obsessed, submerging himself in a world of ever more extravagant displays of indulgence, that it had become the only thing he knew. It was his new normal to value things over people, money over experiences. No, there was no point in discussing anything with him. Asking for answers. She had seen all she needed, to know what kind of life she would have with a man like him.

Slowly, moving as though the floor might tip, she began walking back the way she had come, her foot kicking over the drink which she had forgotten was still sitting there, incongruous on the carpet. She knew she ought to stop and pick it up; someone could tread on it and smash it, someone could get hurt.

But she continued walking. That someone wouldn't be her.

The reception had barely been going an hour but already it was kicking off, the space crowded, revellers hanging around outside on the street. It was more like a club opening than an art exhibition – music pumped from the sound system, waiters moved with practised ease, somehow managing to keep their loaded trays away from the flinging elbows and flipped-back hair that made navigation so precarious. Perhaps it was the perfect sunset outside, or the mix of guests; maybe the playlist or the cocktails, but whatever the 'it' factor was, this party had it.

Elle was already there and looking sensational in her flea-market dress. People kept staring, their eyes drawn to her in the middle of the room as she laughed and swayed provocatively to the music, a head taller than everyone else, even most of the men. Chloe on the other hand had done exactly what she'd promised she wouldn't do and turned up dressed nun-like in her suit after all. Although she wasn't sure nuns drank whisky straight from the bottle.

She watched the action from her secret vantage point, taking in every whispered aside and seductive smile. Life – love – was going on without her, continuing as though nothing untoward had happened. What did any of them care that her world had fallen apart again? That all her months of careful plans and brave resolutions had been undone by him in less than a week?

A trickle of sweat wriggled down her spine – it was another steamy, airless night – and she pulled at her jacket angrily, forcing it open and sending the button flying off. She watched it land on its side and wheel around in ever decreasing circles, finally toppling over; if she had gone home after the meeting after all, she would have changed and at least she would be standing here, looking good, looking a part of things like everyone else, like Elle. And that button would have stayed sewn on to the jacket.

She took another surreptitious slug of the bottle, pressing her hand to the back of her mouth, eyes closed for a moment as the room pulsed around her and she kept the tears held back. No one could see her here; she wasn't even sure why she'd come, only that she couldn't bear – didn't dare – go home. He would go looking for her there again, she knew he would. He was probably there right now, guarding the steps, wanting to know why she'd stood him up at the hotel.

'So this is where you're hiding out.'

She opened her eyes, looking back in astonishment at the bearded ruggedness of Joe Lincoln's handsome face. She'd forgotten she'd invited him.

'J-Joe!' she stammered, trying to force a smile. 'You made it.'

'I've done three fly-bys of this place trying to find you.'

Carefully, keeping her left shoulder behind the corner of the false wall, she reached her left arm back and replaced the whisky bottle on the waiters' supplies table. 'Yeah? Oh, well, I was just taking a quick rest. These things can get pretty . . . hectic.'

He nodded but she sensed a knowingness to the movement. Had he seen her knocking back the whisky? 'It's a great party,' he shouted over the music.

'I know, right?' she shouted back, having to bite down on the impulse to quote back to him his protestations that perks such as this held no interest for him. 'This is what we do. Wherever you want to go, we'll get you in.'

His eyes narrowed fractionally, though she wasn't sure whether it was at her flat tone or her continuing refusal to believe that he wasn't impressed by this. 'Thanks for asking me. It's a great exhibition.' He gestured vaguely towards the wall, some of the canvases marked with red dots.

'Great!' she said, grabbing a passing waiter who was carrying a tray of espresso martinis – they were the drink of the summer. 'D'you want one?'

He handed one to her, took another for himself and they both dispatched them quickly. 'So – have you been here long?'

'Just got here,' she lied.

'But you've come on from somewhere?'

It was less a question than a statement of fact. Could he tell she was drunk? His eyes were on the loose ties of her blouse which were pulling the silk fabric down and exposing some skin. She wondered if she looked as undone as she felt. 'Yeah, I guess you could say that. You?'

'Just got here.'

'Don't tell me, you were pulling another shift at Chimi-changa.' She laughed, a little too loudly.

'Exactly,' he deadpanned.

'That was the funniest thing seeing you there. I nearly died of shock.' She slapped her hand across her chest.

'How do you think I felt?' His eyes glittered – almost; he had a sense of humour that was so dry as to be desiccated. She found it both unnerving and attractive.

'It's my new favourite place. I'd eat there every day if I could.'

'What's stopping you then?'

She sighed. 'Work commitments. Not all our clients are as . . . flexible as you.'

She looked up at him through the dim light and whisky haze, remembering the flash of attraction – the sense of another world opening up – that had zipped between them that Saturday at the food market. She felt flickers of it again now, like a static that crackled, sometimes reaching her, other times falling short. Her chest tightened, anxiety a flare that shot through her. 'My friend thinks you're gorgeous, by the way. She's the reason I invited you to come.' The words came out in a jumble, falling across one another like toppled dominoes. She didn't know why she'd said it, only that she felt gripped by a sense of panic. Oh God, how drunk was she? She tried to remember what she'd had to drink – three mojitos at the hotel, twenty minutes of whisky-swigging here, now a martini . . . Pretty drunk then.

He looked taken aback momentarily. 'And to think I thought it was one of the perks of membership.' That dry tone again.

'Well, I mean I would have told you about it *anyway*,' she said quickly. 'Look, that's her over there,' she said, pointing to

Elle now standing with Julien Sacramento, one of the bad boys of the New York art scene. 'Isn't she beautiful?' she sighed.

'She is,' he nodded, barely looking over at her before coming back to face Chloe again.

'I can give you her number if you like.' No! Why was she doing this? Why were these words coming out of her?

'Is that part of the service too?' he asked coldly, looking at her directly, a wedge of that curtness from their first meeting back in his voice.

'Nooooo,' Chloe groaned, playfully swatting him across the stomach with the back of her hand, trying to lighten the mood.

But she'd clearly misjudged again because, for a terrible moment, everything went still – for her anyway – as he looked down at his shirt. She felt instantly horrified, realizing she had got it wrong again. She had crossed a line, touching him inappropriately, a man she scarcely knew! Her client! Which was the worst of all those scenarios?

She waited, feeling her pulse pound in her ears louder than the dance-floor beat. She watched as he took a breath, as though pressing a 'reset' button. 'Listen,' he said, taking a step closer, his voice becoming louder in her ear. 'I don't actually care why you invited me; I only came tonight because I want to talk to you about Greece. I need to move on it.'

'Greece?' she echoed, feeling relieved he wasn't going to upbraid her for harassing him. 'Greece is *great*. It's going well.'

He looked at her and she could tell from the way he eyed her suspiciously that he definitely knew she was drunk. 'So then you've found something?'

'Absolutely, yes,' she nodded. 'Lots.'

'Even better. A choice then?'

'Well I have found men do like choice,' she mumbled under her breath as another image of Serena and Tom zipped through her mind. Whisky. She needed more whisky.

He frowned. 'Excuse me?'

'Nothing,' she sighed, dismissing the query with another, more feeble, swat in the air. She leant her head against the wall, wanting to go home now. She felt suddenly exhausted. Defeated.

'So when can I see them? Have you got anything I could look at now?'

She arched an eyebrow, looking at him as though he'd just asked her to poledance. 'Now? *Now*-now?'

'Yes. Now-now. Show me on your phone.'

'I can't. I should do it properly – you know, brunch at Sant Ambroeus, laptop presentation. The whole VIP treatment,' she said scathingly, with a roll of her eyes for good measure.

'Chloe, I've already told you several times I don't care about all that; I don't need to be mollycoddled. I just want to see the damned properties.' He fixed her with a stern look.

'Really?' She bit her lip.

'Really.'

'Well, if you're sure . . .' she said, giving a huge sigh and opening up her phone and finding the files in her emails; it took a few minutes. The screen wasn't working properly. Or it was the 4G. Or her fingers.

'. . . Right, so that's one of them,' she said finally, handing over the phone so he could get a closer look. She peered over his shoulder, having to remind herself not to rest her head on it. All she wanted now was to sleep. 'Beautiful sea views, twelve acres. No mains power though and the plumbing is . . . basic.'

'Twelve acres is too small. And I need mains power.'

She gave a sigh that she didn't even try to hide. 'Okay, so then the next one is a really beautiful building.' She reached over him and swiped the screen left. 'The old mayor's house. It has zero land and is in the old town—'

'It needs to be rural, Chloe, with lots of land. I told you I want privacy.'

'Splendid isolation is all very well in principle,' she countered, not liking the way he cut over her. 'But you might find you like having neighbours when you get there.'

'I have neighbours here.'

'But it's not like here, over there,' she said, beginning to feel huffy; he was so *difficult*. 'They'd be different neighbours.'

'How?'

'You know,' she shrugged, wide-eyed. 'Farmers and goats and shit.'

'Farmers and goats and . . . ?' He sighed, looking exasperated by her now. 'Chloe, the entire point of this place is seclusion. I thought I made myself clear on that.' He handed the phone back to her.

'But I haven't shown you the picture yet,' she pouted. 'It's super pretty.'

'It doesn't fit the brief,' he said firmly.

She tutted loudly, her finger jabbing the screen as she searched for the next property. '. . . Oh, this is one, but I don't think it's right: old farmhouse, walled garden, olive groves. About a mile off the nearest road but—'

He took the phone from her hand again and she watched him flicking through the pictures intently, his eyes keen on the detail. He had a good profile. Strong. Manly. She wondered whether he cheated on his girlfriend too . . . Was it all men, or just Tom? Or was it her? Was *she* the problem, lacking in some way?

'I like this one.' He held her phone back and she tore her gaze off his profile to have a look.

'Yeah?'

'It's worth seeing. Have you others like that?'

'Tons,' she said confidently, even though she couldn't remember her own phone number right now.

'Okay – but we'll need to go see them.'

She blinked. Then blinked again; she wasn't entirely sure her eyes were working together properly. 'We?'

'Well of course. I need a woman's eye.'

'But . . . but . . .'

'But what? That's okay isn't it? Surely you're allowed to travel with clients if it's required?'

'Absolutely. I just didn't realize that's what you wanted, is all.'

'Well I do. And time is of the essence for me. I don't want to lose this summer and it's mid-July already. How soon can you get away?'

'I'd have to look at my diary,' she said, feeling disorientated, looking around the room. *Could* she do this? She'd need to speak to Jack. What if Alexander needed her? Or Pelham? What if Poppy woke up? Where was Elle?

Joe turned to face her square on, blocking her view of the rest of the room, his hands jammed in his pockets. He was all she could see; it wasn't a bad view. 'I suppose tonight's out of the question?'

'Toni—?' she spluttered. 'You want to take off for Greece right now, without a moment's notice?'

He shrugged, as if he couldn't see what the big deal was. 'Yeah.'

He was mad. '. . . But we'd never get a flight.'

'Not commercially maybe. But you can get us a jet, can't you?'

'A private jet?' she echoed, sure she was hearing things.

'I seem to recall you telling me you could get me a rickshaw in Bangkok with three minutes' notice if that was what I wanted. Well, I'm telling you I want a plane to get me from here to Greece, *now*.' He looked at her with that intense expression of his again, as though scrutinizing her, looking for the fault lines. 'What's the problem? Have you got meetings that can't be rescheduled?'

'Well, no, but—' Apart from Poppy, she actually couldn't think of any compelling reasons to stay in New York this week. And there was one overwhelmingly good reason to leave.

'So then go pack a bag and we can be on our way.'

'It's just so . . . sudden,' she faltered.

'I'm asking you to accompany me to Greece, Chloe. Not marry me.' His face split into an amused smile, enlivening his features. She noticed he had very white teeth. '. . . Joke?' he added when she didn't respond.

'Oh. Oh yes, of course. I knew that,' she managed. Men joking about not marrying her was too close to the bone, though.

'Listen, spontaneity is money's single greatest gift, Chloe,' he said, watching her. 'Don't overthink it. Let's just go.' She placed a hand on the wall, just to prop it up. She felt harried, rushed. 'You can sleep on the plane and tomorrow, by the time you wake up, we'll be on a different continent. A hangover on a Greek island is surely better than a hangover in New York.'

'Will you be hungover?' she asked, wide-eyed.

His eyes glittered with contained laughter. 'Not me. You.'

'*Me?*'

'Don't worry, a swim in the sea will perk you up.'

'What makes you think *I'm* going to be hungover?' she asked huffily.

At that, he threw his head back and laughed. 'Precisely that!' His eyes flashed, his mood upbeat. 'So what do you say? Are you in?'

Chloe leaned against the wall and looked at him: being on a different continent to Tom by daybreak? She couldn't think of anything better than that at all. 'Hell yes I am – I'm in.'

Chapter Fifteen

The drone was constant, a noise to match the pressure in her head and she frowned without trying to open her eyes, pulling the pillow closer to her and snuggling back down again. Just five more minutes. She would sleep until her alarm went off, no way was she getting up early . . .

The earth dropped suddenly and she flinched violently, feeling as though the bed was falling away from her. Her eyes flew open and, for a moment, she was utterly bewildered by the scene that greeted her – ivory leather everywhere she looked, on the walls, chairs, ceiling even; the small tubular space . . .

She sat up in a rush, a panicky feeling beginning to rush through her as she tried to make sense of what was happening – what had happened last night? – but her head disagreed with the sudden motion and she dropped it in her hands, wondering if she was going to be sick.

A self-pitying groan escaped her as flashes of last night came back in silent cameos: The velvet chairs in the Blond. Serena at Tom's doorway. The mojito on the floor. Whisky on a table. Elle in the centre of the room. Martinis on a tray. Joe—

'Good morning.'

She looked up – again too quickly – an aghast expression

on her face as the man himself smiled back at her. He was standing by the partition that blocked the bedroom she was in from what she could see was a seating area behind him.

Plane. She was on a plane.

'I thought I heard you stirring. There's been some turbulence. Did it wake you?'

'Uh . . .' Her voice was an octave deeper than usual. Her hands went to her hair, her face. Oh God, what did she look like? And – she looked down at herself – how the hell had she got into these pyjamas?

'Don't worry, you were able to do it yourself – just,' he said, watching her slow-dawning panic. 'I thought it was better if you had the bed.'

'Where have you slept?' she managed, every word a croak. Water, she needed water.

As though reading her mind, he came into the room and poured her a glass from the bottle on the burr-walnut side table.

'Thank you,' she mumbled, taking long, thirsty sips.

'I slept back there,' he said, jerking his head towards the main cabin as he settled himself on the arm of a chair across the aisle from the bed. 'And very comfortable it was too.'

'Well, thank you,' she said acknowledging his manners for forfeiting a truly flat bed and proper night's sleep for her. 'Did *I* do this?' she asked, looking around the plane in wonderment. She had booked them countless times over the years but had never actually been in one.

'You were very efficient. I had no sooner suggested the idea than you made a few calls and had it sorted in ten minutes. A very impressive service, Miss Marston.'

Her eyes met his and she saw the pity on his face. '. . . Hmm, not so impressive today though,' she murmured, her free hand going to smooth her hair again, feeling mortified that she had got herself into this state in front of him, her client. 'I'm so sorry.'

His gaze was steady. 'Why? It was a party. You partied.'

She glanced at him. Was that what he thought she was – some high-flying party girl, living the life she flogged to her clients? 'I know, but, I don't usually . . . I'd . . . I'd had some bad news. I was upset.'

He nodded, watching her and she wondered whether he believed her or just thought this was an excuse.

' . . . Where are we going?' It was humiliating to have to even ask.

'You don't remember?'

She shook her head.

'Greece. Specifically the Saronic islands.' He watched the look of horror spread across her face. 'You said you could rearrange your meetings, that there wasn't anything particularly tying you to the city this week.'

'Uh . . . right,' she stumbled. 'Yes.' Had she really said that? She'd been blind drunk. Even now, she couldn't remember her commitments off the top of her head. Had she signed off on the Andermatt deal?

'Are you sure it's okay?' he asked.

What about Pelham – had the river cruise worked? What if Alexander called? 'Well, I'm guessing it's too late to ask the pilot to turn around now,' she said, giving a feeble smile.

'To be honest, yes. We refuelled in London three hours ago. We should be landing in Athens in about forty minutes.'

She'd been asleep all that time, crossing an ocean and a continent? She wondered what Tom would be thinking after she hadn't turned up at his room last night. Had he called?

Her phone was on the little side table but she could see the blue light flashing. She tore her eyes away from it.

'Forty minutes . . . Right.' She finished the remaining water, leaning across the bed to push back the blind. The day jumped in without manners; outside, a symphony of blues was playing: clear skies and cerulean seas, ocean-going yachts merely white pinpricks from here. 'And how long will we be here?'

He shrugged. 'As long as it takes, I guess. It could be a couple of days, it could be the week. It depends what happens on the ground when we see the properties.'

'Uh-huh.' She tried to hide her frustration at the open-endedness of it. How could she have done this – just boarded a private jet with a man she barely knew to come to a tiny island for an unspecified amount of time? Kate would freak if she found out. Her mother would—

He watched her for a moment as though her thoughts played across her face like a television screen. 'Well, I'll leave you to get changed. You were adamant you didn't want to pack anything last night, you kept saying you just wanted to go, so they've left your suit in the closet.' He looked at her apologetically. 'But we can get you some lighter stuff when we get there.' He himself was wearing jeans and a grey-marl t-shirt. Had he been wearing that last night too?

'Absolutely, no problem,' she said, trying to smile again even though the idea of pushing her body into a tailored anything made her want to curl up in a ball and cry. Her head was making her want to cry. Tom and what he'd done . . .

Joe retreated back into the cabin and she looked down again at the Mediterranean view – the purple range of the

Peloponnese mountains like dimpled bruises on the earth's skin, islands threading the Greek seas like dot-to-dot pictures, the horizon blindingly bright. It wasn't just a new landscape out there, it looked like an entirely different world, the bare, scrubbed terrains and plunging chalky cliffs the polar opposite to the thrusting, avaricious man-made, steel-clad intensity of Manhattan.

She felt a small quiver in her soul at the sight of it. It was odd. She had come out here on the screaming delirium of alcohol, but something told her this was the very place she needed to be: somewhere simple, clean and healing, back in the elements.

Clearly it would have been preferable to have Elle here instead of Joe (although the commute wouldn't have been anywhere near as merciful), and she couldn't help but wish that this could have been a girls' holiday to help her get over her broken heart, composed of lie-ins till noon, afternoon tanning sessions and hanging out in bars with pretty Greek boys. That was the way forward surely? She needed to cut all ties with her old life, completely this time. No more half measures.

But not quite yet. Whether she liked it or not, she was here with Joe, and having hitched a free ride here, she couldn't very well ditch the guy; she had a moral as well as professional obligation to do what she had signed up to do when she stepped onto that jet, and that was to help him buy his house.

But . . . if she could wrap up his business here quickly, there was nothing to stop her staying on a while, without him, and working out her next step. Tom was a tumour she had to cut from her life and she had to find a new path now.

She pressed her hand to the glass.

And this was the perfect place to start.

Hydra

It turned out she was excellent at her job, even pie-eyed. The helicopter was waiting on the tarmac when they disembarked, ready to whisk them straight to the island, so that their feet were on Athenian soil for less than fifteen minutes. Its drone through the earphones – significantly louder than the plane's – didn't do her headache any favours, but she supposed since it was self-inflicted, she had no one to blame but herself. And besides, it was worth the freedom.

She spent the short journey with her forehead pressed to the cool glass, gazing down at the islands that she could see in much greater detail now they had dropped altitude. Most of her visions of the Greek islands had been built around the twee perfection of Santorini and Mykonos, their blue-and-white cubiform buildings sitting in dense clusters above the sea; but looking down on the vastly more rustic and underdeveloped islands here, the buildings looked more friendly and familiar, with red tile roofs, pale-grey stonework and brightly coloured windows and doors. Beside her, Joe sat scrolling on his phone, not seeming overly interested in the view for someone who was potentially going to buy a home here.

They began dropping height in ever-decreasing circles, coming to a stop not on Hydra itself but on a tiny outcrop just off the coast; she had read about it during her research: not only were no helicopters or planes allowed to land on the island at all (except for emergency aircraft), nor were any cars or scooters permitted either. Apparently, everything was transported by packs of donkeys, although this she had to see – was it a marketing gimmick? She wasn't sure she believed it.

'Mr Lincoln?' a man in navy shorts and a grey polo shirt enquired, greeting them as they jumped down.

Joe nodded, glancing over to check she was still with him. Out of the air-conditioned coolness of the chopper, she was already beginning to sweat in her suit. It had been, what – four minutes?

'This way, please. Your bags will be sent on.'

They were led to a small RIB tied up by the jetty and within minutes were speeding across the surface of the very sea that she had been looking down upon from the sky, themselves now one of the minuscule dots on the ocean's skin. Chloe tipped her chin up, letting the wind blow her hair back and liking being buffeted by the sea air; it made her feel blown through, as though all the darkness could be swept out of her; the sea spray spritzing her face, cleaning her of the city's grubbiness. They had been here all of five minutes and already her spirit felt lighter, even if the image of Serena standing at that doorway did flash behind her eyelids every time she blinked.

It was only a short hop to the port and both she and Joe straightened up, impressed and excited, as they came into the handsome harbour. It was crescent-shaped and densely flanked by tall, robust houses, white-hulled local fishing boats tethered outside cafes and tavernas, deep-draught gin palaces and yachts moored in the deeper water.

They jumped off, eyes wide as they took in the bustling scene. Most of the tables at the cafes were occupied, the awnings of the waterfront boutiques pulled out as protection from the late afternoon sun; the beautiful blue and white Greek flag fluttered from sailing masts, and everywhere there were indeed donkeys, suited up with saddlebags, heads nodding drowsily in the heat.

'So that's the first thing about this place,' she said, trying to do her job and not just be another hungover tourist (not that she looked like a tourist in her Manhattan suit; in this heat, it was becoming creased and limp and she needed a shower and a change). 'There are no cars, no scooters, no vans, no nothing. If you need to get somewhere or you need something to be delivered, it's by foot, by donkey or by boat.'

He frowned. 'So, if I wanted to get a sofa for the house?'

'Donkey or boat.'

'. . . Interesting.' He didn't look particularly pleased about it.

'Old school, I'm afraid,' she smiled. 'They also get their water shipped in here from Athens.'

A look approaching panic crossed his face.

'You did say you wanted rustic seclusion,' she shrugged.

'I suppose I did,' he agreed. 'So, what now?' he asked, looking around them quizzically. 'View the properties or check in first?'

Chloe felt a rush of panic. Indeed, what now? She had been so focused on getting here – or, in her case, getting *away* from New York – that she hadn't thought as far forward as where they might actually stay. Which was a disaster, no two ways about it, she thought, looking around too. This wasn't a big island and Hydra Town was, from memory, pretty much the only large settlement; any hotels or guest-houses would be found here. There was almost no development inland, and whatever could be found there would be privately owned.

She took in the number of wandering visitors, the occupied tables . . . it was high season – the port was packed. Supply would be exceptionally limited even at their 'money no object' level; you couldn't have what simply wasn't there.

She held a finger in the air, stalling him from saying anything further as her befuddled, much-dehydrated brain went into overdrive, considering their options. She needed access to their database but she didn't want to ring the team in New York for help; she wouldn't give Tom the satisfaction of knowing where she was. Not yet anyway. Let him sweat.

She closed her eyes and concentrated. Jack had given her the name of his contact in Athens, but Rome was their nearest office outpost to here. 'Just give me a few minutes,' she said, getting her phone and beginning to scroll through. 'In fact, why don't . . . why don't we have a drink first and get our bearings? See if you can get us a table at one of the cafes here – unless you want somewhere more formal?' she asked with a look of trepidation. God help her if he wanted a Michelin-star meal right now.

His mouth turned up fractionally at the corners. 'A snack is fine. I'll get us a table. You do your thing.'

With a sigh of relief, she watched him wander off, patting one of the donkeys as he passed by, a wry smile on his face. A couple of Scandinavian-looking girls gave him interested double-looks as they walked past, their brown legs scissoring beneath short flirty floral sundresses, but if he noticed, he didn't look back. She wondered if they could tell he was different, set apart from the masses? That he'd flown here all the way from New York in a private jet? Certainly nothing about him advertised his wealth: not his jeans, not his watch (because he didn't wear one), not his battered Adidas trainers; there was no swagger, no chest-puffing, no man-spreading, and yet he was still unequivocally a man's man; he radiated masculinity in his stillness, the sense of containment about him. Chloe suspected he never lost control, never got messily drunk . . .

'*Invicta, sono Maria.*'

'Oh, hi, Maria, it's Chloe Marston calling from the New York office.'

'Hey, Chloe, how are you?'

'I'm great, thanks. Listen, I wonder if you could help me out . . . ?'

He had managed to bag a table at a cafe halfway along the harbour, blue-and-white chequered cloths on the tables, little wooden chairs painted red; pink potted geraniums that were set on the ground as soft boundary markers clashed terribly but it didn't matter. She took the seat beside him and sank into it, grateful to see that he had already ordered a large bottle of water and some wine.

'Do you mind if I . . . ?' she asked, pouring herself a tall glass of water, draining it and refilling it immediately. 'I'm so thirsty.'

'I'm not surprised. Hungry too, I should imagine?'

She hadn't been able to face the coffee and pastries the hostess had offered on the plane but now she thought she would sell her grandmother for a plate of pasta.

'Ravenous,' she admitted, shooting him an apologetic glance. '. . . Aren't you jaded at all? Not even a little bit?'

'You were way ahead of me by the time I got there last night. I think you said you'd come on from somewhere?'

There was an interested note in his voice but Chloe swallowed and drank some more water. Alexander may have forced her to discuss her love life but she wouldn't be repeating it with Joe.

'God, look at that view,' she said, looking determinedly out to sea, still scarcely able to believe this was her vista. This time yesterday she'd already been played for a fool, kissing Tom like a teenager on a New York street corner and planning their rendezvous at his hotel . . .

A seagull sitting on the crow's nest of a nearby mast squawked loudly, shifting its webbed feet as it eyed the crowds for easy pickings. A marbled cat jumped off the wall and trotted, its tail aloft, in the direction of the large fishing boats that were just docking at the far end and throwing down their nets. A couple of ducks slid into the water off the outboards of moored caiques. It was more wildlife than she'd seen in a month of living in Manhattan (unless under-arm chihuahuas counted).

'Would you like some wine? Or is that a provocative question?'

She smiled. In truth, the last thing she felt like was more alcohol but she had a duty to be good company and do her best for him whilst they were here; he had saved her in ways he would never know and for that she was grateful. Plus, hair of the dog always worked, in her experience. 'A *small* glass would be lovely.'

He took the rosé from a bucket of ice next to him and poured. 'So are we all set for rooms?'

'We will be. I've got the team cracking on with it now. They should be calling back any moment.'

'Good.' He tapped a finger against her glass, watching her. 'I'll admit, I'm beginning to get why people go for this gig now; I wasn't convinced before, but I can see now it's useful being able to just go anywhere in the world at a moment's notice and it all just . . . happens for you. Logistics sorted, no hassles.'

'I know.' She smiled wanly, wishing someone could do it for her for once. 'That's the magic.'

'Do you enjoy it?'

'This?' she quipped, motioning to the idyllic scene laid out before them. 'Hell, no! Who could enjoy this?'

'There must be lots of perks for you.'

'Yeah, I suppose there are,' she sighed. 'And it could be a party every night if I wanted; discounts everywhere.'

He hitched an eyebrow. 'I sense a but.'

Was her disillusionment so apparent? 'I'm just careful to draw the line. It's not *my* reality. I see your world and occasionally I get to live in snatches of it too – like right now – but I know I'm only ever here by proxy. It could be so easy to be seduced into thinking that because I can access it, I'm somehow part of it, but I'm not. I'll never charter a private plane myself or have gold sprinkles dusted on my cornflakes. I don't need the Dalai Lama himself to teach me how to meditate.'

There was a pause. 'I'm getting the impression you find these things all a little . . . ridiculous.'

'No! Not at all,' she said quickly, not wanting to offend. 'It's endlessly fascinating to me to see what satisfies people like you who really do genuinely have it all. Appetite doesn't necessarily dwindle just because hunger is met; it's part of the human condition to always want more than we can have; whatever our level, there's always something else to aspire to and I'm interested in what makes people happy when *all* barriers are removed. So in your case, finding a fantastic rural retreat somewhere like this.'

He nodded, his eyes slitted against the bright light. 'This is pretty great.'

'What you wanted?'

He glanced at her. 'So far.'

'Do you feel the need to escape because your work's so intense?'

'Yes. Exactly that,' he said quietly, looking out to sea. 'I want to be somewhere where no one can reach me – no emails, no texts, no FaceTime.' He glanced back at her. 'No demands.'

'. . . But lots of donkeys?' she asked hopefully as a small train of them walked past, one lifting its tail not three metres from their table and releasing a steaming load of dung onto the ground.

He laughed; it was a glorious sound, throaty and generous, his eyes crinkling at the corners, his teeth flashing white against the growing darkness of his beard. He nodded, drumming his fingers against the table as he looked back at her with amusement. 'Yes, exactly, lots of donkeys.'

Chapter Sixteen

The houses rose up and away from the harbour in narrow streets, old grey stone steps polished to a shine by the generations of inhabitants, travellers and pack animals that trod weary paths up and down them under the blazing sun. On either side, potted, nodding flowers lined the streets, with small wooden chairs set outside, ready for the cooler hours. There was no common consensus on the island's colourway – some doors and windows were fuchsia pink, others a marigold orange, sunflower yellow or cobalt blue – but the overall effect was splashy and vibrant, hot and vivacious. Most of the houses were stippled white, but some of the grander buildings were built from square-cut stones and looked out upon the town with arched windows and balconies. Theirs – for the next three nights anyway – was one such. Known as an *archontikó*, which was Greek for 'mansion', it was an eighteenth-century sea-captain's house and one of the most notable properties on the island. It didn't advertise its rooms but was filled through elite word-of-mouth recommendations. Since it was already fully booked for the week, Maria had only been able to secure the two rooms by offering the existing incumbents complimentary private transfers and stays with one of their partner hotels in nearby Spetses. They had been lucky the offer had been accepted; even Chloe didn't know what they would have done otherwise.

She leant against the low wall of the roof terrace, gazing down upon the striking red roofs that looked almost aglow in the creeping dusk, the jingle of a donkey's cowbell just audible in the maze of streets below as the church bells began to swing and chime.

Though the sun was setting, it was still steamy, the temperature at 29 degrees at almost nine. After lunch, they had briefly shopped, giving her a much-needed chance to buy some more appropriate clothes than her bedraggled cream suit. Joe had been patient, telling her to take her time, but she hadn't listened; she wasn't here to shop, they were here to meet his needs, not hers, and she had bought from the first boutique they'd gone into – a pair of white linen trousers, some chambray shorts, a pale-blue Swiss-dot cotton blouse, two t-shirts, a vest and a navy low-backed silk jersey dress that she was wearing now.

She hadn't realized it was low-backed when she'd bought it; in the interests of expediency, she hadn't tried anything on, simply buying off the hanger, and she had been alarmed to find a bra was simply not going to be an option with it. Still, she figured it would be easy enough to stay facing him, and if she didn't, well – it wouldn't be like he hadn't seen a woman's back before. A back was a back.

'Ah, you're up here.' He was coming up the external steps, two glasses in his hands. 'You *do* like to hide away in corners.'

'I wanted to see the sun set,' she said, taking one of the glasses with a smile as he came and sat beside her.

'Good spot,' he nodded, holding out his glass.

She clinked it. 'Cheers.'

'Cheers. To a successful hunt tomorrow.'

'I've spoken to the agents now. Everything will be ready for us to view – all unlocked, so we can go any time that suits.'

'Agents? But—' He frowned.

'Don't worry, everything we're seeing is either not yet marketed, or is known to them as being uninhabited.'

'But the agents won't be there?'

'No, I explained you wanted privacy.'

'And they were okay with that?'

'It's not standard procedure for them, but coming through us? Yes, it's fine,' she shrugged. 'A lot of our clients prefer to do things anonymously.'

He nodded, looking out across the view. The sky was molten, liquid fire poured above a dark, sleeping sea. 'It'll be good to get started.'

'Well, we've got a boat ready to take us where we need to go from nine. But clearly there's no rush; sleep as long as you want. Jet lag's going to kick in.'

'I never need much sleep.' He looked back at her, his eyes falling momentarily to her bare arms. 'Did you sleep earlier?'

'No. I tried, but—' She shrugged. In truth, she had spent the time listening over and over to her voicemails. Elle had rung once. *'Where'd you go, babe? I saw you talking and looking cosy with your hot client. Have you given him my number?'* Rosaria had left a message demanding she ring back – she hadn't; Tom had rung thirty-three times and left fourteen messages, basically until her voicemail had filled up, blocking him – or anyone else – from leaving any more.

'. . . Where are you baby? . . .'

'. . . Call me back . . .'

'. . . Chlo, what's going on? . . .'

'. . . Are you okay? Has something happened? . . .'

'. . . I don't understand . . .'

'. . . Christ, talk to me . . .'

'. . . Where the fuck are you? . . .'

She could track the growing confusion in his voice, the rising hurt, the building anger. He was so convincing at all of it, the beguiling lover so baffled, that if she hadn't seen what she had seen with her own eyes, she would have believed anything he told her. But she had seen it; she had heard his voice and what he'd said to Serena: '. . . *Call me. Day, night – there's never a wrong time.*' There could be no going back now, no matter how much it hurt. *Fool me once, shame on you; fool me twice, shame on me.*

'Chloe?'

'Huh?' She looked up. Joe was staring at her, a small frown on his brow. 'God, I'm sorry, I was miles away.'

'I could see that. You look pale.'

'Do I?' Her hands flew self-consciously to her cheek, her neck, but there was nowhere to hide with her new chop; the auburn mane Tom had so loved now snipped and whipped into defiant androgyny. 'I guess it's the jet lag. My body clock's out. Not helped by the mother of all hangovers of course.'

'Do you want to go back to your room? I won't take offence if you'd rather have some downtime alone. We've got a busy day tomorrow.'

'No, I'm fine. All good.' She slapped a pretend smile on her face and took another sip of the drink.

Joe didn't look convinced but he shrugged. 'If you're sure.'

They lapsed into a long silence, both of them watching a

small water taxi chugging around the headland, its red light flashing.

Chloe glanced across at him, feeling suddenly awkward. Such had been her haste to escape New York, ergo Tom – and then the twin efforts of dealing with her hangover and organizing their accommodation here meant she hadn't given much actual consideration to the fact that she was basically on holiday with a stranger. He was her client of course so she knew a lot about him – thirty-four, Aries, Vermont-born, younger son, lefthander, medium rare, allergic to sticking plasters – but keeping a list on someone wasn't the same as knowing them, and he knew nothing at all about her, bar her name. Small talk was all well and good, but it was hard to keep up for more than a few hours at the best of times, much less twenty-four hours after the love of her life had smashed her heart into smithereens *again*.

She thought about Poppy suddenly, knowing that she would have found this a breeze, sipping cocktails on a Greek island, entertaining him with a whip-crack stream of anecdotes and jokes, looking after her client, keeping him entertained, giving him the level of service he expected and was paying for . . . Instead, Joe was stuck with her: quiet, defensive, her world in ruins and using him to make her second intercontinental escape in six months. It was pathetic. She was pathetic.

'. . . So.'

She looked up to find Joe watching her. She smiled.

'Why don't you tell me something about yourself,' he said, shifting position as though settling in for the long haul. 'I know you've got a strong whisky game and an ability to sleep through thunderstorms, landing planes and jet refuelling. What else?'

She gave a horrified laugh. 'Oh God, there's really not much to tell,' she said quickly, tucking her hair nervously behind one ear.

'That's not true. I pride myself on being a good judge of character, and you strike me as . . . enigmatic; you're like the moon, constantly slipping behind clouds.'

She didn't know what to say; nobody had ever described her in such terms before. '. . . Well, what do you want to know?' she shrugged.

'Well, clearly you're English. Why don't you start by telling me what made you move to New York?'

Her mouth dropped open. It was an innocent enough enquiry, but of all the questions he could have asked!

'. . . Or *not*,' he said, after a long pause, seeing how she couldn't get the words out.

'Sorry,' she stammered, staring into her glass.

'No, my mistake,' he said shortly and she couldn't help but be struck by how different he was to Alexander; Alexander who needed to know and control before he could trust. 'How about . . .' he rooted, searching for something safer than the unexpectedly explosive bombshell of why she was living in a foreign country. '. . . Family. Have you got any brothers, sisters?'

'Yes.' She gave a relieved – and grateful – smile. 'One sister, Kate. She's four years older than me but you'd think it was fourteen the way she bosses me about.'

'She adores you then?'

'We're very close. Although, she's still in London so . . . not, not physically.'

'No.' He didn't press her further but she could see he was assessing her every reaction. 'And your parents?'

'Living the good life in Northumberland, the north of England. I go back to see them as often as I can. They can't get down to London very much as they have so many commitments – Mum is the local Guides leader and Dad's very involved with the parish council, plus he coaches the little ones for football on Saturday mornings.'

A smile played at the corners of his mouth. 'Have they come to visit you in New York?'

'Not yet. But they will, soon, I'm sure. Going to London is a big enough deal for them so New York really is a huge ask.'

He nodded, still watching, the glass hanging loosely in his hand. 'And you're not married.' It was more of a statement than a question, but before she could respond he pointed to her hand. 'No ring.'

'Oh, right, yes – I mean, no, not married.'

'Boyfriend?'

'Nope,' she said cheerily. Too cheerily.

The sudden change in tone was marked and he didn't reply for a moment. 'Don't tell me – that was the bad news you had last night, and you have terrible taste in men?'

She couldn't help but grin. Hearing it put so baldly . . . She was a living cliché, it was tragic but true. 'Yes. And yes. How did you guess?'

'I've seen that thousand-yard stare many times before.' He shook his head but he looked bemused. 'Usually on women on a dinner date with me.'

This time she couldn't help but laugh. Self-deprecation was something new to add to her list on him. 'How about you?' she asked, determining to take the heat off her.

'Do I have terrible taste in men?' he repeated, a light in his eyes.

She laughed again.

'No. Single. The business has taken too much of my energy recently; I've barely had time for lunch, much less a relationship.'

'Ah. That old chestnut.' She took another sip.

There was another silence and she felt his gaze flit on and off her like a grasshopper. In the distance, they heard another cowbell, rising through the town.

'So, what's so terrible about your taste in men? . . . They all wear bow ties?'

She almost choked on the drink. Who knew he was so amusing? 'Oh, you don't want to hear about this, surely?'

'What else are we going to do?'

She met his eyes. He was staring down at her and, for a moment, she could almost forget that he was her client, that this was a professional commitment and not simply her sitting on a rooftop under a darkening sky, having a drink with a handsome stranger.

Only for a moment though.

'Those bow ties,' she sighed eventually. 'What can I tell you? I'm a sucker for them.'

It was his turn to smile but she saw him register the knock-back, the door being firmly shut and locked on shared confidences. She wasn't Poppy, she couldn't blur the boundaries the way she did; Joe was her client, not her friend, and she just needed to get him to sign off on the house and get back on the plane. The sooner he was gone, the sooner she could fall apart alone.

Turning her face away from him, she looked back out to sea, just in time to glimpse the last sliver of sun drop below the horizon. On the wall, her phone buzzed; she had turned it on to silent so as not to be disturbed by Tom's incessant calling, but her heart still leapt at the sound of it anyway, and she still jumped to see the screen.

It dived again at the sight of Jack's name.

'Do you need to get that?' Joe asked, watching as she resolutely didn't answer it.

'No, it's fine. Just my boss.'

'Oh. *Just* your boss,' he repeated in a wry tone.

'He probably just wants an update on how things are going out here. With you.' He wanted to know where in the world she was, rather. Her brief email to Jack last night had simply told him she was accompanying Joe on a house-hunting trip, no mention of where; she didn't want Tom to have any clue as to how to find her this time.

'If I'm happy with the service, you mean?' That faintly sarcastic note sounded in his voice again.

'Yes, maybe.'

A moment later, the phone vibrated with a new text from him and she read it, her mouth dropping open. *'Thought you'd want to know . . .'*

'What is it?'

She looked up at him with newly bright eyes, the first genuine smile of the day enlivening her face. 'It's Poppy,' she gasped. 'Oh God, I can't believe it. She's awake!'

Chapter Seventeen

'Xan, it's me,' she whispered, sitting up in bed, her elbows on her knees. It was still dark outside, the jet lag keeping her on New York hours; 5 a.m. here, but only ten there. She knew he'd still be up.

'*Chlo!* Where the hell are you?' His voice was almost a shriek and she was forced to hold the phone away from her ear for a moment.

'I'm in Greece.'

'*Greece?*' Another screech. 'What the hell are you doing there?'

'I'm with that client, Joe Lincoln.'

There was a pause. 'The hot one?'

She rolled her eyes; why did everyone call him that? 'Yes. Him. He wanted me to come and see the houses I found for him.'

'Did he now? And there was no one else who could do that for him? Someone like, oh, I don't know – a realtor?'

'This is work, Xan.'

'Yeah, right – come away to a Greek island with me, beautiful lady, and we shall tell no one.'

She couldn't help but laugh. 'It's not like that.'

'Isn't it?'

'No. Look, he came to the Basquiat show and cornered

me there – and yes, I'd had a few drinks so it seemed . . . not such a crazy idea at the time. But I'll be back soon, I promise.'

'Well you'd better, because management's going bat-shit. Jack's been tearing round the place like he's Zeus, shooting bolts of thunder from his eyes, I goddam swear. I haven't ever seen him like that before.'

'Why?'

'Search me. Seems he's always flipping his lid about one thing or another at the moment.'

She closed her eyes, hating herself for what she was about to ask. 'And Tom? How's he being?'

'Well, you know Tom – always the good cop, but he's been off too. I swear to God he spent the entire day standing at the window whilst the rest of us were *working* for a living.'

'Oh God, I'm sorry.'

'What are you sorry for? It's not your fault they keep fighting. Sandy in accounts was coming back from doing a matcha run earlier and she overheard them arguing in the elevators. She said that when the doors opened they were all smiles and floppy hair and "pass the tea, vicar", you can imagine; but in the moments *before* the doors opened, she thought they were almost going to come to blows. Everyone in the lobby heard them. It was totally awkward.'

Chloe frowned. 'But why are they fighting? They're such old friends.'

'Agh, the size of their dividends? Who cares?' he tutted. 'Listen, much more importantly – did you hear the *good* news?'

'Poppy? Yes, that's the reason I'm calling – she woke up? It's actually true?'

'Yeah! Isn't it great? A chink of sunshine amidst the chaos and gloom.'

'Have you been to see her?'

'No, they're still saying family only, although Jack got in somehow; he said she looks really bad – weighs practically nothing; vampire white – I mean *completely* bloodless, he said; she's got black eyes; a fractured cheekbone; broken jaw that's had to be wired shut, a broken arm, broken leg . . . Uh, what else did he say? . . . Oh, they had to shave some of her hair for the op too so that's not helping either. She sounds like a mini-Frankenstein. I think she just sort of blinked at him.' He took a breath, sounding worn down. 'But he thought she recognized him, which is something. Poor guy, though, he looked pretty shaken when he got back.'

'I guess that could account for his mood,' Chloe said quietly. 'He's taken her accident really badly.'

'Yeah, well – that's *another* development and it's not good news I'm afraid.'

'Jeez, I've only been gone a day! What else has happened?' She felt a bloom of dread in the pit of her stomach.

'It turns out the accident wasn't no accident after all; it was a deliberate hit and run. The cops are investigating it as attempted murder.'

His words sounded like they had an echo to them, 'murder' reverberating through her brain like a reflection in a hall of mirrors. So it was out in the open now. Had the police come to the office? Were they interviewing colleagues? Did they need to speak to her?

'Chlo . . . ?' Xan asked when she didn't respond – or at least, not quickly enough. 'Oh my God, did you *know*?'

'I . . . uh . . .'

'You did!'

215

'Yeeaah, sorry – I found out at the weekend. I went to the hospital and spoke to her mum.'

'Jesus, Chlo, and you didn't think to tell me?'

'I'm sorry! I wanted to but Jack asked me not to. He said he didn't want it to get out in case it spooks the clients and lowers morale amongst the team even further.' She bit her lip. 'Do the police know any more?'

'Well, they've been here and taken all her files, if that's what you mean,' he said tartly.

Chloe frowned. 'Her *files*? But why would they need those?'

'Well at a guess I'd say they're investigating whether her attack was work-motivated.' Sarcasm now, too, she noted. Great.

'Xan, I'm sorry, okay?' she said quietly. 'I was trying to do the right thing.'

'Yeah? And how is skipping the country with zero notice, leaving the rest of the team in the shit now we're *two* men down, with a police investigation hanging over our heads, doing the right thing?'

She sighed. He had a point. 'Tonight. I'll get on a plane tonight and be with you by brunchtime tomorrow. I'll make it up to you, I promise.'

'It's not me you need to make it up to. It's everyone else who's had to pick up the slack – you need to watch your back, Chloe; Serena's all over your patch like a fly on shit. I came in to her talking to Rosaria Bertolotti this morning on *your* phone, chatting like they were old friends. God knows how long she'd been there. If I were you I'd get back here sooner than brunch or you might not have a job to come back to.'

Chloe stiffened at the mention of Serena's name; that

bloody woman was everywhere – all over her man and now her job too? '. . . I'll do what I can.'

She narrowed her watering eyes as the RIB ploughed through the docile sea, hair swept back off her face by the wind. They had been going for hours now, zipping between the neighbouring islands of Poros, Agistri and Aegina too, trekking round the various different properties that all had something different to offer – spectacular sea views, acres of land, historic significance – but seemingly not one had everything he wanted.

Overhead, plane tracks criss-crossed the spotless sky and she wondered how many people were looking back down at them, seeing just white pinpricks and imagining their story – holidaymakers on a boat trip – with no conception of the complicated reality that had brought her here: a hit and run; a cheating lover; a mercurial businessman who didn't like to wait.

Joe was sitting beside her, one arm across the back of the seat, his face tipped up to the sun. He had swapped his reading glasses for Wayfarers and she could tell the jet lag was getting to him from the way he was slumped; he'd been awake since dawn, just like her.

'Right, back to Hydra. This is our last appointment, I'm afraid,' she said, as the skipper threw a looped rope over a low bollard and they docked at a small tethered pier; they were on the far side of the island from the port. She had deliberately left this one till last. If splendid isolation was what he really wanted, splendid isolation was what he was going to get . . .

A rickety-looking set of wooden steps zigzagged up the rocks. 'After you,' she smiled, indicating for Joe to lead the way.

'This is the only access point?' he asked, a hand on the balustrade.

She made a point of looking at the boulders either side of them; it was clear the only way forward was up the cliff here. 'By sea, yes. But there's a rough path that comes over the hills if you need to get to town that way. It's a very long walk though.'

He glanced back out to sea at the wide empty horizon and nodded. 'Good.'

They climbed the steep staircase slowly – it was difficult to do otherwise in the fierce heat, their skin feeling scorched, their breath coming in shallow pants by the time they reached the sandy-soiled top. They looked around them, hands on hips, getting their breath back as they took in the aspect: there was scarcely a blade of grass to be seen; instead, jagged rocks littered the reddish, bare earth, ancient gnarled and bulbous olive trees throwing out wild Afro-canopies and scattering tangled shadows on the ground. The land sloped gently upwards, away from the sea, and with no clear path to follow they began to walk through the globes of dappled light, grateful for the fleeting shade. In the background, cicadas scratched and ticked, a butterfly flitted.

They walked through the vast grove, past the remains of an old crumbling well, before the landscape opened up and the remains of a terraced garden spread out before them, two old dry-stone walls with steps between them leading to an upper area. Joe stopped and looked around them again. The sea had dropped out of sight beyond the trees and from this vantage point, they could only just glimpse the top of a stubby chimneystack, the house still well out of sight. He nodded again, seeming pleased. Clearly he wasn't one for the topiaried grandeur of the French Riviera and she hoped he wasn't after one of their pastel-frosted eighteenth-century villas either, because he wouldn't find it in this part of the world.

Chloe didn't say a word as they moved onwards, but she was watching his every move and she felt a thrill of success ripple up her skin as she saw him take in the sight of the house for the first time. His eyes lit up, his mouth opening with pleased astonishment. She looked back at it herself, wondering what it was that appealed to him so much. It wasn't the grandest building they'd viewed today, far from it; nor would it be anywhere near the most expensive (once they established a price for it; the Athens contact had received word that although recently closed up, it wasn't yet formally for sale). She had assumed that with an open budget, he would equate the best with being the most costly but this would be very much at the lower end of the table. Its remote position, with not another house in sight for miles, was a negative for most potential purchasers and it was in fact the reason the previous inhabitants had been forced to move, as – nearing their eighties – they needed to be in the port for their health care.

She looked at the property appraisingly as Joe loped up to it in long strides now. The roof sat low on the building like a slightly too big hat. It was solid-looking and rather classical, if not outright handsome. The old farmhouse had been standing empty only for a few months but it could have been a lot longer than that – a sense of feral permanence seemed to hang over the place, as though the house had always been here, as though the land surrounding it would never be tamed more than this. It was wide, low and squat and looked as settled in the landscape as a boulder that had rolled down a cliff and come to a final stop in the grass. Nothing would move it now – not wind nor rain nor snow nor drought. The walls were thick and dimpled white, the peg-tiles bleached a soft peach colour beneath the merciless Aegean sun; it had enormous arched windows and on the ground floor, shuttered but wide double doors led into rooms which may once have been stables for the livestock – some of the more rural properties had been built with the stables below the farmers' living accommodation. Chloe could imagine that with the shutters thrown back, the space would be flooded with light.

Her footsteps echoed behind his, falling back, giving him space as he walked through the many rooms with his usual briskness, but there was an energy to him that hadn't been there when she'd shown him the much larger, more expensive admiral's house on Poros or the rich Athenian's mansion on Aegina.

The bedrooms – all four of them – were incredibly basic with just one electrical socket and a pendant wire hanging from the ceilings, but they were large and sunny with double-aspect windows, plain white walls, old wooden floors (some with gaps she could get her hand through) and slatted shutters at every window. They had high ceilings, and although nothing was en-suite, there were two bathrooms upstairs, one of which could easily be knocked through to the main bedroom if he wished. As for the bathrooms, they were also undeniably simple – rough-walled showers with plain green tiles in one, blue in the other; the basins were old stone water troughs set on concrete piers, and the toilets came with old-school chain flushes. There was no limestone, no glass, no bronze fittings, but each room had an authentic rustic charm that all the leading-edge designers in Manhattan were aping with overpriced reclaimed pieces and vintage finishes.

Downstairs, she could see the space had indeed originally been used for the animals. The flagstone floor was uneven and heavily worn – and all the more beautiful for it – and there was a sense of a past vitality emanating from within these thick wattle walls, as though the generations of animals that had slept and fed here had somehow seeped into the fabric of the building. The kitchen, off to the right of the stairs, was enormous but clearly a practical area that had been carved latterly from the overall open-plan space. Rustic, hand-made olive-wood units were pressed back against the walls, their surfaces rubbed as smooth as marble; the butcher's block was stained dark from use and a long preparation table ran along the side wall with a stone basin and garden tap at one end. The stove was an electric one that looked fifty years old and fairly kaput, but she supposed that was easy enough to replace and wouldn't threaten the 'immediately habitable' stipulation that he had given in his brief. Personally, she liked best the stone staircase which rose between the kitchen and old stables – chalky and thick, with deep treads and low risers, it was dimpled with dinks, scuffs and knocks from over a century's use.

She had opened up the shuttered doors of the old stables while Joe was upstairs and she watched him as he came back and stood in the centre of the space that could, in theory, become a living room. He had his hands on his hips as he turned on the spot. The roof beams splayed out high above his head, the three walls behind and to the side of him as rough as the cliffs outside, the rockfaces simply painted white. If he wanted any shelves they would have to be free-standing, she mused, although the floor curved in subtle dips in some places. But the three enormous open doors gave onto the small, cracked terrace and the patchy lawn,

drenching the room with warmth and light, as she'd pre-
dicted. If he installed glazed windows here, perhaps Crittall
. . . it could look stunning.

'So, clearly the big drawback with this property is that
there's no sea view,' she said quietly, hesitant to intrude on
his thoughts.

'I don't mind that,' he murmured.

'Really?' It seemed somewhat pointless to her to buy a
holiday home all the way over here, on a Greek island, and
not actually have a sea view; again, it was another reason
she had left this one till last.

'No. The sea's easy enough to get to if I want to look out
over it. I want privacy, privacy, privacy!'

'Oh! Well, good,' she shrugged. It was to be his house
after all. 'And I guess you could always put a bench down
there if you wanted to catch the sunsets. Or even build
something perhaps – a pergola, have a table and chairs.'

'Yes, maybe.' He nodded. 'What about wifi? Mobile reception? Connectivity?'

'Patchy at best. You can get some 4G at the top of the sea
steps and at some points in the garden, but that's about it.'

He nodded, looking pleased. He looked back at her.
'You've done a good job, Chloe. I only briefed you – what,
eight days ago?'

'I leveraged our network; that's what we do.'

'You do it well.'

It was like being praised by her old headmaster when
she'd won the school spelling competition, and she felt ridiculously proud and pleased with herself. She stood back as
he wandered into the kitchen, again watching as his hands
trailed on the deep stone sills, seeing how his eyes narrowed
as he examined the integrity of the wooden windows. She

stayed where she was as he bounded up the steps for yet another look at the bedrooms; let him explore, this would be his playground. She could tell he loved it, and strangely, as unpredictable as he could be – charming one minute, abrupt the next – she liked him all the more for the fact that he wasn't seduced by the more obvious super-deluxe modernist condo or four-storey palatial mansions that his budget could buy. To her, it spoke well of him that he wanted something authentic and fitting. What did a single thirty-something like him need with a ten-bedroom villa anyway? She liked that he valued having peace and quiet over owning a status symbol, that he preferred his trees ancient and wild rather than clipped; that he would rather his only neighbours be wild goats. It said something about him, to her anyway – he had integrity, substance, soul.

Finally, his inspections complete, he came back to where she was waiting, sitting on one of the window sills. 'It's perfect. I'll take it.'

'*If* we can persuade the owners to sell,' she said, having to temper his excitement with a dose of reality. He'd insisted on seeing only not-for-sale properties but that came with inherent risks.

'Don't worry about that. They will. Just give me their details,' he said with a confidence that bordered on arrogance.

'Or I can negotiate for you. I'm used to it. In normal circumstances, I head up our Corporate Partnerships department so I'm more than used to—'

He shook his head, looking back at the room again. 'No. I'll do it myself.'

She felt offended; didn't he believe she could get him a good deal? She pushed herself back to standing. 'Well then, once you've done that, we'll start getting the paperwork drawn up. Procedure out here is that once an offer is accepted, you have to pay a ten per cent deposit to reserve the property.'

'That won't be necessary. I'll pay whatever they're asking, in full, upfront.'

'Well, it may not be that simple. We'll need to sort out importation of funds and that needs to be overseen and approved by the Bank of Greece. But we have a lawyer who can lead you through the process if you'd like, unless you want to use your own team?'

'There's no need,' he shrugged, turning away and walking back into the kitchen. 'The money's already in place.'

She frowned. 'It is?'

He turned back to her and blinked, nonplussed. She could tell he was distracted, thinking about things other than financial practicalities. 'Of course. I have business interests all over the world,' he murmured. 'But there is something else I'm going to need you to do for me.'

She suppressed a sigh, crossing her arms over her chest, feeling frustrated that he wanted her help, yet didn't at the same time. 'And what's that?'

The spreading smile across his face was languid, charming, even excited. 'We're going to need another plane.'

Chapter Eighteen

Provence

Her leg twisted around his like a vine, his thigh muscle firm even at rest, his body banded by tan lines at the wrist, ankle and neck. She rested a hand on his chest and looked up at him. He was dozing, his dark lips parted slightly, lashes throwing spidery shadows on his cheeks, dark hair curling on the pillow.

Across the small room, the thin cotton curtain fluttered at the open window, the babbling sounds of the market below drifting up like a rising tide. One of the pale-blue shutters hadn't been pinned back properly and was knocking against the wall intermittently in the breeze, sparrows fluttering onto the metal balcony balustrade for fleeting moments before flitting to another perch, always in search of the next crumb. Overhead, the ceiling fan whirred, a steady drumming that circulated the hot air, much like the jumbled thoughts in her head.

She dropped her head back on his chest. Why couldn't it always be like this?

His hand tightened around her shoulder. 'What are you thinking?' he murmured, voice heavy with sleep. She knew he was tired; he had been called out twice last night and his clinic had been full again this morning. She wasn't the only person he rescued.

'Why can't it always be like this?' she whispered.

'It can.'

She closed her eyes, one hot tear falling from her skin to his. '. . . No.'

Neither of them spoke. It was an argument they had had too many times; sometimes she started it, sometimes he, but the conclusion was always the same: these moments were the exception to the rule – snatched, stolen, rare; a fantasy for them both. Love wasn't the answer, it wasn't enough, it couldn't break the seal of reality that covered and smothered them both like a plastic-wrap tomb, in sight of each other but always a step removed.

The sound of the grille being pushed back from the pharmacy windows opposite made him sigh; it was the cue they had both been dreading, the moment they had been hoping to keep pushed back with their kisses and urgent touch. But they couldn't stop the clock's incessant march and his afternoon clinic would be starting soon, patients already arriving, their slow treads audible on the stone steps.

He kissed the top of her head, his lips lingering against her hair for several long moments, his stomach muscles hard against her hand. Then he rose from the wooden bed, walking naked across the room to where their clothes still lay in a tangle on the floor by the door.

Pulling the sheet against her, she watched as he stepped into his boxers, shrugging his shirt on with downturned eyes. His body was slim but not built, he spent too much time behind a desk for that; there was a quiet elegance to his physique: long legs and arms, narrow hands, oval face behind wire-rimmed glasses. He was younger than her by three years, but he had been her lifebuoy in the storm, her only safe anchor and she had grabbed on to him with the zeal of a drowning woman. She despised herself for drawing him into the entropy of her world; he was still fresh for life – open and calm, optimistic, hopeful, and she knew without question that although their love might save her, it would ruin him. How could she claim to adore him and yet knowingly continue to put him in harm's path? But the very thought of forsaking him . . . she wasn't strong enough to do this alone. He had saved her in more ways than one.

He buttoned up the white coat, hooking his glasses over his ears, and he looked at her, that familiar mix in his eyes of yearning and resignation that it would always be like this; that it couldn't possibly continue. For how much longer could they go on, sneaking around like this? All it would take was one sighting, one whisper and if her husband ever found out . . . She went cold. He was away for the week but he would be back at the weekend. He didn't yet know that things had changed. 'Thursday then?'

Their day. She nodded. 'Of course.'

A last longing look, the door closed with a click behind him and for a few minutes more, she stared at the painting on the opposite wall – a cliff scene with turquoise seas, white-sailed boats on the horizon. She felt hollow, scooped out, as she always did when their time together came to its inevitable end. It was the only thing she had to sustain her, the only thing that was true in a life built around lies, but the hours here were too fleeting and always, always felt as fragile as a butterfly's wing. She might be crushed at any moment . . .

Feeling the familiar prickle of fear, she rose and dressed quickly, taking care to tread lightly on the boards; his surgery was directly below. She could hear the hum of his voice coming up through the rafters, the scrape of a chair.

She got down on her knees to ensure nothing had rolled under the bed – not an earring or key, any lingering proof she had been up here. The clinic door was opening and closing frequently now, the buzz in the waiting room beginning to grow. But she didn't take the main stairs down. Heading through the small kitchen, she opened the door onto the fire escape and, with her shoes in her hands, silently picked her way barefoot down the iron treads. The feel of the hot ground on her soles was a relief but as she pushed her feet into her sandals, she knew she wasn't in the clear yet; she wouldn't be safe even in the back alleys that would bring her out to the Place Bonnet, three hundred metres away. No. Only when the crowds swallowed her whole and she was one of the faceless multitude could she breathe again and know she would live to see another day. At least until Thursday.

Hydra

They were panting again as they emerged through the pines. The combination of the craggy, hilly landscape and merciless sun made for a bootcamper's dream – in fact, Joe was more like a drill sergeant than an engineering boss the way he'd led their march – and they both stopped with their hands on their hips as they looked down at the view. The bay was small and deeply curved, the water an inviting turquoise, so clear she could see the rocks and stones from here. Some sunbathers were lying on brightly coloured towels on the fine-shingled beach – it was the nearest they got to sand here. A small building hugged the beach at the back, pale-blue wooden chairs and tables shaded beneath a woven rattan awning; she could see people sitting there already, their drinks glasses bubbling with condensation, elbows on the railings as they looked down towards the water. A few swimmers were splashing and playing bat and ball games in the shallows, others floating like starfish; a little further out, a few small motorboats were all bobbing out of time with one another.

Joe looked at her and grinned. He had taken off his t-shirt halfway up and the sweat trickled down his tanned, finely muscled body. She hadn't allowed herself the same privilege – she didn't have any swimwear with her and was wearing plain grey jersey Calvin Klein underwear beneath her new vest and shorts.

'Lunch?'

'Oh God, please,' she groaned. They had been 'exploring' for most of the morning. She had come down to breakfast to find he had already been into the port and 'settled everything' with the elderly couple who owned the farm-house. She had no idea what he'd done or how, but the agent had sent her a follow-up text, confirming the deeds would be with them by mid-afternoon, hence his idea of this excursion whilst they waited.

They began to walk down the slope, the stony path making it hard going with the threat of turned ankles. 'The locals must be as fit as fleas,' she mumbled, grateful that her boxing classes had meant she could keep up with him reasonably well.

Within half an hour they arrived in the bay of Limnioniza and headed straight for the tiny taverna, led by their noses and the wonderful aroma of freshly grilled fish.

'Two, please,' Joe said, holding up his fingers as a waitress met them on the deck.

She led them past a giant tank where lobsters were crawling, their pincers banded shut, antennae twitching and feeling hopelessly against the glass. They sat at a table in the back corner, overlooking the beach. There were only five tables in all and the others were taken, couples talking in low voices, everything in the dim shade seeming muted and gentle out of the fierce heat. Music played quietly in the background, the clatter of pans and the sudden sizzle of fish coming through from the kitchen.

'Last table? We got lucky,' he said to her, as the waitress handed them their menus.

'I get the feeling you were born lucky,' Chloe quipped, sinking back in the chair and basking in the relief that came from finally being in the shade. She checked her shoulders and arms for signs of sunburn. Unlike him, she couldn't expect to just turn golden; any colour she got would have to be earned, emerging slowly from beneath hundreds of applications of SPF.

'I think luck's a state of mind. What's the saying? The harder I work, the luckier I get?' he said, eyes flicking up to her, before flitting off again as he scanned the menu. 'Shall we have beer and the fish of the day?' he asked her as the waitress set down paper napkins and fresh cutlery in front of them.

'Sure,' she nodded, as he ordered that.

She checked her phone. She had missed a call from Pelham. She dialled voicemail and put it to her ear, marvelling that she could get reception here.

'Chloe, darling.' His voice was like warm caramel being poured into her ear. 'The river cruise was splendid! So special. It was raining torrents of petals. Rissa simply loved it.

Well, apart from the petal that hit her straight in the eye when she looked up. We were worried it might have scratched her cornea but the doctor gave her some drops and said it should be fine in a day or two. But apart from that, darling, just wonderful. I don't know how you do it, coming up with these things!' Chloe suppressed a smile. Poor Rissa. Pelham's seduction techniques ought to come with a health and safety warning. 'Anyway, we're just heading over to Washington – the state, not the city. A friend's granddaughter is getting married and they're letting us barge in. I don't suppose you could be a sweetheart and think of a gift for the girl? She's twenty-two I think . . . Is she? Yes, I think that's it. Brown hair anyway.' Chloe arched an eyebrow. That was *it*? She was supposed to find a wedding gift on the strength of that? 'We're just at the airport now but I'll send you our address for where we're staying in Seattle. Thanks ever so – you're a darling. Toodlepip.'

She disconnected with a sigh. Joe was watching her. 'They're a high-maintenance breed, your clients,' he said with a wry look, pouring them both some water which the waitress had brought over, along with olives, bread and oil.

'They?' She gave him a knowing look. 'You don't include yourself in that group?'

He gestured to the tiny taverna. 'Does this look high-maintenance to you?'

'But we came here by private jet. On the turn of a sixpence. That's high-maintenance; it isn't *normal*.'

'Define "normal",' he said, tearing off a hunk of still-warm bread and dipping it in the olive oil.

'For people like me?'

He shrugged as he popped the bread in his mouth, and looked at her, waiting. He had put his t-shirt back on as they'd come into the taverna, which she personally thought was a shame.

'Okay then. Well, I guess I'd say, for most people, normal is eating the same thing for breakfast every morning; it's having to choose between affording a festival or a holiday. It's only ever buying second-hand cars and living to a budget. It's having to go without more times than with. It's working till you're sixty-five.'

'You make it sound so fun,' he quipped.

'Don't mock! You asked and I'm telling you – that's what normal is.'

'And I agree,' he shrugged.

'. . . You *do*?' The scepticism rang out in her voice.

He looked at her interestedly. 'Of course. But if you ask me, normal isn't as mundane as you're making out; some of us might say it's a luxury – getting to live in a house that's a home and not an asset; climbing into bed next to your wife every night instead of having to get on a plane. It's having home-cooked food that someone who loves you has made for you, not the latest star chef. Pets. Kids. The school run. Weekly shopping trips. The whole caboodle.'

She stared at him. 'Exactly.'

'Exactly.'

She frowned, losing the thread of his argument – which side of 'normal' was he on? This was supposed to be a debate, not an agreement. 'But that's not real for you. That's not your reality.'

'I guess we've all got to have something to aspire to,' he shrugged, reaching for an olive.

She wasn't sure whether to laugh or not. Was he being for real? His sense of humour was so dry, so spare, sometimes she couldn't quite tell. Sometimes she even felt like they switched roles and she was the client, the one who was indulged, pampered, spoilt . . .

The waitress brought over their meals – grilled sea bass, roasted tomatoes, sautéed potatoes, wilted spinach.

'I feel so virtuous,' she said, looking at it.

'That's a shame.' And when she looked up at him in surprise. 'Joke!' he said, quickly holding his hands up in surrender. '. . . It was too good to miss.'

She chuckled. The boundaries between them had begun to shift, as she had known they would. It simply wasn't possible to be in the exclusive company of someone else, twenty-four-seven, and not begin to drop her guard.

She checked her phone for messages again but the signal was patchy, to put it mildly. 'Well, the plane landed in Athens an hour ago, on schedule. So the boat should be almost loaded and they'll be en route here shor—' she said, spearing a tomato. Hot juice squirted out of it, straight onto her white vest. 'Oh my God!' she moaned, dabbing at it frantically with her napkin, but the damage was already done. 'I can't believe that just happened!'

She looked up to find Joe grinning. He had a particular way of smiling more with his eyes than his mouth. 'I can.'

'I look like a bloody toddler,' she complained, dunking the corner of the napkin into her water glass and trying again to remove the mark. But she only succeeded in making it look more noticeable as the water stain bled through the fabric. 'Oh great. And now I look like I've been shot too!' She sat back in the chair, her arms falling forlornly to her sides.

'Take it off,' he shrugged, resuming eating.

She looked horrified. 'I can't do that.'

'Why not?' He glanced behind her. 'Everyone else is in their swimwear.'

She turned around and looked at the other diners. Several of the other women were in just their bikinis, the paper napkins spread beneath their legs to stop them from sticking to the chairs.

'Yes, but I don't have any,' she murmured. No way was she sitting here in her bra.

He sighed. 'Chloe, it's a beach. A bikini is simply waterproof underwear. It doesn't matter. Nobody cares.'

Nobody? Well, when he put it like that . . . And it was true her taste veered to the sportier styles. It wasn't like she'd be sitting here in a lace balconette.

Reluctantly, she peeled off the wet vest. She could feel his eyes gallantly staying resolutely glued to his plate as she arranged it over the railing to dry in the sun, and they ate in silence for several minutes.

'So, you were saying – the boat's leaving Athens imminently; what's the time frame?' he asked.

'Well, because there's so much cargo, we couldn't get one of the high-speed craft, so they've said it's a sailing time of three and a half hours to here. Then of course they've got to unload it all and get it over to the house.'

'You've booked the donkeys?' he asked, reaching for his beer.

'I've booked pretty much every donkey on the island,' she said.

He looked pleased. 'So we're talking, what – six o'clock tonight? Thereabouts?'

'Pretty much. The head donkey guy's going to text me.'

'So what shall we do for the rest of the day, then?' he mused, looking out to sea.

Please no more walking. 'Lie on the beach? Sleep? Sleep sounds good to me.'

'Yeah, we could,' he said, his eyes on the water. 'Or we could get a boat.'

'Boat? What kind of a boat?' Oh God, what now?

'I saw a yacht for hire in the harbour earlier.'

'Oh did you?' she asked. She had seen it too. A stunning glossy navy-blue hulled schooner with blonde-wood decks and a mast that seemed to reach to the top of the encircling hill.

'Yeah, in fact, I made a point of getting the number,' he said, rummaging in his shorts pocket and pushing it across the table to her. 'Shall we hire it for the afternoon? They could bring it round here to pick us up.'

'Well I guess that's one way of avoiding the walk back,' she quipped and he cracked a smile at her flippancy as he continued to eat. 'As I was saying,' she murmured, beginning to dial. 'Not normal.'

The yacht, *Olympia*, all forty metres of her, prompted a crowd on its feet as she nosed round the headland. Chloe heard the murmurs of delight as the other beachgoers sat up on their towels, turned round on their lilos and stood in the shallows as it became clear she was dropping anchor.

'There she is,' Joe said, just a few metres higher than her. 'God, she's a beauty.'

It was another few moments before Chloe had scrambled up the rocks to be able to see for herself (given that she was now stripped down to just her underwear, she was insisting he went ahead). This was Joe's idea of 'taking it easy' until *Olympia* arrived – climbing on the rocks like they were children. It was a fun, if unexpected, pursuit for a multi-millionaire engineer. But then, he seemed to defy convention and expectation at every turn. She couldn't get a clear handle on him. Some moments, he seemed so utterly normal – eating in street food markets and little tavernas, wearing jeans and t-shirts like the masses; the next he was dropping money-bombs, chartering jets and yachts like they were pedalos.

'Oh wow,' she breathed, taking in *Olympia*'s sinuous curves and sleek lines. Joe had looked her up online as Chloe had made the booking: she had fifteen-metre over-hangs, two deckhouses and two cockpits, with one of each reserved for the client.

They sat on the rocks and watched along with the rest of the beach as the boat turned in a stately glide, her prow facing out to sea.

'We should probably get back to the beach, then,' she said, glancing across at their pile of clothes still sitting on the sand; naturally they hadn't packed towels. Joe had said he wanted to dive off the rocks; she was planning a much more gentle jump in, holding her nose – losing her knickers was not on the agenda. 'They'll send in a crew with the tender in a moment and it wouldn't do for us not to be there.'

'Yeah. Or we could swim out to her ourselves.'

She looked at him. 'What?'

'Why not? We wanted a swim anyway and she's not that far out.'

'Define "not that far".' It was going to be like the 'normal' conversation all over again.

He glanced across at her, grinning. His teeth seemed extra white against his dark beard, his golden skin. God, he was—

'What about our clothes, though?' she asked, pulling her-self back. 'We can't leave them on the beach!'

'That's fine. They can send the crew in to get those.'

'Uh-huh.' He had an answer for everything, she knew.

There would be no getting out of this. She looked out at the yacht again. It had to be a good three hundred metres away.

'Come on,' he said, rising to a stand, his muscles flexed as he found his balance on the rock and looked down, checking his entry. And then, without a second thought, he pinned his arms above his head and soared through the air. It was like watching an eagle go into a stoop, everything perfectly pitched, taut, braced. He entered with minimal splash, surfacing a second later and throwing his head back, droplets flying through the air like a crystal rainbow. 'Come in!' he yelled up, looking like a god. 'The water's lovely.'

'Chloe?'

'Hi!' She felt a rush of relief to hear Alexander's voice, that he'd been able to catch her. She had cleared her phone of Tom's messages as quickly as she'd been able to yesterday, but she had still been niggled by the fear that she had missed a call from him and that he hadn't been able to get through; he didn't usually go more than a couple of days without ringing in and it had been four now since they'd spoken last. Not to mention, after what Xan had told her yesterday morning, she had concerns that Serena might have tried to muscle in on Poppy's patch and poach her star client. 'How are you?'

'Where are you? The ring tone is different.' His tone was brusque.

'I'm in Greece.'

'On holiday?' He sounded stressed.

She looked across at Joe. He was stretched out on his stomach on the sundeck, reading a Robert Harris thriller and wearing a new pair of khaki swimming shorts with a neon rainbow stitched across the bum.

She got up from her shaded spot on the sunken sofa and walked across to the handrails, looking down into the dappled waters. Sunlight flitted off the refracted surface like electric fairies, tiny silver fish whipping past in tight shoals. A shallow ripple of foam looked like lace against the hull as *Olympia* cut through the sea like a knife through hot butter. She extended a leg and dipped a bare toe into the sunlight. 'No, helping a client, but I'm still absolutely here for you too. What's up?'

'I'm in India.'

'Okay.'

'I've brought a client – one of the investors I was telling you about; he wants to see the Taj Mahal but the idiot concierge in the hotel here has just told me it is covered in scaffolding.'

In the background, she could hear a man's voice: 'But it is being cleaned, sir. An eighteen-month programme.'

'Did you hear that?' Alexander demanded. 'Eighteen months! I can't wait eighteen months! I told my client I'd show him the Taj Mahal.'

'Of course not,' Chloe agreed calmly. 'It's a preposterous suggestion.'

'Prewhat?' he snapped.

'Nothing. Listen, I'm on it. Can you stay there another night? I know it's inconvenient but I'll have it all down for you by tomorrow.' She pinched her temples with one hand; what was she saying?

'Fine.' He still sounded grumpy. 'But tell them the poles must be moved out of sight. I don't want them on the ground, making the place look messy.' His accent was in full colours today.

She rolled her eyes. 'Don't worry about a thing. I'll call you back in an hour to confirm.'

He hung up and she let out an exasperated groan. 'For *fuck's* sake,' she muttered under her breath.

Or so she thought.

'I heard that.'

She looked up to find Joe padding across the deck to her, an utterly amused look on his face. 'Somebody being unreasonable?'

'No,' she said quickly. Too quickly.

He smirked, clearly not believing her, making his way over to the bar. 'Want to tell me what it is?'

She watched him go. It was fast becoming normal to see him half-naked. 'I can't. Client confidentiality.'

'Ah. You take that seriously, do you?' He opened a bottle of Watenshi gin, flashing a glance her way.

'Of course,' she said, almost insulted that her professional integrity should be questioned.

He didn't say anything for a moment and she watched as he poured the gin over crushed ice in two tumblers, then some tonic, before tossing in a piece of pink grapefruit. It was their third of the day – not to mention their beers at lunch – and it was only just gone three o'clock. Currently, they were off the coast of Poros.

'Good,' he said finally, bringing the drinks over and handing one to her, his gaze seeming to snag upon her momentarily before he made his way back to the deck and his book.

She cast a quick look down at herself in the olive-green bikini; her swimwear – like his new, dry shorts – had come with the yacht, a whole drawerful of it in fact: Melissa

239

Odabash, Heidi Klein, Manuel Canovas, Princesse Tam Tam . . . all brand new and tagged.

She glanced back at Joe, startled to find him already looking over at her, his gaze inscrutable behind his sunglasses as he took a sip of his drink. Without a word, he went back to his book.

Heart pounding a little harder than she would have liked in such a revealing bikini, she took her phone back into the salon; unlike him, she was here to work, not play. She had some phone calls to make.

He had fallen asleep when she came back out forty-five minutes later, his Wayfarers dropped onto his book, his left cheek pressed against his hands. He looked different when he slept, that guarded reserve that he wore most of the time shed like a snake's skin. She took in the long stroke of his eyelashes, the small parting between his pinkish-brown lips, the crease between his shoulder blades as the muscles there nudged against each other . . . he had somehow managed to clip back the beard so that it was more of a stubble again. He was a stunning-looking man. Elle had had the right idea wanting his number and that was without even knowing the package that came with him too – that plane, this boat, money no object, a lifestyle where nothing was out of reach . . . It was a crying shame he was her client, she thought to herself, settling herself down on her tummy on the white, navy-piped towelling cushions too and feeling the heat on her skin, closing her eyes for just a minute . . .

She opened her eyes and, for a moment, didn't know what she was seeing. Another eye, up close, doesn't look as it does from a distance and she could see the pupil shrink and bloom, making the cocoa-coloured iris seem to sway and dance. He was watching her now, his hands still folded under his cheeks as though they were lovers in bed, eye to eye, legs interlinked . . .

She felt the colour creep up her cheeks.

'The jet lag,' she murmured as though it was an explanation, an apology, pulling herself away and up onto her elbows and breaking the eyelock.

'Tell me about it.'

'Have you been awake for long?' She wasn't sure she wanted to hear the answer to that.

'A while.' He shifted position, rolling onto his side slightly, resting his head in his left hand. 'Who's Tom?'

'What?' The word snapped out of her as though on a catapult.

He watched her. 'You said the name when you were asleep.'

'I did?' He nodded. 'Oh . . . He's no one.'

He arched an eyebrow, watching her as she moved herself up to a sitting position and made a point of looking at the craggy parched coastline off the starboard side. 'Does he wear a bow tie?'

She ignored the question; it was none of his business and he knew it. Those drinks had gone to both their heads and he was overstepping the mark – watching her sleep, pressing her about her ex; what did he think he was doing? Did he think she came with the membership fee? 'What time is it?'

There was a pause. 'Almost four.'

She saw that they were no longer cruising but had dropped anchor in a small bay, pale rocky cliffs encircling them, the sun a white blaze that bleached the sky; the water here was dappled green and blue, domed rocks far below them sprouting grassy seaweed. It looked so tempting, enticing. She wanted to dive in. They both needed to cool down.

He watched her, reading her mind. 'Another swim?'

'Oh, I should probably check my messages,' she said, pulling back. She needed to be sure everything was being followed to the letter in India, that her order for Pelham's gift was being delivered in Seattle; and she couldn't afford to miss any more calls. 'It's so busy at the moment; I don't want to let anyone down.'

'Well you'll let *me* down if you don't,' he said as she grabbed her phone and began to scroll.

'I *do* have other clients, you know,' she said, shooting him a look from under her lashes.

'But I'm the most important.'

She laughed, a mocking smile on her lips. He was so cocky. If he only knew who her other clients were: nobody but nobody could eclipse the might of Alexander Subocheva. 'Oh, you think so?' she scoffed lightly.

'I know so.' And taking the phone from her hand, he tossed it onto the nearby sofa, out of reach.

'Joe!' She scrambled up to get it but he caught her by the wrist.

'Come on. In!' he said, tugging her over to the side of the boat.

'Joe, no!' she laughed, pulling back into a squat. 'It would be lovely, really, but I have other clients; I have to work.'

'This *is* work,' he said, shocking her with a sudden wink – and then jumping overboard.

She screamed as she was pulled over too, the drop in her stomach as she fell instantly extinguished by the cool embrace of the water. She surfaced, spluttering, pushing her hair back from her face, to find him grinning.

'See?' He pushed onto his back and floated on the surface as though he – they – had not a care in the world. 'Working.'

She worked for the rest of the day. They jumped off the top of the cliffs – only three metres high here – and swam off the rocks. The yacht came with all the toys too, the snorkelling kit being the very least of it, although they whiled away over an hour covering the bay, kicking lazily side by side as he pointed out an octopus to her and she found a starfish. She laughed until she almost cried as he had a go on the aquatic jetpack, face-planting several times into the water, before finally getting the hang of it and looking like Bond as he hovered at deck level and asked for some fruit – just to prove his dexterity and control.

'Ever been on one of these?' he asked later, pointing to the jetbike.

'No,' she replied, knowing exactly what was coming next. She had given up protesting. If Joe Lincoln wanted something, it happened.

'Come on then.'

They watched from the deck as one of the crew winched it into the water, both of them shrugging on the lifejackets.

'I'll go first,' he said, eyeing up the sleek machine. It might as well have been a Lamborghini, he looked so excited by it.

'Oh will you?' she challenged, not even having to say it as he looked across at her.

A second later, they were both in the water, splashing and laughing and coughing as they raced to get to it first, neither one of them aqua-dynamic in the buoyancy vests. Naturally, he won.

'Only because you're taller. You have a height advantage,' she panted, still laughing as she kicked back in the water and looked up, watching him settle on the seat. 'So in real terms, it was a draw. In which case it should be ladies first. If you were a gentleman you'd let me go first.'

He looked down at her. 'That's skewed logic you've got,' he said, a dark light gleaming in his eyes. 'And I've never said I'm a gentleman.'

She stuck her tongue out at him. Not her most eloquent riposte but sometimes, when he looked at her, she felt he tore the words away from her. Or the ground. Or the breath.

'Tell you what, I shall be magnanimous in victory –' He reached down a hand, offering to haul her up too. 'Come on. There's plenty of room.' He shuffled forward slightly on the seat.

'No, I was only joking,' she grinned, kicking away from the bike again, floating easily in the lifejacket. 'You go first. I'll just watch.'

'Get up here.' His arm was still outstretched.

Swallowing – knowing he didn't respond to being told 'no' – she reached up and with a single tug was out of the water, balancing on the narrow lip that skirted around the bike. It wasn't a tandem and although the seat was deep for one, two would be a push.

'Look, it's—' she said nervously.

'Just sit down,' he said, talking over his shoulder.

Biting her lip nervously, she swung her leg round and scuttled onto the seat behind him. There was just about enough room if she pressed herself as much as was possible against his back; the lifejackets didn't make it easy but there were no handholds, nowhere to put her arms.

'Holding on?'

With no other option, she tentatively circled her arms around his waist. He smelled salty and earthy all at once, his arms twice the girth as they came down over hers.

He revved the throttle and she automatically tightened her grip, braced for the sudden acceleration from nought to sixty. When it came, and she screamed, she felt him laugh, the vibrations from his chest pressing through her. The wind whipped back her hair as they zipped across the water's surface, whizzing past the boat. To her surprise, she saw the crew winching down a second jetbike.

'Oh!' she cried, raising one hand to point it out to Joe, to show him.

But he couldn't have seen it or heard her, because in the next moment he took a hard left facing out to sea and sped them away faster and faster, making her scream with delight, the yacht at both their backs.

Chapter Nineteen

She had never seen so many donkeys in her life.

'What's the collective noun for a group of donkeys?' she gasped as they emerged, still breathless from the climb up the steps, through the olive grove onto the dishevelled garden. 'A herd?'

'A drove, I think.'

There had to be at least thirty-five of them tethered to various trees, their colourful leather reins slack around their necks, backs bare of burden as their handlers swarmed, lifting heavily plastic-wrapped sofas, tables, chairs, a small wardrobe, up to the house. The little terrace was almost lost from sight under the amount of furniture deposited there, an entire home set outside on the doorstep, waiting to be carried over the threshold.

Chloe looked across at Joe questioningly. He wanted her to create order from this chaos?

He shrugged. 'It won't be as bad as it looks.'

'You don't think?' she scoffed, looking back at the pile of furniture and boxes. 'I think you've confused me for a big strapping Kiwi house mover.'

He glanced across at her, his quick up-down like fingers raking over her skin. 'No, I *definitely* haven't confused you for that,' he said in an oblique tone.

They walked up to the house and she put her head through the doorway. An assortment of leather-skinned men were milling about – oh God, more boxes, she saw – many of them talking in hurried Greek, some of them shrugging their shoulders, others shaking their heads.

'Hello. Hello. Chloe,' she said, placing a hand on her chest and smiling as they noticed her, the buzz of conversation dying down. 'Thank you.' She gestured to the boxes and furniture that had been placed all around. 'Thank you. Very kind.'

The men looked at her; they seemed to be waiting for something. Then she remembered. 'Oh God, payment. Yes, right.'

She patted her shorts but even as she did, she knew she hadn't put her purse in them; it was still in her bag on the boat.

'Don't worry, I've got it,' Joe murmured from behind her, pulling a wallet out from his cargo shorts and beginning to peel off fifty-euro notes. Chloe looked on in as much astonishment as the men gathered round, all waiting to be paid. How much cash did that man carry?

One by one, the donkey owners filed away in a procession, the retreating jingle of cowbells marking their progress over the dirt road and the long, hilly walk back to the port.

She looked on wistfully as they departed, wishing they would stay and help. 'Oh God, they've carried all that stuff this far, can't they carry it the final few yards?' she asked as the last few walked away over the scorched earth.

'Absolutely not,' he said, watching them leave too. 'This is the fun part.'

Fun? She was about to retort he clearly didn't know the meaning of the word, but the day they had just spent together had been the very definition of it. She hadn't stopped laughing – or screaming; he seemed to take pleasure in making her do one or the other and for a girl whose heart had just been broken – for the second time – she had done a remarkably good impression of being happy. Stepping out of her own life, into his, had been exactly the recovery she'd needed.

'What first then?' she asked.

'Well, if you can take that sofa there, I'll get this,' he said, picking up a small cardboard box.

Chloe's jaw dropped. He had to be kidding?

'*Joking*,' he grinned, walking up and putting the box in her arms. His eyes were positively dancing with merriment and she felt a complicated whirl in her stomach at the sight of it. His teases felt provocative, always unnerving her.

'Haha,' she smiled, dropping her gaze.

They worked well as a team. He had been surprisingly well organized when putting everything into storage in France, the boxes all being marked with different colour dots and each dot signifying a particular room – so yellow for the kitchen, green for the sitting room, purple for the master bedroom, red for the bedroom opposite, orange for the bathroom and so on. She unpacked all but the purple-dotted boxes; he said he'd do those himself.

The big furniture wasn't bad either; even those large pieces which he couldn't move alone were fine when shared between the two of them, although she suspected he was taking most of the weight of everything and she was simply there to balance things. A gentleman after all, then?

The bones of the building were strong – high ceilings, beautiful windows, aged floors – so it was easy to dress; in fact, it was rather like playing house when she'd been a girl.

Almost everything seemed to be vintage and his taste was a lot more eclectic than she would have supposed. They put a faded coral-pink linen sofa in the old stable – or rather, the living room as it was now – with sky-blue linen armchairs at either end and a colourful Moroccan rug was unrolled over the flags; a big painted table and original 1960s rainbow-coloured butterfly chairs were set in the middle of the kitchen; they brought the wooden bedstead up in bits, Joe sitting on the floor for the best part of an hour while he wrestled with screws and nuts and bolts, much to Chloe's amusement. 'You know, as the boss of an engineering con-glomerate, I would have expected you to be rather more . . . dextrous,' she grinned – her turn to tease – as he struggled with an Allen key.

It was dark by the time they finished several hours later, and with the electricity supply not yet reconnected – she made a note to chase it in the morning – they unpacked the last few boxes of towels, bedding and the like by the light of a church candle they had found on a window sill in one of the bedrooms.

'Well,' Chloe said, looking pretty pleased with herself as she looked around at the almost-finished result. It was still sparsely furnished of course, and there was much that still needed to be brought over, but this was a solid start; the rooms had character now, the house feeling more loved already. 'I'll give you this – you've got good taste, Joe Lin-coln. But you *really* didn't need me at all.'

'*Au contraire*. You knock the spots off all the big strapping Kiwis I know.'

She laughed. 'What are we going to do with all this pack-aging?' The boxes were piled six feet high, great sails of polythene wrapping lying in tangled heaps. She bent down to scoop some up, stuffing it into the nearest box where no one could trip on it. She took another box and, setting it on its side, stood on it, expecting it to buckle beneath her weight. But it stood firm.

'Oh.' She wiggled a little and gave several small jumps before the box began to crease and fold. But it wasn't a straightforward collapse: one corner gave out first, tipping her sideways. 'Ohhhh!'

She lurched forwards, Joe just catching her like she was a gymnast as she pitched towards a side table. She felt his arms close like a vice and for a second she was too shocked to do anything but stare up at him, open-mouthed and wide-eyed. But then, the shock abated – and he was still holding her.

She blinked once. Twice. That crackle that kept shooting between them was threatening to catch and ignite. She saw it in the way he was looking at her.

'That would have been nasty,' he said finally, setting her upright again.

'Yes,' she said. 'Thank you.' She felt shaken – not by the fall but the capture. The moment that had flashed between them as his face was above hers, flickering in the candle-light, couldn't be taken back. Ignored perhaps, but it was as though a seal had been broken and air was rushing in. She had a sense of momentum, of inevitability. Every hour, every minute that they spent in each other's company, invisible lines were being crossed.

A protracted silence pulsed between them as loudly as any dance-floor beat. She wasn't sure what to say, where to look, where to put herself as he just stood there, watching her, as though what happened next was *her* decision.

'I guess we should get back to the boat and return to the hotel,' she said finally, turning away.

'. . . Yes.'

He walked across to the candle and blew it out; darkness swarmed but still the air felt charged, alight, as though suffused with electromagnetic rods.

She found the flashlight on her phone and waited on the terrace as he locked up. She looked back at the proud farmhouse, hidden from civilization, the retreat he had wanted so badly, so impatiently. He had seen it for the first time yesterday evening and now it was his, already filled with his things.

She still didn't know the details of how he had made it all happen so fast, but what was it he'd said to her that night at the Basquiat retrospective? 'Spontaneity is money's single greatest gift.' He had simply visited the old couple in the town before breakfast and by the end of the day, he was moving in. That was how things played out in his world. Why wait? If he wanted something, he simply went after it and made it his.

Was he doing the same with her now?

By the light of their flashlights, they walked over the ruined lawn, his hand – accidentally – brushing against hers once or twice as they dodged the larger rocks; they walked past the crumbling stone wall and through the grove of olive trees that looked like wizened statues in the moonlight. Not a word passed between them as they followed their own beams of light down the gentle slope to the sea. What was there to say? She had a feeling any conversation would just be diversion, cover. There was an unspoken truth now that was demanding to be addressed.

At the cliffs, they looked down at the moored yacht

bobbing gently on the dark sea, her lights gentle and discreet on the water, ready to take them back to civilization and back to the hotel, as though knowing what awaited them there. He let her go first down the steps and she stepped back onto the boat with a light foot – and frantically beating heart.

Chapter Twenty

She stood in her bedroom, looking out to sea, arms wrapped around herself as she watched the lights of a far-off water tanker glide across the horizon. She barely dared to move from the spot; she knew exactly what would happen if she joined him for dinner.

The invitation had been innocuous enough – they were after all two colleagues (of sorts), together in a foreign country – but there was an undeniable undercurrent to their conversations now, a buzz in their silences, a light in their eyes that only seemed to be growing, and she couldn't pretend otherwise. Even though he was her client. Even though she had followed him here with the single-minded pursuit of making her life simpler, not of complicating it further with him. Greece was supposed to have been her escape as much as his.

No, staying here, in her room, was the right thing to do, the safe thing, and tomorrow she would catch the ferry to the mainland and the first flight back from Athens. She could leave him here in his Greek retreat, knowing she had done her job. She would fly back to New York, where she would see Poppy, face Jack and of course—

Tom. She had come back to another block of missed calls and messages – they were all frustrated and angry now, her continuing silence the slap in the face that told him everything he needed to know, just not why.

A quiet knock at the door made her turn and she stared at it with a look, as though she expected it to fly off its hinges at any moment. What was Joe doing? Hadn't her refusal of dinner been clear enough?

She stared at it, feeling the blood rush around her head. She didn't know what to do. Should she pretend she wasn't here? That she'd gone for a walk in the port? But, with her heart pounding, she found herself walking across the room.

She stopped behind it, remonstrating with herself. She shouldn't open it. This was a bad idea—

And yet she did it anyway.

'Oh.' She was surprised – and crushed – to find a quartet of waiters standing there. 'Mr Lincoln said you would prefer to have dinner in your room?'

She hadn't ordered anything yet; he had taken the liberty of ordering for her? 'Oh. Yes.' She stepped back, allowing them into the room, watching as two of them brought through a small square table, one a chair, and the other a large tray of silver-cloche-covered food. One of them had a wine bucket, filled with ice and a bottle of sauvignon blanc.

She sank onto the bed, getting out of their way, and picked up a Greek gossip magazine, pretending to look at the pictures as they set up on the balcony; she pretended not to notice her own disappointment, she refused to admit how gutted she felt that he had taken her at her word.

'Dinner is ready, Miss Marston,' the lead waiter said, coming back into the room a few minutes later. 'Would you like me to pour your wine?'

'No, that's fine, I'll sort myself out, thank you.'

She tipped and the four of them left, closing the door behind them with a quiet click.

Well that was that then, she told herself, standing in the middle of the room. Dinner in her room it was. Alone. For the night. Safe as houses.

They were obviously both of the same view after all.

With a sigh, she walked out onto the balcony. The waiters had dressed the table with a mink-grey linen tablecloth, a pale-pink candle flickering in a storm glass, her wine glass a rose-hued dimpled tumbler—

'Good evening.'

The voice to her right made her jump and she looked across to find Joe on his balcony, beside hers. Although not interconnected, they were only a metre apart – and he too had an individual dinner table laid out identically to hers.

'Great idea having dinner in our rooms,' he said drily as she gawped at the sight. 'I like it.' He raised his glass and toasted her, his gaze as steady as her hands *weren't*. '. . . Are you going to sit?'

With a laugh of utter disbelief, she sank down into her chair. The tables had been set at angles, so that the two of them faced diagonally towards each other.

'Would you like me to pour your wine?'

'And how are you going to do that?' she laughed again, imagining him ridiculously leaning over the balcony and risking a forty-foot fall in the name of good manners.

He grinned, picking up his cutlery. 'I wasn't sure what you like to eat so I made a guess for the lamb. Please don't tell me you're a vegetarian.'

'No. I'm not a vegetarian,' she smiled, pouring herself a glass of wine and sipping it.

'Thank God for that.'

She swallowed nervously. Thank God for that forty-foot drop more like, she thought, taking another sip of wine. Across the narrow breach that divided them, the candlelight threw shadows up the planes of his face which, already half covered by beard, only served to emphasize his deep-set, rich brown eyes; they were expressive, still playful.

Picking up her weapons too, she began to carve the cutlet and went to bring it to her mouth – before getting a fit of the giggles.

'This is ridiculous!' she laughed, dropping it on the plate again.

'Why?'

'We ought to have just eaten together downstairs.'

'But you wanted to eat in your room,' he said simply.

'Well yes, but—'

'But?' His look was a challenge, daring her to say it – that she wanted to be alone; that she didn't trust him, or herself to be together now.

'Nothing. This is lovely. Very . . . inspired.'

He arched an eyebrow. 'Could you pass the salt?'

'Huh?'

'The salt?' He flicked his eyes towards the condiment set on her table.

'Oh, yes . . .' She picked it up and half rose from her chair, leaning over the chunky stone wall and handing it to him.

'Thanks,' he said, his gaze catching hold of her as though she really might fall, his fingertips brushing hers.

Was it just her or was it hot out here? She felt the sweat prickle her skin. Ten o'clock at night and still 28 degrees; she would never get used to it. It was definitely the heat.

'So did you manage to make those calls?' he asked, not so far away.

256

'Pretty much,' she nodded; it had been the perfect excuse for getting away from him when they'd got back here. Alexander had called again and left a message – his wife was going to be staying on the yacht for a few nights to catch some sea breeze; apparently it was oppressively humid on the mainland. Could she arrange for two hundred white peonies to be delivered and arranged on board before she arrived tomorrow night? He wanted to make it 'homely' for her. And Mike Greenleve had needed another private medic who would sign a non-disclosure agreement and fly out to Hawaii; the other doctor she'd sourced was refusing to treat his lead artist now and without a methadone prescription, no music was going to be made. Plus Rosaria had called again, this time detailing in exacting fury just why she needed Chloe to ring her back – someone had made the mistake of putting lilies in her dressing room. Someone had to be fired.

'You must need the patience of a saint, doing what you do.'

'Not at all. You are all complete pussycats.'

He caught her ironic edge and shot her a bemused look. 'It can't be all bad, surely. Today was fun. You could hardly classify it as work.'

'You just had me heavy-lifting!'

'You were easily up to it.' His eyes flashed and flipped her stomach easily. 'Besides, the rest was good. Wasn't it?'

The question was loaded and she kept her eyes down. 'Mm hmm, great fun,' she said non-committally, pretending to have trouble spearing a carrot. 'The image of you face-planting in your jetpack will sustain me for many weeks to come.'

'You're supposed to think of me, perfectly pitched,

hovering at the deck in a great display of masculine power.'
He watched her as she chuckled, a faint smile playing on his
own lips. Her amusement seemed to amuse him. There was
a little silence. 'So I take it you're still intending to leave
tomorrow?'

The question caught her off-guard. Still? Was he suggesting
there was a reason her plans should have changed? '. . . Yes.
I'm booked on the first flight.'

'That's a shame,' he said in a tone she couldn't quite
place.

'Well there's a lot going on in New York,' she said, keeping her tone light. 'I've been gone long enough as it is. They
need me.'

'And I don't?'

'No, you don't, my work here is done!' she scoffed playfully, still not looking up. She did not dare. 'How long are
you staying for, anyway?' she asked, determined to move
the conversation along. 'You've got the rest of the summer
ahead of you after all – exactly as you wanted.'

'Actually, I'm going to France tomorrow night.'

'France?'

He shrugged, eating his meal with the same studied concentration as he had at their first lunch together.

'But then you'll come back?' That had been the point after
all, the reason for his urgency: he wanted to spend the
summer here.

She watched him as he stopped eating – as though giving
up on it – and sat back in his chair, taking a slug of wine and
resting his eyes upon her once more. 'Yes, probably.'

A gust of night breeze rustled round them both, blowing
his hair lightly around his face, pressing his shirt against his
torso. The candles flickered in their storm lamps, swaying

dangerously but never blowing out. His face danced in the half-light, all angles and shadows, secrets and promises.

'How lucky,' she sighed, looking out to sea. 'So all this will become routine for you.'

'I don't think this could ever be routine for me.' She had meant the view, the hot night air, the food, this ticklish breeze – but he hadn't. His eyes were on her as certainly as any touch.

She met his eyes this time and saw he was beginning to push. She knew she had to tell him – about her terrible taste in men and how it had nothing at all to do with bow ties, but with fiancées and being gullible. 'Joe, look—'

'Could you pass me the wine?'

She paused. What? 'The wine?'

'Yes, I want to try the sauvignon. I'm not rating the Asti.'

'Oh. Right.' She reached back for the bottle in the ice bucket and half rose in her chair again; he had already come to stand at the wall of his balcony. 'There you go.'

'Thanks,' he said as she held it out for him. But it wasn't the bottle he reached for, his hand closing instead around her wrist. Her gaze fell to her own arm as she felt him pull her up towards him so that they were both standing now – her holding the bottle, him holding her.

It wasn't accidental. He wasn't being gallant. He was bringing into the open the electricity that was surging between them. No more pretending, no more stalling. The clock was already ticking. This time tomorrow she would be on one continent, him another; the story of her life it seemed.

His eyes burned for a long moment in which neither one of them spoke and yet everything was said, before in one swift movement he leaned forward, his other arm reaching out and, clasping her behind her head, pulling her to him, kissing her – mouths together, bodies agonizingly far apart.

She didn't know how long they stayed like that; at one point, he grabbed the bottle off her and tossed it into the ice bucket beside his, freeing their hands, and she felt his fingers entwine in her hair, the soft prickle of his beard against her palm.

When they finally pulled apart, she was breathless – not least from the strain of leaning over. His eyes were still burning; she suspected hers were too. It wasn't enough.

'Where's a ground-floor room when you want one?' he muttered, glancing down at the drop, his breath coming heavily as he kept her in his sights – so near, yet so far.

'Well, there is a door,' she said quietly, taking a few steps back towards the bedroom.

He watched her, like a cat with a mouse, not one movement missed. 'No.'

No?

'No.' He stepped up suddenly onto his chair and put his foot on the balcony wall as though testing it, finding the sweet spot. 'Where's the fun in that?' he grinned. And leapt.

She blinked in the gloom, the new day barely making an impression on the floor as it nudged feebly against the slatted shutters, the vintage bed sheet moulded to her naked form. She turned over with a sigh, then again, trying to get comfortable. The crack of light told her it was still too early to be awake, the jet lag still refusing to release her, cradling her tightly and rocking her awake with thoughts of Tom. Tom and Lucy. Tom and Serena. Tom's lies. Joe.

Joe.

She turned over with a start, remembering – but the bed

was empty, the sheet a tangled rope on his side. He'd gone? She sat up in bed, looking harder, as though it was the dim light hiding him from her, but she was alone. She could feel it.

Oh God. She bent her knees and dropped her head onto them. What had she done? Flashes of last night played on loop through her mind – as unbelievable as they were unstoppable; so much better than it had ever been with Tom, they had laughed, ordering up another bottle of wine. He had an earthy masculinity, the skin on his hands rough, his beard pinking her skin, his body relaxed but also somehow primed; he felt completely 'other' to her and she had felt liberated with him, exhilarated. Joe was the first man she'd slept with since Tom, and she'd been faithful to him for all of their four years together.

And now Joe hadn't even stayed the night. And he was a client.

She moaned, feeling wretched, humiliation washing over her in waves. She was an idiot. An idiot. A bloody fool. He had used her; she was just another thing to own or claim; or perhaps he really did think sleeping with the staff was part of the service. What had she been thinking? Why should she have supposed he'd have thought otherwise?

Angrily, she yanked the sheet off her and stalked across the room, the cool floor tiles welcome relief on her feet; her skin felt clammy and she didn't think the temperature could have dropped below 25 degrees overnight. She poured her-self a glass of water from the carafe and stepped back out onto the small balcony, looking down at the little town with its cascade of stepped red roofs. The port was not yet awake although the fishing boats – like him – had already left; here and there, washing hung limply from lines that had been strung across tiny roof terraces, cats were curled up and sleeping on stone walls, but even the sky was bare of birds.

It was a view that still shocked her with its foreignness – what was she doing here? She thought of her tiny apartment and the fact that the dress she had worn to the opera – and which was supposed to have been returned to Barneys on Monday – was still thrown across the bedroom chair, her underwear balled up in the corner ready for her to hit the laundromat this weekend; the milk would be still fresh in the fridge, her Saturday market flowers probably still sucking up the last drops of water in the vase. She had just walked out of her own life as though it and the people in it meant nothing. *Again.* And now she would be stepping back into it, like her life was a pair of jeans she could put on and discard at will.

God, had she really only been gone a few days? It was Friday morning and she had still been in New York on Monday night. It felt so much longer than that. She was a wreck. Her life was a mess.

She took a deep glug of water from the glass still on the table – her mouth felt like it had been carpeted – and sank despondently against the wall on her elbows, looking out to sea, only vaguely aware of the deep plough lines of the fishing boats' wakes still shimmering on the water's surface. It would be almost ten in New York. What was happening there now? Was Poppy's jaw still wired? Could she do any more than blink? Had Jack calmed down? And Tom – had he guessed she'd seen him with Serena? Or had he given up and gone home, back to Lucy?

So many questions. Ever since that cab ride on Bond Street when the truth had come into crystal clear focus, she had determined to act with conviction from that point on, never to be the victim again, to stay one step ahead of the heartbreak that snapped at her heels. And yet somehow, she was always the one left wondering what was going on.

A small sound made her jump and she turned back to see the latch on the shutters in Joe's room being turned. With a desperate leap, she landed in the shade of her own doorway just as he stepped onto his balcony in his boxers.

Their tables were still where they'd been set up last night, the dinner plates attracting flies. She watched as he threw his arms above his head and stretched like a big cat, the muscles on his stomach and torso like flat, polished pebbles. He walked up to the balcony wall and looked out to sea and across the port, just as she had done. How long had he been back in his own room? Had he waited for her to fall asleep and then just left?

He had his phone, she saw. She watched as he dialled a number and put it to his ear, rolling his shoulders, the muscles in his back clearly defined as he looked out to sea.

'Hey, yeah, it's me.' His voice was low and barely distinct. '. . . I know, sorry about that but reception is patchy here and I can't always get away . . .' Chloe frowned, struggling to hear. '. . . not often alone.'

There was a silence as he listened to the other person, stretching his neck by pressing his head down one side, then the other.

'. . . already sorted. Remote spot. Olive groves. You'll like it. All the furniture's in now.'

Chloe felt her heart beat harder. He was talking about the house – but to whom? He'd told her he was unmarried and single so who was this person he thought would like it – a friend? A business partner? Investor? His parents? But no, she knew from his tone it couldn't be them. His voice was too . . .

confiding, somehow. It reminded her of the early days with Tom, when they'd tried so hard to stay away from each other, working side by side all day and putting on their best professional voices, only to succumb in the lifts or at the photocopier, and he would call Lucy, telling her he was working late. Chloe had hated herself in those moments as she heard him use that voice – the same one Joe was using now.

She closed her eyes, feeling sick, as she realized with utmost clarity that he was on the phone to a woman, that there was someone else and it was happening all over again. Tom mark two.

He began to pace and she pressed herself flatter against the wall as he walked over towards her balcony, his voice becoming louder – '. . . it's all going to plan . . .' – before he turned away again at the wall and his words drifted away like ribbons on the breeze. '. . . Have to be careful not to arouse suspicion.'

What? Her antennae shot up and she shifted position slightly, straining to hear more. What plan was he talking about? And whose suspicion didn't he want to arouse – hers?

She risked a peek round the doorway; he had his back to her, one hand on his hip as he continued to talk. Who was this man who had barged into her life just two short weeks ago? Who had all but insisted she leave the city on a whim. Who was wry and sarcastic and silent one moment, and sweep-her-off-her-feet charming the next. Who leapt balconies to be with her but crept from her bed to ring another woman.

She leant forward further, straining to hear more and placing one hand on the hinge of the shutter; it creaked loudly and she saw him start to turn. She ducked back in again but not before she caught sight of the water glass she'd just left sitting on the wall. She had forgotten about it when she'd heard him coming out but now it sat there conspicuously – showing she had been out there too. Not to mention one gust of wind would send it flying forty feet to the ground below. If someone should happen to be walking past . . .

She heard his bare feet pad over the tiles, glimpsed his hand as he reached over to her balcony and picked it up. Was he looking back towards her room? She pulled as far back out of sight again as she could, pressing herself flat – flatter – against the wall, but even if she was out of sight, he would clearly be able to see that her shutters were open, that she must be up too. She held her breath, not daring to make even that sound; if he leaned across his balcony – or, God help her, jumped again – he would see her here, naked as a baby and spying on him, a man she had just heard had a plan that was grounds for suspicion.

A short silence followed. What was he doing? She scrunched her eyes shut.

'. . . Yeah, yeah, sorry, I'm still here . . .' She heard the soft suckering sound of his bare feet on the tiles again, his voice retreating and the rasp of the latch on the shutters.

She peered around the doorway. His balcony was clear. She felt her muscles release.

But not a moment later, she heard the click of a door out on the corridor; she darted back into bed, pulling the sheet over herself and forcibly slowing down her breath to a steady, sonorous beat. A moment later, her own door opened again and she heard him come back into the room, his feet on the tiles and then the mattress sagging, rolling her towards him slightly as he lay down on it beside her. For several seconds, all was quiet as she felt the weight of his stare on her face as she pretended to sleep; and then she heard the soft clink of her water glass back on the bedside table – he must have taken it with him as some sort of safety-first gesture.

But safe wasn't how she felt around him now.

Chapter Twenty-One

'Where are you going?' His voice was heavy with sleep, a low groan escaping him as he glanced at the time on his phone, falling back into the pillows again.

'I've got a plane to catch,' she half whispered, doing up her bra and bitterly wishing she could at least have got her clothes on without him waking up. She didn't want to ever see him again; she didn't want him to see *her* again, especially not half-clothed.

'Get another one then. Come back to bed.'

The intimacy in those words . . . She closed her eyes, feeling the bitterness curl. He had another woman and he could just trot out commands like that to her? But it wasn't his infidelity that was making her get out of there so fast; it wasn't the fact that he was a cheat that made her feel so frightened. And she *was* frightened. In the three hours since he had come back to bed, falling asleep almost immediately, she hadn't slept for a minute; she didn't know this man, not what he really wanted or what he was up to. But he was up to *something* – she could smell it now, like off milk – and she knew that she had to get out of there and away from him as quickly as she could. She hadn't been able to leave any earlier, as she needed a ferry to get off the island and they didn't start running till breakfast. She also didn't want to arouse his suspicions that she had hers – a perverse double bluff that everything was absolutely normal.

'I can't. I need to catch the first ferry back to Athens.' She wouldn't look at him; she might give herself away, the anger and the fear intermingling in her blood and worn on her skin like a pox. She busied herself instead with fiddling with the buttons of her Swiss-dot blouse.

'Chloe.'

The way he said her name . . . It was both a command and a plea. Her fingers stopped moving as a shiver ran up her spine. She closed her eyes for a second, feeling confused by the way her instincts reacted to him. He thrilled her, he intimidated her, he delighted her, he frightened her. She managed to throw a non-committal half-smile over her shoulder, not making eye contact. 'I'm sorry. I really do have to go.'

She walked over to the chest of drawers and pulled her tiny capsule wardrobe from it, keeping her back to him as she rolled the pieces down and pushed them into her handbag; she could buy a travel bag at the airport.

'Do you though?' She heard the first trace of suspicion in his voice.

'I told you last night. My flight is first thing.'

'So why am I getting the distinct vibes you're running? Do you think this was a mistake?'

She closed her eyes again, grateful she could hide her reactions. Now he wanted to play hurt? The victim? 'Of course not.'

'Look at me.'

She threw another half-glance his way; he was sitting up in bed, the sheet fallen down to his hips and revealing the dark hair on his chest, that incredible physique. He had an animal physicality that was almost compelling to watch. She looked away again. It was more than enough, far too much.

'I mean properly. Look at me.'

She turned with a sigh, rolling her bag in her hands as she forced herself to make eye contact with him at last. In spite of everything, regardless of what games he was playing here, why did he have to look like that? Why couldn't he have just stayed asleep? She'd been so quiet; it had taken her twenty minutes just to get her first foot on the floor, sliding out as silently as she could from beneath the sheet.

'What's really going on? Why are you running? And *don't* say you've got a flight to catch.'

She steeled her nerve, knowing she could do this. 'Joe, you're my client.'

'I realize that.'

'So this . . . this is wrong. It should never have happened.'

His eyes narrowed, not believing her, refusing to accept her account. 'Why not? People meet through their work all the time. Clearly it's not an ideal scenario; I get that this makes things tricky, for you particularly, but if it's not an issue for me, why should it be for you? This is between us. Two consenting adults. It has nothing to do with the company you work for.'

'They wouldn't see it like that.' Tom. He definitely wouldn't. 'It was completely unprofessional of me. I can't believe—' She pinched the bridge of her nose, feeling the emotions close in on her. What had she done? How could she have done this?

'Chloe—' He moved forward in the bed, coming towards her.

'No!' Her tone stopped him dead in his tracks. 'This was a mistake.' She enunciated every word with crystal clarity;

she didn't want to be misunderstood. 'When I get back to New York, I'll transfer you to my colleague – her name is Serena Witney.'

'I don't *want* Serena. I want you.' She heard the petulance in his voice then; the arrogance of a man used to having everything – and everyone – he ever wanted. There was no 'no' in his world. But then he'd said exactly the same about Poppy too; he'd wanted her and only her in the beginning, and now look at him.

He saw her expression, the determination in her eyes. He sat back again. 'Okay then, fine – put me on to Serena. You're right – it will simplify things; technically I won't be your client.'

And . . . ? Did he think that 'solved' the problem? She stared at him, open-mouthed. He thought this was a negotiation? She knew exactly how he wanted this to play out – an easy affair; she would be the 'other woman' all over again and history would just keep on repeating itself.

Yanking her gaze from his, she looked into her bag. Her passport was still there. She could go. She looked back at him. 'Joe, we won't see each other again. Last night was . . . what it was. Nothing more.'

It was his turn to look stunned now as he saw she was really doing this; she was leaving him high and dry in her own bed. She bet he couldn't believe it; she bet no woman had ever done this to him before and, for a fleeting moment, as their eyes locked, she felt gripped by uncertainty – memories of yesterday, of last night, propelling her back to him. But then she remembered his whispers in the early hours. The *plan*. Some deal he had going on? She didn't even care. She had come to Greece to escape the lies, to be rid of men like him and Tom.

'Goodbye, Joe.'

'Chloe—'

She slipped from the room without a backward glance, emerging moments later onto the street, her footsteps on the cobbles the only sound to be heard as even the donkeys slept on.

New York

She stood on the corner of Madison and East 86th and stared into the traffic as the cab pulled away, her body feeling physically assaulted by the wall of noise as the sharp staccatos of hydraulic drills mixed with car horns and shouts, squealing brakes and whirling sirens. She felt tiny, insignificant; steel tower blocks thrusting skywards all around her, dissecting the sky into small blue parcels. It was all so different to the quietly billowing, tented sky of Hydra in which birds soared – gulls chasing the fishing boats, pigeons crossing from red roof to red roof, sparrows flitting greedily around the cafes and market.

It was another beautiful day, the temperature in the high eighties, but the heat was as different here as the sky – more intense, oven-like. Her clothes didn't stand out in the same way as her Manhattan outfit had in Hydra though; a girl in blue shorts and a white dot blouse? She could be on her way back from lunch with friends, or en route to a creative media meeting downtown, shopping at Bergdorf's or heading for the Jitney, ready for her weekend decampment to the Hamptons. Let the weekend commence! Certainly nothing indicated she had come straight off a plane; even the rucksack over her shoulder, barely filled with her feather-light holiday wardrobe, gave no sign that she was freshly returned to the city that had become her asylum.

She had intended to go into the office for a couple of hours; with just a few hours left of the working week, it was the very least she could do – offer to pick up the slack. But she couldn't seem to make her feet move.

She didn't particularly care about whether she still had a job to come back to – she certainly didn't care whether Alexander's client had got his perfect picture of the Taj Mahal, or if the medic for Hawaii had signed the non-disclosure agreement, or if Rosaria had found a head to roll. Right now, she couldn't seem to care about much. It wasn't that her heart was broken; Joe, with all his sexy charm and money, couldn't do that, simply because he couldn't break something that was already smashed – Tom had got there first and seen to that. But she did feel changed. Empty somehow, as though she'd been bled of trust. Hope.

She sent a text to Elle. *'Back! See you tonight?'*

Less than a minute later, her friend replied in emojis: dancing woman and cocktail glass.

It made her smile. It made her feet move. She could always rely on her girlfriends. Poppy would have rallied round her too . . . if she could.

Poppy.

She began to walk, but not towards the office. It was twenty blocks to the Mount Sinai hospital from here and as she walked through the doors, she felt an odd sense of dislocation. Had it really only been five days since she had sat here with Poppy's mother? Three since Poppy had woken up? It felt like a month ago to her. She had been in a different time zone, living a different life, with a different man—

She shunted him from her thoughts with a cold determination. No. No brooding. No obsessing. She was done.

Knowing exactly where to go, she travelled up in the elevators, feeling conspicuously empty-handed amongst the other visitors laden with flowers and gifts . . . She got out on the eighth floor and walked towards the Intensive Care Unit.

'I've come to see Poppy Langham,' she said quietly at the desk, peering down at the banks of paperwork spread on the counters.

A plump, dark-haired, dark-eyed nurse looked up at her. 'I'm afraid it's family only.'

She didn't even hesitate. She was done with this too. 'Yes, I know. I'm her cousin.'

'And visiting hours have just ended.'

'Please, I've come straight from the airport. I've flown in from London. Even if it's just five minutes. Then I can come back later?' She swallowed, lying fluently. 'We're really close. I know it would lift her to see me.'

The nurse gave her a quick once-over: similar ages; English accent; the airline tag on her bag . . . 'Fine, but just for five minutes. She's in Room 822. I'll take you there myself; as you know, she's still under protection.'

'Yes.' The thought of it made her feel sick that Poppy was still a target. How could anybody want to hurt her?

She followed the nurse, glancing through the slatted blinds at every window, at the patients motionless in their beds, hooked up to IV lines and monitors, charts on hooks detailing their progress and prognosis.

. . . 820 . . . 821 . . .

A black-uniformed police officer sitting in a chair beside the door stood up at their approach.

'Hey, Charlie,' the nurse said to him. 'This is Poppy's cousin from England. I've said she can have five minutes.'

The police officer looked across at her. 'Name?'

'Chloe Marston.'

He made a note of it and nodded. 'I'll be watching from out here.'

She swallowed. Did he really think that she might do something? Was everybody under suspicion? 'Of course.'

'Five minutes,' the nurse said, before walking off.

Charlie opened the door for her and Chloe felt her heart miss a beat at what she saw. It was one thing to know what had happened; even to hear the details of it from Jack, via Xan. But actually seeing Poppy lying there . . .

She shuffled in, already regretting her decision to come, lying her way in. She had wanted to see her friend, to talk, to confide, to unload, as though she'd expected to find Poppy propped up with pillows, surrounded by flowers and chocolates, daytime TV on and a pair of Jermyn Street pyjamas, ready for a girlie gossip. Instead, she was inert, almost invisible on the semi-recumbent bed. She had been wafer thin to start with but now her bones – her knees, her hips – could be seen poking through the sheets; her blue eyes seemed three times the size in her face, her shrunken frame distorted further by the grotesquely oversized casts on her left arm and leg. And her head was wrapped, top and bottom, in bandages so that only her mouth, nose, cheeks and eyes were visible.

A small sound escaped Chloe before she even knew it was coming and Poppy's eyes opened to slits. Then properly. She moved her head up to vertical as Chloe pigeon-stepped into the room. Did Poppy even want her here?

But her good arm rose up, outstretched towards her and

with a gasp of relief, Chloe rushed over. 'Oh, Pops,' she whispered, her eyes flying over her frantically, as though trying to absorb the trauma in one sweep, to get it over and done with. Seen. Understood.

Poppy gave one long blink in reply, squeezing her hand weakly.

Carefully, she looked for somewhere to perch on the edge of the bed, terrified of hurting her or catching on the equipment. 'God it's so good to see you. I've been desperate to come but they wouldn't let us in.'

Poppy nodded and it was then that Chloe saw the wire around her lower face.

'I lied,' Chloe whispered, pulling an aghast face, trying to joke. 'I told them I was your cousin . . . That's okay, isn't it?'

To her delight, Poppy managed a sort of wink and smile.

'How . . . how are you feeling now?' It was a ridiculous question, she knew that. How did she suppose Poppy was feeling after being mown down by a car, left for dead, enduring brain surgery and now lying around with broken bones and a wired jaw? 'Are you in pain?'

A slight shrug.

'Do you want me to call a nurse?'

Fractional shake of the head.

'Are you tired? Do you need to sleep? Should I go?' Perhaps this was a mistake; maybe she shouldn't have come. Now she understood why access had been so severely restricted. This wasn't a game.

Another fractional shake of the head and she felt a squeeze of her hand. Then Poppy swivelled her head, looking towards a small white board with a black pen on it.

'You want that?' Chloe asked, reaching for it.

She had to hold it for her; one of Poppy's legs was in a

275

cast and the other . . . well, she was no doubt too weak to bend it herself. She waited, holding it, as Poppy wrote something, the effort visible on her face.

When she had finished, Chloe turned the board towards herself and read it; the words were spidery and weak, barely legible. *Suntan? Tell.*

'Oh.' Chloe felt the positivity drain from her. What could she say? She couldn't burden Poppy with her disastrous fling with a client, the client Poppy herself had lined up – and now she had sabotaged it. She felt Poppy squeeze her hand, watching her, wanting to hear. 'I just went to Greece for a few days; that new client of yours wanted a holiday home on one of the islands so I was helping him scope out the options and get it set up.'

Poppy squinted, quizzical.

'You know, that Joe Lincoln guy?'

Nothing.

'Tallish, athletic-looking, designer beard. Dark-brown hair and eyes. The engineer? You had lined him up as a new client?'

She waited as Poppy began to write on the board again. Not possessing the strength to wipe it clean, she simply wrote in a corner, the spidery letters overlapping the previous message. Poppy handed it over to her, watching as she read it. *No Joe.*

Chloe summoned a faint smile, but fear was what she felt. She knew a level of amnesia was to be expected, having googled the mid- and long-term effects of head injuries. Poppy may have survived the operation and woken from the coma but that didn't mean she would escape entirely unscathed. There would always be repercussions from such a major trauma and some temporary – or even permanent

– memory loss would be the least of it. She easily could have been left with motor function problems, or worse, brain damage.

Chloe tried not to stare at the wire looping her friend's head, taking her hand gently instead and squeezing it. She didn't want to frighten Poppy. 'Well, anyway, don't worry, it's all in hand. And I'm back now – home to reality and keeping everyone else on track. Poor Pelham is still tying himself up in knots trying to win back Clarissa. They're in Washington State at the moment at a wedding. Who knows – maybe he'll get on one knee himself after the "I do"s.' She rolled her eyes. 'As for Rosaria, honestly, I don't know how you put up with her; she's so rude. So, someone put lilies in her dressing room at the Scala this week – *in spite* of my reminder call beforehand – and now she's absolutely freaking, saying someone's head has got to roll. I mean, hello? Why so vindictive?'

She slumped slightly, running out of steam. It was hard keeping up an entirely one-ended conversation.

'And Alexander's in India this week – I had to get the scaffolding for the cleaning works around the Taj Mahal taken down so that his investor contact could take a picture, can you believe it? What am I saying? Of course you can.' She patted Poppy's hand in solidarity. 'He's pretty wound up at the moment now that the One Stop deal's officially been shot down; he's getting a new group of investors in, I think, but it wasn't his preferred choice and he's been in a pretty filthy mood whenever he's called,' she sighed wearily. 'But, on the plus side, his J Class yacht has arrived in the South of France and he seems happier about that. He's flying there right now, actually.'

Poppy gave an interested nod, although the prospect of

moving freely, flying halfway across the world just to see a boat, probably seemed a lifetime away from here.

'He was telling me he bought one of the only three original models left in the world and had it completely restored. Did you know?'

Poppy nodded weakly.

'Of course you do. I bet you found it for him. Anyway, it's entered for the Saint-Tropez regatta next week so hopefully that'll chill him out a bit.'

Poppy took the board, feebly rubbing away the previous message with her gown. She began writing but the door opened and Charlie stood there again with the nurse.

'Time's up, I'm afraid. Your cousin needs to rest now,' the nurse said.

Chloe nodded, turning back to Poppy. 'I'll come back tomorrow, okay?' she said quietly. She wished she could kiss her cheek, hug her, but everywhere on her body was broken and fragile; she was like a robin held together with sticky tape. The board had fallen from her grasp as Chloe had turned away and now lay flat on her lap. Chloe lifted it – *mol*, she read upside down. Huh? Frowning quizzically, she put it down on the side table. 'Rest now. You can tell me tomorrow.'

Poppy's eyes grew bigger and Chloe felt her heart rate quicken at the sight of her, stranded there – everyone coming and going whilst she was immobile and silent.

'Don't worry. I'll be back tomorrow, I promise.' She got up and walked across the room; turning at the door, she winked. 'Bye, cuz.'

Chloe had barely set foot out of the elevator before Xan had run over and accosted her, diverting her over to the kitchen, in the opposite direction to Tom and Jack's offices.

'Girl, you are in a whole heap of shit,' he hissed. 'Where've you been? I thought you were getting back yesterday.'

'I got delayed,' she shrugged. 'Joe wanted me to help him move his stuff in so we had to wait for it to come in from France. Why? What's happened?'

'Jack and Tom have had some huge fight.'

'Another one?'

'They're barely even talking now.'

She folded her arms across her chest. 'Do you know why?'

'Your guess is as good as mine. All I can tell you is they can barely even be in the same room together. They can't *look* at each other. And every five minutes I've got one or the other of them coming up to me: Where are you? Have I heard from you?'

She put a hand on his arm. 'I'm really sorry, Xan, I don't know why they're so agitated.' Well, not Jack at least. 'I'll go and speak to them now. I didn't realize me being out of the office for a few days would cause so much upset. It's not like I haven't been dealing with the others; I've been picking up all my calls.'

'Not all. Like I said, someone's been sticking her fingers in the pies. Oh, talk of the devil,' he muttered, rolling his eyes and turning away as footsteps approached. Chloe half turned to see Serena coming straight for her. She felt the blood rush to her cheeks, her hands tightening into balled fists. She wouldn't dare, she wouldn't dare come up to her and act like nothing had happened, would she?

She would, stopping when she was only a foot away. 'Chloe, hey,' Serena smiled, a bunch of papers in her arms clasped to her chest. 'You're back.'

'Looks like it.' Chloe's voice was clipped and she refused

to smile, to pretend to be friendly to this woman after everything she'd done.

Xan pretended to make himself useful, switching on the coffee machine and throwing open the cupboard doors, looking for their favourite capsules.

Serena ignored him, as she always did, and if she had picked up on Chloe's abruptness, she wasn't showing it.

'Thank God you're back. I'm sure you've heard it's been *so* crazy here this week. I don't know what's going on – something in the air.'

Chloe didn't reply; she refused to do anything that might make Serena comfortable: speak, smile . . . There was a short silence.

'So anyway, I fielded a few calls for you while you were abroad. I hope you don't mind?'

'It's a few calls, Serena. Hardly my *job*.'

Serena, picking up on the atmosphere finally, gave a hesitant smile. 'Yes, well . . .' She looked down at the papers in her arms. 'Well anyway, I was just signing off on some of the paperwork that's come through and there's an invoice here for Mr Subocheva from a florist in Provence – 2,000 peonies to dress a yacht?' She pulled a face. 'I don't think so, do you?'

'Why not?'

'Well, that many flowers in a confined space seems a little . . . overwhelming.'

Chloe's eyes narrowed as she watched Serena thinking she knew it all; striding around here with her paperwork and officious, fake smiles. 'Or perhaps Alexander thought it would be a romantic gesture for his wife, given that she's staying there on her own.'

Chloe straightened herself further; it felt good to have the upper hand, to know something Serena didn't, for once.

Serena looked chastened. 'Oh. I see. Well, yes, I can see how he might have . . . that's very romantic indeed.' She gave a wan smile. 'I-I just wanted to be sure it was a valid claim, you understand; you know how some of these suppliers get – the bigger the budget, the more they think they can slip a fabricated claim through and no one will notice.'

'I placed the order myself, Serena. He's my client. The claim is legitimate.'

Serena shifted weight uncomfortably. 'Okay, great.' She gave a lackadaisical shrug. 'Well I guess that's okay then. Thanks for clarifying.' She walked off, tossing her sleek hair over her shoulder as she went. Xan was by Chloe's side in a flash.

'Bitch,' she muttered under her breath, watching her go.

'Well, take a look at you, Frosty. You showed her.'

'I hate that woman.'

'Yeah. Getting that,' he said with lifted eyebrows. 'Care to share?'

Chloe looked back at him. She wished she could, to start from scratch and tell him all of it . . . But, well, it was a long story now. She had transgressed quite enough political lines as it was – becoming involved with her boss *and* her client? It required a context she really didn't have the time or energy to give, especially not now. She closed her eyes as she heard the voices coming down the hall – those British accents carrying like red balloons in the sky – unmistakable, unmissable.

She turned again to see Jack, closely followed by Tom, striding down the office towards her, looks of fury and relief marbled on their faces.

'Oh, shit,' Xan whispered as the two bosses bore down upon them. 'I promise I didn't tell them anything.'

'It's fine,' she smiled, straightening up slightly as Jack got to her first. 'Hey, Jack. How are you?'

Tom was only two strides behind, his eyes shining with a thousand silent accusations.

Jack stared at her, as if in disbelief at her nonchalance, before jerking his thumb behind him and almost stabbing Tom in the eye. 'Conference room, Chloe. *Now.*'

Was this glass bulletproof, she wondered as they sat in the conference room, because the way Tom was shooting looks at her . . .

Jack was just as mad. He had spent at least five minutes shouting at her and giving the rest of the team a good mime show: if they couldn't hear his words, they could certainly tell by his body language that she was being hauled over the coals, with his arms flying, his floppy hair tossing first one way, then the other.

Xan kept walking past the windows, behind Tom and Jack's backs, with hilarious written signs: *Medical emergency? Death in the family? Gun?*

It was all she could do not to burst out laughing; she couldn't take any of this seriously – their anger and indignation. She didn't care any more. She had had enough of being used, of being disposable; second best. Let them rage, she thought to herself, watching as Jack brought his fist down on the desk, Tom beside him with his head in his hands. She realized she wasn't even listening to what they were saying – something about responsibility . . . pulling together as a team . . . time of crisis . . . danger . . . Lincoln . . .

Perhaps she should quit? It would probably be better than waiting to be fired; at least then they'd be obligated to give her a reference.

Wait, what?

'What did you say?' she asked, cutting in over Jack, leaving him silent in surprise again.

'I *said*,' he sighed exasperatedly, 'anything could have happened to you and we would have had no idea where you were.'

'Xan knew where I was.'

'No. He knew only that you were in Greece. That was no more helpful than saying you were in Europe.'

And whose fault was that if she didn't want to be found? She looked at Tom coldly. He looked back at her with a blank look of defeat. 'So?'

'*So* – you were off God-knows-where, doing God-knows-what, with God-knows-who. Isn't it bad enough that we've already got one employee in the hospital under police guard?'

She tipped her head wearily and sighed. God, this melodrama was getting dull. Exactly why were they trying to draw a parallel between her work trip and Poppy's predicament? 'I'm sorry but I don't get what all the fuss is about. Joe Lincoln is a client, I was helping him with this overseas project.'

'Except you weren't, were you?' Jack demanded.

Chloe felt her face burn, her eyes automatically flashing to Tom's; she saw him jolt in recognition of her guilt as the truth teleported between them in silence. Surely Joe hadn't rung in and told Tom and Jack what had happened between them out there? No, that made no sense. Why would he do such a thing? Unless . . . her mind was racing. Unless it was revenge for the way she had left him like that, still in bed, rejected? Was her job the scalp he demanded in return?

She couldn't believe it of him. She didn't. Whatever he was, he wasn't petty.

'If it hadn't been for Tom, we'd all still be labouring under the illusion that this guy was who he said he was.'

What? 'What do you mean?' Her voice had turned thin.

'Well, if he hadn't FaceTimed you and seen this Joe Lincoln for himself, none of us would be any the wiser even now that he wasn't who he said he was.'

She felt sick; dizzy. This couldn't be right. His voice sounded far away, her thoughts pressing in on her so that it was another moment before they registered and she felt the floor drop beneath her chair. 'When . . . when did you Face-Time me?' she asked Tom, looking straight at him.

'Yesterday. You were on some boat?' His words were clipped, the unspoken accusation dripping from them. He knew.

The boat – she had been asleep, her phone beside her.

'He answered, said you weren't available,' Tom said, the words hot with anger. 'Asked who *I* was and then hung up on me.'

'*Who's Tom?*' Joe had asked . . .

'It was only then we realized the guy you were with wasn't who he was claiming to be,' Jack said, just as hotly. He pushed a piece of paper in front of her. It showed a company logo of DCS Engineering and beside it, a photo of a very pink, balding man in his early sixties. 'Thank God Tom had followed due diligence and checked him out.'

'But *I* did!' she protested. But even as she said the words, she saw where her failure lay – she had gone on the DCS website, checking the company was real. She had seen his name come up and that had been enough for her. Everything checked out at first glance, she hadn't felt the need to go forensic on it. But she should have done – looked for a photograph, double-checked the age . . .

284

'When Xan said you were with Joe Lincoln, and then Tom saw him . . .' Jack looked at her with an inscrutable expression, as though he barely dared say the words. '. . . *That* man there is Joe Lincoln,' he said, stabbing at the picture.

'Not your pretty boy,' Tom snapped.

'He's not my anything,' Chloe snapped back. 'I was doing my job.'

They glared at each other but she knew her blushes had betrayed her.

Jack looked first at her, then at Tom, picking up on the arctic freeze between them. There was a long three-way silence, Tom still communicating unspoken accusations with his eyes. She had left him again and she had slept with Joe, he knew it . . .

'I think it's probably best if I hand in my notice,' she said quietly, tearing her gaze away from him and looking over at Jack. 'This isn't working out.'

'Oh no. You're not getting off that lightly,' Jack snapped.

'I'm sorry?'

'Christ, you must think I'm an idiot,' he murmured, dropping his voice now, sinking back into his chair, fingers interlaced, elbows out. 'You think I don't know what happened between you two?'

Both of them looked back at him in surprise. Tom looked especially stunned.

'Of course I bloody well knew! But I turned the other cheek, didn't I? You were discreet, it didn't affect work. I mean, I thought you were a bloody idiot for what it's worth,' he snapped, glaring at Tom. 'Lucy deserves better frankly—'

'We both did,' she cut in hotly, refusing to be cast as the villain in this. 'He kept telling me he'd finish it! I had zero desire to be his bit on the side, let me tell you!'

Jack shot his old friend a weary look of disdain, although it wasn't like he could take the moral high ground himself.

'Well, whatever happened between the three of you was your own business,' he muttered. 'I didn't care then and I don't care now.' He looked at Chloe again. 'But when you turned up here five months ago with no warning, I knew exactly what had gone down and, frankly, I thought it was the best thing for everyone – I didn't want this company to lose you, Chloe; you've been good news for us, no two ways about it. So I held my tongue and let you two get on with . . . playing your charade! But when you bring your shit in here – *you* turning up out of nowhere last week,' he spat at Tom before turning back to her. '*You* running off to nowhere a couple of days later? Well, then I'm obliged to get involved.'

'Piss off, Jack – you're not,' Tom said, rallying, his own cheeks flushing with anger. 'Chloe and I have always kept our private life well away from the office. What is or isn't happening between us is nothing to do with the matter in hand.'

'Oh, is that so?' Jack sneered again. 'So then, you're telling me she would have disappeared in the middle of the night with that man – whoever the fuck he is! – even if you two *hadn't* had some lovers' quarrel?'

Neither of them could reply, but they both knew it was the truth. Tom still had no confirmed idea why she had gone.

'You're overreacting,' Tom mumbled instead. It was no defence.

Jack stabbed the desk hard with his finger. 'We've got Poppy lying in a hospital bed like Flat Freaking Stanley, with God-knows-who after her,' he hissed at his partner. 'And then Chloe disappears to some Greek island with a man going under a stolen identity and you tell me I'm overreacting? We have no idea who he is or what he wants. Just like we have no idea who hurt Poppy or why. For all we know, he's the same guy! He could have hurt Chloe too, don't you get that?'

The words echoed around the room, shocking them all. *Had* Chloe been in danger? She had certainly felt frightened after she'd overheard his secret phone call.

Tom's face crumpled at Jack's harsh words, his clear, boyish beauty folding into rough pleats as he raked his hands into his hair, sliding his head down, his forearms and his body heaving with huge, silent sobs. Chloe couldn't breathe as she saw the scale of his devastation, his despair an avalanche sliding down the face of him. Her eyes slid to the glass windows – the entire team was watching, Xan standing at his desk and looking over, his mouth hanging open at the sight of their mime. Suddenly it wasn't so funny.

'But . . .' She couldn't think straight, she couldn't take any of it in. She tried going back over what they'd told her: that Joe wasn't Joe, that was why they'd been so worried about her; that he might have been the one who'd hit Poppy? Maybe?

And she'd shared a bed with him.

Everything seemed warped; it was like looking at the world in a fairground mirror: truth and reality stretched and distorted so that nothing looked as it should. *Plan. Arouse suspicion.* So she'd been right. She *had* been in danger.

'Christ, Chlo, the thought of anything happening to you . . .' Tom sobbed.

'But it didn't. I'm fine,' she said, reflexively reaching an arm over the desk and squeezing his hand, her voice barely a whisper as she remembered the softness of Joe's touch on her skin, the way he'd murmured into her hair . . .

'He didn't hurt you?' Tom croaked, looking back at her with red-rimmed eyes. 'I swear to God, I'll ki—'

'He didn't hurt me,' she assured him. Not like that, anyway.

Chapter Twenty-Two

Sergeant Mahoney didn't blink much, although she noticed he twitched his moustache a lot when he thought she was lying; and right now, he seemed to be struggling to comprehend what she was telling him, as though it was too fantastical to be true.

'So you're telling me that in all that time you were in Greece together, you didn't once take a photograph of this man?'

'That's right,' she nodded, wondering how many times she had to say it.

'Not a selfie at dinner?'

'No.'

'Not a sly side shot when he wasn't looking?'

'No.'

'Perhaps when he was sleeping?'

'He was my client; why would I have seen him sleeping?' she said firmly, looking outraged and hoping to God he hadn't talked to the hotel; the chambermaids would surely have seen that his bed hadn't been slept in the morning after they checked out?

'Well, I never thought I'd see the day,' he muttered, a wry grin on his thin lips. 'One of you *millennials* who isn't on Instagram.' Sarcasm oozed from the words and he seemed to be pretty pleased with himself for labelling her as such.

'I didn't say I'm not on Instagram, only that I didn't post to it,' she clarified.

Her calmness seemed to irk him and the smile faded from his lips as he looked down at his notes again. She concentrated on the badge on his shirt, reminding herself she was being interviewed, not interrogated; she had done nothing wrong.

She was still in the conference room although the office was deserted now. It was Friday rules – half the team had caught the 3 p.m. Jitney, the rest sloping out on the dot of five, everyone disappearing in the elevators and talking about what had gone down this afternoon. Even Jack had manhandled Tom out of the building for a drink, insisting she be left to talk to the police without him hanging around, making things worse. Emotions were running too high as it was.

'So you said he bought this house on the *far* side of the island?' As though it was the far side of the moon.

'That's right. He wanted somewhere remote, no neighbours. He didn't want to be contactable.'

'Did he say why?'

'He said it was his escape from the pressures of his job.'

'And you didn't question that?'

'Why would I? Most of our clients have incredibly pressured lives. Many of them have holiday homes to retreat to.'

'But this *obsessive* need to be out of touch?'

'I think it's fast becoming the new luxury,' she shrugged.

'Hmm.' His moustache twitched again. 'We've had the local police go over and take a look at it for us – it's a farmhouse by all accounts.'

'Yes, that's right.'

'There was no one there.'

'No, there wouldn't be. He was flying back to France today.'

'Did he say to where exactly?'

'No.'

'Did he say why?'

She shrugged. 'I didn't ask.'

He looked frustrated. 'Well did he say when he was coming back?'

'No.'

'Did you arrange the travel for him? Book his flight?'

'No.'

'Even though you had arranged the flight over?'

'Yes. He had wanted to leave immediately on the way out. It was all very last-minute.'

'Didn't you think that was odd?'

'Not really. He believes the greatest gift of money is spontaneity.'

Sergeant Mahoney's eyebrow shot up, unimpressed, and she imagined he could think of its many other gifts that might be considered greater than that. 'Why was he in such a rush?'

She suppressed a sigh. 'Because he said he didn't want to lose the summer. He wanted to get on and buy somewhere.'

'But August is a sneeze away. He left it a bit late for looking for a holiday home in the middle of July, didn't he? These things take months to go through.'

'Which is why he came through us rather than an agent. I sorted out a shortlist for him in under a week.'

'But the paperwork? And the money?'

'I wasn't involved in that. He said he had business interests there – he said the money was already in place.'

He took a deep breath, his eyes narrowed to slits as he

watched her closely. 'Miss Marston, were you aware that he paid the owners for the property in cash? That he gave them a huge bung to hand over the deeds immediately?'

Bung? She went still. 'No. I didn't know that. I had assumed it would be a bank transfer.'

'Why do you think he would have paid three million euros, cash, for a property that's worth less than half that?'

That was what he'd spent? She was taken aback. 'Well, many of our clients will spend whatever they see fit to secure what they want,' she said slowly. 'At a certain level, money ceases to become as important as time.'

'Lucky them,' he said sarcastically and she could only shrug in response; it wasn't like she was one of them. 'And so you booked a second plane on the . . .' He checked his notes. 'On Wednesday night, coming to the island from the South of France?'

'Yes. Montpelier. He had furniture in storage that he wanted to be brought over for the house; it landed mid-morning on Thursday.'

'That's an efficient service you provide.'

'That's the point of our service,' she said shortly.

He tapped his pen against the top of his notepad, thinking deeply, watching her. 'It all seems very strange to me – the urgency; the cash. And the house itself doesn't seem like the kind of thing a man with his presumed level of wealth would want. There are bigger, fancier places available for sure. Why fly all the way out there on a private jet, only to buy a ramshackle farmhouse?'

'Actually, it was rather charming.'

'But the journey alone would have cost almost as much as the property.'

She shrugged. 'Horses for courses, I suppose. I was personally rather gratified by his choice. It gets tiresome only ever dealing with clients who want trophy houses and phallic jets.'

The police officer openly studied her. 'It sounds like you liked him.'

She swallowed. 'It's in my best interest to like my clients, Sergeant, given how closely I have to work with them.'

'It was nothing more than that?'

'Well, I suppose I found him a little intriguing. He's not like most of our clients.'

'No? How would you describe him?'

She thought for a moment, remembering how he'd leapt across the balcony, arms outstretched, eyes ablaze, coming to claim her – in that moment, she had never felt more beautiful, more desirable, more wanted, all the things Tom had made her doubt. He had been free and wild, spontaneous, sexy as hell . . . 'I guess I would say he was personable, intelligent, understated. But he could also be brusque at times. Distracted. Impatient too.'

'Do you have any idea why he targeted you?'

'He didn't *target* me,' she protested. The very suggestion gave her the chills.

'No? But you said earlier there was no record of his alleged appointment with Miss Langham in her diary; that he just turned up at the office the very first workday morning after her accident. Don't you think that timing was a little strange?'

'Not really,' she mumbled, but even as she said it, she remembered Poppy's message on the board. *No Joe.* What if it wasn't amnesia? Had she been trying to tell her she *didn't* know him? That there had never been any appointment arranged between them?

The sergeant must have seen her sudden doubts because he leaned in, pressing harder now. 'And then of course, he turned up on Monday night *insisting* you accompanied him to Greece – not giving you a moment to think, to tell anyone even.'

'I don't know if I'd put it quite like that,' she mumbled. But she wasn't so sure now. Had it been that way, really, and she'd just been too drunk to sense a sinister undercurrent?

'*Did* you tell anyone?'

'Well, no, but—'

'Tell me, when you were in his company – did you ever feel intimidated by him? Frightened?'

She remembered the phone call; the way he had watched her pretend to sleep as he'd climbed back into bed, as though knowing she was faking. She could still remember the feel of her own rapidly beating heart against the mattress springs. She had been scared that he knew she'd overheard him, that he had done the very thing he didn't want and aroused her suspicions. So, yes, she'd been scared. As well as humiliated and ashamed. Take your pick.

'Miss Marston?' Sergeant Mahoney was watching her closely, seeing how she had begun to wring her hands. 'If you saw or heard anything at all, even if it doesn't seem particularly important to you, you need to share it with us; let us decide what is and isn't relevant.'

She swallowed. It wasn't like she owed Joe anything; he had used her, lied to her. He wasn't what he'd said he was: thirty-four, from Vermont, engineering firm . . . had anything he'd said been true? 'I heard him on the phone this morning.'

He looked interested, her hesitation pricking his curiosity. 'Okay. What time?'

'I'm not sure exactly. Dawn, whenever that is out there.'

He arched an eyebrow. 'That's very early.'

'He was jet-lagged, we both were; we kept waking and sleeping at odd times. My room was next to his and my doors were open; I heard him on the balcony.' It was technically true.

'And who was he talking to?'

'I don't know, but it was a woman, I think.'

'You think? How could you tell?'

She shrugged, looking down at her hands. 'It was just the tone he used, I guess.'

He inhaled deeply, considering this; her. 'And what did he say to this woman?'

'Just that he hadn't been able to get away and it was difficult to talk . . . And then he said something about not wanting to *arouse suspicion*.'

The police officer leaned forward again, like a hound scenting blood. 'Go on.'

'Well, that was it. My door creaked and he stopped talking; he went back into his room after that. I couldn't hear the rest of it.'

A look of annoyance rippled across his face. 'Nothing at all?'

'No. And besides, it wasn't like I was trying to overhear; I don't make a habit of eavesdropping on people, Sergeant.' Although perhaps she should, she wondered.

'Even after what you'd heard?'

'I didn't know what I'd heard, what it meant.'

'So you didn't bring it up with him?'

'Of course not. It was none of my business and I was leaving that morning anyway.'

'So you just . . . went your separate ways? You flew back here and he went to France?'

'Exactly. I had done what I was required to do, there was no further reason to remain there.'

'You weren't tempted to stay on?'

'He was my client,' she said firmly.

'No, he's not that, Miss Marston. At the very least, he's a conman.' He snapped his notebook shut and looked her straight in the eye. 'And at most, he's something much, much worse.'

Mediterranean Sea, off the coast of Provence

She stood on the teak deck and looked out to the dark horizon, her back turned to the sparkling lights of the Côte d'Azur; they held no appeal for her any more. She didn't care about the parties in the beautiful villas, the gowns on the beautiful hostesses, the men in silk jackets with promises in their eyes. There was one such event going on right now, populated with faces she knew, the night sky colouring red, purple and green as fireworks exploded on and on in a lavish display. She wasn't sorry to be missing it; she had lived in that world and found nothing below the surface – nothing to nourish or sustain her, no real friendships, no reasons to keep her there.

Now it was the blank space that lured her, the dark horizon she felt pulling her away from here. She wanted silence. Peace. Oblivion. She couldn't go on another day. Everything was a lie. She knew this was her only way out.

Behind her, she heard the slow, heavy tread of one of the

security guards patrolling the deck, a gun in his waistband. If it was supposed to make her feel safe, it didn't.

She fussed with the skirt of her billowing gown as he passed; it was sea-green silk, suitably – a voluminous to-the-floor sundress that could almost have doubled as a parachute – but it wasn't from the sky that she would fall.

She waited for his footsteps to recede, watching as his shadow disappeared around the curve of the stern. She would only have a few minutes now. She didn't want him to stop her, to save her. It would be no mercy. He might think he saw her life from the inside, but he had no idea of what happened behind those closed doors, just a few feet away from where he walked.

Glancing round to make sure no one else was near, or watching, she climbed over the rail. The ledge was narrow and she turned inwards, facing the deck to get a better grip – to have one final look.

Overhead the sky split gold, fountains of colour raining down as thunderclaps rattled the stars, ready to camouflage a splash. With a deep breath, she looked over to the dining area where her wine glass still sat, where she had undertaken the private ritual of her final meal, all alone.

And then she closed her eyes – and let go.

Chapter Twenty-Three

New York

Chloe looked up at the ceiling, a helium balloon bumping against her shoulder as they all squeezed in to make room for a man in a wheelchair being pushed by a nurse. Her shoes squeaked slightly when she walked.

Chloe watched the numbers rise agonizingly slowly, having to suppress a sigh every time the doors opened – more people getting out, others coming in – at almost every floor. When finally they got to the eighth, she had to stop herself from sprinting down the corridor to the nurses' station.

'Hey,' she said, almost breathless, seeing that the same nurse was on duty as a few hours earlier. How much had changed since then. 'I've come back to see my cousin, Poppy Langham.'

The nurse looked at her, blankly for a second, before recognizing her. She got to her feet. 'Her cousin, you say?'

'Yes, I came in earlier but I could only stay for five minutes.'

Folding her arms over her ample chest, the nurse squared up. 'Turns out that was five minutes too long.'

'Excuse me?'

'I told you, family only.' The nurse stared at her coldly, daring Chloe to lie to her face again.

Chloe swallowed and said nothing, her eyes sliding down the corridor towards Room 822. The police officer was still sitting in his chair outside; he looked incredibly bored.

'Her parents weren't too happy when I said Poppy's cousin had dropped in,' the nurse said, her expression and tone becoming more frosty by the second. 'They knew your name – you *work* with her. They don't like that you lied and neither do I.'

'I'm so sorry; I didn't want to, but—'

'What do you think this is? A zoo? You get to come in and ogle the animals behind the glass?'

'Of course not—'

'Don't you understand how serious this situation is? You think that cop's sitting there for fun?'

'No, of course I don't—'

'I could have lost my job.' The nurse's dark eyes shone angrily.

'I'm so sorry, but that's the thing: it's *so* important that I see her. I have to ask—'

'Oh, you won't be doing anything of the sort. You're leaving.'

'But if I could just—'

'*Now.* Or do I need to call security?'

Chloe took a step back. She desperately needed to get clarification on whether Poppy had ever met Joe and arranged for him to come to the office. She was the only one who could prove whether everything he'd ever said to her was a lie, whether he was what the police were saying. Tom and Jack had proof he wasn't Joe Lincoln – of DCS Engineering anyway – but only Poppy knew if he had truly been lined up as a client. Because if he hadn't, then what had he been up to? And did it mean he had targeted her specifically, as Sergeant Mahoney seemed to think?

An idea came to her and she grabbed a pen and piece of paper from the jotter on the desk. 'Okay, fine. I'm going. But can I ask you to please get this to her? Show it to her parents first, it's fine.'

'I'm not doing anything of the sort. You've caused quite enough trouble. You need to leave.'

Chloe quickly scribbled the message and handed it over regardless. The nurse stared at her, not moving to take the note from her outstretched hand.

'Please. It's incredibly important. It's to do with the case.'

'I can't have her getting upset.'

'I promise, it won't upset her; she doesn't know the context. All I need is a yes or no answer from her.' She proffered the note another inch closer. '*Please.*'

With a worn-down sigh, the nurse's gaze fell to the note and she read the message. *Did you ever meet a man called Joe Lincoln?*

Clearly it seemed innocuous enough. 'I'll give it to her parents when they come out,' she said finally, taking it from her. '*They* can decide whether to show it to her.'

'Thank you. Thank you,' Chloe said gratefully.

'Don't thank me. I'm not doing it for you.' The nurse arched an eyebrow. 'Now go. And do not come back.'

'No, I won't,' Chloe said, moving away, back in the direction she'd come. 'Thank you.'

She walked over to the elevators again and waited, her mind racing, trying to make connections. Poppy had been deliberately hurt and now the police thought Chloe herself had been targeted too. Possibly by the same man. Joe Lincoln.

She still couldn't believe it. She didn't want to. And yet hadn't she felt unnerved by him at times – how he switched from being oblique and diffident to charming and open, as though he was two different people? A lover and a fighter? She had felt that sense of menace when he'd climbed back into bed. Had she really slept with the enemy?

The doors opened and she stepped in, dodging a man carrying a giant teddy bear almost as big as himself. She sank back against the wall and waited for the floors to count back down again. She was spent; this afternoon had not been what she'd been expecting, what with two hospital visits and a police interview. She needed some time out, to be with someone she could really trust. A few drinks in a quiet bar somewhere with Elle, perhaps a takeaway, and everything would feel better. It was all just a storm in a teacup, as her mother would say – a string of unfortunate coincidences and it would blow over soon enough. Whatever had been going on, she knew she was through the worst of it.

'Make it stop.' The voice was muffled, coming from deep beneath the duvet.

'Huh?' Chloe shifted position, rolling onto her stomach, squeezing her eyes tighter shut.

The groan came again. 'No.'

Chloe lifted her head from the pillow, her hair falling over one eye as she tried to compute. Where was she? What had she done? Why was she feeling so bad?

She saw cherry-pink toenails, a long, gleaming ebony leg emerging at one end of the duvet, an Afro at the other. An empty bottle of tequila was lying on its side on the floor beside the bed, a half-empty bag of nachos sprinkling paprika dust on the ivory sheepskin rug, a pale upside-down leg stiff and straight just behind her.

Oh. She realized it was her own and pulled it back in under the turquoise fringed silk shawl that appeared to have doubled as her sheet. Slowly, even her eyeballs moving at half-tempo, she saw she was on the sofa, not in bed at all, her shorts and blouse crumpled into a heap beneath her cheek and seemingly used as her pillow.

With another groan, she sat up. Her body was stiff from lying awkwardly and she tried a stretch, abandoning it halfway through. Elle was all but obscured under the duvet and showing no signs of waking up.

Not quite sure why she was awake herself, Chloe got up tentatively and made her way to the bathroom. Her brain seemed to knock against the inside of her head as she walked and she spent a good five minutes staring at her reflection in the mirror – mussed-up bed hair (in the bad way), wearing a two-day-old bra and knickers, bags under her eyes that could double as hand luggage and breath that could kill a dog.

She looked away with a weary sigh; as in life, so on her face – the chaos was there, writ large for all to see. Tom. Joe. Poppy. The three of them chugged through her mind one after the other. All interconnected, disrupting her life in their own, individual ways.

She staggered into the kitchen – as Elle optimistically called it – and boiled the small kettle, steam rolling around the tiny space; it was like cooking in a cupboard but she somehow put a coffee together and pushed up the kitchen window, climbing out onto the rear fire escape.

She didn't know what time it was but it must have been late morning, judging by the position of the sun, the roar of the traffic and the already intense heat. The iron stairs felt cool against her skin and she lay back, allowing the sunlight to warm her stiff muscles and soothe her battered body. Thank God it was the weekend. A red-brick tower block looked down upon the alley, anyone could be watching, but she didn't care. So what if she was in her underwear? It was no different to being in a bikini. That was what Joe had said anyway.

Joe. Tom. Joe. Tom.

She lay there for a long time, trying not to think about either of them. She knew that in being here she was hiding again, doing precisely what she'd promised she wouldn't, but she needed time to think. Tom would have been on her steps *again* last night, of that she was certain, and she wasn't ready yet to deal with him. The way he'd fallen apart when Jack had spelled out the danger she'd been in with Joe, that she could have been hurt too . . . He had been devastated and she had seen that – in spite of everything, his weakness, his inability to commit – he did love her. She didn't doubt that.

She had comforted him out of instinct, habit, and he had seized it. He knew what she'd done with Joe; she knew what he'd done with Serena and yet still, still he wanted to continue? To try again? How many times could they do this – keep going back to each other, leaving again? They were toxic, no good together. Surely one of them needed to draw a line in the sand? She thought she had done that by moving here. Seemingly not. It was their same old story, just in a different city.

A movement at the window made her jump suddenly,

almost spilling her coffee over herself, and she slapped a hand over her chest as she saw Elle standing there, a most unamused expression on her face as she held out Chloe's phone. Her hair, wild as a box of springs, looked fabulous.

'If you don't answer this thing, I will drop it out the freaking window, you hear me?' she mumbled, barely coherent.

'Oh, babe, I'm sorry,' Chloe gasped, taking it from her. 'Did it wake you?' She glanced at the screen – six missed calls. An unregistered number. Tom? Using another line?

Her stomach contracted. What if it was Joe? The police had told her to contact them if and when he got back in touch.

Elle groaned dramatically, reaching an arm up to the window frame and leaning against it, looking like she might go back to sleep standing up. She too was in just her underwear, although hers was a lemon satiny set from Victoria's Secret and she still managed to look like she was modelling for a catalogue. 'Ugh, why did we do that?'

'Because it was fun?' Chloe leaned back against the steps again, face tilted to the sun like a sunflower.

'*Fun?*' Elle was quiet for a moment, her head still on her arm, before a small smile curved her lips. '. . . Ha, yeah, I guess it was.'

'God I'm tired,' Chloe mumbled. 'I just need to sleep. That's twice this week that I've drunk myself into oblivion and in between, I've been house-hunting in *Greece*. I'm so jet-lagged and hungover, my body literally can't take it.'

'That's the jet-set for ya. No one ever said it was easy.'

'Well, I'm not getting on another plane for at least a year.'

'You say that like you want sympathy.'

'I *do*. I deserve it. I've had a shit week.' Her phone rang in her hand and she jumped. Unregistered number again. She stared at it as it continued to ring.

'Jeez, answer it, why don't you?' Elle said grumpily. 'I've had enough of whoever that is disturbing my morning.'

Chloe looked up at her, panicky. 'But I think it's Tom.'

Elle rolled her eyes. 'Your freaking love life . . .' she muttered. 'You need to sort it out, once and for all. At some point, you need to stop running away from your problems and start facing up to them.'

Chloe bit her lip. Elle was right.

'Hello?' She pinched her temples with her free hand, waiting for his voice, that beseeching tone that he had taken to using with her now, always so certain she was about to hang up again.

'Where have you been?' The demand was furious.

'*Alexander?*'

'I have been trying you for hours!'

'I-I'm sorry. I didn't recognize the number.' She frowned; his anger was like a Saharan wind against her face, scorching her.

'That's because it is a new one. I always change my number every month.'

'Oh.' Was she supposed to have known that? Was it in the files? 'Is everything okay?'

'Okay? How can it be okay? Have you not seen the news?' His tone was incredulous.

'I . . .' She squinted, trying to catch up, sober up. Last night she had gone straight from the hospital to the bar to back here. 'No, I'm sorry. What's happened?'

There was a pregnant silence and she braced herself for the next ballistic round. And when the words came, they were indeed like gunshots. 'My wife is missing. Believed dead.' In a flash, his anger had gone, his voice quiet, young, flat – like these were lines he was being forced to say, but didn't believe. Couldn't.

The entire soundtrack of New York fell away as the words echoed in her head. She had seen photos of his wife; she was incredibly beautiful, a former model; Chloe thought she recognized her from some campaigns a few years back. 'Oh my God, Alexander, I'm so sorry.' Her voice was thin, insubstantial, shredded with shock. 'Oh my God.' She slapped a hand over her mouth. 'What can I do? Tell me how I can help?'

'Get over here. I need somebody I can trust.'

'Of course. I'll leave right away,' she said, already pushing herself up to standing. 'Where are you?' His apartment was on Park.

'The South of France.'

She ran all the way back home, twelve blocks in nine minutes. A Swiss flight was leaving JFK at one-forty; if she could pack and be at the airport within the hour, she could make it.

She didn't notice her loose rattling brain as she ran or her ragged breath as she took the steps outside her building two at a time. There was no time for a hangover now, no such thing as a weekend. Her hands shook as she tried to get her keys in the lock, throwing off her dirty, travelled-in, partied-in clothes on the floor as she darted through the apartment in a pale streak of limbs and panic, showering in three minutes and stepping out with wet hair – God, she loved having short hair – towelling it roughly before throwing open her wardrobe and looking for something clean to wear. Dropping the towel on the floor, she noticed again last weekend's opera dress still on the chair. Would she ever get a chance to return it? It had cost over $2,000. She didn't want to have to pay for the damned thing, she'd never have the occasion to wear it again.

But there was no time to return it now. Again.

She slipped on her white jeans and a Breton top; she was just sliding her feet into her new Gucci trainers when she heard a sound.

She looked up and almost screamed.

Tom was standing in the doorway to her bedroom, watching her.

'Jesus! You almost gave me a bloody heart attack!' she cried, almost weak with shock.

'You left the door open. You need to be more careful. Anyone could have come in.'

She looked at him – his assumption that he wasn't anyone was a bit rich. She sighed, taking in his day-old stubble, the reddened rims of his true-blue eyes, and she knew what he'd come here for; but just like that dress – it wasn't the time. Opening her wardrobe, she grabbed her leather hold-all from the shelf. 'Tom—'

'Where are you going?' he asked, part-incredulous to see her begin packing up again, part-resigned. 'Oh, for Chrissakes, don't tell me you're leaving again!'

'This is *work*. For *your* company!'

His expression changed, darkening. 'Joe Lincoln? He cal—?'

'Alexander Subocheva,' she said, reaching down for her nude ballet pumps sticking out from under the bed. 'I take it you've heard about his wife? Apparently it's all over the news.'

He frowned. 'No. What?'

'She went missing last night; she's presumed dead.'

'Jesus!' He visibly paled. 'What happened?' He came further into the room, stepping over her wet towel, not thinking to pick it up.

'I don't know the details yet but he wants me to join him in France.'

'Why?'

She shrugged. 'He says he needs someone he can trust.'

Tom watched her as she ordered an Uber.

'Well when will you be back?'

'I have no idea.'

She started throwing clothes into her leather holdall – lightweight trousersuits in sober colours, a black shift dress for the worst-case scenario . . .

'You must have some notion?'

'How? How can I know?'

He looked agitated. 'So then talk to me now. Look at me.'

'I've got a flight to catch, Tom.' She checked her passport was still in her handbag; she always carried it with her.

'But I might not be here when you get back. I can't stay out here forever. I've got to get back to London.'

She kept her eyes on her packing, rolling up her knickers into balls and stuffing them in her shoes. If it had been intended as an ultimatum, it had failed. 'So then go.'

There was a pause, his stare becoming weighted. '. . . Just like that? That's it then?' His voice sounded flattened, steamrollered.

'Yep.'

Another long silence. She could feel his frustration build; she knew him so well. Five seconds, ten. The pressure was building up inside him as she moved with hasty efficiency.

Sure enough . . . 'What the actual fuck, Chlo? Do I not even get an explanation? Monday, you—'

'You know exactly what happened,' she said, talking over him, a quiet, calm voice. She turned her back to him, climbing onto the bed and looking for her sunglasses in one of the boxes on the high shelf.

'No! I don't!' he cried. 'I waited in that room all fucking night for you and you never showed. You didn't answer my calls. You didn't turn up to work. And then the next thing I heard you were with *him*.'

The way he said it – her eyes met his. 'Be careful, Tom. People in glass houses and all that.' Finding the shades, she jumped back down again.

'What?' He threw his hands out furiously. 'What are you talking about?'

She threw them in the bag and stopped. 'I'm talking about Serena, Tom.'

He paled, as instantly and completely as if he'd been doused in milk.

'I saw her coming out of your room. I was standing right there. I heard you both. "Call me – day or night," you said.'

He wetted his lips, looking ashen, desperation in his eyes. 'Oh Jesus, Chlo, look, it's not what you think—'

'No? So you're denying it then?'

'I . . .' He stared at her, his arms hanging helplessly by his sides.

She gave a silent snort of contempt. 'I didn't think so.' She stared into the bag, her life packed into it as she prepared to blow away to the next chapter, on the road again. 'Just go back to Lucy, Tom. Or Serena. Whatever. *Whoever*.'

She zipped up the bag, just as her phone buzzed. She checked it – the car was outside.

'But I don't want them. I want you. I came over here for you. Everything I told you on Monday was true.' He was pleading now, begging, as he saw her straighten up, getting ready to go.

She looked at him. He was the second man in two days to ask her to stay; the second man in two days to betray her. She wouldn't do this any more. 'I don't believe you, Tom. You're too late. You *had* me! I was there, by your side, every day for four years. I would have done anything for you. I adored you; you were the man I wanted to spend the rest of my life with.' She shrugged, feeling her own tears gather. 'But you've blown it. I just don't trust a word that comes out of your mouth any more.'

She picked the bag up off the bed.

'Please! Don't go,' he said, reaching out and stopping her, his hands on her arms. 'Let's talk about this.'

'There's nothing to say.'

'Really? So what about Joe? Or rather, the guy *masquerading* as him? Is there anything to say about that?'

Chloe felt winded by the sound of his name again, the memories raining against her like blows.

'Because I know what happened. It was written all over your face in the meeting.'

'I know you do,' she said calmly. 'But *this* isn't about him.'

'I disagree!' he cried. 'You slept with him, Chlo! Are you going to tell me it was a mistake?'

She didn't reply. Was she? Clearly, logically, it had been. The man had done nothing *but* lie to her. How could she condemn Tom for the same crime and not Joe too? How could she? And yet . . . ? 'Of course it was.'

'Do you *bitterly* regret it?'

'Of course I do.'

'But it just happened, right?'

'Yes.'

'It was just a terrible error of judgement; something you would change in a heartbeat and would never repeat if you could go back in time . . . ?'

'Don't try to make out I'm the same as you, Tom.' Her voice sounded tired. She didn't want to argue with him any more. 'This is about you and the fact that I cannot trust you.'

'But you can! I'm telling you the truth. None of it was a lie. We just made bad decisions, both of us. But we can come back from them. I can forgive if you can. *Chlo?*'

She looked around the messy flat – clothes everywhere; life interrupted again as though she couldn't settle here, no matter how hard she tried. She looked back at him with a flat stare. 'You need to pull the door hard on your way out, okay?'

Chapter Twenty-Four

Though her body was still, her eyes were gliding over the salon like they were on skates. This yacht was an entirely different animal to the one she'd been on earlier in the week, in a different sea, with a different client. It was five times the size, for starters, with none of the sinuous lines of the schooner, no sense of understatement. And this wasn't even the main attraction but merely Subocheva's shadow yacht, the auxiliary vessel to his prized J Class and now the headquarters for coordinating the search for his missing wife.

More like a tanker to look at, it was low slung and blocky; white hulled and double-tiered with blacked-out windows and a double-storey below-decks hull. Its principal mission was to carry sails, all the smaller craft and toys, provisions and a helipad, but if it had originated as a workhorse, it had been outfitted to a billionaire's expectations of comfort: there was a lap pool on the top level, the main stateroom was all pocketed white suede sofas and French-polished walnut; it slept eighteen in nine majestic suites and had an army of twenty-five staff, all clad in red shorts and navy polos. Not that their presence had done anything to protect their owner's safety.

Chloe had learned what she could on the flight, reading every newspaper report and watching the news channels over and over for new information. But in spite of the story being repeated on a loop, it seemed the news agencies were low on actual facts – Elodie Subocheva had disappeared from her yacht overnight; her disappearance had not been discovered by staff until the following morning and no body had yet been found. Accident. Possible Suicide. These were the words being repeated by the chief of police tasked with investigating her disappearance but it seemed to Chloe that the story was being treated by the news services less as a human tragedy and more as an opportunity to run clips of the Subochevas' glamorous lifestyle – shots of the two of them together on the red carpet, Elodie slight and ethereally beautiful beside her big cat of a husband, her hand like a child's in his; archive footage of her walking in the Yves Saint Laurent show, all Bambi legs and big eyes; aerial footage of their magnificent pale-pink villa in Cap d'Antibes, a holding shot of the yacht Chloe was now sitting in.

Alexander himself was broken, locked away in his suite, a stream of staff trying to go in with messages, questions, phones, food – only to be thrown straight out again; even Anjelica wasn't granted access to the inner sanctum, in spite of her steeliest glares and low-voiced threats to the guard on the door that she categorically had to see her boss.

Chloe was sitting on the suede sofa in the stateroom, keeping as still as she could and doing her best to stay out of the way. Alexander had been informed of her arrival forty minutes earlier but she knew he would see her when he was ready. He had called her here for a reason; she was here by personal request.

There was an air of barely suppressed panic on board; the staff looked terrified – they were being interviewed in turn by the police; they would all most likely lose their jobs, but that wasn't what was making them look so worried: they had failed their employer, a powerful man who was known for pressing for his pound of flesh. If foul play should come to be suspected . . .

From what she could ascertain, the biggest hindrance to the investigation was that no one knew exactly what time Elodie had disappeared. According to the staff interviews, she had taken a light supper on the main deck at eight, sitting alone, reading her book – *The Unbearable Lightness of Being*. One of the security guards patrolling the boat had seen her standing by the handrails on the port side just before nine-thirty; she often did this; she had been looking out to sea and was wearing a green silk dress. It was the last known sighting of her; by the time the guard had completed a lap around the boat and come back, she was gone. He had assumed she had retired to her room.

Her bed had not been slept in but the book was back on her table. The maids were adamant they hadn't returned the book to the room themselves so this posited two scenarios: one, that Elodie had returned the book to her room after dinner but then went back on deck a short while later to watch the stars. The other was that she had not returned to the room at all, until after the security guard had seen her on deck.

The chief of police – a Monsieur Desfils – seemed to think this was important. If it was the former scenario, then her disappearance could be tagged to those minutes around nine-thirty, falling – or jumping – overboard in the time it took the security guard to patrol a lap (three minutes nineteen seconds apparently; the police had had one of their officers walk and time it). But if she had only returned the book to her room after standing on deck, then she had to have left her room again later, which could have been any time in the night.

And there was the problem. The alarm hadn't been raised until 8 a.m., ten and a half hours later. The yacht had been moored but the strong winds and local currents last night meant they were looking at a search radius of almost 300 nautical miles. They were in a race against time. Even if Elodie had survived the fall and a night in the water, she was still in grave danger. She would be tiring fast by now and these were busy waters, with very many large vessels – fishing boats and ferries, as well as privately owned yachts – ploughing turbulent channels; and whilst this might create some hope she would be spotted, there was a greater fear she would not be seen in the dark, in time, that she would not be able to move away . . .

Not that there seemed to be much realistic expectation by either the police or the coastguard that she was still alive; Chloe – watching them – could see it on their downturned faces, the grave shakes of their heads, the flat timbre of their voices. Seemingly, it was only Alexander's raging grief and wide-reaching political connections that were keeping them going through the motions of exploring these faint hopes.

She kept looking down at the text that had just come through. It was from Poppy's phone.

No Joe.

The reiteration of those two little words that told her so much. He wasn't Joe Lincoln, that much she already knew, but now she could add that he had never been lined up as a client; that Poppy had never met him; that he wasn't supposed to have been there that morning. So what did he want? Who was he, and as Sergeant Mahoney had asked, why had he targeted *her*?

A security man came and filled the doorway that led from the stateroom down to the suites. Chloe looked across. 'Mr Subocheva wants to see you.'

She rose to follow him, feeling Monsieur Desfils's cool gaze upon her as she left. He had demanded to know who she was when she'd stepped on board, and discovering that she was the victim's husband's *lifestyle manager* hadn't endeared her to him. In fact, he had regarded her with outright suspicion, as though already predicting that whatever she was asked to do, it would no doubt be an interference with his job. He was probably right.

A door was opened for her and she walked into a suite; only, it was more like a war room with generals everywhere. In the centre of the far wall, in front of a TV set to a news channel on mute – Elodie and Alexander's own faces flashing across it frequently – there was a nautical map on a white screen with several red crosses and one large irregular circle drawn on it, a team of men huddled over a table. It was clear that this was the true nerve centre of the investigation, the hub of the action. The police would be hampered by red tape, bureaucracy and laws, but with Alexander's unlimited resources, he was going to leverage everything in his power to find his beloved wife. Alexander himself was sitting on his own, staring at the map with a focus that, if concentration alone could bring the solution, would have already yielded the answer.

'Alexander,' she said quietly, sitting on a chair off to his side, not bothering to wait to be asked. This was no time for pleasantries. 'I'm so sorry. Tell me how I can help.'

He looked across at her, his eyes red-rimmed and blank. He looked dead inside, as though his missing wife had snatched his soul with her as she fell from the deck. He

opened his mouth to speak, but the words came from someone else.

One of the men at the table had turned round. 'We need
helicopters.'

Helicopters? Plural? Chloe glanced between him and
Alexander, back to the man again. It was clear he was the
war general, dictating strategy, calling the shots.

She straightened up. 'Okay. How many?'

'Twelve.'

Twelve?

'All military. Fully fitted with infrared telescopics –
they've got the range and the equipment we need. And I
want four paras in each – two front, two back.'

Chloe was quiet for a moment, taking it in – he wanted
twelve decommissioned military helicopters and forty-eight
former paratroopers to find Alexander's wife? She knew it
could be done. But could it be done in time?

She glanced back at Alexander again; he was staring at
the map – into it, as though seeing into the very sea itself,
his wife's lifeless, beautiful body drifting below the surface.
His grief was palpable, he looked completely undone.

'I'll see what I can do—'

'No. Don't see, *do* it,' the man said harshly. 'I want them
in the air within the hour.'

Chloe felt a wave of fear wash through her. That simply
wasn't possible. Their contacts didn't extend to mercenaries,
to arms dealers! These things he wanted couldn't just be
pulled from a file.

A phone rang somewhere in the room; someone else
picked it up.

Chloe couldn't take her eyes off Alexander; he had barely
moved in the time she had been here. She wasn't even sure

he was aware that she was here; he had looked at her but she wasn't convinced he had seen her. Her eyes fell to his hands – he was holding one in an unnatural fashion, upturned on his lap, inert.

She reached over and slowly, gently, turned it over. It was grossly swollen, the knuckles purple.

'Alexander, have you seen a doctor?' she asked him. No answer. She looked back at the general. 'Someone needs to look him over. His hand looks broken.'

'He's fine.'

'No. He's in shock and he needs medical attention.' She surprised herself with her tone of authority.

The general hesitated a moment, before nodding to one of his team. 'Get the doctor.' He looked back at her. 'And *you* – get those choppers.'

'—call you back.' Another sound entered the fray as someone suddenly turned on the volume on the TV, wheeling the white screen with the map on it out of the way. 'Mr Subocheva, you need to see this.'

They all looked up at the screen that was now tuned to a financial news channel, red ticker tape running across the bottom with numbers that made little sense to her. Arrows pointed up. Others down. A silence spread as they all listened to a suited reporter in a bright studio. Chloe took a moment to tune in, wondering why the hell they were listening to this when Alexander's wife was missing.

'. . . *shares in Gelardi Hotels are expected to drop when the markets reopen on Monday as the market weighs the details of this shock bid. The mixed shares and cash offer that was put to the board late last night values Black Pearl at $9.6 billion. It is believed that the bid would push Gelardi's gearing to 145 per cent, with the credit agency Standard & Poor's poised to put the company's* *rating of A on watch with negative implications. However, many on Wall Street are saying this is only an opening shot and that . . .'*

The TV was turned to mute again, the anchorman continuing to hypothesize and report in comic silence as everyone in the room turned to look at Alexander. He was still sitting, still not speaking, but something had changed – his back had straightened, life was coming back to his eyes. Whatever that reporter had been talking about had got Alexander thinking hard, his breathing beginning to quicken.

He got up, his right hand still hanging limply at his side as he began to prowl in heavy silence. No one disturbed him. Chloe scarcely dared breathe. It was clear from the tension in the room that this was the first Alexander had heard of the bid and she realized it was probably the cause of Anjelica's extreme agitation outside; she hadn't been able to update her boss on this other, lesser, problem.

Chloe watched him pace. As if he cared about business at a time like this. She knew how much Black Pearl meant to him but compared to the human tragedy unravelling here . . .

'. . . This changes things,' he said finally, his voice little more than a growl.

Chloe looked up, baffled. It did?

'In fact, it changes everything.' He looked around the room with a clear, fresh gaze, beginning to nod slowly as if understanding now.

'What does it change?' the general asked.

But Alexander looked instead at her. 'We will not be needing the helicopters.'

'Uh . . . Okay.' She wanted to ask why but her voice wouldn't work; she ought to have felt relieved, but all she really felt was frightened. His physicality had changed. In one movement he seemed to have gone from prey to predator. Gone were the hunched shoulders and dropped head; in their place, a rolling, gathering intensity, as though he had swallowed a thunderstorm.

'Alexander?' the general prompted.

It felt like a long time passed before he replied, as though he was running the words through his mind several times over. He tapped his index finger thoughtfully to his lips. 'My wife is not dead. I do not believe she is even in the water. She never was.'

What? Chloe looked around the room, everyone else's expressions as confounded as hers. What on earth had just happened to make him suddenly come to that conclusion? She looked back at the muted television again. Surely that bulletin hadn't had anything to do with it?

'But how can you know that?' the general asked, looking concerned.

'Because this –' he gestured to the room, the boat, them – 'all this is a decoy. A distraction. Something to keep me busy.'

There was a confused pause as the general looked from Alexander to the TV screen, back to Alexander again, joining up the dots. 'You think Lorenzo Gelardi is behind *this*?'

'I know he is. Do you think it is a coincidence that within hours of my wife's mysterious disappearance, he makes the move he has been plotting for years?' Alexander growled. 'He was the one who torpedoed the initial merger; I know it, and he knows I have been exploring other avenues for refinancing the Black Pearl Group; he also knows that if I am successful in that, he will never be able to get his dirty hands on my company. Ever.' His eyes blazed with frightening intensity. 'This is Gelardi's only shot.'

Chloe watched him, she could see how his mind was working, tarring his rival with his own brush: 'Adversity is simply Opportunity turned inside out,' he had once told her. She glanced out of the window – the night was flashing blue and red as police boats and the coastguard came to and from the yacht like it was a hive. Everyone was working to find her, a fragile slip of a woman in fathoms of water. And now Alexander was saying she wasn't there after all?

'I know Lorenzo,' he continued, talking to everyone and no one. 'I know how his mind works. I know what he wants and I know he will stop at nothing – *nothing* – to get it.' He stared at them all with trembling anger. 'Elodie is not dead. She is collateral.'

Collateral. The very word had a transactional connotation.

'But . . . but to take your wife hostage?' Even the general sounded incredulous.

'Not hostage; there will be no ransom demand. She is quite safe. Whoever took her for him will be under orders to treat her very well. Gelardi is not a monster, after all. Just a businessman.'

His jaw clenched as the words left him; the calmness in his face was terrifying, unnatural. The worse the situation became – and surely this was a turn for the worse? – the more he seemed to rise up. Didn't it occur to him that his wife could be in as much peril at the hands of his bitterest enemy – her long-forsaken fiancé – as she was in the water?

'Yes, that is the game here. Gelardi knows she is the only reason I would drop the ball. She matters above everything, even Black Pearl. He is forcing me to make a choice: find her or fight him.' Alexander's words came slowly, purposefully. He was still calculating the plot.

Chloe tried to keep up. She couldn't believe this was actually being posited as a scenario – creating this mayhem simply to distract from a business move happening halfway across the world?

Alexander was still pacing but there was an energy in him that hadn't been there five minutes ago. He had come alive, now that he felt his wife wasn't dead. 'That is it. That is exactly it,' he murmured, agreeing with himself. 'Gelardi is banking upon me being here, blinded with grief; he thinks I will not leave until she is found. He thinks I will think of nothing else.' He looked over at his men. 'But he thought wrong – that is *not* what I am thinking.'

'What are you thinking?' the general asked dutifully, watching his boss's face like a dog does his master.

Alexander's eyes narrowed. 'I am thinking about how it was that he came to know my wife was on the yacht. Without me. This was no mere coincidence – it would have needed planning. And that means he would have needed help.'

The room fell silent, everyone asking themselves the same question: if this was true, how had Gelardi known?

Slowly, like a cannon being wheeled into position, Alexander turned – coming to a stop as he looked at Chloe. His eyes were narrowed and hard. Chloe's mouth parted in fright. There was threat in his demeanour, his hackles up. She felt the sweat prickle the palms of her hands.

'What did you tell him, Chloe?'

She blinked, feeling afraid. He couldn't . . . he couldn't be serious? He couldn't honestly think . . . ? But everyone was staring at her with cold, expressionless eyes.

'How did Lorenzo Gelardi know my wife would be on the yacht, alone?'

'I . . . I don't know,' she stammered, feeling the cortisol spike.

'I think you do.'

She blinked, scarcely able to breathe. This couldn't be happening. 'Alexander, no. I didn't tell him. I would never do that,' she whispered. 'I've never even met the man. I don't know him.'

He walked towards her, all the more menacing for the dead arm at his side. 'But you know me. And you knew my wife would be here alone – you, me and Anjelica were the only ones who knew. This is the perfect place for an ambush: they could come in at any angle, silent, in the dark. There are no cameras. No dogs – no trace left in water. Security is limited.'

'Alexander . . .' She was beginning to tremble. He couldn't seriously think . . .

'You knew about the investors; you knew I was close to putting together a deal to shore up operations.'

'But I didn't . . . I would never . . .' The words wouldn't come. Panic was blinding her brain.

'Did I not make myself clear in New York, my need for absolute trust?' Ice threaded every word and she saw the whirling wilderness behind his eyes. It wasn't trust he wanted, it was control.

'I've never done anything to betray you, Alexander. I wouldn't.' Her voice was quiet and thin. But she was holding up. She wouldn't cry in front of them all. She wouldn't beg; she sensed it wouldn't help her anyway. 'I don't know anything about what's happened to your wife, or the history between you and Gelardi. I don't know anything about it. I came out here to *help* you.' She was shaking. Was the truth enough? Did he believe her?

He shook his head slowly, tutting quietly. It was more frightening than if he'd pointed a gun at her. Possibly.

'The thing is – I *know* there is a mole, Chloe.' His voice was quiet, calm, studied.

Mole?

'This is not the first leak but I thought it had been . . . sealed.' Alexander gave a tiny shrug, as though that was inconsequential now, beside the point. 'I see I must have been wrong.'

Chloe stared at him, her jaw slack but her body rigid with terror and confusion. He thought there was a mole? And what did he mean by 'sealed'?

Mole.

Mol-? With an almost violent shock through her body, she remembered what Poppy had been trying to write at the hospital, when they'd been interrupted by the nurse. Her stomach swirled acidically. Had Poppy been trying to tell her there was a mole? That Alexander suspected there was a mole? Oh God – her stomach dropped as she was hit by a terrifying thought. Had Poppy been trying to tell her that Alexander had thought *she* was the mole?

There was a horrible logic to it: Alexander was right. Poppy *had* had access to his diary and movements in a way that almost no one else did – always knowing where he was in the world and with whom: which hotel and room he was staying in, what he'd ordered for dinner, the name of his driver . . .

But it prompted a question so terrifying, she wanted to throw up. Because if Alexander had thought that, then what had he done to silence her?

She gasped, looking at Alexander in horror. 'Oh my God, it was you,' she whispered, clasping her hand over her mouth, tears rushing to her eyes. *He* had been behind Poppy's accident? Chloe began to tremble. Afraid. Angry. He wasn't a businessman, he *was* a monster – she'd seen in Poppy's hospital room exactly what he was capable of when crossed, when given a motive.

He stared back at her – a slow blink, unhurried, and she felt time spool out as they watched and assessed one another, both looking for the truth in the other's eyes. The police were in the next room, buzzing around outside these very windows – but they were still too far to help her. These walls were soundproofed – she had read the yacht's spec in Poppy's files – and the world had contracted down to the walls of this suite; she was surrounded by men who could hurt her without even having to try, to think. Because if he'd thought Poppy had betrayed him, then he was suspecting *her* of the same now.

Whatever Alexander might have believed before, he knew Poppy couldn't have done this; she wasn't the one to betray him this time, under police guard in a hospital bedroom, more broken than alive under wires and casts and tubes. Gelardi had taken his wife in pursuit of breaking up his empire and someone else had to have helped him; someone on the inside.

Someone like her.

Standing not a foot away from him, she could see the violence in his eyes and she realized with utmost clarity that he would show her no mercy – take away the silk-cashmere suits and the expensive toys and all that was left was the brute. She had flattered him in assuming that he had become someone greater, more noble than his past; she had chosen to believe he had evolved from the embittered young businessman who had bought a company purely to destroy his own father, that his philanthropy came from purer motives than vaingloriousness. But why should she have made those assumptions? Simply because Poppy was fond of him? He was a man shaped from abject poverty, grown from a boy starved almost to death. In the ashes of communist collapse, whilst others burned, he had risen like a phoenix from the flames. He had not just survived his childhood, he had thrived from it, and all it had cost him was his humanity. He was a gangster, capable of anything.

Chloe knew there was nothing she could say to convince him. He would trust only his instincts and minutes passed, no one speaking, no one coming to her aid as he watched her – assessing, deciding, reading the fear and disgust and anger in her eyes, because he wasn't the only one to sense an ugly truth now.

But finally, almost imperceptibly, he nodded and turned away. In a flash she went from being the most interesting, important, potentially most dangerous person in the room, to the least. Chloe felt she might slide to the floor but her knees remained locked. What . . . what had saved her? Her defiance? Her inability to lie? He had read her correctly that day in the Rarities bar. Had he just done the same here?

'What do you want to do?' the general asked, stepping forward, breaking the deadlock. 'Shall I notify the police? Get the coastguard to call off the search?'

'Yes.' And then he frowned. 'Wait. No. I have no proof of what I know to be true and trying to explain it to them will only waste valuable time.' He narrowed his eyes thoughtfully. 'No. Let the authorities continue their enquiries. It will be better for us if we allow the public charade to continue.'

He nodded his head towards the flashing-light emergency playing outside the windows. 'Gelardi will think his plan is working and that I am here – giving me time to get back to New York and call an emergency meeting of my investors.'

Chloe saw a look pass between the two men. Conspiracy. Agreement.

Alexander glanced back at her, as though remembering she was still there. Still listening. 'My driver will take you to your hotel, Chloe. Or the airport if you prefer it. I am sorry your trip here has been wasted.' They were back to the veneer of civility again.

'. . . No, not wasted,' she murmured. Even ignoring the implicit threat that had just hovered over her like a swinging axe, even aside from what she knew now he had done to Poppy, she felt disgusted by what she was witnessing here. He couldn't know for certain that his wife wasn't in the water – not a hundred per cent – but he was prepared to follow his gut, to go with the hunch that this was a hustle. It was business as usual, no matter that he was playing Russian roulette with his wife's life.

One of the men opened the door, her cue to leave, and she walked slowly towards it, not sure her legs would hold up, just as a security guard walked through. 'The doctor to see you, Mr Subocheva.'

'Ah yes,' Alexander murmured, raising his injured hand and cradling it, as though noticing for the first time it was broken. 'Chloe,' he called after her, just as she got to the door. She turned. '. . . Your loyalty has been noted.'

What did that mean – that she was safe? Because it still seemed like a threat, a warning of sorts. She was on his right side – *just*. She gave a half-nod; she just wanted to get out of there. She didn't see the man coming through the doorway until they almost collided.

''*Scusez-moi,*' he said, his eyes meeting hers for only a second as he continued into the room, a medical bag in one hand. The door closed behind him.

Chloe did a double-take and stared back at it, wild-eyed, her heart thumping erratically. For a moment, she'd thought it was Joe. The broad strokes were the same – strong-shouldered, dark hair; but of course that could have been describing a quarter of the male population. It was just a similarity, a passing coincidence. In spite of all the terrible things everyone had told her about him, it was just wishful thinking.

Chapter Twenty-Five

Chloe stood at the window of her bedroom, unable to look away. Her hotel was set on the promenade and Alexander's yacht's lights were actually visible from here. She was riddled with exhaustion, the adrenaline on board now ebbing away and leaving her almost feverish – jet lag, so much transatlantic travel, sleepless nights . . . She wanted to stop, to collapse into her bed and submit to oblivion. Her head was swimming, too much was going on for her to handle. Everything was piling up and she felt buried, but she couldn't pull herself away from the window, watching as the search helicopter's beams swept the sea, vast cones of light brightening the dark water, high-speed RIBs zipping over the surface with whirling lights.

But they wouldn't find what wasn't there. Alexander was so sure of it, he was staking his wife's life on the arrogance that he could outwit his rival, that he could best him even in his darkest hour. As far as he was concerned, Gelardi had set up a dilemma – save his business or save his wife – certain he couldn't do both. And so now Alexander was doing precisely what his foe had calculated he wouldn't, and had abandoned his focus on his beloved wife's whereabouts to throw himself back into the boardroom fray.

But even if he was right, even if Gelardi *had* orchestrated the whole thing, Alexander was still taking a huge risk in calculating that Elodie would not be harmed; that she was simply a distraction and not a target. If Alexander did successfully stop the takeover, what then? Would Elodie simply be released anyway, a useless pawn who had served her purpose? There were billions at stake here and men had killed for a lot less.

On the yacht, she saw red lights begin to flash on the helicopter, the fresh drone of rotors adding to the melee out there. She couldn't see any people from this distance – she couldn't make out his bulk as he strode across the helipad, a god ready for war – but she watched as the sleek, light helicopter rose up, up, blowing rosy circles on the sea's surface, its nose tipping forwards as it rotated and headed towards the shore. His jet would be already fuelled and waiting, ready to take him to New York. To hell with Gelardi and Elodie and Poppy. He would win. No one would get in his way.

She sagged against the wall, still trembling, not knowing what to do. How do you fight a man like that?

A quiet knock at the door made her turn. Somehow, she recognized it. It had a pattern to it that her ear had long since become attuned to.

As if in a daze, sleepwalking, she opened it. Tom blinked back at her. He looked as dreadful as she felt – ashen, hollow-cheeked.

'What are you doing here?' she asked in a disbelieving croak. Could she trust her eyes? She was so tired. She hadn't slept, hadn't eaten . . .

'I was worried about you. I had to check you were all right.'

'Here?' she whispered, wanting to cry. 'You followed me

here?' It was so good to see him. After everything she'd been through tonight – the terror, the shock, the horror of it all – he was the sun to her snow. Whatever had passed between them, he was still her safety, her reassurance. Wasn't he?

'Of course I did. I'll follow you wherever you go, Chlo.' His eyes were swimming with regret; he looked as broken as she felt and for a long moment neither of them said anything. 'But . . . if you're fine, then . . . I'll—'

'No.' Her arm reached out, catching his; he turned back. 'Don't go. Stay with me.'

'. . . Really?'

He looked at her with an expression almost of disbelief and, in truth, she couldn't quite comprehend it either. But then, nothing in her world was recognizable any more, least of all her sense of what was right, what was best. Her days now seemed to have become populated by strangers who lied to and deceived her, threatened to hurt her, *had* hurt her friend . . . Where was her safety? Who could she trust? Tom had slept with Serena, yes, and she couldn't forgive that, not yet – it was still too raw. But what if he had been right, back in her apartment, and Serena and Joe had just been momentary weaknesses, just distractingly *there* . . . ? Didn't everything, always, ultimately come back to the two of them? After all, hadn't he always been honest with her about the real emotional ties in his life? She had seen for herself the bind he was in with Lucy, what with her father being a primary investor in his company and Lucy so vulnerable . . . She knew he was fundamentally a good man, albeit a weak one, trying to do the right thing between the two women he loved.

A chink of hope fluttered across his features and she saw the draw of breath swell his chest slightly, daring to fill him up. 'Oh, Chloe.' He cupped her head in his hands and, hesitating – as though anticipating an incoming right hook – kissed her tenderly.

She let him, her eyes open as though needing to see it to believe that he was here, she wasn't alone. It would all be okay now. He would make it okay. He would know what to do. 'I was so frightened, Tom,' she said, hot tears beginning to fall in sheets down her cheeks as they pulled apart and she looked back up at him. She was worn down, worn out.

'Frightened?' A look of consternation crossed his face. 'Why? What happened?'

'It was h-him. Alexander.'

'What was?'

'Poppy's accident. He thinks she betrayed him to Lorenzo Gelardi.' A sob hiccupped out of her. 'He thinks she's a mole.'

'*What?* My God!' He looked aghast, the blood draining from his face so that even his blue eyes seemed to pale. 'Are you sure? I mean, how do you know?'

'He as good as said it,' she replied, the sobs beginning to pile up, making her breath judder. 'And there were all these men there, his s-security . . . And the police were on board too but they couldn't hear me . . . I was so frightened, Tom. I couldn't get out.'

'Did they hurt you?' Tom's fingers gripped her shoulders, desperation on his features as he looked her over.

'N-no,' she managed, shaking her head. 'But Alexander – he thought it was me, that I was the one who told Gelardi that his wife would be alone on the boat.'

Tom looked confused. He realized that they were still in the doorway, their conversation audible to anyone who might choose to listen. He pushed her gently back into the room and closed the door behind him. 'Wait, I don't understand,' he said in a low voice. 'What has Lorenzo Gelardi got to do with Subocheva's *wife*?'

'Alexander is convinced Gelardi's team have taken her to distract him from what's happening in New York – they've launched a hostile takeover bid.'

Chloe wouldn't have thought it was possible for Tom to pale further, but somehow he did. 'You have *got* to be kidding.'

She shook her head. 'What can we do? He hurt Poppy. He tried to have her killed. What if he tries again? What if he . . . what if he comes after m—?'

'No! Don't say it! Don't even think like that.' His grip tightened on her arms again.

'But he confessed it, Tom. He knows that I know what he's done.'

Tom stared at the carpet, looking concerned. He was quiet for a long time. 'Then he must also know you can't prove it. He wouldn't expose himself like that unless he was sure.' He looked back up at her, worried. 'You *can't* prove it, can you?'

She slumped. 'No.' She was a minnow to his shark, with neither the resources nor connections to make such an allegation stick. She was no threat to a man like Subocheva. She was nothing.

'Well that's something,' he muttered.

'Tom, it's not! He tried to have Poppy killed and he almost succeeded! He can't get away with it.'

'Listen, I don't like it any more than you do but if anything should happen to you . . .' His voice splintered. He raked his hands through his hair, turning away from her. 'Christ, it's all such a fucking mess.'

'But if we speak to Sergeant Mahoney—'

'And tell him what? That Alexander Subocheva put his hand up to having Poppy run over because she was informing on him to his rival?'

'But she wasn't!'

'I know. I know in all probability she wasn't.'

'*Probability?*' The word was like a slap.

'Chlo, I know Poppy's your friend but this is serious shit. Can you say with one hundred per cent certainty that you know *for a fact* Poppy wasn't informing on him?'

'Yes!'

'No. You're saying that from loyalty – and it's one of the reasons I love you so much. But none of us knows exactly what has gone down and we won't know till the police have been able to question her.' He grabbed her hands and kissed them. 'Listen, don't look at me like that. I'm with you, okay? I adore Poppy too. I'm just playing devil's advocate: what if Alexander does know more than us? What if he is right and we're wrong?'

'He's not.'

'He gets security debriefs on everyone he comes into contact with. He has access to way more resources than us. Plus, let's not forget his paranoia.'

'Tom, Poppy would never have done what he's accusing her of. I know it. End of.'

He nodded. 'Okay. But it's still his word against yours. You can't go making accusations against him. Just take a moment to imagine the lawyers he'd hire. They'd rake over your life, Chlo, they'd destroy you.'

'But I don't care. I don't care about any of that. Let them! There must be proof somewhere.' She stared at him, feeling desperate as he sighed and walked away from her, going to stand by the window, his gaze on the search and rescue operation. It couldn't just dead-end like this. Poppy deserved justice. There had to be something they could do. 'At the very least we need to report it, for Poppy's sake,' she said, watching him.

'No!' he said forcefully, his eyes popping white as he spun back round. 'Chlo, you're not getting it. You don't make an enemy of a man like Alexander Subocheva – not unless you are *sure* you can win. He is too powerful. He could do anything, he's already proved that.'

'But—'

'No buts. I'm not prepared to do anything that risks your safety. That he already knows you know is risky enough, but if he hears that the police are beginning to link him with the accident, he'll come after you then, you can be sure of that.' He strode back over and held her by the shoulders, his eyes blazing with hot angry tears. 'I am so sorry about Poppy. You know I am; I wish there was something we could do to get her justice. But I need *you* to be okay more. I cannot and will not let you do anything that jeopardizes your safety. I don't know what I'd do if . . .' His voice broke and he dropped his head down, his own tears falling now. 'Jesus, Chlo.'

Chloe watched him, taken aback yet again by the scale of his emotions: all this fear, all this love . . . She stared at him, the man who was everything she'd ever wanted. For four years, her life had revolved around him. Alexander had been right on that one point after all: Tom had missed his cow when he'd found the stable empty because now he'd followed her to New York, chased her here to France, was protecting her . . .

He read her eyes, watched as the tears tracked silently

down her cheeks. '. . . Chlo, I know I don't deserve you, I know that. I've made so many mistakes, things I can't forgive myself for.' He hung his head, two red spots of shame pinking his cheeks. 'I know I should be a better man than I am and let you find someone who deserves you. But I can't. I just can't do it. I love you . . . Give me one more chance.'

Was it too much to ask? He'd given up Lucy, told his friends and family he'd been living a lie, risked the company's financial stability by angering her father, a key investor; got on a plane not once, but twice, to try to win her back. Of course, Serena flashed through her head again but she blinked her straight back out. Everyone makes mistakes. And besides they were even now, she thought, as she remembered Joe's dark eyes hungrily watching her as she slept on the boat, his bold, irreverent laugh as he'd pulled her into the sea. She blinked him out of her head too. Tom had had his indiscretion and she had had hers. The important thing was that they had come back together. United. Stronger.

And besides, after everything that she'd just learnt and endured this evening, a one-night stand wasn't the dealbreaker it had seemed a fortnight ago.

She reached up on tiptoe and kissed him lightly on the lips again, her eyes closed this time. It wasn't like that first kiss with Joe, his hand gripping her wrist and pulling her urgently to him. But it was nice. Familiar.

'Forgive me, Chlo,' he said, smoothing her hair back with his hands and clasping her head affectionately. 'I'll do better this time. I'll be a better man.'

She looked into his blue eyes. 'I know.' She felt his hands skim her waist, beginning things between them again, making her his, but she placed her own hands over them, stopping him. 'Do you know what would be better than anything right now?' she whispered.

He nuzzled his cheek against hers, running his hands through her hair and getting used to the feeling of it, short, between his fingers. 'Shall I run the bath?' He knew her so well.

She jerked her head towards the bed. 'Sleep with me.'

She saw the lust darken his eyes, felt his body straighten.

'No –' She put her hands on his chest, stopping him as he bent his head again. 'I mean, let's *actually* sleep.'

Chapter Twenty-Six

New York, mid-August, three weeks later

'Holy mother, who the crap *ever* had a waist small enough to get into these things?' Elle cried from the other side of the curtain.

'They used to wear girdles in those days, remember,' Chloe called back, reluctantly replacing the emerald-green dress she'd tried on the rail; it was beautiful but pointless. Where would she ever wear it? Kate was at the next stall across the aisle, browsing the vinyls and sporadically crying out 'How much?' in an indignant tone and then in an excited one: 'Hey, Chlo, remember this?'

This was her perfect Saturday morning, pretty much. A lie-in, walk in the park, a bit of shopping and soon, lunch. Who could ask for more? The weather was perfect, her sister was over from London.

It was perfect. Just perfect.

She sighed, reminding herself how lucky she was. This was the life she had always wanted and now she had it. Tom was being amazing, having offered to take Orlando to the swings while the girls had the morning together; he was so considerate like that. Kate was only over for the weekend – here for her birthday and flying back after lunch on Monday

– and every minute together felt precious. She had even brought Orlando with her, in spite of the craziness of travelling all that way with a toddler, just because she knew how much Chloe was missing him and that she had to feel the heft of him as she held him in her arms and marvelled at how much he had grown in five short months.

It was almost more than she could bear, having them both here, in the flesh, and several times, Chloe had had to hold back the violent urge to grab her sister by the arm and beg her not to leave, to move here too. Suddenly, London felt an awfully long way away and several times over the past few weeks, she found herself wondering why she and Tom were still here. She had only come here to set up a new life away from him; wasn't it ironic then that her new life here was *with* him? She wondered what Alexander would have to say about that. New York hadn't been anywhere near far enough away in the end. Not even close.

But London wasn't the warm home it had once been to Tom, for one thing. The break-up with Lucy had proved messy and many of their friends, scandalized by his long-standing affair, had sided with her. His home town wasn't going to be welcoming him back with open arms any time soon.

He kept trying to persuade Jack to do a job swap and move back to London instead, the headquarters needed one of them there after all, but Jack was proving resistant. Things were still strained between them both, for reasons Chloe didn't fully understand, and as Jack argued, he'd already been the one to uproot his life once before; why did it have to be him making the sacrifice again? (To be honest, Chloe thought he had a point.)

So, as a temporary measure, Tom had moved in with her;

it was just for while they decided on their future and what it looked like, but her apartment was tiny even just for one and they had already begun to bicker as they tripped over stray shoes and ran out of toothpaste. Tom had looked at various fancy apartments on the Upper East Side but they were all far too big and expensive for just one person and Chloe wouldn't discuss moving in together; not yet. Wanting things to work between them wasn't the same as wanting to rush headlong into the future; those four years of lies and deception were proving harder to forgive or forget than she'd anticipated and she needed time to come to terms with everything that had happened. Her head couldn't quite catch up with her heart. Or vice versa, she wasn't sure which it was.

'Forget it,' Elle said, tearing back the curtain in a huff and thrusting the prom dress at the stall owner. 'Like *anyone* is ever going to get into that.'

'Don't mind her, she's just hangry,' Chloe said apologetically to the poor woman.

'I am not!' Elle protested. 'I'm just fed up with clothes being made for anorexic midgets.'

'You're always evil if you don't eat every ninety minutes and we're now . . .' She checked her phone. 'Yes, we're in the red zone.'

Elle frowned, before noticing Chloe's empty hands. 'Wait, you're getting that green dress, right? Where is it?' She looked around them as though it might be on the floor.

'I put it back.'

'*Why?* It looked gorgeous on you.'

'No it didn't.'

'I'll be the judge of that and I'm telling you it did. Go get it.'

'Elle, even if it did suit me, I can't afford it. Plus I don't need it. You are forgetting that I am now the unworthy owner of an incredibly expensive Elie Saab gown that I am going to have to spend the rest of my twenties paying for.' She nodded her head towards the record stall. 'Come on, let's find Kate.'

'You're approaching that all wrong,' Elle called after her. 'Remember what I'm always telling you: cost per wear! The more you wear it, the less it cost you. I'm down to $150 on my Preen dress and I only got it in June. Gimme another few weeks and I'll be back in credit.' She gave a 'beat that' shrug.

Chloe tutted as they reached Kate. 'Well on that basis, I'd have to spend three years wearing it to the gym, to bed *and* to the office before I could break even. I will never need another dress for as long as I live.'

'Now we all know *that's* not true,' Elle smiled, joshing her with her elbow. 'Tom's so going to propose to you – isn't he, Kate?'

Kate hitched her eyebrows up. 'I bloody hope not,' she muttered, pulling out a sleeve of *The Thin White Duke* and turning it over to read the song list.

'Kate!' Chloe protested.

'What? You know my views,' she mumbled, squinting.

'Yes, you've made them perfectly plain! But how many times do I have to tell you? We've sorted everything out. We've, you know . . .' She gave a big shrug. '. . . Forgiven all the other stuff.' She mumbled the last bit; she and Tom seemed to have fallen into an unspoken agreement not to discuss either Serena or Joe. 'Bygones.'

'Oh. Bygones. That's what you're calling it, is it?'

'Kate, please—'

'Chlo, don't ask me to be happy about this when you

know and I know perfectly well that he is only going to hurt you all over again. Maybe not this month. Maybe not even this year, but once a cheater, always a cheater.'

Chloe felt her bottom lip tremble. 'People are allowed to change, you know. We all make mistakes, that's how we grow. We can't all get the fairytale romance like you and Marcus. If I can forgive him I don't see why you can't. This is everything I've ever wanted.'

Kate tipped her head to the side, a pitying look in her eyes. 'Is it though?'

'What does *that* mean?'

'I don't know,' Kate sighed, dropping her shoulders two inches. 'I guess I'm just not quite feeling it.'

'Oh, *you're* not? Because it's about your feelings?' Sarcasm dripped from the words.

'I don't mean it like that; I guess I just . . .'

'You just what?' Chloe demanded, feeling upset. 'You know, Tom's falling over himself to get to know you better but it's not easy for him when you're always making him feel like the bad guy.'

Kate looked at her sympathetically. 'And I get that, I can see he's trying. I guess I'm just wondering if the fallout was worth it. I know it's what you say you wanted, but now that you've got it . . . ?' She shrugged.

'What? You think we don't love each other?'

'No. But I just wonder whether you love the *idea* of each other more. Now that you've got him, does the reality match the hype? You just strike me as a little . . . flat. Strained. Like you're playing the part.'

'Like an actor? You think I'm acting out my life? I can't believe this,' Chloe said, shaking her head, looking between her sister and Elle. 'I can't believe you're saying these things.'

Kate took her by the arms, forcing her to make eye contact. 'It's only because I love you. You're my baby sister. I just want you to be happy.'

'And I am!'

Kate blinked, looking at her in long silence before dropping her arms again. '. . . So, okay then,' she sighed. 'Fine, that's great. Then I'm really happy for you.'

'No you're not. You're just saying that.' Somewhere, in the back of her mind, Chloe was aware that she sounded ten years old again, arguing with her big sister about who set the table last.

'If you tell me that this is what you truly want and you are truly happy, then I am one hundred per cent behind you. All the way,' Kate said firmly, her green eyes burning. 'Just do me a favour, okay?'

'What's that?'

'Don't rush into anything. Not yet. No engagement. No ring. No dress.' Kate shot a warning look at Elle. 'And don't you encourage her. My sister is quite impetuous enough.'

'I'm not!' Chloe protested again.

Kate threw her hands out. 'Uh, hello, are we or are we not standing in New York City, which you decided to move to within twenty minutes of finding out your boyfriend had got engaged to someone else?'

Elle grinned. 'She's got a point. And you did do the exact same thing all over again when you skipped off to Greece with the hot client.'

'Could we please not discuss that? It's entirely different. That was work. This is my personal life,' Chloe said in a low warning tone to her friend; she did not need Kate finding out about the Joe situation. 'And besides, don't call me impetuous when *you're* the one talking about wedding dresses!'

'Yeah, and given that's not happening any time soon, even more reason you should have bought the green one.' Elle folded her arms across her chest again, her point made.

Kate threw her arms around her sister and kissed her affectionately on the cheek. 'Look, I promise, Sis – if Tom can prove through his actions, sustained over the course of *many* years, that he loves you and deserves you, then I will love him as a brother and welcome him to the fold.'

'Heaven help him,' Chloe sighed, rolling her eyes but sinking into the hug anyway.

Kate kissed her on the cheek, before straightening up and checking her watch. 'In the meantime, he is looking after my beloved only child and I'd quite like to check that's all going to plan.'

'They were only going to the playground,' Chloe smiled. For all her briskness, Kate was like any other mother: anxious and worrying whenever her child was out of sight.

'Yeah, but you haven't seen Orlando in the sand pit. God help any child that tries to grab his bucket and spade.'

'Fine, I'll text him now and tell him we're done. Where shall we meet him?' she asked, looking across at Elle, the phone poised in her hand.

'How about that food market?' Elle suggested. 'I'm up for some more of those taco-things. I'd thought we were going to be making a habit of going there at the weekends.' She gave a pout that suggested this oversight was Chloe's fault.

And perhaps it was. Memories of Joe flickered in front of Chloe's eyes again: her surprise as he'd turned around that day; his surprise as he'd seen her, the plates outstretched in his hands. It had felt too risky going back there, in case he was helping his friends again (unless that had been a lie too?). She wasn't ready to chance seeing him, even though she knew he was more than likely spending these last few days of summer at the beautiful house she had found him in Greece. It was hard enough keeping him out of her mind as it was, without having him made flesh and blood again, and it took all her powers of persuasion to convince herself to see him as the police and Tom and Jack described.

'Tacos?' Kate echoed as they linked arms and wandered out of the market, past the yellow school gates. 'At this time of the day? But it's not even twelve.'

'Or noodles? I could totally do noodles.' Elle shrugged. 'Or pizza.'

'We have to feed her; Elle's not good on low blood sugar,' Chloe explained, banishing Joe from her thoughts with a determined toss of her head. 'Something to do with all that height, I reckon.'

'Hmm, well you look like you could do with an extra meal or two yourself,' Kate said, giving her a quick up-down. 'How much weight have you lost?'

'I wasn't aware I had.' Chloe glanced down at herself uninterestedly.

'Are you eating properly?'

'Yes!' Chloe groaned. 'God, you sound just like Mum!'

'Because she'd have a fit if she could see you. You're getting thin.'

'Chill! There's just been a lot on, that's all. I was running around too much. But things are quieter now.'

'Now that you've got fewer clients, you mean?'

'Exactly. I'm down from six to four now, which is far better,' she said, thinking how much quieter things were now that Joe and Alexander were out of her life. 'And I've stopped all that travelling.'

'Don't tell me – Tom's hidden your passport?' Kate cracked herself up laughing, Elle joining in too.

'You're funny,' Chloe said in an ironic tone. 'Really funny.'

'Hey Kate, has there been coverage of the "clash of the titans" in England?' Elle asked, looking across and down at Kate.

'Clash of the what now?'

'One of Chloe's former clients is locked to the death in a boardroom battle that's like . . . masters of the universe. Alexander Subocheva?'

'Subocheva?' Kate shot a concerned look at her sister. 'But the guy's a crook. You never told me he was one of yours.'

'Because I'm big on client confidentiality, thank *God*,' she muttered to herself, remembering again that terrifying hour on the yacht. It had become something of a regular occurrence since then, to wake in the night with a gasp, her heart pounding, Alexander's pale eyes boring into hers as he decided whether she was loyal, trustworthy, believable . . .

A jogger ran between them, splitting up their little group momentarily.

Kate frowned as they swerved back together again. 'His wife went missing, didn't she? The model?'

'Yes. Disappeared from their yacht,' Chloe murmured. 'It's coming up to a month ago now.'

'And they still haven't found her body?'

'No.' Chloe felt sick about it. Alexander had been wrong after all – that or he had underestimated what his rival was prepared to do to win. In public, it was purely a boardroom battle: Alexander had won the first round, holding off the takeover bid with a last-minute alliance with the potential investor from the Taj Mahal; the terms for Subocheva weren't as favourable as they might once have been, shrinking his personal holding in the group by 24 per cent, but he was still the largest shareholder and it had been enough to stabilize the ship in this storm – at least, temporarily. But last week Gelardi had upped his offer again and judging by the markets, it was winning growing support from the board.

That was the public face of the battle, but in private . . . ? If distraction had been Gelardi's intention whilst he made his move, that moment had well and truly passed; it had ended the moment Alexander's jet had touched down in Manhattan and he had thrown the full might of his attention onto the offer. He had made his choice between ostensibly saving Elodie or Black Pearl and he had chosen the latter. So why should Gelardi have held on to his wife? The eyes of the world were on the two men. It was far too risky and keeping her, hiding her, now achieved nothing.

If they'd ever had her.

It had made no sense to Chloe then and it didn't now. She had her own theory and it was bleaker than a woman being taken as collateral in a business feud; Elodie hadn't been taken by Lorenzo's men, and she hadn't fallen either. As far as she was concerned, that poor woman had jumped; Chloe had seen for herself the whistling hollowness in Alexander's eyes that night, the blackness of his soul. His entire life was about possession; Elodie would simply have been the most cherished object in his collection.

'It's so sad,' Elle said. 'I always thought she was so pretty. Did you see the Dior campaign she did a few years back?'

Kate shrugged. 'I had other things going on. Like pregnancy and labour. And how to mop up sick off your shoulder and make fruit purees with just one—'

'Yeah, yeah, we get it,' Chloe groaned as they stopped at a street crossing, waiting for the lights. Crowds gathered on their side and opposite. The cars rolled past – commuters, cabs, trucks, buses . . . everyone moving on to somewhere else. Faces in profile, nodding dogs, stacked ladders, stickered logos . . . It all rumbled along as the crowd of waiting pedestrians grew, some stepping off the kerb and walking along the gutter in their hurry to keep moving.

'Hey.' She felt hands squeeze her waist, a kiss on her cheek as Tom beamed down at her, looking very pleased with himself and panting lightly. 'I saw you from half a block away.'

'Did you?' she asked, feeling self-conscious that Kate was watching them. What did she see that was missing between them?

'Well, you're an easy trio to spot, to be fair,' he grinned, nodding towards Elle – already a head and shoulders above everyone else even *before* the Afro. 'Orlando and I sprinted to make it before you crossed. I've got to say, I'm pretty nifty with that thing,' he said, looking down at the stroller, before meeting her eye again and giving her a confiding wink.

She looked away, not quite sure what he was trying to tell her – beyond that he could navigate a pram.

'So – did you have fun?' he asked, taking her by the hand and kissing the knuckles.

'Yeah. You?'

'Sure did. He's a great little chap, Kate,' he said, addressing her directly on his right side. 'We had such a ball.' He looked back at Chloe again. 'I think I'm a bit of a natural, actually. I can see me being a dad.'

Chloe saw Kate's look of horror on his far side; she gave a nervous smile but said nothing.

The lights had changed, she realized. 'Oh—'

The crowd propelled them forwards into the road, bodies hustling for space between the stopped cars, meshing with the oncoming rush from the opposite side of the street. Tom was forced to let go of her hand as the two sides bled into each other. Kate, hampered by the stroller, fell back slightly. Chloe could hear her clipped accent in the crowd. 'E*xcuse* me.'

But it suddenly sounded far away, Chloe becoming aware that something had changed, as though the city had paused. She felt the static charge of an electric stare. Her head lifted as though in slow motion, her gaze seemingly flick-kicked up by another, straight into the beam of a pair of chocolate-brown eyes, steady and unreadable, coming straight towards her.

Joe.

He looked radically different, he had shaved for one thing, but she could still see the faint tan lines of where his beard had been and she recognized his walk, the sheer physical animal presence of him. Her lips parted in silent surprise as he passed right by her, he was there almost before she could process it and she felt a shock as his fingers brushed against hers, his gaze as direct and steady as ever. But he passed by without a word, without turning back, leaving her standing there and watching after him. Time had become fractured, noise muted, colours leached as he disappeared into the mass of bodies and all that remained were the remembered sensations of those eyes, those lips, still warm memories from under a Grecian sun, an Aegean moon.

She felt her entire body wake up. It didn't matter what everyone told her about him – what he was and who he wasn't – his was the face that walked through her dreams, waking her night after night, her head saying one thing, her body another . . .

'Hey, Chlo, you okay?'

Noise returned. Colour. Sense.

Kate was standing beside her, holding her by the elbow. The lights had changed and Tom was was already almost at the opposite kerb with Elle. 'We need to move. The lights are changing.'

'Oh—' Chloe let Kate grab her by the elbow and steer her across the road, but she kept twisting back, trying to glimpse one last sight of him.

'Do you know him?' Kate asked, following her stare. 'That guy?'

Chloe looked across at her sister and blinked. What could she possibly say? How could she explain? 'No, I don't know him,' she croaked. 'I don't even know his name.'

'This has to stop, you can't carry on like this – that thing's becoming a fire hazard,' Xan quipped as the cake was carried over to the table, the entire restaurant looking over and singing 'Happy Birthday' to her.

'Well, the problem is – I'm not sure I much like the alternative to getting older, Xan,' Chloe grinned as it was set down in front of her, all twenty-seven candles throwing out some serious heat. They were burning down quickly.

'I don't think there's time for you to make a wish,' he wise-cracked, pretending to look flustered. 'Quick, just blow them out.'

Chloe laughed and glanced around the table at the flickering faces gathered there – Kate, Tom, Elle, Jack and Xan. The closest she had to a family out here. Poppy too, but of course she couldn't be here. Not yet. 'Well before I do, I just want to say, this is my first birthday here and it means so mu—'

'No, absolutely not, you're playing with our lives,' Xan said quickly, blowing them out for her instead. 'We'll all be burnt to crisps.'

'Xan!' she cried, as everybody laughed, relaxed on good wine and full bellies. It had been a great evening, made even more wonderful by the fact that everyone had managed to keep it a surprise. Chloe had thought they were just having a quiet girls' night.

Across the table, Tom was watching with a soft-eyed expression. She had already received his present this morning – a deep box of La Perla lingerie (although there was nowhere to store the box in the apartment, and she'd said her drawers were so full, she might need to wear all the underwear at once), a rose-gold Cartier nail bracelet and tickets for the US Open final next month. He'd gone all out on spoiling her (even though she knew he would have received deep discounts on the brands and that the tickets would have been freebies) but she had still felt a twinge of disappointment that his gifts of lingerie and jewellery had been so *generic*. She had been dropping hints about a small still-life of apples that she'd seen in the window of a gallery in SoHo but he had ignored those, probably on the grounds it wasn't showy enough.

'Come on, open your presents now,' Elle said, clapping her hands, more excited than anyone.

The small collection of gifts had been stacked by the waiters on the shelf behind them and Jack turned round to hand them over.

'Open mine first. It's the biggest,' Elle said.

'Well, clearly that's the most important thing,' Chloe dead-panned, pulling the black ribbon on a pink tissue bundle. The emerald dress she had fallen in love with, but tried to resist for practicality's sake, fell open in a spray of silk chiffon, blooming against her hands like a rose. 'Oh, Elle—'

'Sometimes you need to have something frivolous and beautiful, even if it isn't the most practical thing. And *don't* say you can't accept it,' Elle said gruffly. 'No returns, the lady said. I already checked.'

Chloe smiled, knowing full well the stall owner had said nothing of the sort. 'You're so bad. I love it, thank you.'

Elle's stern face dissolved into the sweetest of smiles as Chloe reached over to hug her.

'Happy birthday, Miss Marston,' Xan said with a wicked tone as she picked a small rectangular package from the front of the pile. She took it with a suspicious glance, shaking it lightly. It rattled.

'Hmm. Should I be worried?'

'Yes!'

'Should I open it now or later?' she asked, seeing how he kept glancing over at Tom with wicked looks; he was still recovering from the shock revelation of not just her and Tom being together but their clandestine relationship history too – she had broken it to him over drinks when she'd returned from France, rather than letting him find out with the rest of the team via the brief but official acknowledgement that she and Tom were together. She hadn't wanted to go public with the news, not yet, but Jack had insisted – it was the very least they both owed him after all the subterfuge last time and besides, she understood his concern that keeping it secret was doomed to failure and would prove corrosive in the interim. 'Is this going to embarrass me?'

'*Moi?* Embarrass you in public?'

'So that's a yes then.' She lifted the lid and gave a huge groan. 'Oh God!'

'What? What is it?' Kate asked.

Chloe dropped her head in one hand, grinning and blushing as she pulled out a pair of furry handcuffs.

'Mink, don't you know,' Xan said, sounding like a duke, as Jack slapped Tom on the shoulder as though in congratulations. 'And I got a copy done of the key, just in case you should ever, you know – lose it. Just call me and I'll come straight over.'

'Thank you, Xan, *so* thoughtful,' she said with a sarcastic grin, glancing only fleetingly at Tom. 'You just think of everything.'

'I certainly try to,' he said, throwing a wink Tom's way.

'I'm afraid mine is rather less exciting,' Jack said, handing over what was clearly a book.

'Does it go glug?' she asked, tipping it over and pretending to guess.

'How did you know?'

She tore open the wrapping, but still gasped at what she found. A third-edition *The House at Pooh Corner*, the red cloth cover dusty and friable, faded at the corners, the thick pages yellow with age. 'Are you kidding me? I *love* Pooh!' she cried, hugging the book closely to her chest.

'I know. I'm afraid first editions are pretty hard to come by,' he said, almost apologetically.

'Uh – not to mention pricey!' she laughed. 'Jack, it's far too much as it is. I don't know what to say.'

'Well, I wanted to do something to, you know, make things up to you.'

'But you don't have anything to make up to me, Jack,' she said, casting him a quizzical smile. But he just shrugged.

Across the table, Tom shifted position and she could tell he was jealous. Did he suspect she preferred Jack's gift to his?

'Right, Kate . . . what's it going to be?' She reached for the small flat rectangular box left on the table. 'Is it an . . . inflatable flamingo for my pool?'

'You don't have a pool,' Kate laughed.

'For my bath then?'

'That either.'

'Is it . . . a tennis ball?'

Kate shook her head.

'A single shoe? I've always wanted one Louboutin . . .'

Kate laughed.

'How about a . . . oh my God.' Chloe's eyes widened as she dramatically pressed a hand to her mouth. 'Don't tell me it's a car key. Have you got a brand-new car sitting outside for me?'

Kate laughed. 'You're a riot, Sis. But I'm afraid my present to you is my *presence*.'

Chloe threw her arms round her neck and planted a kiss on her cheek. 'Best present ever.'

'Good. Because I'm afraid that little beauty is nothing to do with me at all.'

'So, then, who's it from?' Chloe asked, sitting up and holding the box up to the table. But everyone shook their heads.

'Uh-uh. I already spent my fifty bucks and I'm not spending one cent more,' Xan said, crossing his hands primly in front of him.

They all looked at her. Her eyes met Tom's questioningly

– was it an extra one from him? – but he looked back at her blankly.

'Well, a mystery gift. How intriguing,' she said dramatically as she slid off the ribbon and lifted the lid. She froze.

'Well, what is it?' Jack asked. 'Show us.'

'Aw, it's . . . *sweet*,' Elle said, reaching in and pulling out the gift.

'That is not sweet, it's naff. And totally pointless,' Kate said with a grimace. 'What are *you* supposed to do with that?'

'Isn't it self-evident?' Elle asked, trying it on herself before dropping it in disdain; even she couldn't make it work. 'Huh.'

'Come on, hands up who bought it,' Chloe said again, a smile wobbling on her lips, but her heart rate was beginning to speed up. Her eyes scanned the room, looking at the other diners, out past the windows, checking the waiters to see if any of them were watching her. But they were occupied and seemingly oblivious.

'Well, I'm not surprised they're staying quiet,' Kate said, sipping her wine. 'It's bloody grim. Whoever bought that thing has *terrible* taste in bow ties. Am I right, Chlo?'

'Yes,' Chloe murmured. 'You're right.'

Chapter Twenty-Seven

They lay on the bed, legs intertwined; matching pedicures, same-shaped feet – their father's. The green dress was draped over the bedroom chair for them to admire, the box of lingerie already a trip hazard by the door; Kate had fastened the bow tie around Marmalade's neck. The little TV was on, a bottle of merlot half drunk on the floor beside them as they channel-hopped.

'I don't think I will ever get used to American TV,' Chloe murmured, skipping from channel to channel in the vain hope of finding something that wasn't adverts.

'I think there's a lot of things you won't get used to,' Kate sighed, shifting position so that her head was resting on Chloe's shoulder.

'Like what?'

'Like having to say "jelly" for jam.'

Chloe snorted, rolled her eyes. 'God, yeah. You're right – I'm moving back.'

Kate dug her in the ribs with her elbow. 'Like whenever you buy something, you're going to have to hand over payment *without* saying thanks; and when someone walks into you on the subway and you can't say sorry.'

Chloe chuckled, finding an old episode of *Friends* and stopping on it.

'Like not being around to see your nephew grow up.'

'Oh don't—'

'Like not seeing me every weekend.'

'Kate—' she frowned.

'Just saying,' she shrugged.

'I miss you more than you could know. But I made a decision and I have to stick to it; my life is here now.' She bit her lip, wondering why it sounded like some sort of grim mission statement and staring at her fingernails, which had never been more perfect – one of the great perks of living in this city, there was a nail bar on every block.

A short silence bloomed, interrupted only by a spray of canned laughter from the studio audience. 'Well at least you've got good friends here, I can see that. Tonight was fun.'

'Exactly. Elle and Xan and Poppy . . . I just adore them.'

'And of course, now Tom's living here . . .'

'Exactly.'

'It's all perfect,' Kate shrugged.

'Exactly.'

'He's amazing.'

'Exa—' Huh? Chloe slid her eyes over to her sister suspiciously.

'No, he is, I mean it,' Kate said, looking back at her with a clear-eyed gaze. 'He adores you, a blind man could see that; and how many other men would go back to a hotel room to relieve the babysitter just so that his girlfriend could spend a few more hours with her sister?'

Chloe held her hands out. 'I know, right?'

Kate nodded.

They fell quiet again, watching as Joey ran around with a turkey on his head.

'So why don't you tell me what's really going on?'

Chloe's hands dropped. 'What?'

'I can't leave here till you tell me. I know something's not right with you, Sis. Everything's flat. You keep smiling but it never reaches your eyes; you tell me everything's perfect like you're reading out a recipe.'

Chloe's mouth opened but no words came out; her sister had fixed her with that gaze that made hiding so impossible.

'Well?' Kate pushed, jogging her in the ribs with an elbow.

Chloe curled up, jumping off the bed in sudden agitation. 'I don't *know* what's wrong. That's the truth.' She threw her arms out. 'I feel unsettled and I don't know why.'

Kate crossed her ankles, watching as she began to pace. 'Are things moving too fast with Tom?'

'I dunno. Maybe.'

'Is he still going on about you moving in together?'

Chloe cast a withering glance around the apartment. 'Well, this place isn't exactly designed for two.'

'So he can move out then, and you stay here,' Kate said, as if it was really that simple. 'Why not? Things seemed to go supersonic between the two of you after your trip to France. But after everything you told me – about that girl—'

'Bitch,' Chloe corrected.

'Indeed. That bitch at the office – why would you take him back? I just don't get it.'

'We have history. It's complicated and it's deep and I get that it's not the fairytale or a straightforward romance but . . . sometimes getting through all the shit and still wanting to be together counts for more than all that.'

'But after all those things he's done—'

'It's not like that.'

'Isn't it?'

'No, because he wasn't the only one to mess up. I'm no saint either, Kate.'

Kate paused for a moment, regarding her. 'Oh crap – you cheated too?'

'No, it wasn't cheating,' Chloe said hotly. 'Tom and I weren't together when it happened. And in fact, technically speaking, we hadn't been for over five months.' Ten minutes of kissing on a street corner could hardly count as being back together again.

'But then . . . when? *Who?*'

Chloe sighed, sinking onto the end of the bed, and tucking one leg beneath her. 'Does it really matter?'

'I think it does, yeah,' Kate argued. 'Have you seen him again?'

'No. Well, sort of.' She frowned, shaking her head. 'Agh, no, not really.'

'That makes no sense. Yes or no?'

Chloe knew she had to pick a side. 'No.'

Kate stared at her through narrowed eyes. '. . . Is he here? In New York?'

'He was. Then he wasn't. Now – I don't know.'

Kate pulled a bewildered expression. 'Jeez, Chlo, who the hell is this guy?'

'I don't know, okay?' Chloe cried, jumping off the bed. 'That's the whole bloody point! I don't know anything about him. He lied about everything – including his name. I slept with a fucking ghost!'

Kate sat up suddenly, her back straight, watching her.

'What?' Chloe swallowed.

'Oh my God. The guy in the street.'

'*What?*'

359

'The one with the intense eyes. He touched your hand. I saw the way you looked at each other.'

Chloe couldn't speak. She didn't want to think about him. She didn't want to remember – *arms outstretched as he flew between the balconies* . . . She looked away. 'I need some water.'

She disappeared down the tiny hall into the kitchen and ran the tap.

'Chlo, tell me what happened.' Kate was right behind her.

Chloe reached for the glasses, stalling for time, trying to think of ways to explain it, explain it away.

'It was just a holiday fling,' she said, handing over the water glass, her eyes down. 'A total disaster from start to finish. He was a client so . . .' *Watching her sleep on the boat.* She shrugged and pushed past her sister, heading back to the bedroom again. Goddammit, there was nowhere to go. A girl couldn't even pace in peace.

'Well, what does that matter?'

'It's unprofessional for one thing.'

'Yeah it is. But it's hardly the end of the world either. People fall in love at work all the time.'

Chloe glanced at her; it was exactly what Joe had said too. They resumed their positions on the bed, Kate crossing her legs and staring at her sister. They were back where they'd begun, no escape route in sight; there really was nowhere to go in this godforsaken flat. Chloe picked up the remote and began avidly channel-hopping again.

Kate took it from her and turned the telly off. 'So you had a fling with a client. Whatever. But clearly you have feelings for him.'

'No, Kate, I have confusion. Because it turns out he wasn't a client.'

'But you just said—'

'He wasn't a bona fide one, I meant. He was using someone else's identity.'

'Why? For what? Tickets to Madison Square Garden?' she scoffed.

Chloe looked at her. She knew what would happen once she told her sister about this whole sorry mess. She would want action. Results. 'You really want to know?'

Kate nodded.

'I think – and the police think – he was using us as a front for money-laundering.'

There was a stunned silence. Tom had reacted that way too, when she'd first said it to him, but it was clearly what Sergeant Mahoney had been implying with his questions . . . But where Tom had given her worried looks and beseeched that she 'stay out of it' and 'let the police do their jobs', Kate threw back her head and laughed out loud. 'No fucking way!'

Chloe double-blinked. 'Yes way, Kate. It's the only thing that makes sense. I've gone over and over it in my mind and . . .' It was the least of the disaster scenarios that played over in a loop in her mind. 'Look, he got us – well, *me* – to source him a house in the middle of nowhere, okay? Which he then paid for in cash, at more than double what it was worth.' She shook her head. 'The whole thing was suspicious as hell. He was throwing money around – flying in private jets, chartering a yacht – and all of it was paid for, upfront, behind my back – so to speak,' she frowned. 'I thought it was all going on his account. I didn't find out he'd paid them all till I got back here and chased for their invoices and they told me the accounts were already settled.'

'I don't suppose you checked his bags?' Kate quizzed. 'If

361

he was carrying around that much cash, he must have had a lot of suitcases. Money is heavy. So they tell me,' she muttered.

'Kate, this is serious. Besides, he has an account with a very private Swiss bank.'

'Right.'

'But it wouldn't surprise me if he had brought money over in one of the jets. They rarely check on the private flights, you know.' Chloe stared into space, going back over the memories and picking at the scar they had left till it bled again. 'Oh – and plus he had a whole container of furniture all ready to move into it, which he then brought over *again* by private charter. Looking back, it was like he was trying to spend as much money as he possibly could.' She arched an eyebrow. 'I mean, have you ever met a man who bought the contents before he bought the house?'

Kate shook her head. 'Don't they just go out and buy a washing machine and kettle the day after they move in?' She squished her lips together as she watched her sister for signs this was a wind-up after all. 'Damn, so you're actually serious about this. He was money-laundering.'

'Well, that's just my opinion. And the police's – possibly. They've got a number of theories.'

'What does Tom think? It's his company.'

'Tom thinks he works for Alexander Subocheva.'

'No way!' Kate shouted. '*That* guy? On the street? He didn't look like a heavy!'

'Not as security. Tom thinks he could have been working for him as a mole – keeping tabs on us; well – *me*.' Chloe felt another stab from the words. It was idiotic that it should hurt her more that he might be a corporate spy than a money-launderer. Neither scenario made him marriage potential, as her mother would say, but if he had been tasked by Alexander to get close to her, to find out what she was doing, then it meant everything that had happened between them had truly been a lie. 'Alexander thought we were leaking details of his movements to his rival and Tom reckons he used Joe to get close to me, to see if I would tell.' She had remembered his questions on the boat, trying to find out who she'd been on the phone to – trying to get her to give up the names of her clients, what they wanted. But every time she had resisted. Thank God she had resisted. Tom was convinced that was what had made Alexander let her go – Joe must have reported back that she was discreet, dependable.

She didn't know what to think. She felt like she didn't know anything any more.

'But you didn't?' Kate looked worried. 'Tell, I mean.'

'Of course not.'

Kate sat back, digesting the revelations. It was a lot for anyone to take in. 'So going back to the money-laundering thing – was it just the one house he bought, then? Because you'd think he'd buy more than one if this was a ring.'

'I know, but he might have planned more and he just didn't get that far. After we . . . hooked up, I told him I couldn't represent him any more.'

'Why?'

'Because I heard him on the phone to someone. A woman.' She looked up to the ceiling, feeling the tears threaten; they always felt just below the surface at the moment. 'Because what are the chances he's married? Y'know, just to add to everything,' she groaned. 'So I got the hell out of there and told him Serena would help him from now on. But she hasn't heard from him.' She sighed; she had devoted surprisingly little thought to Serena since getting back from

Greece. 'Unsurprisingly, I suppose. I came back here to a huge shit-storm with Tom and Jack; by then they'd found out Joe wasn't who he'd said he was and they'd got the police involved, worried he was behind what had happened to Poppy and that I might be in danger too. I guess he must have caught wind of it all somehow because no one's heard from him since. Whatever his game was, at the very least, he knows he's been busted as a fraud.'

'So we're looking at fraud, spying or money-laundering? Christ, those are big guns pointing at him, Chlo,' Kate said, looking anxious, and Chloe knew what she was thinking – where there was smoke . . .

Chloe remembered the whispered phone call on the balcony . . . *Arouse suspicion* . . . 'I know. And I know he is guilty of something bad,' she nodded.

Kate leaned in, looking at her more closely. 'But?'

'But . . .' Chloe sighed, pressing the heels of her hands to her eyes, as though rubbing out the world, even though the tears were falling anyway. 'Everyone's so dogmatic about him – the police, Tom, Jack – they're all telling me what they think he is and what they know he isn't. It's like . . . It's like they're trying to control what I think about him. And yet—'

'And yet you're still mad about him.'

'They don't know him! I do!' Chloe looked back at her, feeling a rush of despair, flooded with a desolation that until this moment she hadn't allowed herself to acknowledge. 'And when I was with him, it didn't feel like a lie. It felt real.' Her voice was barely audible, shame coating every word.

Kate looked back at her sympathetically, reaching over to rub her knee. 'But, Sis, if he's even one of those things that they're saying about him . . .'

Chloe sniffed, feeling stupid. 'I know, I know that's what

people like him do,' she said, looking away. 'He has to be convincing, a master manipulator.' She gave an embarrassed shrug as the silence extended. She wanted her big sister to bluster them through this; there was always a way with Kate. But even she couldn't tell Chloe what she wanted to hear; no one could. How could anyone possibly argue in favour of a man wanted for questioning by the police? A man who might very possibly be working for the man who had arranged for Poppy to be hurt? It was a mess, there was no upside, and after several minutes she forced a smile, forced him back out of her thoughts again. There was no point in this, trying to find solutions to fit – it achieved nothing. 'So you see,' Chloe said, taking a giant breath, trying to rally. 'When you consider the alternatives, Tom really isn't the duff option you thought, now is he?'

Kate forced a laugh but it sounded as contrived and false as it really was. 'Well, now that I come to think about it, he has been growing on me . . .' she murmured, still looking worried.

Chloe's eyes slid over to Marmalade, resplendent in his new harlequin silk bow tie. 'Yeah. My taste in men isn't *that* bad.'

It was commotion, people everywhere wheeling bags across the concourse, their eyes up as they scanned the display boards. Someone – Tom most likely – had told her once that at any given moment, around the world, there were always a million people in the air. And now her sister and little nephew would make up two of that number.

Chloe jigged Orlando on her hip as Tom helped Kate collapse the stroller over at the outsized baggage area. 'Now, no crying on the plane, you hear me? You're going on a big, exciting adventure back to Daddy who has missed. You. So. Much.' She tickled his tummy, making him shriek and wriggle with delight. 'And don't kick the seat in front because . . . well, it's really annoying.' Orlando put his thumb in his mouth and began sucking it; he looked tired already. 'And don't sleep too soon. And make sure you look after your mama for me when you get back, okay, little fella?' she said, chucking his plump cheek between her fingers.

Orlando blinked back at her, all eyelashes and dribbly lips and white-blond curls. 'God, I'm going to miss you,' she said, kissing his head as Kate and Tom came back.

'You're never going to believe this,' Kate said, her eyes bright and clutching Tom's arm excitedly. 'Tom's only gone and secured us an upgrade! To first class!'

Chloe smiled, looking across at him. 'I should jolly well hope so. There's got to be some perks to having the owner of a luxury concierge business as your sister's boyfriend.'

'Here, let me take my pal,' Tom said, taking Orlando from her with a groan. 'He's a heavy potato, aren't you, dude?'

'Not a topato,' Orlando pouted, making them all laugh.

'And what did you promise?' Tom asked solemnly.

'Not to eat peas on my knife,' Orlando said by rote, looking very proud of himself.

'Exactly. Because, trust me, I've been there and done that – and when it goes wrong, it *hurts*.' Tom pulled a face, making Orlando kick excitedly.

Kate turned to look at Chloe, tears already shining in her eyes. 'Oh God. I hate this bit.'

'Me too.' They hugged, so tightly their fingertips blanched. 'I wish you didn't have to go.'

'You're going to be fine,' Kate whispered into her hair.

She nodded. 'I know.'

'And I take it all back. Tom's amazing. He's fallen over himself to get to know me and Orly this weekend – and he clearly *adores* you. You could do a lot worse.'

'I know,' Chloe nodded again. 'I'm very lucky.'

Kate's grip tightened. 'You are. You are.'

Chloe felt her sister's fingertips tense on her shoulders and wondered which one of them she was trying to convince. They pulled away. 'FaceTime me when you get back, okay? Just so I know you're there safely.'

'Hey, who's the big sister here?' Kate demanded with a grin, taking Orlando from Tom and giving him a warm kiss on each cheek. 'And you look after my girl,' she said sternly. 'She needs it.'

'I will,' Tom said solemnly, taking Chloe by the hand. 'I promise.'

Tears dropped silently onto her cheeks as Kate nodded, looking at them both for one last time before she turned and walked into the bag-check area, she and Orlando waving frantically at the boundary before finally slipping out of sight.

Chloe felt a part of her going with them. She kept staring at the point where they'd gone, in case they should reappear. It was all she could do to keep herself from breaking into a sprint and joining them.

Tom turned to look at her. 'Well, I guess it's just you and me again, babe.'

Chloe nodded. Was it supposed to sound such a bleak prospect? 'I guess so.'

'Coffee?'

She sighed; smiled. 'Sure.'

Chapter Twenty-Eight

She'd brought flowers this time – a tall spray of palest blue delphiniums that held their own amongst the helium balloons and fruit baskets in the lift. Everyone rode up in silence, progression stilted as they stopped at almost every floor again, dropping off some only to pick up others.

She walked down the corridor; it was exactly the same as when she'd been here the other week, just with different faces. She couldn't see the nurse who had thrown her out last time, and it wasn't Charlie sitting outside her door. In fact, no one was.

'Hi, I'm here to see Poppy Langham,' she said, her eyes going back to the unguarded door.

'Name?'

'Chloe Marston. I'm a friend.'

'Room 822, down the corridor there—'

But Chloe was already walking. She slowed as she reached the doorway, steeling herself. Seeing her friend last time had been a traumatic experience.

Taking a deep breath, she popped her head round. 'Hey . . .' she said quietly. And then '—Hey!'

Poppy looked back at her with an almost-smile. She was sitting up, an iPad propped on her legs. Her left leg was still in a cast but her arm was supported in a foam sling now. The bruises and cuts had faded and there was real colour in her cheeks. But best of all, the bandages and wires around her head had been removed. She looked like Poppy again, no longer Mr Bump.

'Well, I don't need to ask how *you* are. I can see!' Chloe grinned, rushing into the room and carefully hugging her. 'I can't believe the difference.'

'What can I tell you – an alkaline diet, daily Pilates, gold facials and you too could look like me.'

The words were still a bit of a mumble but Chloe laughed. 'Oh, I have missed you.' She put the flowers on the table and sat gently on the bed. 'Nothing's been the same without you, Pops.'

'Eventful, I gather.'

'Oh . . .' Chloe felt her smile falter; she didn't want to distress or burden Poppy with the horrors that lay below the surface. 'You know, so it goes on. Want to hear Pelham's latest?'

'But of course.'

'Hot air balloon ride above the Serengeti.'

'Nice.'

'You'd think.'

Poppy managed a grimace. 'Tell me.'

'A bird flew into it, tore the canopy and they landed in the middle of the park with nothing to protect them but a wicker basket.'

'No!' Poppy gasped.

'Luckily, they were already descending when it happened so they weren't as high as they might have been; and the bright colours and the flapping of the balloon meant the animals were too scared to approach before the rangers got to them.'

'That *is* lucky. Were they okay?'

'He's got a nasty whiplash and she's got a fractured hand. But otherwise they're fine.'

'Which hand?' Poppy winced.

'Left.'

'Please tell me he got the proposal in first?'

'Of course not. He'd been waiting till they were over the caldera in Ngorongoro apparently. That poor man is destined to carry that ring around in his pocket.'

'Well, it's not going to go on her finger any time soon now, that's for sure.'

'Poor Pelham,' Chloe smiled, suppressing her laughter. 'Why he can't just get down on one knee at the breakfast table and ask her, is beyond me.'

'And how's our diva?'

'Well her affair with *el presidente* is raging on. She's back in Brazil at the moment so she's been pretty quiet for the last week. You know she had her hair cut?'

'No.' Poppy looked shocked. Rosaria's long raven hair was as much a part of her branding as her famous bosom and soaring voice.

'Naturally she regretted it within the day so I had to get the clippings recovered from the bin, sorted from the other clippings—'

'Ew!' Poppy pulled a face.

'—And made into a hairpiece. They managed to put it on clips so it just sort of looks like she's had layers put in now.'

'God, I'll have to google it,' Poppy said, eyes wide. 'And Mike?'

'Back from Jamaica now. He just about managed to get the album laid down, and he's in post-production now. Did you hear about the lead singer's OD?'

'Yeah. What happened there? I thought they were watching him like a hawk.'

'They were. We had several private doctors managing his prescriptions. But apparently he ordered a cake for the wrap party and it turned out to be dusted with cocaine. Everyone thought it was icing sugar. And on top of everything else he'd taken . . . '

'Unbelievable,' Poppy muttered.

'Mike's furious because it means the album can't be supported by a tour now and that's where the money is.'

'How selfish of his lead singer to have died on him like that,' Poppy said drily, shaking her head. But her smile faded. 'Honestly, this world. What's wrong with everyone? When did we all stop being *kind*? When did it become normal to care more about money than each other?' Poppy sank her head back into the pillow, watching her, and Chloe detected a shift in her mood, like a car moving down a gear. They both knew where they were heading. '. . . And Christopher? How's he?'

'He's happy,' Chloe said, trying to find the positive stories. Depression was common after a major head trauma. 'The festival went well – his new film was runner-up for the Palme d'Or at Cannes. He's in Sardinia at the moment on Coppola's boat so he's not calling in much. Although I did help out his daughter last week who had travelled to Belarus without sending ahead the paperwork needed for a visa.'

Poppy rolled her eyes. 'That's always fun.'

'Tell me about it. I must have spent five hours on hold.'

'Ugh.' A silence bloomed and Chloe knew what was coming. She could see it in the way Poppy looked at her; she could see it wouldn't be stopped. '. . . And Alexander. How is he?'

Chloe met her gaze. How could she tell her he wasn't with them any more, without explaining why?

'. . . Have they found Elodie?' Poppy said, before the words could leave Chloe's mouth.

'You know about that?' Her eyes travelled to the TV on the far wall. 'Oh, I see.' Of course Poppy knew about Elodie's disappearance; what else was someone bed-bound with broken bones going to do but watch TV? She probably knew more about the case than anyone – well, anyone apart from Chloe; she hadn't been able to tear her gaze from the fallout of Alexander's hubris, she couldn't bear that his wife had been the tragic victim of his craze for power, that his hunch had been wrong after all and his bluff had backfired. 'No. The search was called off two weeks ago.'

'The official one, yes, I know. But surely Alexander has his own team looking? He'll be so devastated. Losing her would destroy him. She's his world.'

Chloe didn't know what to say. 'Uh, no, he doesn't have a team out. He never did.'

Poppy looked stunned. '*What?*'

Chloe wet her lips, not sure where to begin, what to leave out. 'He didn't believe she'd fallen in the water . . . He thought Lorenzo Gelardi had taken her.'

'Lorenzo?' The colour drained from Poppy's face. 'But why?'

'As a distraction whilst he made a takeover bid for Alexander's hotel group.' She bit her lip, watching as Poppy digested the news. She looked fragile again, her earlier bloom of health fading fast. 'Which is crazy, clearly and *not* something we should be discussing anyway. I came here to cheer you up, not—'

'But this . . . no. This can't be.' Poppy's words were a croak, her gaze settling into the distance. 'The takeover . . . ?'

Chloe's shoulders sagged. Had Poppy kept up with the business news? How much did she know? 'Yes. They're still fighting it out but it looks like Gelardi's going to do it. Alexander had brought a new investor in, but from what I understand it's not enough and the majority of the board are now in favour of the new offer.'

Poppy looked back at her, dismay on her face. 'And Alexander thought Lorenzo took Elodie?'

'Well, I don't know if he still thinks that, but he did in the beginning.'

Poppy looked at her. 'Do you?'

'No. I don't think it was anything to do with Gelardi – other than a freak coincidence of timing.'

'Do you think she's still alive?' she asked hopefully.

'No.' Chloe shook her head, her tone flat. 'I think she jumped.'

'*Suicide?* But why? That makes no sense. He adored her. He gave her the perfect life.'

Chloe looked away – the more she imagined what Elodie's life might have been like with Alexander, the further away from perfect it seemed to get. 'Alexander wasn't . . . he wasn't the man he appeared to be, Poppy,' she said quietly, hoping they could leave it at that. She didn't want to have to tell her the full truth of what she knew about him; it would devastate her and terrify her in one blow.

'No, it's not *Alexander's* fault.' Poppy's voice was vehement. 'No, this is . . .' Her expression crumpled. 'Oh God, this can't be happening.'

Chloe took her hand and squeezed it. 'What can't?'

Poppy looked straight at her. 'Lorenzo did take her. And it's all my fault.'

Her words exploded like smoke bombs, filling the room, hissing in the silence. A mole . . .

'. . . *What?*'

Poppy swallowed, seeming to struggle to gather her voice. 'The night before my accident, I was working late.'

'Yes, I remember. You'd organized Alexander's dinner on the iceberg and you were staying to check it had all gone to plan.'

'Exactly. No one else was in the office, it was just me. And after a while I went out to get some dinner. I took my bag and was gone maybe forty minutes? None of the lights were on because it was still light.' She gave a tiny shrug. 'I suppose it must have looked like everyone had gone for the weekend.'

Chloe watched her, feeling a rising anxiety trickling through her nervous system. Where was Poppy going with this? Poppy's mouth had turned down slightly at the corners, paling, her voice becoming more strained.

'So imagine my surprise when I got back, to find someone sitting at my desk.' Her attempt at wryness failed. 'She didn't hear me come back in because of course I did my usual and took the stairs, not the lift; I must have watched her for a good twenty, thirty seconds before she realized I was there.'

'She?' But even as Chloe asked the question, the answer came to her.

Poppy's eyes blazed. 'Serena. She was going through my files – I hadn't bothered logging out because I was coming back and I thought no one else was there.'

'Oh my God.' Chloe felt winded, as though the air had been punched from her lungs. 'Serena was the mole.'

Poppy caught on her words. 'The mole? So then you knew too?'

Chloe met her gaze; there was no hiding it now. 'Alexander thought it was you,' she whispered, watching how Poppy's eyes slowly filled with tears as the intimation became clear. Alexander thought she had betrayed him – so he had betrayed her right back. He was behind the accident. He had tried to have her killed.

Poppy looked away, unable to stop the tears falling, her eyes shining in the setting sunlight as she looked towards the window, understanding it all now. 'Well, I suppose he would have thought that,' she whispered. 'What else *could* he have thought?'

As if that made it okay? Justifiable? Chloe grabbed her good hand, clutching it tightly. 'Poppy, listen to me, none of this is your fault.'

But Poppy just stared out at the city that had continued without her, not missing a single beat; guilt sat on her as heavily as a bear. 'Yes it is. It's all my fault.' Her voice was scarcely more than a whisper. 'I was careless. I should have logged out. Alexander depended on my discretion; he trusted me to safeguard his privacy and I let him down. Because of me, Serena was able to give Lorenzo what he needed and now Alexander's lost everything.'

Chloe dropped her head, not knowing what to say, how to talk her out of shouldering all this blame. 'What happened with Serena? Did you confront her?' Chloe asked quietly, eventually.

'*Confront* her?' Poppy scoffed, a strangled snort escaping her. 'Hell, I practically threw her out of the office by her hair. It'll all be on the CCTV, just wait till you see it. I told her not to bother coming back, that I was going to tell Jack everything, that she was out. Done.'

But of course, things hadn't played out that way; Jack had been in Palm Beach and Monday had already been too late. The very next day, Alexander – suspecting the wrong life-style manager – had exacted his revenge. Chloe remembered Serena's fake concern on the Monday, pulling rank on her, trying to intimidate her, trying to find out what she knew. It made her feel sick to realize everything had already been in motion by then, Serena covering her tracks, and then moving in on Poppy's other clients whilst Chloe was away . . .

Oh God. Her stomach lurched as she realized something else: Serena with her clipboard, the day Chloe had arrived back from Greece, questioning the florist's invoice. Chloe, quick to put her in her place, had told her she had placed the order herself, that it was a romantic gesture from Alexander to his wife whilst she was on the boat alone. Chloe *had* betrayed his movements after all, to the very person who was reporting back to her own client – Alexander's sworn enemy.

Chloe stared at her friend – if Poppy was guilty, so was she. They had both been lax, they had both been at risk. 'Poppy,' she said gently. 'You have nothing to berate your-self for. You always acted in his best interests. The man is a gangster. A monster. He tried to *kill* you.'

But Poppy just looked back at her with a dead-eyed gaze. 'And can you blame him?'

Tom was sitting on the fire escape outside the bedroom when she got back, a small blanket spread over the iron tread steps, a bottle of Bollinger sitting in an old red fire bucket she had seen hanging in the communal corridor and which he had filled with ice.

'Hey.' His eyes brightened at the sight of her. 'You're back! My God, I was going to send out the sniffer dogs. What took you so long?'

She sighed, dropping her bag on the floor. Not now, she thought. She couldn't deal with this now. The last thing she felt like was a clichéd seduction on the steps, sipping champagne as the sun set. His relentless romancing was beginning to grate; having lost her not once but twice seemed to have left him almost needy, desperate to show her – and perhaps himself too – that they were doing the right thing, that all the upheaval and heartache had been worth it. '. . . I stopped by the hospital to see Poppy,' she mumbled. 'They've removed the wires from her jaw.'

'Oh! Well that's great. How's she doing?'

'Yeah . . .' she faltered. 'Much better.' It was true, physically, at least.

'I really must get in to see her. I feel terrible I haven't been in yet.'

Chloe didn't reply, she didn't have the energy. She pushed her shoes off and walked barefoot across the bedroom; he watched her through the open window as she began to take off her work clothes, weariness in every movement.

He frowned as he watched her, sensing her low mood. 'She must be desperate to get out of there.'

'Yeah.' She pulled a pair of grey sweat shorts and a t-shirt from the wardrobe.

'God, the boredom, just lying there day and night for weeks. Can you imagine?'

'I'd rather not.'

'Any idea when they're going to release her?'

'I don't know. I didn't ask.'

He laughed. 'What *did* you two talk about?'

She shot him a look. Like he'd want to know.

'Girl stuff, huh?'

'Mmm.' She crossed over to the bed; but rather than climb over it to the window and join him outside, she sank down on it instead.

'Hey, what are you doing?' he asked as she flung herself back and stared up at the ceiling. She felt like crying.

'I'm just tired,' she mumbled, wishing she could be here alone.

'Well, tough. You and I are celebrating. Get out here.' Slowly, she turned her head and he winked at her as he pulled the gold foil off the top of the bottle.

'. . . What are you celebrating?' She was reluctant even to ask as she realized she actually didn't care.

'Come out here and I'll tell you.' He waggled his eyebrows at her.

She stared at him for a moment, the first time she'd looked at him properly since she'd come in, in fact. She could see he was as fizzy as the drink; clearly something big had happened. With a sigh, she scrambled over the bed and climbed rather inelegantly out of the window. He held out a hand and pulled her through.

The cork flew off with a satisfying pop, clattering down through the steps to the street below. He poured them each a glass, handing hers to her, and she watched him expectantly as he held his up for a toast. 'To Invicta – and her new owners.'

Her mouth fell open. '*What?*'

'We sold the company.'

'*What?*' she asked again. '. . . Since when?'

The grin spread almost from one side of his face to the other. 'The deal was inked today.' His beam grew as he watched her disbelief. 'Aren't you going to ask me how much?'

She frowned. 'Okay, how much?'

'Thirty-four million. Seventeen mill each,' he added, in case she couldn't do the maths.

'My God, Tom!' she whispered. 'I can't . . . I can't believe it. I didn't even know you were looking at selling.'

He reached over and kissed her, the excitement literally buzzing from him like an electrical charge. 'I couldn't say. Everything was massively hush-hush, it had to be. We couldn't tell anyone.'

'But not even to *me*?' She wasn't just anyone, was she? How could he not have told her about something as big as this? Didn't he trust her? Didn't her opinion matter? Quite apart from their personal relationship, she was the company's longest-serving employee.

'Believe me, I wanted to, but you've had so much going on lately, Chlo, and I know you've been missing Kate, worrying about Poppy. I didn't want to add to your stress with this.' He shook his head. 'Honestly, it's been a fucking nightmare – one minute it was on, the next it was off again. And Jack took a *lot* of convincing. He wanted us to wait and see out our ten-year plan – but this offer, it was too good. Even he could see it wouldn't come around again.' She remembered what Xan had said about their arguments and fights, the sulks and silences. Had it all been about this?

He drew a breath, his eyes dancing with delight. He was almost giddy on the success, knocking back the champagne like water. 'Hurry, hurry. Drink up. Tonight, we are going to get well and truly trollied.' He poured himself another glass, topped up hers, the bubbles fizzing over the sides and making her fingers sticky. 'Just think, the world's our oyster, Chlo – we can get a new place. Something incredible. Something *huge*!' he laughed. 'We can go away on a round-the-world trip. Whatever you want.' He took her hand and kissed it excitedly. 'This is it; we've done it. We're set for life. We can live the dream, have everything we ever wanted.'

She looked at him in dazed bewilderment. He was already drunk on the success. 'I don't know what to say. I'm stunned,' she said honestly.

'There are terms of course – we can't ride off into the sunset just yet; Jack and I have to remain as managing directors for three years and 20 per cent of the price will be issued as shares in the parent company.'

'Which is what?'

'A high-end hotel group. In addition to running their core business, they want to develop another strand to Invicta and roll us out as a facility for their guests.'

'So you mean, you're taking Invicta in-house? You're giving up all those contacts and relationships with *all the other* luxury hotels in the world, to be associated with just one?' The scepticism rang out loud and true in her voice. How could he have done this? Finding and building those partnerships was her job. Going in-house with one brand was going to severely restrict their members' movements. How many of them would want to only ever stay in or drink in or eat at that one brand? Variety and choice was what their members paid for.

'Well it's worked well for the Soho House Group.'

'But you're not Soho House! You have an entirely different business model.'

'Well, clearly,' Tom snapped, not appreciating her assertions. 'But by aligning ourselves with this parent company, we can still be a truly global concierge service but with a physical presence – now we're not just a voice down the phone or a name on an email. It's a perfect synergy. Our members are given a premium booking discount incentivizing them to stay at the hotels within the group, and their paying guests – once they've sampled our services – are given a membership discount if they want to sign up with us. It's a win-win.'

Chloe stared at him. He just didn't get it. Notwithstanding her concerns about the restrictions this imposed upon them all, she was the Head of Corporate Partnerships; or had he forgotten that? Her opinion on this should have been valuable – crucial – and yet he'd cut her out. 'So who is it then? Which group? What are their hotels?'

Tom took a deep glug of the champagne, tipping his head back in the amber sunlight. He swallowed and smacked his lips together happily. 'The Ritz Barcelona, Palazzo Parigi in Rome, The Royal Post in Lisbon . . .'

Chloe stared at him. She frowned, feeling a buzz begin in her head as the blood began to rush. 'But . . . But those are Alexander's hotels.'

Tom's gaze skipped on her and off again. 'Not any more.'

She stared at him, feeling the world begin to speed up. 'Gelardi.'

'Yes, the board accepted their offer this afternoon. Subocheva's out, Gelardi's in. You're not drinking,' he chided, topping up her glass needlessly, almost to the brim. He refilled his again. Was this excitement? Or agitation? He couldn't return her stare, she realized.

'Tom . . .' she said quietly, looking at him. She had a

growing sense of dread in the pit of her stomach. 'What's going on?'

He glanced at her, away again. 'Hmm?'

'What have you done?'

He frowned, gave a small shrug. 'I don't follow.'

But she did. The wheels were beginning to slowly turn in her mind. Gelardi had been successful in his bid, a bid that was only possible thanks to the confidential information Serena had supplied; Poppy had taken the fall for it, she'd almost been killed because of it. And now, on the very day Gelardi finally beat his old rival, he bought the company which had leaked the information to him in the first place?

That wasn't a coincidence. And that wasn't business, it was bribery. She looked at Tom, feeling cold suddenly, in the sun.

'You were in on it,' she whispered as she watched him, beginning to see it now.

'In on what?'

But she wasn't fooled by his disingenuousness, not any more, and Tom went still as he saw the understanding begin to dawn across her features. The silence that erupted between them was as loud as a thunderclap and just as startling. '. . . Now just listen, I can explain.' He reached for her but she withdrew; even his touch would be toxic.

'You were working with Lorenzo. This payday only happened if you delivered him the material he needed to destroy Subocheva. And Serena—' The words were snatched from her as the full implications hit her head-on. 'Oh God. She was reporting to *you*.' The blood drained from her face as she looked at him, seeing him now as if for the first – the only – time. 'You didn't cheat on me with her; that wasn't why she was in your room that night.' She thought back, remembering how he had stilled as she'd confronted him with the truth that she had known Serena had been in his hotel room. 'You let me *believe* that you had slept with her because it was better than admitting what you were really doing together.'

She got up and turned away. She felt sick as she remembered it – he hadn't made any excuses, put up any defence when she'd confronted him about it. Infidelity, he had reasoned, could be excused, possibly forgiven. After all, she'd succumbed to temptation too, right? He'd tried to make her believe that they were guilty of the same crime.

What other crimes was he guilty of? Oh God – she froze. What else had he done to stop the truth from coming out? 'Did Serena tell you that Poppy had found her spying?' she whispered.

No reply.

'And did you then tell Lorenzo?' A sob leapt to her throat as the words left her. 'Poppy was mown down the next day, Tom! You knew, didn't you? It wasn't Alexander at all, it was Gelardi! And you knew and you did nothing!' She spat the words at him, unable to hide her disgust any longer.

He shook his head, panic in his eyes. 'No. I didn't know, not for sure.'

'Stop lying to me!'

'I'm not!' he cried. 'I didn't know that what happened to Poppy wasn't an accident. Not at first.'

'That is *bull*shit! You want me to believe that within hours of your scam being discovered, Poppy ends up under the wheels of a car and that timing isn't suspicious to you?'

Tom's face crumpled suddenly, like a piece of paper crushed in a fist. 'Okay, yes, look – I admit I had my suspicions. But I swear, I *never* knew he would do that, Chlo, you have to believe me. When I warned him that Serena had been busted, it was to get him to withdraw, to backtrack from going ahead with the bid. The timing was all wrong, it was too dangerous. I never thought . . . not for a moment that he would do something like that . . . I swear.' The sobs shook his shoulders. 'I love Poppy. She was never supposed to get hurt.'

'But she did! Because of you!'

'I know! And I've got to live with that. But I'm not a bad man, Chlo. You know that. I'm not like them. I was just trying to set up our future.'

Our?

'No!' Her finger was in his face, her eyes wild. 'Do not bring *me* into this. This is not about me. It was not done in my name!'

'Okay, no,' he held his hands up. 'You're right. I'm sorry. I didn't mean to imply . . .' He slumped, looking at her from reddened eyes. 'But everything I've done since has been to keep you safe, I swear. When Jack told me you were taking over Poppy's patch, it almost killed me – because it *could* have been Alexander too. I didn't know for certain who was behind the accident; it could have been either one of them. They're both capable of it, they're both fucking scumbags, as rotten as each other. If Alexander had found out information was getting out from Poppy's files, I wouldn't have put it past him to retaliate like that. We both know what kind of a man he is. You even said it yourself when you came back to the hotel – you said he'd confessed to it!'

It was true. She had. *He* had. But as she fell back into the memory of that terrifying encounter on the yacht – '*I thought it had been sealed*' – had he really? She had taken those words as an admission of culpability for what had happened to

Poppy, but he was the first to admit he saw opportunity where others saw hardship. Alexander might well have believed Poppy was the mole, but what if he also believed her accident had been exactly that? The last he'd heard, she was barely alive; at the very least that meant she wouldn't be selling his secrets any more. It was a terrible tragedy, of course, but it had solved a problem for him too. None of that made him guilty.

'That was why I followed you to France – don't you see? I knew that once he heard about the bid, if he worked out there was another leak . . . I didn't know what he might be capable of.'

She looked at him in disbelief. Was he really trying to come over as the hero in this? Her knight in shining armour? 'You didn't follow me there to make sure *I* was okay!' she cried, beginning to shake with anger suddenly. 'No, Tom! You were checking your secret was still safe and that Alexander didn't know you were selling him out!'

'No.' He shook his head vehemently. 'You're wrong. It was about you. I was trying to protect you.'

'You?' she scoffed. '*You* thought you could protect me? You actually think you could do that? *You're* the reason any of this has happened! Your greed is what led to it all! How could you save me, Tom, when you were the one who threw Poppy and me under the bus!'

'I never would have let him hurt you,' he cried, looking pained.

'How? You told me yourself there's no protection from men like that. They're too powerful. You said you don't make an enemy of them unless you are certain you can win. And you knew nothing of the sort.' She was openly shaking now as her own tears came in hot rushes. 'How could you?

385

How could you do this? *You're* the scumbag!' She smashed the glass down on the step, and it shattered everywhere, raining down minute crystal shards to the street below.

He sprang back, seemingly not daring to reply, and neither of them spoke for several minutes. An entire life – one not yet lived – was ending. Even he could see that. 'Whether you choose to believe me or not, I swear I love you,' he said quietly. 'I never cheated on you with Serena, I—'

'Fuck Serena!' she yelled. 'I don't give a damn about her and what you did or didn't do.'

'. . . All of this – it was just business.'

'Business. Wow,' she murmured, forcing a big inhale and rubbing the tears away with the heels of her hands. 'Tomato; tomato,' she shrugged. 'You say business. I say corruption.' She turned to look at him, disgust flaring in her eyes, her mouth drawn into an angry slash. 'I wonder what the police will say?'

His expression changed then. 'Now, look, I'm sorry it's come to this, Chlo,' he said in a low voice. It was colder, harder now. 'But before you go running to *anyone* about this, you should realize there's absolutely no proof. I made sure of that.'

Chloe stared at him for a moment, chilled by the man standing before her. How could she ever have thought she loved him? 'Oh, I see,' she said, realizing what he was telling her. 'You wiped the CCTV the day you got here, didn't you?'

He merely blinked in reply but the glimmer of victory was in his eyes.

She looked away, enraged, impotent. Without video footage showing Poppy confronting Serena at her desk, there was no way to establish conclusively that Serena had been spying for and reporting back to Gelardi; that the information she had supplied had enabled him to put together a bid that would rob his oldest foe of everything – including, possibly, his wife. Everything was thought through – all neatly tied up and plausible; after all, the addition of these prestigious hotels to Gelardi's business portfolio called for a sideline deal that would seemingly give them an edge over their competitors, but was in reality a way to legitimately make payment for services rendered.

And they would get away with it – all of them: Lorenzo, Serena, Tom.

'Jack? Was he part of it?'

'. . . Not initially, no.'

She remembered Xan telling her about their fight in the lift, Tom telling her he'd wanted to see through the ten-year plan. Had the lure of the cash won him over in the end? She remembered too what he'd said at her birthday dinner about wanting to make things up to her; it had struck her as odd at the time, but now she wondered: did he already know by then that he was going to take the cash? Had he already decided to turn a blind eye to the nefarious activities that had got them to this point? Maybe he had convinced himself that *knowing* what had happened, wouldn't *undo* what had happened? That this wasn't so much a choice between doing the right thing and the wrong, as it was between winning and losing?

And there were so many winners: Lorenzo. Tom. Jack. Serena undoubtedly would have been rewarded too. Even Alexander hadn't lost in this. Yes, he'd been outmanoeuvred by Gelardi on this deal but there would be others; after all, he was richer than ever now. And though the price of his misjudgement was that his wife remained missing, presumed dead, billionaire widowers tended not to stay that way for long.

No, it was Elodie and Poppy who were the losers here; as Alexander had said so presciently, they were the collateral. Chloe herself . . . well, she had got away lightly. What was a broken heart to a broken body? She shuddered to think how close she'd been to Tom all this time, sleeping beside the man at the heart of it all.

'Get the fuck out of here,' she said in a low, menacing voice. She looked at him with withering disgust and she saw him flinch from it. He had lost her and perhaps that was the price *he* had to pay for his win. Maybe he really did love her as much as he claimed – just not more than the money.

'I'm sorry, Chlo.' The broken glass crunched underfoot as he trod over the stair and went to pass her to get to the window – but without conscious forethought, her arm shot out and she gave him a sudden, violent shove. He yelled as his arms wheeled for a stretched-out second, before gravity imposed its might and he fell, the staircase shaking as he tumbled awkwardly down the five steps to the platform below where the staircase turned. It wasn't enough of a fall to seriously hurt him, just enough to prove a point.

'No. You leave *that* way!' she snarled down at him, before climbing back through the bedroom window and locking it shut, trembling violently. The parting sight of him, bleeding profusely from a split lip, lying in a crumpled heap, would have to suffice as her revenge; it was certainly the only justice Poppy would get.

She stepped back from the glass, watching, waiting for him to suddenly reappear, bloodied now, his fist raining blows against the window. But nothing came and after a few minutes, she could make out the sound of his footsteps retreating on the stairs; they sounded uneven. Was he limping? She sure as hell hoped so.

She stared out at the fire bucket still sitting on the steps, the ice now melting, the Bollinger bottle opened and half drunk. Five minutes ago, it had been the very vision of romance, of success. Now, it was a tableau of a deserted feast and broken dreams. She sank onto the end of the bed and let the tears come, knowing he would take the first flight home; with the deal done, he had got what he'd come for. He was gone, this time for good. She would never see him again.

New York was far enough, after all.

Chapter Twenty-Nine

Aegean Sea, six weeks later

Dolphins were chasing them, tracing arcs through the air before splashing seamlessly back into the water and weaving through the boat's wake. Chloe watched them play, her cheek resting on her forearms as she leant on the rails. Poppy was sitting on one of the bucket seats on the main deck behind her, looking after their bags and enjoying the still-sizzling temperatures. After so long spent recovering indoors, she was still weak; the muscles in her leg had withered quickly and she could only walk for short periods before having to take a break – or 'martini stop' as she called it – but she was doing better than anyone could have expected; they had even gone clubbing one night.

They had been right to come here, in spite of the doubters. Her parents had just wanted her home, back on the lawns of their Shropshire estate and doing nothing more taxing (or dangerous) than watching the lambs graze; the doctors would have preferred her to rest in her apartment for another month and work with a physio first before embarking on any kind of long-haul holiday. But all she had wanted to do was feel the sun on her face and the wind in her hair; to leave Manhattan and the memories of that awful incident far behind her. Like

Chloe, quitting Invicta had nullified her work visa so they were free to go wherever the wind blew them, and in these last dog days of summer, Poppy had wanted to go where the sea was bluer than the sky and warmer than their drinks; it was her way of closing the door on a season spent indoors, under fluorescent lights, to the soundtrack of machines.

The dolphins became outriders, falling back, peeling away. The island was growing ever closer, the rocky cliffs the walls that kept outsiders out. She could see people sunbathing on the rocks, their bare bodies bright against the stone, a few local boats bobbing in the shallows.

With a sigh, Chloe straightened up and went back to the main deck. Hidden behind her shades, Poppy looked asleep, mouth slightly open as her head tipped back. It would be several months before all the drugs completely left her system and she would begin to feel properly well again. She had had her hair cut short, a pixie cut that blended the new growth that was coming in fast from her operation; the origins of her look were set in trauma but with her sharper-than-ever cheekbones and thin-as-a-rod thighs, kicking back in her bikini top and denim shorts, she probably looked to most people like an off-duty model.

'We're almost there. Are you ready?' she asked, sinking into the seat beside her.

Poppy slid back up the chair. 'Born ready, babe.'

'There were dolphins just now, chasing the boat.'

'Why didn't you come and get me?' Poppy gasped, whacking her lightly. 'I *love* dolphins.'

Chloe groaned. Of course she did. 'Don't worry, there'll be others.'

An announcement came over the speakers, making them wince – it was both blaring and inaudible at once. They picked up their backpacks and, shrugging them on, wandered over to the exit. A queue had formed already. They watched as ropes were thrown, caught and wound tightly as easily as a schoolgirl doing her ponytail, waiting their turn to step out onto the bright, bleached cobbles.

'You're gonna love this place,' Poppy said excitedly. 'I've always wanted to visit it. Plus, I've sent quite a few members their way over the years so it should be the red carpet treatment for us.'

'Even though we're not with Invicta any more?'

'Ah, but they don't know that,' Poppy winked. 'And I've still got some business cards on me. You?' Chloe nodded. 'Sorted then. We are VIP all the way, baby,' she said, taking Chloe's hand and raising it in the air, like a girl power salute. Chloe laughed.

They ambled at a leisurely pace along the harbour front, Poppy pressing her face to the glass at almost every boutique window. She was like a starved woman in Fortnum's food hall, scarcely knowing where to begin. Her small, quiet monochromatic cell had been replaced by a vividly technicolour world of foreign shouts and native aromas, strange faces and searing heat. Every sense was jarred, shaken, woken up again. It felt that way for Chloe too; she could only imagine the amplification for her friend.

A sudden gasp made Chloe stop dead in her tracks and she looked across in panic to find Poppy's mouth as wide as her eyes, sheer delight radiating from her. She looked back at Chloe with childlike excitement. 'Oh my God,' she squealed. 'I bloody *love* donkeys!'

Perhaps it was the Invicta link that saw her put back in the same room as last time. Poppy had a room on the ground floor on account of her still weak leg, as there were no lifts in the old hotel.

She stood on the balcony, the skirt of her emerald green dress billowing in the breeze – she wore it as often as she dared these days; Elle had been right, it was important to have beautiful, frivolous things in her life, not everything had to be practical. Her hair was still wet from her shower, her make-up not yet on, as she looked over the stepped red tile roofs, enjoying the breeze that slunk around her neck like a cat's tail. A water tanker on its way back to Athens skimmed along the horizon at a stately pace, and she spotted the first of the fishing boats coming back in, heralded by the flock of seagulls overhead in aerial convoy.

She kept staring out, forwards, directly ahead; she was so determined to look only there. But gradually, inevitably, she succumbed to the lure of looking right – over the balcony to what had been Joe's room. The shutters were closed with only two lounge chairs out there and a potted bougainvillea. It looked so . . . proper, now. Anonymous. She didn't need to even close her eyes to see him leaping over the balcony wall, to remember their dressed dinner tables set up identically and turned towards each other, candles flickering, wine chilling . . .

She turned away again.

Poppy was in her room, resting after their short but steep hike earlier to the nearby village of Kamini. They had lunched at a taverna right on the beach, the chairs sinking into the sand as they drank wine from a thick earthenware jug, before buying bright pink lilos at a beach shop and bobbing on the sea for several hours, holding hands lest one of them should drift away. A small group of local guys had trod water beside them for a while, trying to get them to join them for drinks that night, but neither she nor Poppy were interested. In their own different ways, they were both here to recover.

Chloe couldn't help but notice the irony that she should be seeking refuge on this very island for a second time. And Poppy had been disappointed when she'd come clean that she had not only been here before but stayed in this same hotel too.

She walked back into the room and lay down on her side of the bed, the embroidered cotton sheet cool against her skin. The mattress was harder than she remembered and she felt as though she was lying on the surface of it, rather than sinking in. An allegory for her life these days, she thought.

She swept one hand across the sheet, her gaze on the plumped-up pillow beside her, the bed noticeably too big for one as her eyelids closed. Sleep coming . . . bringing relief.

'. . . doing well. All set up now . . .'

She turned her head, trying to shake him from her dream. Those eyes watching her as she slept.

'. . . very comfortable . . .'

His hand on hers, pulling her into the water.

'. . . of the heat . . .'

His fingers against hers as they crossed the street.

'. . . not sure yet . . .'

Impostor.

'. . . few more weeks . . .'

Mole.

'. . . be sure it's safe . . .'

Something much worse.

She awoke with a gasp, her heart beating rapidly, shame

pouring through her as she realized she had dreamt of him. Again. Almost every night it was the same, his ghost stalking the palaces of her mind, finding her though she tried to hide from him, rooting her out. It left her feeling traitorous to her own self. Confused. Helpless.

She was surprised to see she was sitting up on the bed. How long had she been asleep for? Her gaze fell to the window. It was still light outside, not yet dusk, but the strong white afternoon light was becoming richer, more golden. Forty minutes? An hour?

She checked her phone. Poppy had said she would text when she was up again. But noth—

'. . . okay, bye . . .'

She froze, even her heart forgetting to beat. She hadn't dreamt it? The voice was low, accented . . . She stared at the balcony, seeing the tip of a shadow pass over hers for a moment, and then the click of the shutters being closed. Silence.

It was several moments before she could move. She heard the sound of a door nearby being closed in the hall, footsteps on the stairs . . .

She ran out onto the balcony and looked across. It couldn't be what she thought. It just couldn't.

But there, drying on one of the chairs, was a pair of khaki swimshorts, a retro rainbow stitched across the back.

And she realized that it damn well could.

She knew it was crazy. As the taxi zipped across the water, she knew she shouldn't be doing this. Curiosity had killed the cat – why not the Chloe? She knew she couldn't trust him and yet the thought of leaving here without knowing why he had done what he'd done, who he really was . . . she wasn't sure she could live with that. After everything that had gone down with Tom, she was done with running away. She wanted to always face the truth now, no matter how ugly or brutal, and this might be her last chance to find out. After all the theories about who and what he was, she just wanted the facts. He couldn't be worse than Tom – could he?

She felt her stomach clench as they curled around to the far side of the island, the cliffs rising sharply. A couple of goats – their coats silken black – peppered the rocks and even from a distance she could make out the haphazard stairs that were bolted to the rocks. The little jetty looked half rotted in the water as the driver cut the engines and they glided up to it in silence.

'You call me?' he said, confirming their agreement.

She held up his card. 'Yes. Thank you,' she nodded, hopping off tentatively.

Her flip-flops seemed noisy as they slapped against the wooden treads; the staircase seemed steeper – and more precarious – than she recalled too and for a moment, her courage abandoned her. What was she doing? Everyone (the police, even Kate) had warned her about this man, so what was she doing chasing him here to a remote house on the far side of the island? But before she could change her mind and turn back to safety, she heard the water taxi at her back, pulling away from the shore, white wake frothing behind it.

She closed her eyes and steeled herself. Well, there was nothing else for it now. Apart from anything, she couldn't get phone coverage down here by the water. She would at least need to climb the steps.

Her knuckles blanched as she gripped the rope handrail, swearing under her breath as tiny, chalky stones skittered down the cliff either side of the staircase; but within minutes she reached the top with an expressive burst of expletives as she dared to look back down.

Eyes glancing left, right and left again, checking her arrival had been unobserved, she walked hesitantly into the olive grove that seemed almost to sparkle with shadows and light. Her hand reached for some of the ancient stippled, gnarled trunks; the trees were laden with fruit, much more so than when she'd been here earlier in the summer, fat juicy green olives speckling the canopies. She ducked low, avoiding some of the more bent-over and low-hanging trees – some of them appeared almost cleaved in half, others had stubby trunks no taller than her but so wide she couldn't close her arms around them.

She remembered how charged the air had been as she and Joe had come back down here together that fateful last night, how they had almost skipped over the roots, returning to the boat with an unarticulated promise suspended between them.

Soon, though, she was through it and she stood at the edge of the grove, heart hammering, as she looked up towards the crumbling stone wall. Beyond it lay the garden and the house. Was he even there? He surely had to be, didn't he? Why buy a house only to continue to stay in a hotel? It didn't make sense, unless he was doing building works? But then, seemingly nothing that man did made sense. Everything about him was illogical and elusive.

Scanning the ground area one more time, she ran across the open expanse to the steps at the bottom of the wall and waited. There was no sound that she could make out, nothing to suggest he or anyone else was nearby. Tentatively, she climbed the steps and peered round the wall into the garden, her eyes opening wide at the sight that greeted her.

The difference was astonishing – it had been turfed, beds cut in around the perimeter and laid with lavender, rosemary, thyme and sage; a gardening fork was still stuck in the ground, a kneeling pad and trowel beside it. A beautiful cubed teak furniture set with sofas, armchairs and a table had been positioned on the grass; deep, palest-blue linen cushions softened its angular lines, and from here she could see the pages of a magazine fluttering upwards in the breeze on one of the seats.

On the terrace, some plush orange beach towels were drying across the backs of chairs grouped around a vast slate dining table, storm candles on the surface burnt down low.

Her eyes settled on the house, her ears straining for sound – a TV on, music playing, voices from a bathroom . . . But all was still. Nothing moved behind the glass, no lights shone. That was perhaps the biggest change since her last visit – as per her advice, glazed Crittall doors had been put in behind the ground-floor shutters which lay flat against the wall now. The stables had become a living room properly now.

Balling up all her courage – knowing that in moving from this spot, she would be fully exposed to anyone looking from the house, especially in this dress – she stepped forward. Blood was rushing through her ears and she half expected an alarm to suddenly blare, floodlights to find her; but she continued to put one foot in front of the other, creeping her way up to the building.

Feeling like a comedy villain, she pressed herself flat against the glass, trying to hear anything at all apart from the thud of her own heart and the caw of the wheeling seagulls overhead. She peeled herself away and peered in through the kitchen window. A chopping board was on the table, two lemons and a knife positioned there as though awaiting a Dutch master to paint them. She saw a cookbook – Trish Deseine's *Petits Plats Entre Amis* – lying open on the wooden counter and several brown paper bags still twisted closed at the top. Some plates, glasses and cutlery were lying on the draining board; the water rivulets still running down the sides told her they'd been freshly washed. A laundry basket was on the floor in the far corner and she squinted, trying to make out the jumble of clothes from this distance: she could see cuffed shirt sleeves, the elasticated waistband of boxers, and then – she stilled as she glimpsed a cream bra strap dangling distinctively over the side.

She felt almost winded by the sight of it, even though she had already known he had a woman; she had known that first night just by the tone of his voice. This, then, was merely confirmation – one of the truths she had come looking for.

Why should she be surprised? Why should it hurt so much? But her head dropped, a tightness in her chest spreading. What point was there in staying now? This was enough surely. Why torment herself with further evidence of the life he had set up here? With his wife, or whatever she was.

But she couldn't help herself. With masochistic zeal, she crept around the rest of the building, cupping her hands around her face as she peered in, unable to stop herself from looking, her frantic, hot breath fogging the windows as she flayed herself with the vignettes of a happy home: a gauzy blanket draped over the sofa – the same sofa *she* had lifted and put there – the cushion positioned side-on as though someone had used it as a pillow for a nap; a stack of paperbacks on the floor, a wireless tall floor speaker, a large brown leather holdall at the bottom of the stairs; a—

She froze again, forgetting to breathe as she caught sight of something tucked away to the side of the window; she could barely see it from where she was standing and she ran around the corner to try to get a better look, but it was exactly the same from this vantage point; it hadn't – couldn't – miraculously morph into something else. It was and always would be a cradle, wooden with turned spindles and hanging on a rocking frame. She blinked, blinked again, one palm pressed flat against the glass as she struggled to accept this inviolable truth.

He had a baby.

It was the sucker-punch she had needed; the only thing that could knock some sense into her and make her think clearly again. She had romanticized this man; even as *everyone* had warned her off, she had found ways to excuse or pardon him. An impostor, a fraud, or 'something much worse' – that was one thing; incredibly, she'd told herself perhaps he had 'reasons'! But a husband and father?

She had to get out of here. There was no point in prolonging the agony. Whatever his reasons for doing what he'd done, these were irrefutable facts that rendered any explanations pointless anyway.

Her phone buzzed suddenly and she jumped. She had signal here? *'Hey! Where are you? Room empty.'*

Chloe texted back as quickly as she could. *'Soz. Went for a quick walk. Heading back now.'*

She pressed send and turned, only to find herself facing some sort of summer nativity – for there, just a few metres away, was a trinity of figures: a woman on a donkey, a man standing beside her. And in front of them both, Joe.

If he was surprised, he didn't show it. 'Hello, Chloe,' he said quietly.

Looking back at them, just for a moment, she thought their group looked more shocked, more scared, than she. But that was ridiculous of course, she was heavily outnumbered. To her ear, her own breath sounded like a howling wind; everything was hollow.

'I believe you know everyone,' he said calmly, introducing her as though they were at a dinner party and he hadn't in fact just caught her trespassing on his property, spying through the windows; that he wasn't a man who had lied to her about his name and God knows what else . . . 'You've met my brother Lucas.'

She swept her gaze over to the dark-haired man holding the donkey's reins. She squinted, a frown puckering her brow. Why on earth did he think she knew his brother? She didn't even know who *he* was . . . Although . . . now that she looked at the man, he *did* seem familiar, somehow . . .

Everyone was silent, as though waiting for her to catch on, to catch up.

Her sudden gasp was the sign that she had. 'The doctor,' she whispered. 'On the boat.' They had looked so alike, it had been like passing Joe's ghost, even though she had known it was impossible . . .

Lucas nodded but still there was no smile, no flicker of friendliness. They were all locked in some sort of holding pattern, as though waiting to see who would do what next.

'And of course . . .' Joe's arm swept round to the woman sitting on the donkey. With the sun behind her, she was largely silhouetted, but as she held her hands out to Lucas to be helped down, Chloe saw the ripe swell of her belly.

Lucas handled her carefully, setting her down as though she was made of glass. Chloe remembered the large leather holdall at the bottom of the stairs – a doctor's bag, ready for anything, delivering a baby for example.

'Chloe, it is good to meet you at last.' The woman walked towards her, still more shadow than light; but her voice, though quiet, was accented and . . . again, familiar. Where had Chloe heard it before? Why was it hitting bone, demanding to be acknowledged? 'You have done so much for me. I am glad I can thank you in person.'

'Th-thank me?' Chloe stuttered, bewildered. '. . . You mean, for finding the house?' A love nest for her and Joe and their soon-to-be-born baby?

'For saving my life.'

The woman was only a couple of metres away now, taller than she had seemed from a distance, her face coming into clear, beautiful view. Only then did Chloe understand.

'Elodie.'

Chapter Thirty

They were sitting on the garden chairs when Poppy appeared at the top of the steps, out of breath and looking a little wild-eyed. 'Oh, thank fuck for that! I thought the driver was having a laugh!' she panted, leaning on the wall for support as she saw Chloe sitting with the others. 'Those bloody steps,' she managed, one hand pressed over her jack-hammering heart.

Everyone smiled at her dramatic entrance, the flame from the storm candle beginning to throw out long shadows as the sun dropped below the horizon.

'It is a bit hard to find,' Chloe said, jumping up and running over to her. 'Although that's rather the point.' Poppy straightened up as Chloe gave her a relieved hug. 'I'm glad you got here.'

'All okay?' Poppy asked quietly, concern in her eyes.

Chloe pulled back and nodded, smiling widely. 'Come and meet everyone,' she said as they slowly walked over the grass, arm in arm. Poppy was so weak still, perhaps she ought to have sent a donkey for her; but it would have taken three times as long to get here and she'd had the driver on standby in the port anyway . . . She hadn't been able to wait any longer than was necessary. 'Did you sleep okay?'

'Yeah. But what's going on? Why are we here?'

'Well, rather a lot happened while you were resting,' Chloe said, just as they arrived back with the others. 'Pops, I want you to meet Lucas Inkham – orthopaedic surgeon extraordinaire.'

'Jeez, you're going to love me then,' Poppy quipped, holding out a hand. 'I'm more metal than bone these days.'

Chloe swept her arm round to indicate the woman next to him. 'And this is Elodie—'

In a flash, Poppy's smile vanished, her mouth dropping open in a perfect 'o' as she met the gaze of the beautiful woman. '*Elodie?*' She looked in stunned amazement between Elodie and Chloe, for confirmation.

Chloe nodded.

'Elodie Subocheva? You're alive?' Poppy whispered, slapping her hand over her mouth in disbelief as tears gathered in her eyes. She sank down into the nearest sofa, her already weak legs too tired now to keep holding her up. Chloe sat beside her and squeezed an arm around her; she knew that Poppy – regardless of how Chloe tried to argue it – still blamed herself for what had happened to Elodie. She had been the weak link, the channel through which Gelardi had managed to steer his dark ambitions, and although she had come to accept that Alexander's behaviour had been equally as monstrous as his rival's, she had refused to forgive herself for her lapse.

'I am alive, very much so.' Elodie's own smile flickered as she smoothed a hand protectively over her bump, before looking up again. 'But I am not Subocheva any more. I go by my mother's maiden name now: Fournier.'

There was only a short pause as Poppy caught up, her back straightening as understanding settled over her. 'Ah yes. Much nicer,' Poppy said, still wide-eyed.

'And safer,' Lucas said quietly, his hand resting lightly on Elodie's thigh.

Poppy's eyes swivelled between the two of them, and her smile widened. 'How excellent,' she whispered, making Elodie laugh. It was a hesitant sound, as though rarely made, Chloe thought as she watched on.

'And, last but not least, this is Joe.' The name felt gravelly in her mouth as she said it.

'J—?' Poppy did a double-take. 'As in No Joe?'

Chloe grinned. 'The very same.'

Poppy leaned over the coffee table with an arm outstretched. 'Well, pleased to meet you, No Joe.' But just as he went to shake her hand, she looked back at Chloe quickly. '*Am* I pleased to meet him?' she stage-whispered.

Chloe laughed. 'Yes!'

'Well, then, how do you do.'

Joe – eyes glittering with amusement – cracked a small grin and Chloe could see he liked her friend; but whenever he glanced over at her, his eyes somehow made her blood spin, making her feel like she was falling. They had yet to talk alone. Things had been so . . . overwhelming since finding him and his brother and Elodie here. It had been all she could do to have the presence of mind to ring the taxi driver and ask him to bring Poppy round. There was still so much to say, to understand, but she wasn't sure where to start – or when.

They settled back into the chairs again and, for a moment, the two parties looked at each other in the dusky light. There was welcome in the air but also trepidation and Chloe sensed this invasion by the Brits took their small group into uncharted waters. They were all off-plan now.

'Well, this *is* unexpected,' Poppy said lightly. 'So, is this the land of missing people or what?'

Everyone laughed again, put back at ease.

Chloe looked over at Joe, deciding to start it. She wasn't sure she could wait another minute. His presence was filling up her head, her heart, her limbs. Blood had never raced around her so fast. All she wanted to do was look at him but she could scarcely bring herself to do it. 'So what *is* your name?' she asked him, feeling her cheeks flush as his gaze settled upon her with typical intensity. 'I know it's not Joe Lincoln.'

He looked at her – always so steady, so calm. 'It's Joel.'

She blinked at him. His brother was Lucas Inkham. 'Joel? *Joel Inkham?*'

'Joe Lincoln. Joel—' Beside her, Poppy burst out laughing at the phonetic echo falling back in the cushions. 'Oh, I love that!'

But Joe – though he was smiling too – kept his eyes firmly on Chloe. 'If you have to tell lies, keep them as close to the truth as you possibly can.'

'His nickname in high school was Dual Income, if that's of any interest,' Lucas quipped. 'He had a sideline in selling our father's beer from the back of his car.'

Poppy slapped her thighs. 'Oh my God, you lot! You're brilliant,' she cried. 'That's the best thing I've heard in months!'

Joel. Chloe remembered Ariane at Chimichanga had called him that but she had assumed it was an error. Chloe tried the name on for size, rolling it around in her mouth, running it through her mind. She couldn't take her eyes off him; nor he her.

He reached forward and poured Poppy a glass of wine; she was already spearing olives in the olive bowl with a cocktail stick.

'Thank you, Joe with an L,' Poppy said, taking the glass from him and sitting back, devilment in her eyes. She looked back at Elodie. 'Shit . . . I *still* can't believe you're here.'

'It was the only way.' Elodie's hands smoothed over her taut stomach protectively. 'Once I found out about this little one, I knew I had to get out. I had to do it not just for me, but for her.'

'You're having a little girl?'

Elodie nodded.

'I *love* little girls,' Poppy sighed, clapping her hands together and resting her cheek against them. Chloe groaned. It was like sitting next to a puppy.

'So do I. Already she has given me such strength.' Elodie's voice was quiet but fierce. 'For years I knew that leaving my husband was too dangerous: he is such a controlling person, so obsessive. I feared it would not even be possible, that he would rather I was dead than I left him . . .' She swallowed, looking down at the ground. Her arms tightened around her bump. 'But when I learnt about this little one, I knew I had to try; I had to get away before it became evident because then we really would be trapped. He would never let us leave him then.'

Poppy's expression had changed. 'He hurt you?'

Elodie met her gaze and nodded.

Chloe suppressed a shiver. Alexander was a big man in every way – ego, power, and in bulk too. It would be no exaggeration to say that Elodie probably weighed little more than his leg. To think of him bearing down upon her, fists flying, eyes glaring . . . She remembered her own fear that night on the yacht as he stood inches away from her, deciding her fate; it had been so physical she could taste it, a metallic element in her mouth.

'I'm so sorry,' Poppy said, looking crestfallen.

'Why?'

'Because . . . I helped him,' she shrugged. 'I thought he was a top guy, completely misrepresented by the press, libelled by his enemies. I felt pretty sorry for him much of the time actually. I used to go out of my way to make things great for him. I had no idea . . .'

'And how could you have done? He is a charismatic man. He fooled me too, for a long time. Why do you think I married him?' Her fingers had laced together but the knuckles were pressed white. 'I had been in some . . . toxic relationships before I met him. The world I moved in made women like me seem very disposable, and I had no sense of self-worth. But when we met, he was different to all the rest. At first, we were just friends. He would fly in whenever he could to whichever city I happened to be working in, and we would just walk and talk, go for meals. It was all so innocent and romantic. Nobody had ever treated me like a person, before.'

'So when did it change?'

'About five months after we were married. He didn't like the way a man I was talking to at a party had been looking at me. He was certain we were having an affair.' She rolled her lips together. 'He threw me down the stairs that night.'

Both Poppy and Chloe gasped. 'Oh my God,' they uttered in unison.

Lucas, sitting beside her, reached forward and squeezed her hand. 'It's how we met. I knew Alexander from Chicago. I had been working a residency at the Weiss hospital and had operated on him for a particularly nasty ankle break. He had been pleased with my work and kept my number. I happened to be in London for a conference when he rang, saying he had a "sensitive case". She had broken her leg in three places.' His voice tremored at the memory and, this time, it was Elodie who put her hand on his thigh and squeezed.

'After that, I relocated to Paris and he would send Elodie to me whenever she needed medical attention . . . which was regularly.' His mouth had flattened into a line, his eyes as hard as stones. 'He trusted me to be discreet and in return he paid me hush money to keep quiet, to keep her looking beautiful.' His hand brushed down her bare arm as he gazed at the woman now sitting beside him; she in turn looked back at him with an adoration that made Chloe feel intrusive. 'She would always be covered up – long sleeves, long dresses – to hide the bruises . . . He was a monster; I couldn't bear that he thought I was colluding with him, but it was the only way I could help Elodie – even if it was only afterwards.'

'He was the only one who knew the truth, the only person I could trust,' Elodie said in a voice so low, the breeze almost spirited it away. '. . . Sometimes, when my husband hurt me, I was almost happy because I knew then I would be able to see Lucas.'

Lucas's hand found hers again. He looked back at them. 'I begged her to leave him; he would kill her one day, of that I was certain; but she was too terrified – like a deer in headlights, she couldn't move. The security guards supposedly keeping her safe were more interested in reporting back her every move to him. She was trapped. How do you escape a man like that? A man who has the resources to scour every last square inch of this planet.'

'By faking your own death,' Chloe said quietly.

'I had been hiding money away for years,' Elodie said. 'I

had an account in a bank in Switzerland that was so secretive, even my husband would not be able to gain access to it. I didn't think I would ever use it, but when I found out about the baby, everything changed – especially because it was not his. I would not have put it past him to have the baby DNA tested, to be sure. And then he would have killed us all.'

The silence that followed was chilling. No one doubted it was the truth.

'Did he ever suspect you?' Chloe asked, looking at Lucas.

'No. We were incredibly careful. And restrained. No phone calls. No emails. Ever. We would sometimes go months without seeing each other, and when we did, we never met anywhere but at my clinic. I would schedule follow-up consultations for as long as I thought I could get away with.'

'And when that stopped, we would wait for the next beating,' Elodie added simply.

'Jesus Christ,' Poppy murmured. 'So what changed?'

'You, Poppy.'

'*Me?*'

'When I rang that Monday morning, I had been wanting to ask you to get Alexander tickets to the World Cup in Russia. He is fanatical about football and I thought being back in his homeland too, it would help keep him away for another few days at least. I could not bear the thought of him coming back again. I had begun to suspect I might be pregnant but I wasn't ready to confirm it – I knew it would be a life sentence if I was. But then, when you answered, Chloe,' Elodie looked over at her. 'And told me about Poppy's accident, as terrible as it was, I realized it gave me a short window in which to make my move. I knew it was now or never.'

Chloe nodded, remembering the phone call with the

unidentified woman that morning. She had hung up. Chloe had assumed it was Rosaria, but of course, she famously never used her voice before noon.

Elodie looked across at them both with fierce eyes. 'I am ashamed to admit the accident provided me with an opportunity and with you deputizing for Poppy, Chloe, I knew it would be a while before you were standing on your feet. Joel was living in New York so Lucas rang straight away and asked him to go to your offices and sign up as a client. I couldn't go and buy a house myself – anything in my name meant Alexander would know about it within the minute – but the discreet service you provide at Invicta meant you could set up a whole new life for me.'

Chloe looked across at Joel – but he was already watching her. 'And it would all be independent,' she murmured. 'Even if Alexander had become suspicious, there would have been nothing for him to trace – you were an entirely separate client, using a false name. The worst that could happen was that he would learn you were the far-away brother of his doctor. A coincidence perhaps, but nothing more alarming than that.'

Elodie gave a small, bashful smile that appled her cheeks; she was epically beautiful. 'It was almost delightful that Alexander's own concierge, who always made his life so perfect, should be helping me to leave him.'

'It's bloody excellent, is what it is,' Poppy grinned. 'And do you know what? I am happy to have obliged with my own little bit part! A couple of broken bones to help you escape? Totally worth it!'

'It was more than a bit part!' Chloe smiled, but now didn't seem like the time to bring up brain surgery. 'So . . . what now?' She looked back at Lucas. 'Are you still working for Alexander? You were there the night Elodie went missing . . .'

'No, but we had to stage it carefully. It would have looked suspicious if we had both disappeared at the same time,' Lucas nodded. 'So after Elodie disappeared, I continued as normal for another month, then closed my clinic, putting up a notice saying I was retiring from clinical practice and taking up a research fellowship in Tokyo.'

'But wouldn't that be easy for Alexander to trace? How many Doctor Inkhams can there be working in orthopaedics in Tokyo?'

'None, of course. Should he ever bother to look, he will find that I have disappeared too – but I doubt he will; with Elodie gone now, he won't be needing my services on such a regular basis. And besides, Elodie and I have *both* taken her mother's maiden name. New identities for us both. It is the only way to be certain we are safe.'

'For what it's worth, I don't think he will look. I think he truly believes you are dead.' Chloe looked across at Elodie. 'Did you know Alexander thought Lorenzo Gelardi had taken you?'

'Really?' Elodie was still for a moment and a wave of pain seemed to tremor through her.

'He assumed you were taken to distract him from Lorenzo's takeover bid. And by the time he realized you weren't . . .'

'. . . Well, that does not surprise me,' Elodie said after a long pause. 'The human element always comes after the financial one for him. He is incapable of seeing anything outside that context. And it would not once have crossed his mind, of course, that I might have committed suicide. To him, I had the perfect life – houses around the world, couture wardrobes; why would I want to kill myself when I had all that?'

She released Lucas's hand and sat further back in the cushions, wrapping her arms around her unborn child. 'I have more here than he could ever understand.' She gestured to the gardens, to Lucas, her tummy again. 'My life is far richer now than it ever was with him.'

'Hoo-bloody-rah to that,' Poppy said, swinging her long leg and raising her glass. 'But there's something I want to know – exactly how *do* you disappear off a yacht in the middle of the Med in the middle of the night?'

'Ah well,' Elodie smiled, nodding towards Joel, who had been sitting quietly all this time, off to the side. 'Lucky for me, my brother-in-law is ex-Marine Corps. He was a commando in Afghanistan.'

Chloe's jaw dropped open. Well that certainly explained a few things! Her gaze met his again, which wasn't hard; he hadn't taken his eyes off her at all during all this. It was like wearing a coat.

'Joel taught Lucas to teach me how to jump into the water from a height and make minimal splash—'

Chloe remembered his dive from the rocks, his rampant fearlessness. The memories seemed to play between them, hanging in the air.

'But still . . . it was so high! You must have been terrified!' Poppy said in awe.

'It was. I was so scared. But Joel had said the boat gave me the best chance of disappearing without trace. Obviously I had to wait till we had dropped anchor and the engines were off. Then it was just a matter of waiting for night to fall. He had hired a small daytrippers' boat and was moored a small distance further away. There were lots of smaller boats moored for the night so it did not arouse any suspicion.'

'But wouldn't the guards have heard another boat, even if they couldn't see you?'

'I'd brought an inflatable dinghy onto the boat,' Joel said. 'As soon as it was dark enough, I rowed over, clamped myself to the stern and waited.'

'But what if the guards had seen you?' Chloe asked, scarcely able to believe the audacity of the plan – he had just attached himself to the side of the boat and waited?

'They wouldn't have seen me, even if they'd looked down. The hull bellies out there, so I was pretty well hidden from the decks.'

'We had some bad luck, though,' Elodie added. 'There was a big party on the coast that night and they had a fireworks display. The sky kept lighting up. I was so frightened they would see us.'

'Agreed, but I think it worked to our advantage,' Joel said, looking over at Elodie. 'It meant they didn't hear your entry into the water and I think it actually bought us time – they were watching the display along with everyone else.'

'I don't know what to say,' Chloe mumbled. 'It's all so much to take in.'

'I know. We can scarcely believe it ourselves,' Elodie smiled, dropping her head on Lucas's shoulder.

'. . . So why Greece?' Poppy asked. 'Why here? I mean, apart from the stunning seas, gorgeous views, perfect weather . . .'

Elodie laughed. 'My grandmother was Greek so I had many happy summers here as a child. It has always represented safety to me. And of course, it is still quite unknown to the rest of the world. I like that it is more . . . rustic. It feels real and that is what I want after so long of being caged away.'

'I get that that must feel good *now*.' Poppy wrinkled her nose. 'But won't it get a bit lonely, going forward?'

Elodie sighed contentedly. 'I know it will seem that way to most people, but I have seen the world. I have lived on every continent and drunk the finest wines. I have sat at dinner with princes and presidents and none of it was as satisfying as sitting in this garden with the birds and the goats.'

'And the donkeys!' Poppy added. 'I bloody *love* the donkeys.'

Elodie laughed. '*Exactement!* Perhaps in a few years, we will find somewhere in a village, nearer a school, for this little one. But I can *never* afford for Alexander to discover I am alive. My life must remain small if it is to stay safe and that is a price I can pay. I came to Greece to escape.'

'Well I'll drink to that,' Poppy said, holding her glass aloft in a triumphant toast of solidarity. Though she wouldn't get the justice she deserved, this at least was vengeance of sorts. 'To your Greek escape.'

Chloe's gaze slid over to Joel's again. Hadn't they all come here for that? Broken hearts and broken bones had driven the three women here, one way and another.

Chloe stood in front of the shutters, knowing that one latch was the only thing standing between her and her future. She had already heard the rasp of his next door. It was a sound her ear had become attuned to.

Taking a breath, she unhooked it and walked out. He was already sitting on the wall of the balcony, waiting, a couple of bottles of beer in an ice bucket chilling nicely.

His eyes met hers in silent conversation. It was the first time they'd been alone all night.

'I thought you were married,' she said quietly, by way of explanation for her quick morning-after exit, as he handed her a beer; the glass felt cool against her palm. 'I heard you on the phone, that night.'

He nodded. 'A fair assumption.'

She hesitated. 'Then when I got back to New York I was told you were an impostor . . . a fraud . . . a conman . . .'

He nodded again. 'Hard to argue against . . .'

'Then I thought you were a money-launderer! What?' she laughed, seeing his expression at that. 'It was the only thing that made sense.'

'. . . I guess I can see that, too,' he concurred.

'And then, finally, I thought you were a corporate spy. Working for Alexander.'

His mouth opened but he didn't seem to know what to say. He frowned. 'It's hard to know how I can live up to these staggeringly exciting expectations,' he said drily.

'I'd rather you didn't.'

'Really? You're not disappointed that I'm just the proud owner of five Mexican food carts and a lease on a new premises in Greenwich Village.' He grinned outright as he watched her expression change.

'That food truck was *yours*?'

He shrugged. 'Doing pretty well too.' His eyes flicked upwards. 'Although nothing like as well as owning a multinational engineering company.' The querying look in his eyes surprised her. Did he think it would make a difference to her to learn that he wasn't rich after all? 'I won't be buying VIP membership at Invicta any time soon.'

She smiled. 'That's okay. I'll offer you a preferential rate for Langton Concierge instead.'

'Langton?'

'That's one of the names we're thinking about. Poppy and I are setting up on our own – Langton is a mesh of our surnames. Langham, Marston . . .' She shrugged.

'Interesting.'

'Well, we've got the contacts, the clients, the experience . . . and a nice amount of seed money to get us going.' She and Poppy had staged a coup at Jack's apartment the week Poppy was discharged from hospital, the two of them waiting for him as he came home steaming drunk with a couple of brunettes. He had been quick to see that – although they had no *actual* proof of Serena and Tom's industrial espionage – a phone call to the police would nonetheless shine an unfortunate spotlight on both the timing of Invicta's sellout, and to whom: questions would be asked, people would talk . . . And what with the departure since of several high-profile clients (Pelham and Greenleve had both followed Chloe and Poppy out of the door) *and* an investigation by HM Revenue & Customs for suspected payroll fraud (prompted by an anonymous tip-off which Chloe was sure had come from Lucy's father, who had also just cashed in his stake), the murky stench of corruption was beginning to stick. One phone call to Tom later, and she and Poppy had 'resigned' with a $500,000 golden handshake each.

'It looks like you've got everything figured out,' he said, pinning her up with that gaze again.

'Not quite everything,' she said quietly.

He watched her. 'Still having trouble with men in bow ties?'

'Funnily enough, no.' Kate had taken particular delight

in reading out to her a report of Tom being blackballed from the East India Club on account of 'being rather too full of himself' (perhaps it was merely a coincidence that Lucy's father was a member there; then again, perhaps not). And she had heard from several of her old London mates that he was struggling to find even enough friends to make up a game of tennis; it seemed she wasn't the only one to have seen through him at last. She arched an eyebrow. 'But Marmalade, my childhood bear, does look particularly fine in his . . .'

He nodded, allowing a smile to creep into his eyes.

'Had you been following me?' she asked, watching him closely. She had often wondered about it since that night at the restaurant – how else could he have known it was her birthday? How else could he have known they'd be there?

His gaze flicked from her to his glass and back again. '. . . Perhaps.'

'So I was being stalked by a commando on the streets of Manhattan,' she murmured. 'And I didn't even know it.'

'Ex-commando. And that was the point.'

'It wasn't a coincidence that day, crossing the road, was it? You planned it.'

There was a pause. 'I just needed to see you again. I knew it was hopeless and that I wouldn't be able to talk to you . . . that I couldn't explain . . . But I thought that seeing you face to face again, even just for one more moment, would be enough.'

'And was it?'

'No.'

Her eyes met his and she felt like she was fizzing inside, her blood carbonated; she felt on the verge of overflowing. 'But if I hadn't come here and just *happened* upon this, you still wouldn't have told me the truth, would you?' she asked, feeling chilled by the very thought.

He shook his head. 'Couldn't.'

No. The stakes had been too high for Elodie and Lucas – they couldn't risk anyone knowing the truth, Alexander was too dangerous, too powerful. Joel losing her would have to have been the 'collateral' in that arrangement; but his eyes shone and she knew it would have hollowed him as it had her.

'You're a good man, Joel Inkham,' she said quietly.

A beat skipped between them. '. . . Not that good.' And she saw his leg lift as he stepped onto the chair.

Oh God! He was going to do it again. 'There is a door you can use!' she laughed, slapping her hand over her mouth in excitement and fright as she saw him brace for the leap.

A sudden dazzling smile enlivened his face, his white teeth gleaming against his tan and stubble, his eyes dancing with mischief. 'I know,' he winked. 'But where's the fun in that?'

Epilogue

HYDRA GAZETTE

Births

*Mr and Mrs Fournier are delighted to announce
the safe arrival of their baby girl, Liberty Poppy Chloe Fournier,
weighing 7lb 4oz on 21 February. A treasured first child.*

THE TIMES

Marriages

*The marriage is announced between Clarissa, Lady Hungerford,
of Chelsea, SW3 and Pelham, Lord Hungerford, of Belgravia,
SW1, on 21 February at Kensington and Chelsea Register Office,
following a whirlwind engagement.*

THE TIMES

Engagements

*The engagement is announced between Rupert Oliver
Valentine, elder son of Mr and Mrs James Cranmer of Painswick,
Gloucestershire, and Lucy Clementine, youngest daughter of
Mr and Mrs David Yorke of Fleet, Hampshire.*

The Greek Escape

CRAIGSLIST, NEW YORK

For rent

Fifth Avenue, Greenwich Village, Downtown Manhattan.
1 bed. 1 bath. 1,000 sq. ft.
Doorman. Elevator. Pre-war. Hardwood floors. Laundry in unit.
$5,700. Couple preferred.

Acknowledgements

It's not often the humble donkey is considered a muse, but this book started for me with memories of some long-ago holidays to the island of Hydra and the sound of cowbells chiming as they plodded through the cobbled streets. Revisiting Greece last summer – albeit a different island – I fell in love all over again with the historic olive groves and modest stone houses and knew I wanted it to be the location for my next book, so I do hope you now feel you've been there too.

As ever, getting a book to publication is like bringing a ship to launch – so many different teams and specialists are involved. Amanda Preston, my agent, is my rock and sounding board, giving me the courage to 'go for it.' Caroline Hogg, my editor, is endlessly encouraging when I feel panic setting in, and the entire team at Pan Mac makes producing bestsellers look easy when it's really not. (They also host fabulous parties and our meetings always involve champagne!) Thank you guys, hard work is such fun with you all.

And to my family, I know having a writer for a wife/mum/daughter/sister isn't easy and that I always seem to be working at the wrong times. But no world I ever create and no love I ever depict, could come close to the life we share. You make everything perfect.

Christmas
UNDER THE STARS
by
Karen Swan

Worlds apart. A love without limit.

In the snow-topped mountains of the Canadian Rockies, Meg and Mitch are living their dream. Just weeks away from their wedding, they work and play with Tuck and Lucy, their closest and oldest friends. Meg and Lucy are as close as sisters – much to Meg's real sister's dismay – and Tuck and Mitch have successfully turned their passion for snowboarding into a booming business.

But when a polar storm hits, tragedy strikes. Alone in the tiny mountain log cabin she shares with Mitch, Meg desperately tries to radio for help – and it comes from the most unexpected quarter, a lone voice across the airwaves that sees what she cannot.

As the snow melts and the friends try to live with their loss, the relationships Meg thought were forever are buckled by tensions, rivalries and devastating secrets. Nothing is as she thought and only her radio contact understands what it is to be truly alone. As they share confidences in the dark, witnessed only by the stars, Meg feels her future begin to pull away from her past and is forced to consider a strange truth – is it her friends who are the strangers? And a stranger who really knows her best?

The CHRISTMAS SECRET

by
Karen Swan

When the lies stop, can love begin?

Alex Hyde is in demand. An executive coach par excellence, she's the person who the great and the good turn to when the pressure gets too much – she can change the way they think, how they operate; she can turn around the very fortunes of their companies.

Her waiting list is months long, but even she can't turn down the highly lucrative crisis call that comes her way a few weeks before Christmas, regarding the troublesome – and troubled – head of an esteemed whisky company in Scotland. Lochlan Farquhar, CEO of Kentallen Distilleries, is a maverick, an enigma and a renegade, and Alex needs to get inside his head before he brings the company to its knees.

It should be business as usual. She can do this in her sleep. Only, when she gets to the remote island of Islay, with the winter snows falling, Alex finds herself out of her comfort zone. Memories she would rather forget come back to haunt her. For once she's not in control, but with Christmas and her deadline fast approaching, she must win Lachlan's trust.

Yet as she pulls ever closer to him, boundaries become blurred, loyalties loosen and Alex finds herself faced with an impossible choice as she realizes nothing and no one is as they first seemed.

The Rome Affair

by
Karen Swan

A love that can't be stopped. A secret that can't be kept.

1974 and Elena Damiani lives a gilded life. Born with extreme wealth and beauty, no door is closed to her, no man can resist her. At twenty-six, she is already onto her third husband when she meets her love match. But he is the one man she can never have, and all the riches in the world can't change it.

2017 and Francesca Hackett is living *la dolce vita* in Rome, leading tourist groups around the Eternal City and forgetting the ghosts she left behind in London. When she finds a stolen designer handbag in her dustbin and returns it, she is introduced to the grand neighbour who lives across the piazza – famed socialite and Viscontessa, Elena. Elena is overjoyed: the bag contains an unopened letter written by her husband on his deathbed, twelve years earlier.

The two women begin to work together on the Viscontessa's memoirs. As summer unfurls, Elena tells her sensational stories, leaving Cesca in her thrall. But when a priceless diamond ring is found in an ancient tunnel and ascribed to Elena, Cesca begins to suspect a shocking secret at the heart of her new friend's life . . .